Cool Cat

Cool Cat

by
Dan Leissner

Midnight Marquee Press, Inc.
Baltimore, Maryland, USA

This story is entirely fictitious and all characters are imaginary and have no relation to any persons living or dead. This also includes places, names, companies, religious orders or any other names whatsoever.

Cover design by Jeff Duke
Cover layout by Patrick Hurley
Interior layout Susan Svehla

Copyright © 2007 Dan Leissner

Without limiting the rights under copyright reserved above, no part of this publication may be reproduced, stored in or introduced into a retrieval system, or transmitted, in any form, or by any means (electronic, mechanical, photocopying, recording, or otherwise), without the prior written permission of the copyright owners or the publishers of the book.

ISBN 978-1-887664-72-1
Library of Congress Catalog Card Number 2007922772
Manufactured in the United States of America
First Printing by Midnight Marquee Press, Inc., March 2007

For "Cool Cats" everywhere

CONTENTS

CHAPTER 1: SUMMER IN THE CITY — 8

CHAPTER 2: FAMILY — 22

CHAPTER 3: TORTURE TIME — 35

CHAPTER 4: ON THE ROAD — 47

CHAPTER 5: FREE LOVE — 61

CHAPTER 6: STRIP SEARCH — 75

CHAPTER 7: A STRANGE INTERVIEW — 90

CHAPTER 8: ROUTE 66 — 104

CHAPTER 9: SECRET ARMY — 123

CHAPTER 10: THE RAID — 137

CHAPTER 11: DOUBLE AGENT — 148

CHAPTER 12: HIT SQUAD — 163

CHAPTER 13: NOT OF THIS WORLD — 178

CHAPTER 14: COUP D'ETAT — 193

CHAPTER 15: STATE OF EMERGENCY — 207

CHAPTER 16: THE MASTER RACE — 223

CHAPTER 17: A RECKONING — 239

CHAPTER 1
Summer in the City

Hot night glowed red on a skyline of tenement blocks, jagged like black broken teeth. A thin, distant wail of police sirens pierced the thud-thud-thud of jungle drums and pulsing bass, the call-to-war song of ghetto funk and soul. Fires burned on street corners and across great scars of waste ground. The flames made pools of light in a vast maze of darkness where fleeting figures darted, seeking the shadows. There was a hint of tear gas in the air. Smoke seeped up from heaps of rubble, a simmering volcano that was set to explode.

The long limo took forever to glide to a halt, the bright lights sheening on its polished flanks, its tinted windows as black as jet. It had twin escorts, like fast tanks, armored with chrome.

The convoy's arrival triggered a reflex of chattering shutters and a constellation of flashbulbs. There were always cameras, waiting at the Glitter Dome, and a crowd, jostling behind a cordon of red velvet ropes, craning for a glimpse of a famous face. The Glitter Dome—"where the Scene comes to be seen"—its façade a monumental jukebox of blazing neon, a polished marble forecourt transformed into a lake of rainbows.

"Hey!"

"Here he comes!"

Towering doors of glass and steel swung outwards effortlessly. The crowd let out a great collective sound of anticipation. The shutters clattered and flashbulbs detonated like a bombardment of star shells.

"It's him!"

Two tall, broad-shouldered dark men strode into view, out onto a ribbon of red carpet, stretching from the doors to the waiting limo. Their hair was cropped close to the skull, eyes masked by identical, impenetrable shades. They wore the same black suits, with the same leopard-skin lapels.

The crowd murmured, impressed. Then a collective shout rose up, amidst another volley of flashbulbs.

He was a coal-black, blue-black African, a handsome man mountain in gorgeous, flowing robes and pagan gold. Tribal scars etched on his cheeks made him all the more imposing. He stepped out with a slow and stately measure, as his advance guard accelerated till they reached the doors of the limo.

Tall men in shades and leopard-trimmed suits flanked the African as he made his regal progress along the red carpet. Clenched black fists rose above the bobbing heads of the crowd and the war cries rang out. Watching from the fringes, white faces in blue uniforms looked nervous. The African looked neither right nor left, and merely raised a golden baton, like a twig in his massive fist, in acknowledgment of the excitement he was generating.

There was someone with him, in the procession. Whose presence prompted another surge of sound from the crowd.

At the African's side, a precise half-pace behind, there was a woman. A beautiful blonde woman, in a revealing white silk halter top and billowing flares worn perilously low on her hips. A large, white leather shoulder bag with decorative tassels was draped casually over her shoulder.

She shone in the glare of the flashbulbs. She was young, in her early twenties. Her fair hair hung down to the small of her back, framing green eyes over high cheekbones, eyes like a cat's, slanted just a little, just enough to make her fascinating. Her nose was slightly tilted, just enough to be bewitching, and her lips were ripe and pouting, just a little, just enough to make her ravishing.

She was tall, not too tall, but tall enough to make her formidable. Her shoulders were strong and supple and her breasts filled the daring halter-top to perfection. Lightly tanned and golden, her bare midriff was superbly trim and toned. Her fine hips swung with a kind of lazy insolence as she moved past the gaping crowd with a lithe, athletic swagger.

"Jeeee-sus!"

The white cops groaned out loud as the woman paused, striking a pose with one hand on her naked hip, not condescending to look at anyone in particular, but seeing everything that was going on, aware that now everyone was looking at her.

Synchronized, dark-suited bodyguards opened the doors of the stretch limo. The great African made one last flourish with his baton to the crowd, as the chanting began and the clenched fists rose again. With a courtly gesture, he ushered the blonde woman into the car. Stooping, she vanished behind the black glass. As the remainder of his entourage formed a watchful semi-circle around him, the African followed her.

With military precision, the bodyguards split into two groups, moving swiftly to the hulking escort cars, stationed front and back. Doors slammed, engines revved. The white cops stepped forward to wave them away but the convoy was off before they had a chance, and left them stumbling in its exhaust, to a flurry of clenched fists and cheers, in one last fanfare of flashbulbs.

The road wound on and on, through the plush wooded hills. Below, the city sprawled to the glowing horizon as a grid of lights and twinkling towers, stained by blotches of pulsing deep red where the ghetto burned.

The progress of the limo and its escorts was marked on the dark road by the long splashes of their headlights. The road, a snake of deep blue shadow twisting between the dark slopes, was deserted. Occasionally, they passed tall gates fortified with spikes and razor wire, caught the glimpse of a sprawling mansion stark amongst the trees, bathed in bright security lighting.

Ahead, rear brake lights showed red as the lead car slowed in anticipation of a tight bend.

In the limo, the African glanced at a heavy gold Rolex, its dial surrounded by diamonds. Across from him, the blonde woman appeared to be dozing. Behind his shades, a bodyguard watched the regular rise and fall of her half-exposed breasts.

A second bodyguard was riding beside the driver. He pressed the button to lower the glass partition.

"We'll be there soon, Sir," he said back over his shoulder. "Just a—"

A spear of orange fire hurtled down from the dark, thickly wooded slopes above. Descending in a shallow arc, it struck the lead car amidships. First there was a dull thud. Suddenly weightless, the vehicle appeared to levitate, all four wheels leaving the ground. Then there was a shattering roar, an enveloping ball of flame, which rose up like a writhing bubble, shrinking as it vanished upwards. A mangled, smoking ruin, the car came crashing down.

The woman's eyes flashed open. A small hole appeared in the limo's windshield, fine cracks radiating from it like the spokes of a spider's web. The driver grunted, sagging forward onto the steering wheel. The limo slewed sideways and slid to a ponderous halt.

An identical hole materialized in the windscreen of the following car. The door opened and the driver fell out sideways onto the road. The bodyguards came leaping and tumbling out, gleaming automatics in their hands, moving protectively towards the trapped limo. The muzzles of their guns probed the dark slopes.

Muzzle flashes twinkled in the surrounding darkness. There was a prolonged rattle of machine-gun fire. Sparks and spurts of dust danced around the bodyguards' feet. Their guns clattered on the tarmac. One by one, they crumpled and fell beside them.

Silence. Somewhere, a night bird clucked nervously. Crackling tongues of flame licked at the charred wreckage. The bodies lay twitching in a spreading lake of blood.

Men walked out of the darkness, wading into the deep blue pools of shadow on the road. They wore olive drab and mottled camouflage, chests criss-crossed with ammunition belts, their identity concealed by black hoods. One carried an elegant sniper's rifle, fitted with a long scope. Another balanced a short, portable rocket-launcher on his shoulder. The rest cradled business-like AK-47's.

One had the bearing of a leader. He stepped forward, approaching the stationary, silent limousine.

"Mr President....?"

There was no reply. The leader lifted the muzzle of his AK-47 and fired a single shot into the night sky.

"Out of the car!"

The car door opened slowly.

"Hands in the air!"

The two surviving bodyguards edged out awkwardly, their hands up above their heads. A short burst cut them down.

"Sir…?"

A pause. Then the resplendent African rose slowly into view. He gazed at his assailants impassively.

Two hooded men stepped forward to drag the dead driver from the limo.

"Mr President, you will be continuing your journey with us. You will—"

For the first time, they noticed the blonde woman, sitting motionless in her seat.

The hooded men gasped, their eyes, through the slits in their hoods, roving all over her.

"You!" said the leader. "Come out, now!"

Her face expressionless, the woman slid out of her seat and exited the limo lithely. Her flesh was pale and glowing in the moonlight. The hooded men sucked in their breath with an audible hiss.

"What a waste," the leader murmured, lowering the muzzle of his AK-47 till it centered on the woman's chest.

The blonde's right hand was deep in her fancy shoulder bag. Suddenly, the bottom of the bag charred, flamed briefly and burst. There was a short and muffled ripple of machine-gun fire, a spitting muzzle flash.

The leader dropped on the spot with a surprised look in his eyes. The men behind her let the dead driver fall and struggled to un-sling their AK-47's. The woman spun around and dropped smoothly into a crouch, firing again. One man flung up his arms with a yell and fell backwards. The other fired his AK-47 over her head and there was a yelp behind the woman, from the man with the rocket launcher. The woman fired another short burst.

A sophisticated sniper's rifle is a clumsy weapon at close quarters. The woman shot the sniper as haste made him fumble with the bolt. He was dead before he hit the ground.

The last man threw away the rocket launcher and clutched at his leg, cursing loudly. With his free hand, he clawed a big pistol from a holster at his belt. Hobbling towards the woman, he opened fire. Unflinching, the woman flicked away the charred remains of the shoulder bag. A compact 7.65 Skorpion machine-pistol was revealed, clutched in her hand, a wisp of smoke curling from the muzzle.

She fired. The hooded man stopped shouting and fell flat on his face.

The pale and ghostly image of the yacht billowed gently, reflected in the calm, dark waters of the Bay. Its lights glowed like amber, against the black velvet of a summer night.

Soft candlelight gleamed on exotic wood, crystal twinkled. Slow music played seductively. Sheathed in a silken kimono, the blonde woman reclined on a colorful confection of deep cushions. She was in a waking dream. On the mirror top of a small side-table there were some scraps of foil, and fine lines of white powder.

In her dream, the woman made a soft sound and stirred, arching her back lazily. A deep rumbling seemed to fill the large, luxurious cabin.

The mighty African stood and looked down at her, chuckling. His bass resonance made the crystal chandelier tinkle.

"Do you like my candy...?"

The woman said "mmmm...mm..." and squirmed deeper into the cushions. Her hair fell across her face in a fine veil of gold.

"I have a present for you."

His sumptuous robes flowing, the African crossed the expanses of the cabin, ankle deep in the plush white carpet. He opened a drawer, then took something out and brought it back to her, draped in his hands.

The woman laughed, a mellow sound, like honey. She rose in one long, fluid motion and as she soared, the silken robe slithered from her shoulders and puddled at her feet.

"Aaahhh....!"

The African groaned, deep in his chest, ecstatic.

Her nakedness was spectacular. In the candlelight, she had a golden aura.

Reverently, the African decorated her with a leopard skin sash, hung with tassels of gold and adorned by a great star of flashing sapphires and diamonds.

"My country thanks you..."

The night was alive with the sparkle of champagne and gemstones, and the glow of a woman's skin.

The fizz was Coca-Cola and the only perfume was the spicy tang of a red hot chilli dog.

"Boy, I needed this!"

The cops took a break. They stood on either side of the parked black-and-white, stretching their legs, easing the kinks out of their spines. One sucked on a cigarette while his partner took a chunk out of the oozing chilli dog.

The patrol car was drawn up to the chipped kerb, by the empty yard of a derelict warehouse, ringed by a teetering wire fence that was hanging loose in places.

"Another busy night," the smoking cop looked up at the red sky.

His partner nodded, mouth full, wiping his chin with the back of his hand.

"Yep," the smoking cop continued. "That radio will be—"

Suddenly, a spray of something hot and sticky splattered his face. He wiped his hand across it and stared at the thick red smear on his palm. He thought his partner had flicked chilli sauce at him.

"Hey!" he complained. "Grow up, will ya…!"

His voice trailed away. He couldn't see him.

Yanking his pistol from its holster, the cop threw away the cigarette. It skidded across the broken slabs of the sidewalk, making sparks.

He ran around to the other side of the patrol car. His partner was lying on his back with his legs splayed out crookedly. One hand was on his chest, still clutching the chilli dog. His eyes were wide and staring.

There was a small dark hole in his left temple. The right side of his face was gaping and raw. A black puddle was spreading across the asphalt.

"Jesus!"

The cop twisted about, his gun jabbing in all directions.

There was a sharp *Whack! Whack! Whack!* and dust and bits flew off his dark blue shirt, in a neat pattern between his shoulder blades. With a grunt, the cop fell on his face and lay spread eagled. The pistol rattled on the ground.

"G RLS—GIR S—GIRLS!!! ! SEE T EM   DANCE !!"

The broken neon flashed intermittently, in red, white and blue.

"**RUDY'S AR**"

On the wrong side of town, the night throbbed with a dull red glow. A smell of burning drifted from the empty lots. Waste paper skittered fitfully in the gutters. The wail of the sirens ebbed and flowed. Hunched figures moved urgently, like ants, on a mission. They met briefly to rub antennae in the shadow of a boarded-up doorway, hand over cash and grab a little packet of fleeting happiness, then darted off in opposite directions.

Rudy's Bar was a long low single-storey grubby white shack that stood on a bleak street corner. A slash of waste ground piled high with building rubble divided it from rows of derelict tenements with barred doorways and glassless windows like empty eye sockets. Metal grilles protected its windows, where the light pulsated in time with the muffled thump of music.

A shadowy figure opened the door a sliver, making a thin slice of light spear the dirty, dark sidewalk, just wide enough to slip inside, in a brief gust of sound.

"Heeeyyy, my man, what's happenin'?"

The bar-room was a warm blast of voices and the jungle beat. With a sepia glow, a pall of tobacco smoke and the sweeter stuff made the hanging brass lamp-light fuzzy. The long bar with its twinkling Christmas trees of bottles and glasses and illuminated beer signs had a chrome top covered in swirls and scratches that looked like bundles of copper wire in the lamplight. Serious drinkers rubbed hunched shoulders, side by side on scuffed plum-colored leather swivel stools, not talking much, just drinking. Across from the bar, divided by a narrow alley of floor that was a tiled checkerboard of yellow and brown, the social drinkers reclined in the curve of padded booths in the same plum hide tacked down with brass studs. The varnished, tarnished wooden walls were hung with mottled pictures of half-remembered ball players and boxers. At the far end of the bar there was a floor space, with some small round tables crammed together and plain wooden chairs wedged around the tables. The tables were crowded with men, some playing cards, some doing deals. Some watched a scantily clad Hispanic girl as she gyrated on a small platform beneath a display of alternating colored lights that pulsed in time to the bumping and grinding beat.

"Yo! What's goin' down, brother?"

Rudy was a squat butterball, his beer belly straining a red T-shirt emblazoned with a huge gold star. In the lamplight, his broad, flat face looked like smooth brown leather topped by a ragged mop that stood bolt upright, in permanent shock.

"Solid, man, everythin's cool."

The new arrival was a lean mean dark man, a man in black. His jaunty jockey's cap was shiny black leather. His jacket was rugged black leather and he wore it over a high collared black silk shirt with pearl buttons up to his chin, tucked into soft black leather trousers as supple as a second skin. His shoes were black snakeskin, with pointed silver toecaps.

"Yo foun' dat quail....?" Crooked yellow teeth slurred Rudy's ponderous diction.

The lean man slipped off shades with narrow octagonal lenses. His eyes glittered viciously, like hard black pebbles. His face was narrow, the dark skin stretched taut over sharp bones.

He reached into his jacket pocket and produced an old-style cut-throat razor, its ivory handle inlaid with silver wire.

"I done that bitch, fo' sure," he said.

With a practised flick of his wrist, he made the blade flash like brass in the lamplight.

"I carved her good. No bitch o' mine gonna think t'go running to the Heat no mo'..."

The cop in the driver's seat looked at his watch for the hundredth time.

"Will you cut that out!" his partner complained. "Our shift don't end for another hour!"

The patrol car rolled up in front of a small corner supermarket, with a sign that said "Open All Night."

"Aw, now what?"

"I need some smokes. I'll just be a minute."

"Jeez!"

He came running out again when he heard the blare of the horn, long and unbroken.

"What the—!"

The driver was slumped forward, his head come to rest on the hub of the steering wheel. His partner grabbed his shoulder and hauled him upright. The horn went silent.

"Oh fuck!"

There was a small hole just above his ear, the hair matted and dark.

His partner jumped back from the car, pulling his gun.

Whack! Whack! Whack!

The music faded. The Hispanic girl waved to acknowledge a raucous ovation and left the stage.

New music blared from the PA system, a raunchy groove. The hubbub choked suddenly, and then swelled up again, in a concerted exhalation of astonishment and delight.

"Ow! Mama!"

Curtains at the back parted and the new dancer took to the small stage with a long and gliding swagger.

"Ooooo! Ooooo! Ooooo!"

She was tall and and obviously athletic, her eyes masked by mirror shades, her pouting lips scarlet. She wore a snow white Stetson hat from which a mane of auburn curls flowed down to her strong, bare shoulders.

Her costume was a star-spangled blue brassiere with a short white fringe; a red G-string and white boots. Girdling her naked hips, was a narrow silver gun belt, with twin holsters from which protruded toy gun butts in dark plastic, embossed with long-horned steer's heads.

The music was a dirty low-down, rhythm 'n blooze bump and grind. Spreading her long sleek thighs the girl flexed her body slowly, making her hips swing and rotate.

"Oh, baby!"

In the tobacco glow of the lamplight, her bare skin shone like pale gold, the red curls like burnished copper. Barely contained, the quivering mounds of her breasts glistened. Her toned belly and smooth strong thighs gleamed, as she lithed and writhed and undulated.

"Oh yeah!"

"Go baby go!"

Even some of the serious drinkers made the effort to swivel frontward on their stools. In the booths, the social drinkers twisted and craned and stood up for a better view. At the tables up front no one was playing cards anymore. Everyone was staring bolt upright at the stage.

"C'mon, red! Oooooh, mama! Gimme! Gimme!"

The man in black was at the front now, standing amongst the tables.

"Gimme, baby! Gimme! Show me yo' stuff!"

The sheen of her pale flesh lit up the room, her whole body working. She plucked the left-hand gun from its silver holster.

"Yeah!"

They could see it was a small, tin-plated cap pistol, with the little red tongue of the caps protruding from the top.

"Aw, watch out! She's dangerous!"

"A bad momma!"

She raised the little gun above her head and popped a cap at the ceiling. Hip-swaying, she pointed the muzzle here and there, all around the room.

Pop-pop-pop...

"Mercy!"

She holstered the cap pistol and took its right-hand partner from its silver sheath.

"Aw no!"

"She got's more!"

"Ooooo, mercy, mama!"

Fixated by her shimmying breasts, her undulating belly and flexing thighs, they didn't notice that this gun, with its silly plastic handle, was different, blue-black.

Her lips parted slowly. Her tongue tip teased her perfect white teeth. The man in black could see his reflection twinned in the lenses of her mirror shades, as she looked straight at him, where he stood between the tables.

"Oh yeah, baby. I'm yo' man!"

She lifted the gun high in the air, held that pose for a moment and then brought it down slow. All he could see was the straining, glistening tops of her breasts and the sheen of sweat on her thighs.

"Yo Baby! Yo' mine!"

Her smile was dazzling.

Bang!

A black dot appeared on the man's forehead, right between the eyes. The leather jockey cap took flight as the back of his skull erupted in a pale pink halo. For a second the man in black stood there, still posing, thumbs hooked into his expensive belt. Then his knees turned to water and he buckled, crashing down across a table before rolling onto the tiled checkerboard floor.

The card players sat there stunned, splattered in blood and brains. Everyone stared at the corpse, twitching in a spreading puddle of blood.

When they thought to look back at the stage, it was empty, nothing but the blank curtains at the back, swaying slightly.

The unmarked car cruised the dark streets, patrolling the grid map of its territory, looking for trouble.

"No way," said the thin detective. "No way are the Forty-Niners gonna take the Packers. Not in Green Bay."

The fat detective kept one hand on the wheel, digging into a jumbo bag of potato chips wedged onto the dash.

"You just wait and see," he mumbled through a mouthful of crumbs. "The Niners are goin' all the way to the Superbowl this year."

His partner snorted.

"Fifty says they ain't."

"Fifty? Make it a hundred and you're on."

"A hundred it is then."

"I'll look forward to spendin' it."

"In your dreams, buddy. The Niners ain't—"

A line of neat holes was drilled across the windscreen, a web of thin cracks radiating from them.

Whack! Whack! Whack! Whack! Whack!

The detectives were slammed back in their seats. The potato chips fell on the floor.

The car made a slow turn and mounted the sidewalk with a jolt. It buried its nose in a boarded-up storefront and came to a halt, the engine grinding, grey smoke billowing from the exhaust.

Potato chips floated in a lake of blood.

The toilet window swung open onto a dark and narrow alley. The window was small but the dancer slithered out comfortably, without effort. A light rain was falling. Pausing, she savored it on her hot and crawling skin. With a "huff," she expelled the fug of the bar, emptying her lungs. She sucked in a long, deep breath, her breasts rising, filling herself with fresh air. But the air in the alley wasn't very fresh and had a tang of trash and stale urine, and she laughed, grimacing.

She heard urgent voices. A head jutted from the toilet window. Snatching the black pistol from its holster, she took aim coolly and parted the head's afro. There was a yell of alarm and the head vanished.

At a trot, the dancer moved down the alley, her feet scuffling scraps of paper and grazing empty bottles and tin cans.

"Err…uumm..phhh!….wha….whazzat…?"

A shapeless bundle of rags lay sprawled on a heap of rotting cardboard. It was roused from an alcoholic fog.

"W-who….wha…whaddaya wan…?"

The bum's blurred vision cleared somewhat. He struggled to sit up straight, gawping at the near naked vision standing over him. The dancer looked down at him. Holstering the gun, she reached behind her and unhooked the starry brassiere.

The derelict's eyes crossed and then uncrossed slowly as he strained to focus on the impossible feast displayed for him. His mouth opened and shut but all that came out were tiny strangled noises.

Leaning down till the spectacular tips of her breasts were inches from his bulging eyeballs, the dancer draped the bra across the greasy top of his head, so he wore the warm cups like earmuffs.

"No one will ever believe you."

There were muffled voices far behind her. She turned on her heel and moved on to the end of the alley. Beyond lay a broad scar of bulldozed, flat waste ground, and beyond that empty streets with no streetlights, the jagged gap-toothed skyline and the pulsing red glow in the night sky.

She came to a tall fragment of wall with holes where windows had been. In its shadow there was what appeared to be a mound of garbage. The dancer bent to tug with both hands, the muscles cording down her strong bare back. The garbage was clever camouflage netting and slid away like a blanket.

The dancer stood back, smiling.

"Hello, sweetheart."

In the night, it was a pale phantom. A yellow T-top Corvette ZL-1, its shark-like snout traversed by a broad black stripe that tapered dramatically as it raced rearward. In their chrome sheathing, the gleaming side exhausts proclaimed extravagant power.

"Did you miss me?"

The roof panels had been removed and she reached into its dark interior. On the passenger seat there was a fat brown paper parcel. It disgorged a pale blue sweatshirt and grey tracksuit bottoms, a pair of pink tennis shoes.

"Oh."

Reaching up, she took off the white Stetson. She fiddled for a second, and then tugged. The red tresses detached.

"Ow."

She paused to look around. The wasteland was deserted. Nothing moved on the dead streets.

The blue-black gun was wrapped in the wig which was stuffed into the hat and the hat was dropped on the ground.

"Oops!"

She plucked off the red G-string, wrapped it around the mirror shades and shoved them into the hat with the wig and the gun. Bending, she unzipped the boots and tugged them off, laying them on top of the hat.

She froze. Three men were sprinting down the street that bordered the far side of the waste ground. Guns glittered in their hands. They skidded to a stop and turned this way and that, looking all around. They were cursing, gesticulating.

She stood stark naked by the Corvette, submerged in the deep pool of shadow. Her blood was racing. Excitement was a hot and cold electricity that tingled up and down her spine.

A big black sedan with blank windows came barrelling round the bend and accelerated towards the three men. Brakes squealed. Doors slammed. The engine revved and tires smoked. The car was gone. The street was empty again.

Delving into the Corvette, she came out with a tin of lighter fluid.

The wig flared up into a fireball, consuming the G-string and corroding the shades. The hat and boots charred slowly. She kept adding squirts of fuel until all was ashes. The plastic gun butt had melted and the gun was now an untraceable ruin.

She touched the ashes with her bare big toe.

"Goodbye, 'Candy'. It was fun."

Reaching up again, she felt for the last few pins. Long blonde hair like golden silk descended to her naked shoulders. She shook her head and ran her fingers through it.

Suddenly, she was very cold, fingers of ice playing over her bare skin. She looked at her hands. They were shaking.

She laughed.

In an instant, she was dressed, and was cinching the drawstring of the tracksuit bottoms. She didn't bother to bury the wrecked pistol. Like all the rest, this patch of waste ground was littered with discarded guns and knives, and body parts.

The all-black cockpit of the Corvette fitted her like a glove. She inhaled deeply, revelling in leather and all those car smells. She wanted to hear the engine's roar, but she just started up and let it rumble away gently.

When she was far away, she took it onto the freeway and drove for miles to nowhere in particular, out to where there was nothing but a vast empty darkness in all directions. She made motor music, up and down through the scales, with the wind in her hair. And then suddenly, in the middle of nowhere, she turned round and rode home with Sly and the Family Stone.

The phones rang at exactly the same time in every newspaper office and TV station. The message was the same:

"Six pigs died tonight. More will follow. The Power will be destroyed. The black man is a slave no more!"

The beach house was a bright white one-storey affair with a sloping roof that shaped it like a blunt wedge. It stood on stilts, all the way back from where the rhythmic tides lapped at the sandy shore, up against a rust-colored cliff topped by a thatch of tall grasses.

A balcony with a wooden rail ran all along the front of the beach house. The blonde woman was standing there, gazing out at the sea.

She wore an Indian headband embroidered with multi-colored beads; a tan leather halter top decorated with whorls of tiny silver studs; and faded blue jeans secured low and snug on her hips by a silver and turquoise belt buckle, tucked into suede boots.

There was a white plastic table and chair on the balcony. On the table was an oblong tobacco tin. The woman looked at her watch, a chunky, steel military piece on an olive drab GI strap, with a black dial and luminous markers. She smiled. She sat down and opened the tin. Everything she needed was there.

With practiced dexterity, she manufactured a joint, just a small one, a mild one, a morning joint. The sun was climbing into a flawless sky and the sea and the sand were like pale pink gold, the red cliffs glowing. It was going to be a beautiful day.

Inside, the beach house was simple and sparse, woven mats on the bare wooden floor, a few large cushions thrown down casually here and there. Beaded curtains masked a small, functional galley and a bedroom bare except for a tall wardrobe and a Japanese-style bed on the floor. Posters on the walls advertised bygone jazz festivals. A portable TV stood on a stool in the corner, covered in dust. The telephone was on the floor, with the receiver off the hook.

A tangle of cables was connected to a hi-fi deck and its twin speakers, spread wide apart in opposite corners of the main room. Mellow funk oozed from them, the horns like spooned honey. With the joint in her hand, the blonde woman came dancing in from the balcony, making her hips swing slowly from side to side. She hip swayed and bellied around the room, laughing as she surfed on the mats, sliding on the polished floor.

She looked at her watch again.

"Fuck!"

With a flick of her finger, she propelled the stub of the joint in an arc, through the wide open sliding doors, out over the balcony and onto the sand.

"Sorry guys....."

Stooping, she killed the music. She drained the lukewarm dregs from a chipped enamel coffee mug, making a face and wiping her mouth with the back of her hand.

"Ugh!"

Snatching a baggy canvas satchel from on top a heap of cushions, she slung it across her shoulder and vanished through the beaded curtain that led to the bedroom.

She crossed to the tall wardrobe, plain and functional. She opened the doors. She stepped inside.

The room behind the wardrobe was a polished steel strongbox. Neon strip lights lit automatically as she entered, her movements making crazy, jangling reflections.

"Hmmm......."

Racked securely on the wall there was a lightweight .25 Colt automatic carbine, fitted with a sniper scope; the stumpy black Skorpion; a Remington pump shotgun with folding skeleton butt; and a government-issue M-16.

She walked past these and the steel shelves packed with cartons of ammunition, the stack of wooden boxes stencilled with military specs and codes that denoted smoke and gas and fragmentation grenades. She ignored the compact, portable rocket launcher and its attendant missiles.

She reached a steel cabinet mounted on the far wall and opened it, twiddling the combination lock briskly.

No, not the Smith & Wesson .357 Magnum; nor the .45 Colt automatic; or the 9mm Beretta. Today, she felt like the chromed Walther PPK, with its pearl grips. She plucked the cartridges from their little box and thumbed them one by one under the lip of the magazine. She slapped the magazine into the butt with the flat of her hand.

She looked at her watch again.

"Damn!"

A flight of wooden steps led down sideways from the balcony to the golden sand of the beach. She came flying down two at a time.

The way to the garage was under the house, mounted on its lofty stilts. Long grey steel doors were set into the wall of the cliff. A concrete driveway turned sideways sharply and vanished in a twist. Hidden from view behind rising mounds and tussocks, it climbed in a spiral, up a notch in the rock face, to the highway that ran along the cliff top.

The woman pressed a button on a little black plastic gizmo in her hand and the doors whispered open, rising smoothly. Passing through, she broke the beam of a magic eye and the lights came on.

So many choices, so little time. The yellow Corvette was sleek and seductive.

"You've had your turn, baby."

The Chevy Chevelle SS 454 was midnight blue with white racing stripes streaking along the hood and basic black inside with few frills and trimmings. A brute with its massive prow like a battering ram, it was just the thing when you were in a hurry. If you saw that filling your rear view mirror, you got out of the way quick.

She never let anything get in her way.

CHAPTER 2
Family

The mansion at the end of the long leafy driveway was mock-Southern Plantation, with white columns and climbing ivy. Every blade of grass and bush and tree on its sun-dappled lawns was planned meticulously. It had decoratively wrought porch swings and hanging baskets of flowers and a stately silver-grey Bentley parked outside.

"Be it ever so humble..." she grinned, turning up the volume so the sultry beat boomed out of the rolled-down windows, as the bullish Chevelle shouldered its way down the drive, shredding the tips of the lush rhododendron bushes.

The dark blue brute came barrelling onto a broad gravel forecourt, much too fast, leaning over, wallowing on its suspension. It skidded perilously before sliding to a sudden halt, stopping with a jolt and scattering pebbles that pinged on the grey flank of the Bentley.

She let the music pound for a few more bars, then flicked it off, flung open the car door and swung gracefully out of the driver's seat. A pale, disapproving face was watching from a downstairs window. Laughing, she waved jauntily. The face frowned and disappeared.

Her long blonde hair swinging, she bounded up the porch steps. The polished doors opened as she reached for the ornate brass bell pull. An ancient oriental bowed low before her. With skin like parchment, thin as a rake and with a few wisps of grey hair combed across his skull, he was a bygone figure, in a baggy frock coat, striped pants and white gloves.

"Hi, Hiroshi!" she breezed by, slapping him on the shoulder and nearly knocking him over. "Haven't they driven you mad yet? I don't know how you put up with them."

Winded, the old man leant on the doorframe.

"Hey? Where is everybody? Where are you hiding?"

She sailed through the vast entrance hall with its cascading chandeliers and broad, soaring staircase. Entering the main drawing room, she stood with her hands on her hips, drinking it all in. Like the rest of the house, it was all in the best possible taste, wealthy conservative, good solid Republican taste.

Crowding the marble mantle over the impressive fireplace, there were the same old pictures: Dad shaking hands with the Vice-President; Dad with a fraternal arm around the shoulder of Senator so-and-so; Mom and Dad with the grateful President and his First Lady, at yet another campaign fundraiser.

There wasn't a single picture of her.

Smiling, she shook her head.

"You've never liked this place, have you, Catherine?"

Catherine. He always called her Catherine. It sounded so unfamiliar.

She took a deep breath, and then turned around slowly.

"Hi, Dad."

He was a tall, handsome man in his early fifties, wearing an immaculate blue blazer, crisp cream flannels and heraldic club tie. His tan was expensive and his perfectly groomed iron grey hair was all his own. He had the hard, chiselled, patrician look of a man who knew what he wanted and how to get it, the look of a successful man, a man who subjected himself to a rigorous physical regime, who had never had a day's illness in his life.

They stood looking at each other. Their eyes locked, until with a tiny twitch of anger at the corner of his mouth, he looked away.

He glanced at the window.

"Another new car?" His voice was pure Harvard Law School.

"Yes, another new car." Her voice was the sun and the sand and the surf.

"It's an obscenity. That kind of thing is driven by oafish louts, by Negro drug pushers and pimps..."

She smiled.

"Well, I like it. It's fun."

Her father sneered.

"Yes, you appear to be getting a great deal of pleasure out of spending your Uncle John's money."

She shrugged.

"Well, Dad, that was the idea. That's what he wants me to do."

"He must be mad. I can't believe he's my brother! He must have gone out of his mind. He had it all, prestige, a career, a position...to throw it all away like that...!"

She turned away and moved to the window. The light was soft on her face.

"He's happy."

She turned back suddenly.

"Are you happy, Dad?"

He stared at her.

"What would you know about happiness? You who've never done anything with your life!"

She made a face, looking down at her feet.

"Yes! You who wasted all the benefits and privileges that you were born with, all the gifts that were given to you!"

Her father looked her up and down, at the beaded headband, the skimpy leather halter-top and the low-slung jeans.

"And look at you! You dress like some sort of beatnik, like a street corner prostitute!"

She raised her head and gazed at him sadly.

"Is Mom here?"

The anger faded from his face and was replaced by a kind of blankness.

"She couldn't wait for you any longer. She had an important meeting to go to."

Cat nodded.

"I see."

Suddenly, he looked defensive and embarrassed.

"Your mother doesn't tell me her plans...I'm not responsible for—!"

His daughter smiled.

"Don't worry, Dad. I didn't expect her to be here."

She looked back at the window, moved her feet, making the strap of her bag more comfortable on her shoulder.

"Anyway, I only came to let you know that I'm going to be away and you may not hear from me for a while, so not to worry."

Her father made an exasperated sound.

"What is it you do exactly?" he demanded. "Where do you go? You never tell us anything!"

She laughed, rolling her beautiful eyes.

"Oh, this and that. Here and there. You know..."

She sprang forward, light on her toes, to plant a quick peck on his cheek.

"Bye, Dad. Be seein' ya."

She was gone. He heard the rumble of the engine, the crunch of tires on the gravel. He stood by the fireplace, next to his pictures, a blankness in his eyes.

Brown fingers blurred. Long gold-glitter fingernails clicked rapidly on the keys.

Glowing green characters marched out onto the blank screen, forming ranks and filling it with words:

PERSONNEL FILE
(Classified Level 1)

"Field" name – Cat
Real name – *classified*
Age – 23
Nationality – American
Base of operations – Bay City HQ
Place of residence – *classified*

• • • • • •

Cat took the road that ran by the beach, where she could taste the salty tang in the wind that washed her face, rushing through the rolled-down window, and watch the brassy ball of the late afternoon sun race parallel to her and the inviting, glittering froth of the surf roll onto the glowing sand.

The road was the long way to anywhere and in a world where everyone was in a hurry, it was almost deserted, in the middle of a working day. She passed some kids hanging out their arms and laughing, in a psychedelic Beetle with surfboards strapped to the roof. They waved and she grinned and waved back, envying them.

She shifted gear and the blue Chevelle's engine changed key, climbing a notch in intensity. The sun slipped behind her shoulder.

> Special skills – all-collegiate heptathlon champion in her freshman year: can swim, ski, ride, fence and shoot; proficient in several of the martial arts
>
> Weapons – authorized: Colt .25 automatic carbine; Smith & Wesson .357 Magnum unauthorized: no information available

· · · · · ·

A colored speck in her rear-view mirror began to grow. She watched it close the gap and expand until it identified itself as a candy-apple red open-top Porsche.

"Hmph!"

The Porsche pulled out and slid alongside her, matching her speed. The driver sat with one hand resting casually on the wheel, a slim man with long sandy hair and a cowboy moustache, wearing blue-tinted shades and a gaudy Hawaiian shirt over denims cut off at the knee. He had Rock Promoter written all over him.

"Hey, baby…." He called out to her.

She ignored him.

"You in a band, baby? You oughta be in a band. You got it, baby."

She tilted her nose skywards and made the Chevelle draw ahead. Instantly, the Porsche was alongside. Some lost salesman in an anonymous sedan, coming in the opposite direction, had to swerve to give them room and honked his horn in alarm, its diminishing whine disappearing behind them.

"You wanta be in a band, baby?"

The Promoter reached into his glove compartment and produced a little plastic bag sealed with a rubber band, full of white powder. Holding it up between his fingertips, he waved it at her.

"You wanta meet the band, baby? Any band…I know 'em all."

Amusing herself, Cat nudged the Chevelle forward and sure enough, the red Porsche was beside her. The Promoter was still flourishing the little bag. Cat gave it a quick glance, which made the man laugh knowingly.

"Ya want some, sweetheart?"

With a flick of the wrist, he tossed the bag through the open window of the Chevelle. It landed in her lap.

"Yeah! Let's party, baby. Plenty more where that came from!"

Imperceptibly, she made the blue monster go faster. The needle was climbing towards 100. There was a slight hesitation from the Porsche, but then it was right there again.

> Education: all the best schools – *classified*
> Was inevitably expelled from most of them; dropped out of college in search of excitement and adventure

Rock steady, Cat twisted to lean her head towards the open window. She kept it like that, looking at him. When the Promoter turned his shoulders to look right back at her, the Porsche wavered and he had to put both hands on the wheel.

"Whoo! Your place or mine, baby?"

Smiling, keeping the Chevelle as straight as an arrow, she looked the Porsche over from stem to stern.

Same old story, too much car and not enough man

Slowly, elegantly, she gave him the finger.

"Drive American, numbnuts!"

Her head snapped back inside. The Chevelle gave a little nudge sideways and then roared, leaping forward.

> Homes – a fashionable penthouse apartment - *classified*
>
> but tends to live at the beach – *classified*
>
> Transport – *classified*
> Made an impressive debut and considerable impact on the local racing circuits at the age of 18 but was banned after only five races for over-aggressive driving

· · · · · ·

"What the f—!"

The Porsche swerved, dipped down the shallow grassy embankment at the side of the road and careered, its back end bouncing, onto the beach, its engine grinding shrilly, crunching to a sudden halt, its spinning, sinking wheels raising a yellow cloud of sand.

> Status – agent in final phase of probation. Has performed all of her assignments with conspicuous success. Agent is cool and resourceful. However, her flair for improvisation has a tendency to spill over into reckless self-indulgence

• • • • • •

Cat played a parting fanfare on her car horn, a derisive bugle call. She plucked the bag of white powder from her lap and stowed it in the secret place.
"The best things in life are free."

She came into the city by the back way, with the late afternoon sun beating like a brass gong on a scene of destruction and dereliction. An industrial wasteland, empty warehouses, vandalized with spray cans, every window shattered, silent factories slowly corroding or reduced to charred bones, gutted by fire.

Waste paper swirled in the wake of the blue Chevelle as she weaved down the avenues that ran between the hollow warehouses, swerving to avoid heaps of tumbled bricks and lumps of concrete with rusted spars jutting from them. The open windows sucked in the smell of decay and Cat wrinkled her nose, longing for sea breezes.

The avenues became alleyways. She slowed down and squeezed the big car down ever-narrower passages, with an inch to spare, looking left and right, worrying about her custom paintwork. With a surge of relief, she saw the light at the end of the tunnel, which expanded into a broad plain of glaring concrete with tall weeds sprouting in its cracks, strewn with rubbish and rubble.

Rolling to a halt, she let the motor idle, delighting in its deep grumble. On the far side of the bleak concrete, where once fork lifts had scurried and trucks lined up to load, there was the towering, corrugated frontage of a massive warehouse. Its high windows were sightless pits, its bristling hoists and cranes rusty. Corporate banners emblazoned on its vast doors were faded and ghostly, green livery scarred and flaking.

Cat shook her head, smiling. The Chevelle rumbled across the broken concrete, bits of debris crunching under its wheels. She let it roll on and on and just when it looked like there was going to be a collision a section of the corrugated wall swung inwards and the car vanished into the inner darkness. The wall swung shut behind it.

The Chevelle rolled into a huge steel cage. She switched off the engine. Iron shutters descended, closing off the way she came.

The cage was lit by a baleful yellow light. Cat looked at her reflection in the rear-view mirror and teased her hair a bit. She felt the swift descent in the pit of her stomach. It lasted for a full minute.

There was a slight jolt as the cage stopped. Then a muffled beeping and the front gates of the cage rose quickly. The beeping was louder, insistent.

"Okay, okay!"

With a last glance at herself, Cat opened the door and swung out of the car. Striding out of the elevator, she advanced into a white world, a half-circular area with stark walls and a snowy carpet, from which long gleaming corridors, punctuated by polished doorways, radiated like the spokes of a wheel, as far as the eye could see.

All that brightness made her blink, as it always did, but she quickly got used to it.

"Ah, Cat. There you are."

There was a young woman walking briskly towards her, down one of the corridors to her left. Cat smiled when she saw her, a Japanese girl with a face like a deadly kitten, in a crisp pale blue blouse and dark blue skirt, carrying a thick clipboard under her arm.

"Oh, hi, Aiko," Cat hoped she looked appropriately apologetic. "How are you?"

The Japanese girl frowned.

"It would be much appreciated, Cat," she said. "If just once you could be on time."

Swivelling neatly, Aiko set off rapidly down the central corridor that ran straight ahead of the exit from the elevator, tapering to a far distant vanishing point.

"The Boss is waiting for you."

The blonde had to jump to catch up with her. The white corridor was very bright, and all along its length young women in pale blue blouses and dark blue skirts were exiting one door and entering another, laden with files and documents. They all gave Cat a long, interested look as she passed by, looking her up and down, in her revealing halter top and bold, low-slung jeans.

"We don't often get a visit from a field agent here," said Aiko. "You're a celebrity."

"Aw shucks!" Cat replied, laughing.

Aiko frowned.

"You really ought to take the work more seriously."

The corridor did have an end, and finally they reached it. This door wasn't like the others. It was padded green leather, with sparking brass studs.

Aiko pressed a button on a brass panel. A buzzer sounded and the door opened inwards.

"Go in."

The office was huge, with a plush maroon carpet and a rainbow of exotic tapestries on the walls. There were fearsome tribal masks, grotesque statuettes of angry gods and leopard skin rugs.

"There you are. Nice of you to join us."

The voice was a slow, Southern drawl, like golden syrup. Her face, framed by a towering afro, was the color of rich mahogany. Hers was a proud, fierce beauty, with her slanting eyes that burned with a dark fire, her high, broad cheekbones, strong nose, full lips and determined chin. A beauty that belonged to an ancient, royal race, a culture that built stone cities and cultivated and wrote songs and fought and conquered, on an undiscovered continent, while Europeans still scratched themselves in their mud huts.

"Sorry, Selena. I got sidetracked."

The office was dominated by a massive, curved desk, lavishly carved with animal heads and tribal scenes. On the wall behind it there was a panoramic map of the United States and a battery of TV screens. In front, a semi-circle of high-backed conference chairs, upholstered with zebra-skin.

"As always...."

Selena rose from behind the desk. Cat looked at her appreciatively. She was magnificent. It was hard to guess her age. She could even be forty, but she was straight and tall, taller even than Cat, and powerful, dressed in a simple pale green robe that draped down to her golden sandals, gold thread trimming its collar and billowing cuffs.

"You perform your missions like a well-oiled machine. But otherwise..."

Cat laughed.

"Well, you know me, when I'm off-duty I let it all hang out."

Selena crossed the office. The strength of her body was evident in the way that she moved, the long robe flowing. Framing the beautiful blonde head between her long brown fingers with their golden nails, she looked deep into Cat's jade-green eyes.

"Okay?"

Cat took a deep breath, held it for a moment, and then released it in a long sigh.

"Okay."

"Good."

Selena returned to her desk and made a motion with a gold-tipped finger. Cat settled into the zebra-striped upholstery.

Selena opened a buff-colored file that lay on the carved desk-top.

"You did a good job," she said quietly. Mister Mean won't be turning school-girls into junkie prostitutes any more."

Cat frowned.

"It would have been better," she suggested. "If they hadn't waited to call in the Agency until he cut up a nice white co-ed. It didn't seem to matter when all his victims were poor kids from the ghetto."

Selena shrugged.

"That's the way it is. As long as all we're doing is killing each other. They woke up when Mean got ambition, moved uptown and started supplying those rich college boys and girls."

"And one of them just happened to be a big wheel's daughter and that's when the phones started ringing."

"Co-rrect!"

"Well, as long as he got his in the end. Good riddance to bad rubbish."

Selena looked down at the desk, leafing through the file.

"You gave him his for sure. Right between the eyes. I like your style."

"Thank you. I enjoyed it."

Selena opened a desk drawer, producing a somewhat fatter file.

"Not half as much as you enjoyed your assignment with President N'Bonga."

Cat squirmed in her chair.

"Oh don't tell me! You've got it all on film."

Selena looked mysterious.

"Oh, you never know when it might come in useful. In case we ever need a favor from the President."

"The Father of the Nation in sex and drugs scandal with mystery blonde?"

"Something like that."

"Yeah, all men dance like puppets if you dangle them on that string."

They both laughed. Then suddenly, Selena was serious, turning back to Mr Mean's slimmer file.

"Rumor has it that there's an old bum staggering up and down Corneil Street wearing a new hat that looks a lot like a star-spangled bra."

Cat turned a shade of peach and stifled a giggle.

"It's not funny," Selena said sternly. "Sometimes you enjoy your work too much."

"I'm sorry," Cat chuckled.

"Well I hope you won't be. Mean's mob is still out looking and someone may put it together."

Cat sobered quickly.

"Yes, you're right. It won't happen again."

Selena nodded, closing the file.

"Yes, well, in the meantime, you'd best get out of town for a week or two, while we do some background and find out if they're on to you. They're bad boys and it won't look good on their record if they don't avenge their leader's death. It would be hard for them to get another job."

Cat looked reluctant.

"I'd much rather be looking into those cop killings. Something's fishy there."

Selena smiled.

"You could be right. But we have to wait to be asked."

Cat shrugged.

"They won't ask if they've already made up their minds. Maybe we should go and take a look for ourselves."

Selena's golden fingernails tapped out a rhythm on the desktop.

"So you don't believe that it's the Militants?"

Cat shrugged again.

Selena got up and walked round in front of the desk. Cat gazed up at her as she ruffled the soft blonde hair.

"Go on, honey. Take a holiday, you deserve it."

The Deputy Mayor was enjoying his vacation.

Fifty miles down the coast, a whole world away from the big city, was his secret retreat, a hacienda secluded on a wooded hillside, overlooking the golden crescent of the beach.

"Catch any, honeypie?"

The motor cruiser was a dark silhouette on a sea of shimmering brass, basking in the late afternoon sun.

"Are they biting?"

The woman who wasn't the Deputy Mayor's wife was a strapping, well-stacked blonde in a floral print bikini. Bearing a tray with a foaming beer glass she sauntered to the blunt stern of the boat.

"Thanks baby."

The Deputy Mayor laid down the long fishing rod. He was a squat man with receding fair hair and a fleshy pink face, his glistening paunch spilling over the waistband of gaudy Bermuda shorts.

"No luck yet," he chuckled. "But then I'm not here for the fishing."

He wrapped one hand around the chilled beer glass, clamping the other on the blonde's ample buttocks. The girl squirmed, giggling.

"Oh, Freddy! The crew are watching!"

The Deputy Mayor squeezed her rump.

"Don't you worry, babe. They're deaf, dumb and blind."

His fat arm snaked around her wide hips.

"Now you know I didn't bring you here to type any memos."

Way down below decks in the darkness, a clock was ticking.

"Freddy! You naughty man...!"

It was an alarm clock. It was set for precisely that moment. That moment had arrived.

"Now Babs honey, why don't you get down here and—"

There was a dull *Whump*! deep down. The boat, like a tiny toy on the great shining sea, seemed to lift clear out of the water.

The Deputy Mayor and his secretary barely had time to look surprised, only a fraction of a second to register the end of their lives.

There was a shattering roar, an engulfing ball of bright orange flame that rose upwards, writhing and consuming itself, becoming a pall of dense black smoke. Scraps of wood and metal came raining down out of the smoke, splatting on the water.

After a while, the smoke began to fade to a grey smudge, a thin haze that drifted away slowly, the sun showing through it as a pale yellow disc. Seagulls shrieked with excitement, wheeling and dipping down through the grey veils, swooping to snatch dead fish and shreds of human meat from the water mottled with oil.

The Global Tower was a monumental phallus of gleaming steel and tinted glass, a symbol of the city's corporate virility. Boasting that it touched the sky, it gave the finger to the storm clouds of recession. It dominated the Bay City skyline, a constant reminder that when the poor got poorer, the rich got richer.

All the way up the glittering shaft, were the nerve centers of the city's capital and enterprise. The biggest banks and brokers headquartered here, the most expensive law firms, most of the major TV networks and some of the large publishing houses and broadsheets. This is where the politicians came cap in hand. This is where the Power lived.

Men in pin-striped suits were flowing in and out of an array of revolving doors. They all stopped in mid-sentence to stare at Cat in her skimpy street threads. Some looked offended, some lustful, others exchanged knowing, man-of-the-world grins. One or two knew who she was and muttered to their companions: "That's J. Spencer Warburton's daughter…"

Cat ignored them all completely. The tide of suits parted for her as she swaggered by with that long, lithe stride, across the polished forecourt, towards the whirling doors.

Trailing in her wake, a flustered flunkey in a comic opera uniform flapped his white-gloved hands, indicating the brutal, blunt Chevelle, left blocking the constant ebb and flow of multi-colored taxis and stretch limousines, now all honking in irritation.

"Hey! You can't leave that there, Miss. You—!"

A colleague took him by the arm and murmured something in his ear.

"Oh…!"

Cat lobbed the car keys back over her shoulder.

"Park it for me, won't you?"

While the suits gaped, she sailed through the revolving doors and entered the spectacular entrance hall. It was a whole world of its own, of shining marble and chrome, with trees and hanging gardens and towering waterfalls and cascades and melodic fountains. The air was cool and perfumed, and encouraging, uplifting music was piping everywhere. An entire population in business suits came and went across its gleaming expanses, in a brisk and businesslike manner, with places to go and people to see.

Cat's long, loose stride seemed to throw the suits off their timing, and several had to stumble to get out of her way. She treated them as though they were invisible.

There were at least twenty elevator doors, each a shining modern evocation of art deco. And a twenty-first, which was smaller and less conspicuous, just a simple grey slab. But this one had its own sentry, a middle-aged man with a pleasant dark brown face, in a pale blue uniform, wearing a gun.

"Hello, Miss Warburton. Long time no see."

"Hi, Fred, how are you?"

She paused to exchange pleasantries. Suits waiting for the nearest elevator observed her curiously.

"Staying long?"

"No, I'm just here to pick up a few things from Uncle John's old apartment and then I'll be gone for a while."

"I miss your Uncle. He used to stop by when I was on my coffee break to talk Jazz and baseball."

Cat gazed upon Corporate America, hustling and bustling all around them.

"This wasn't the life for him. He's much happier now."

The guard smiled.

"That's good. It's nice to know someone is."

Cat touched his shoulder.

"I'll get him to call you the next time I see him."

She glanced back towards the revolving doors, at the marching columns of suits filing in and out.

"Listen, I'd better get moving. I want to be out of here before Dad shows up."

The guard pressed a button. They shook hands as the doors slid open.

"Well, it's always a pleasure to see you, Miss."

"Good to see you too, Fred. Take care."

The phones were ringing all over the Global Tower, in the newspaper and TV offices.

"The Deputy Head Pig is dead. There is no hiding place where the hand of the black man cannot reach you. The Power will fall. The black man is a slave no more!"

The special elevator to the penthouse was a polished steel box. It went very fast, up and up and up and up. She felt it in her eardrums and swallowed to make them pop.

The elevator door opened directly into the penthouse suite. Cat burst out laughing as soon as she saw it. She just couldn't help it, it was the same every time.

The penthouse was the essence of a swinging bachelor pad. Inspiring nudes adorned the intervals between long panoramic windows that gave a vertiginous view of the entire city, guaranteed to impress a lady, especially at night, when all the lights would be twinkling like a galaxy. There was a lavish, exotic cocktail bar that belonged on a beach in Hawaii, and the very latest in Swedish kitchens. The stacked hi fi system boasted wrap-around quadraphonic sound and there were control panels that fine-tuned lighting that could even simulate the romantic glow of firelight.

The lounge was immaculate as always, but the air was stale. It had the feel of a place that was used occasionally but never lived in. There was nothing about it that spoke to Cat. She scarcely looked around her as she crossed to the master bedroom where she kept her things.

When she opened the door she saw the enormous round water bed with its black silk sheets and, of course, the mirrors on the ceiling. She never slept in that bed, on the rare occasions she stayed here, when she was in town and too stoned to make it back to the beach. It was ridiculous, so she just slept on some cushions on the floor.

She started towards the tall clothes cupboards set into the far wall, wanting to be in and out as fast as she could.

On the edge of her vision, she caught a slight movement in the mirrors.

Cat turned quickly, but not quick enough.

CHAPTER 3
Torture Time

Cat struggled back to consciousness, clawing her way out of deep dark waters. The pounding in her skull became a dull throb, and then a queasy ache. The room span round and round.

She tried to stand up, but her legs were like rubber. She waited a few seconds and tried again. She met with an invisible resistance.

The dull throbbing resurged with a sudden spasm of nausea. Her vision swam in and out of focus.

Ice twisted in her belly and a cold sweat broke out all over her as she realized that her hands were tied behind her to a chair. The chill of sweat on her skin told her that the halter-top had gone. She was naked all the way down to her hips.

"Yo 'wake, bitch?"

Frowning, she made her eyes focus.

"C'mon, baby, yo come back to us."

Four men occupied the stylish, ultra-modern furniture. They stood up slowly, like they had plenty of time on their hands, and strolled towards her, where she sat bound to the chair in the middle of the room.

They were bedecked in their gangster regalia. The obvious ringleader was short and wiry, sporting a modest afro, long sideburns and a pencil-thin Zapata moustache. A spotless white suit hung on his narrow shoulders, with outrageously flared pants, black silk shirt and white tie. His white shoes were Italian and he was twirling a gold-topped ebony cane.

The man on his right was at least six-foot-five and immensely powerful. He had the battered features and dulled look of a retired boxer, his hair cropped to a shadow on his glistening skull. He wore a matching jacket and bell-bottoms made of a quilt-work of leather patches in every possible shade of brown, his feet encased in cowboy boots tooled out of alligator hide.

On White Suit's left was the Boxer's twin, only slightly less scarred and with more hair and a heavy moustache. Bare chested beneath, his costume was a parody of workman's overalls, made of shiny leather that looked like yellow plastic, excessive flares flapping around red and white stack-heeled shoes.

The fourth man, standing behind Yellow, in his straining red T-shirt with the gold star, was Rudy, the fat bartender.

"Hey," Cat muttered, her head still fuzzy. "The circus is in town."

The men formed a line in front of her. They stood and looked at her in detail, a vicious glitter in their eyes. Cat looked straight back at them, her face expressionless. She sat absolutely still except for the subtle, tantalizing movements of her breathing.

White Suit glanced at Rudy, who even with Cat tied up like that, was sweating nervously.

"Is that her?"

Rudy licked his lips.

"Uh…I think so…"

Yellow grabbed his fat forearm and made the bones creak, dragging him forward.

"Whaddaya mean, yo think so?" he rumbled. "Is she or ain't she?"

Rudy swallowed hard, his jowls trembling like jelly.

"Yeah! Yeah! That's her alright!"

Cat looked remarkably relaxed, for a woman half-naked in a room with four men, with her hands tied behind her back. Inside, she was boiling with anger, furious with herself. They must have bluffed their way in with the anonymous army of cleaners and maintenance men and could have been waiting here for days.

"Sorry man," she said casually. "Have we met?"

White Suit stepped forward and leaned over her. The full force of his aftershave made her vision blur again.

"Yo met a friend 'o mine, Mistuh Randall Mean. Yo 'met' him in Rudy's Bar."

Cat smiled politely.

"Sorry. Don't know the man."

White Suit's hand blurred. There was a crack like a whip as he slapped her hard across the face.

She didn't make a sound. Her head rocked sideways, the long blonde hair flying.

He hit her again, harder, with the back of his hand, whipping her head the other way.

"*Ah!*"

Satisfied that he'd got a noise out of her, White Suit took a step back. Cat's body had twisted in the chair, her head turned away, long hair masking her face. Spots of bright red blood fell on her bare shoulder.

White Suit was wiping his hand with a silk handkerchief.

"Wise-ass honkey bitch!"

Cat sat up straight and turned her head slowly to stare at him with a face like stone. Her hair was in disarray and there was a vivid mark on her right cheekbone. A string of blood ran down from the corner of her mouth. Scarlet droplets formed slowly on her chin, then detached and made dark dots on the denim sheathing her thigh.

She could feel the sweat, suddenly scalding, crawling on her skin. She was breathing heavily now, and the glistening palpitations of her exposed flesh made the twin giants stare harder, their lips parting to show their teeth.

White Suit glowered at his soiled handkerchief.

"Goddamn!"

Cat was working her mouth slowly. Without warning, she spat, a gob of thick pink blood and saliva that found its mark unerringly on White Suit's lapel.

The giants recoiled in horror. White Suit went crazy. He screeched and capered. He pulled a slim, gold-plated automatic and pointed it at Cat's head. Cat ducked, folding in the middle till her head almost touched her knees. Two bullets went over her and made neat holes in the exotic cocktail bar.

"Cool it, bruthuh!"

Yellow grabbed White Suit's arm.

"Tha's too easy, man!"

Cat sat up warily. She stifled a smile. She'd just learned something. The three-bar chair back to which her hands were tied had shifted just a little. It wasn't as strong as it looked.

White Suit shrugged Yellow off. He stowed the pistol back in his shoulder holster.

"Okay, okay. I'm cool."

Frowning, he watched impatiently as the Boxer scrubbed his lapel with a small bar towel.

"Uh...doan' yo w-w-worry, man," his slurred diction was punch drunk. "Dry cleaning will git it off..."

White Suit pushed him away. He glared at Cat, from a safe distance. She had caught her breath and now sat calmly in the chair.

"It ain't gonna be easy, bitch," he hissed. "Yo gonna hurt fo' a long time. Yo gonna beg us t'kill yo befo' we's done!"

White Suit nodded at the Boxer. The big man's ruined lips twisted in a vicious leer, his eyes rolling all over Cat's bare torso. Cat stared into space somewhere beyond him, her face a blank. Behind her, her fingers were busily probing the knots.

The Boxer disappeared off to the side. Out of his shadow, Rudy was fixated by the rise and fall of Cat's splendid breasts. He rubbed his chin, stubble rasping.

"Uh...why don' us have some fun with 'er first, man?"

Cat gave him a hard look and he took a quick step backwards.

Yellow laughed harshly.

"Jee-zus! She done tied up, bruthuh, an' yo scared o' her!"

White Suit curled his lip.

"We don' fool wit' white meat, man."

Reaching into his jacket pocket, he produced a switchblade and made the mean-looking blade snap open.

"We here to punish the bitch, man. We here to make 'er feel pain."

The Boxer reappeared, carrying a small bedside table lamp from the bedroom. White Suit shook his head, raising his eyes to the ceiling.

"Whatya bring the whole thing for, motherfucker? We don' need the whole thing!"

The Boxer mumbled an apology. Effortlessly, he ripped the wire from the base of the lamp and handed the long flex to his leader, the three-prong plug dragging on the carpet.

Wielding the switchblade deftly, White Suit exposed an inch of bare copper. Looking at the Boxer, he pointed at the plug on the floor. The Boxer bent to pick it up then lumbered towards the wall. He crouched down by an empty socket.

White Suit moved the blade in the air.

"Yo gonna burn, real slow...an' then I slice that white skin off, an inch at a time..."

White Suit approached, brandishing the wire. Cat closed her eyes and began to breathe slowly and deeply. Behind her back, she had managed to hook a fingertip into the knot. She tested the bars of the chair back again and felt them shift a little and bend.

"That's right, bitch," White Suit muttered. "Let's see some sweat...sweat make the heat work better..."

A white '65 Mustang was parked across the busy street from the Tower. The driver frowned, fingers tapping on the steering wheel nervously.

She was taking her time. She never lingered long here. She hated the place.

Something's wrong...

The Mustang's door swung open and slammed shut. The driver sprinted recklessly through the traffic and leapt into the revolving doors.

Cat's body jumped in the chair. The muscles in her midriff spasmed. Red sparks exploded behind her eyes, screwed tight shut.

Her body jumped again. Sweat glistened and rolled. Her eyes opened wide, glaring up at the ceiling, as her head jerked back, the sinews cording in her neck.

She clenched her teeth till the bones of her jaw line showed, strangling the scream that rose in her throat.

"That was jus' a tickle, bitch..."

Fred the guard took a step sideways to bar the penthouse elevator door.

"I'm sorry, this one is private. You can use…"

The smile disarmed him. The pinching fingers, where his neck met his shoulder, put him to sleep.

She subsided, panting.

Her body glistened all over and the sweat was streaming down it. The undulations of her rapid, heavy breathing made the men stare and lick their lips. The room was suddenly hot and smelled strongly of sweat.

Her head was lolling, her chin on her chest. Lank strands of hair hung down over her face.

White Suit waited for her to catch her breath.

"Hurt, don' it? This only the beginning, bitch…"

Cat made her head rock limply from side to side, letting her body go slack. She fabricated a muffled groan.

"Yo ain't felt nuthin' yet…!"

Behind her back, her fingers worked on the knot. She flexed her strong forearms carefully and felt one of the bars pop out of its socket.

White Suit bent towards her again.

"Now, c'mon bitch, we wants t'hear yo scream…"

Fred slid down gently, guided onto the chair that was there for when his legs got tired. None of the busy, preoccupied suits noticed. It just looked like good old Fred on duty as usual.

The button was pushed. The arc of small lights above the doors showed that the elevator was at the top and was going to have to come all the way down.

Come on, come on, come on!

Cat's back arched till she thought her spine would crack. Her muscles flexed uncontrollably. Her body jerked and juddered. A torrent of sweat was a perfect conductor and a thousand red hot needles flayed every inch of her flesh.

"Mmmgghh…nnnnghh…ggghhhh…!"

Her wide eyes were wild, lips twisted and grimacing, drawn back from her clenched teeth. Her long hair thrashed from side to side, spraying drops of sweat.

"NNNNGGHH…MMGGGGHH…HHH…GGHH…!"

She made the noises a woman makes when she doesn't want to scream. Her sweat soaked body humped and strained.

"C'mon, sing for me, white meat…"

The faces of the men swam before her glaring eyes. Her silent screams split her skull. But at her core there was crystal clarity, a sharp lens through which she could visualize the knot that bound her wrists unraveling.

"Let me hear yo scream…"

Her muscular convulsions were too much for the chair. The wooden struts splintered with a crack like a pistol shot.

"Hey—!"

The knot fell apart.

"Look ou—!"

The sudden release propelled Cat forward and up. The top of her head, solid as a rock, smashed into the point of White Suit's chin, as he stooped to apply the wire. He jerked bolt upright and ran backwards all the way until he crashed into the wall. Eyes rolling like glass balls, he stood stock still for a moment, then fell flat on his face and lay motionless.

Finally! The elevator reached the bottom.

A shocked silence.

White Suit lay still. Yellow, Rudy and the Boxer just stood there and stared at him.

Cat had been jolted back onto the backless remains of the chair. Now she stood up carefully. Her whole body ached, there were stabbing pains in her joints and when she moved nausea was a cold fist twisting her guts.

"ughh…"

The sound made the three men turn. They stared at her, mesmerized.

"Ssssssss….!" Yellow's breath hissed out between clenched teeth.

She was gleaming, naked to the hips. Sweat ran down her face, dripping from her onto the floor.

"Ooooooohh….!" Rudy groaned.

All they could see was a feast of glistening flesh, hypnotized by the heaving of her breasts and the provocative panting of her belly.

Cat's bowels churned again and she bent over slightly, wincing. Rudy came waddling forward, his fat hands grabbing.

"YAAAAAGGHHH!"

The bartender stopped in his tracks. He had a stupid look on his face.

"Aw shit!" said Yellow.

Rudy stumbled backwards then stood looking down at himself. A jagged wooden spar was protruding from the mound of his belly. A darker stain was spreading across the red T-shirt, dimming the gold star.

"M-m-m-mother…f-f-f-fucker…!"

His eyes bugging with disbelief, Rudy slowly deflated. His knees crumpled and he sat down slowly. His head fell forward, arms hanging limply at his sides. Blood pooled in his lap and began to form a lake around him.

Cat shook her head to clear her watery vision. She was only half aware of what she'd done.

"Bitch!"

Yellow jumped. He moved with astonishing quickness for such a big man. He grabbed Cat's arms and pinned them behind her, almost wrenching them from their sockets.

She writhed, slippery with sweat, her body straining. Her struggles made the nausea twist her bowels again and a sudden wave of weakness washed over her. Yellow felt her sag in his grip and laughed savagely.

"C'mon man, give 'er some o' yo stuff!"

His scarred lips twisting in a lop-sided grin, the Boxer lumbered towards them.

"See how y'likes 'dis, sweets…" he mumbled.

As big as a ham, his fist looped in a deceptively lazy arc into Cat's midriff. The room echoed with the impact of knuckles on sweat wet flesh.

"UH!"

Reflexively, Cat clenched her abs just in time. Surprise lit dimly in the Boxer's dull eyes. She went red in the face and puffed out her cheeks, but her belly didn't crumple like he expected it to. He expected to enjoy watching his fist sink in wrist deep; instead it rebounded off solid muscle.

Perversely, the blow had jolted the fog out of Cat's brain. The Boxer was amazed to see her grinning at him.

"Is that…all you've got…?" she panted.

Glowering, the Boxer drew back his fist again.

The elevator doors hissed open.

"Two against one. That's not fair."

Aiko stepped into the room. Her shining, blue-black hair hung down to her shoulders, her face with its almond eyes and pouting lips like that of an evil kitten. She wore a black silk blouse, tied up to bare her supple middle, billowing black slacks and simple sandals. Compared to Cat, she seemed short and slight, but looks could be deceptive.

"Go get her, man!"

The Boxer turned his broad back on Cat and plodded towards the newcomer. Aiko looked tiny in his huge shadow, and simply stood waiting for him, her arms down by her sides.

Cat's belly ached but her brain was as clear as a bell. Lifting her right leg, she brought the sharp edge of her boot heel scything down onto Yellow's shin.

"YOW!"

For one split second, his grip relaxed. Cat cracked her skull back into his face, at the same time twisting her body violently and thrusting outwards with her arms. Yellow lurched backwards, stumbling into the cocktail bar. His hands flew to his face, blood spurting through his fingers.

"Owww! Bitch! My nose is broken!"

Cat whirled. She jumped. Her rigid fingertips stabbed like sword blades into his solar plexus, left and right, one-two! one-two!

"UUUUURRGGGHH!"

Yellow's wall of muscle crumbled and he doubled up, his bloody features creased in pain. With blind instinct, he staggered forward, his great arms swinging. Cat stepped lightly to the side. As he reeled past her, she wrapped her right arm around his throat.

"Ugghh!"

With a grunt, she put on the pressure. Arms flailing, the big man heaved and struggled, making loud choking noises. Cat planted her feet astride, her face contorted with effort. Beads of sweat fell from her forehead. Her biceps bulged, the muscles of her gleaming back rippled.

One punch would break this little Nip into pieces. The Boxer was sure about that.

As he came forward, she retreated, moving back and sideways in a semicircle.

"Aw…hol' still, why dontya, slant, an' I make 'dis quick…"

Aiko stopped. She was dancing on the spot, up on her toes, her arms flowing, hands fluttering like butterflies.

The Boxer blinked, puzzled. What the fuck was she doin'?

She struck like a snake. With a quick flick of her wrist, Aiko made her fingertips flicker across his eye sockets. The Boxer screamed in agony, clutching his face.

"OH SHIT! I'M BLIND!"

She seemed to just touch his throat. His Adam's apple exploded. Vomiting blood, he staggered and collapsed on the floor, rolled around, his arms and legs thrashing.

Yellow was making gargling sounds. His struggles were getting weaker. His eyeballs bulged and his tongue was sticking out.

Slowly, he sank to his knees. Cat went down with him, maintaining her grip.

"Unnnngghh…ghh!"

Grunting, she put her thighs, belly, biceps, back and shoulders into it. There was a muffled crack. Yellow jerked just once, and then went limp.

The Boxer's convulsions diminished into a spasmodic twitching. Then he lay still.

"Hah!" said Aiko.

Cat rose to her feet and lifted her arms above her head, stretching gingerly. She was drenched in sweat, her long blonde hair a shade darker, lank and matted and clotted with dried blood. There was blood on her chin, a livid bruise on her cheek and blood spotted and smeared all over her skin. Here and there, on her stomach and the splendid slopes of her breasts, small dark smudges marked where the wire had touched her.

"Jeeeeeeeee-sus!"

She had a dull, pulsing headache. Every muscle was throbbing and hot daggers stabbed her joints. That fist was still gripping her intestines.

"Any permanent damage?" asked Aiko.

"Only my pride," Cat replied.

Aiko looked at her admiringly.

"You're fantastic".

"You're not so bad yourself. What took you so long?"

"You knew I was watching you?"

"I thought Selena might send someone to keep an eye on me, as long as these boys were still on the loose."

"Well, they won't be bothering you any more, you—"

"Look out!"

His face crusted with blood, White Suit was up on one knee, aiming the gold-plated automatic.

Cat twisted her body sideways and felt the wind of the bullet fanning her cheek.

Aiko pressed her right elbow against her ribs. There was a faint click and a little silver Derringer popped onto her palm. The bark of the automatic drowned the thin crack of the hideaway pistol, but White Suit missed and Aiko didn't. He grew a third eye in the center of his forehead, a small red one with a black edge, and crumpled in a heap.

"He'll be upset about that," Cat observed. "You've made him crease his suit."

She looked down at her battered and soiled body.

"I need a shower," she said. "And then we'd better get out of here."

Aiko surveyed the scene of carnage. She looked at Rudy, sitting cross-legged in a pond of blood with his chin on his chest and the piece of the chair sticking out of his big belly; Yellow curled up on his side at the foot of the cocktail bar, with his tongue sticking out and his head at a peculiar angle; the Boxer sprawled spread eagled, his face a frozen mask of agony, drowned in his own blood; White Suit all crumpled and creased, staring back with his little red third eye.

She made a move towards the phone that was perched on the bar.

"While you freshen up I'll call in the Agency to clean up the mess. An hour from now it'll be like it never happened."

The bathroom, a glitter of chrome and sheen of black tiles, lay beyond the master bedroom. Cat sat on the waterbed to tug off her boots, wincing at every little jab of pain. It took some effort to peel off the tight blue jeans, glued to her thighs with stale sweat.

She luxuriated in the warm balm of the shower, lathering herself slowly and extravagantly, shampooing twice and then a third time, for good measure.

"Hey, come on!" Aiko tapped on the bathroom door. "It's been half an hour. The crew is here."

She had to go back and knock again, when she heard the sound of the electric hair dryer.

"Finally!"

Cat emerged from the bedroom carrying two small suitcases. Her hair shone like golden silk again and her face was glowing. The bruise on her cheek was cunningly disguised with make-up, the slight puffiness of her lower lip barely discernible. She had a spring in her stride, clad in a simple denim jacket over a candy-striped shirt that hung down to her knees and a favorite old pair of faded blue jeans, their frayed cuffs brushing battered red sneakers with a white star on them.

"Better?" asked Aiko, smiling at her.

Cat smiled back.

"Much."

The room was full of people, men in crisp white boiler suits and baseball caps, with badges embroidered on their chests that said "Acme Cleaning Co." As Cat re-entered, White Suit and Rudy were being zipped into black rubber body bags. Yellow and the Boxer were wheeled out in large laundry wagons, into the elevator. The blood soaked carpet was being lifted, with replacement rolls waiting. A replica of the shattered chair was substituted and the bullet holes in the walls and the cocktail bar were filled in.

"Now that's what I call service," Aiko chuckled.

Her brow clouding, Cat put the suitcases down.

"Hey, how did you get past Fred?"

Aiko grinned.

"Fred had a fainting spell but he'll be fine. He won't remember a thing."

She hesitated, pursing her lips.

"Oh, I hope I haven't lost him his job."

Cat laughed.

"Don't worry. I'll make sure he doesn't. Not unless Dad wants a Civil Rights demonstration on his front lawn."

Cat glanced at the telephone.

"I'd better give Selena a call."

There was a tiny panel on the underside of the phone. Lifting it, Cat exposed four push buttons: red, yellow, green and blue.

"What's the code today?"

Aiko rolled her eyes.

"Honestly, Cat, do you ever use the code books?"

"Oh, they have a hundred uses around the house. Very absorbent."

Aiko sighed, stepping back to let a brisk figure in white get past.

"It's yellow, blue, green twice then red three times."

"Marvellous."

Selena always answered the phone within three rings. Distance gave her voice a slight echo.

"Yes Cat?"

"Hi Boss. You were right. Mister Mean's gang set a trap for me but they're not going to be a problem anymore. The cleaning crew are tidying up right now."

"Are you alright?"

"Slightly shop soiled. No, I'm fine. Thanks to Aiko. You'll get all the gory details in her report."

"I'm sure that it'll make fascinating reading. Now listen. Even with Mean's mob off your back I still think that you should take a vacation. In fact, it's an order."

"Yes Boss."

"You take care."

Cat picked up the bags again. Aiko took one from her.

"I'll spare your blushes and give Selena the edited version of my report. You can save the real story for your memoirs."

They strolled towards the elevator, side by side.

"Much appreciated," Cat grinned. "I'm still trying to live down giving my bra to that tramp for a souvenir."

The elevator doors slid shut behind them.

"Have a good vacation," said Aiko. "Any idea where you're going?"

Cat laughed, shaking her head.

"That's a secret! I don't want to find you in some motel room, standing guard in the closet."

Suddenly, she dropped the bag, flung her arms around the Japanese girl and squeezed her tight.

"Thank you! Thanks for being there."

Aiko returned the embrace. Their eyes locked. They smiled.

"Any time."

"We all agreed then?"

The pool of light in the middle of the room was a deep dirty yellow, cast by a single naked bulb. The curtains were pulled, the corners sunk in shadow.

The faces around a plain table, hunched forward under the light, were close and conspiring. They kept their voices low.

"We goin' t'make the call?"

All the heads were nodding. The faces were dark and hard and serious. There were afros and long sideburns, shaven skulls, moustaches and goatees. Some even wore shades in the semi-darkness. All wore black leather coats and jackets.

There was a stubby M1 carbine on the table and a Colt .45 automatic, both stolen from a National Guard armoury. Next to the guns was a telephone. A strong brown hand picked up the receiver. The dial whirred.

"Hello?"

• • • • • •

"Yo. It's me."

• • • • • •

"Yeh, that's right. The pigs gonna lay this shit on the bruthuhs an' y'know it ain't our bag…"

• • • • • •

Yo' damn right it wasn't us! We's here to protect our people. We ain't no motherfuckin' terrorists!"

• • • • • •

"Uh-huh…uh-huh…uh-huh…"

• • • • • •

"That's right. We needs t'know what's really goin' down. Befo' the pigs come down on the 'hood with tanks and we have a goddamn massacre."

• • • • • •

We needs yo' magic. Y'got people who kin go places we can't."

• • • • • •

"Right on!"

CHAPTER 4
On the Road

This stretch of highway was where they sent your career to die. When you'd rubbed someone up the wrong way, this was the assignment they handed you at roll call and told you to just stick at it, till they forgot all about you.

The sky was a glaring blue blank, except for the regular mile-high jet contrails made by people going somewhere interesting, the blue fading to a colorless wash on the flat horizon. The highway was a slate grey ribbon going straight from West to East. It divided the desert in half and the desert was a flat baked ochre that melted into the shimmering grease of the heat haze and wasn't interesting at all.

"Shit...!"

All he had for company was flies.

Cursing, the Highway Patrolman dragged out his damp kerchief and mopped the back of his neck. The noonday sun was directly above and was cooking the tin toy black-and-white cruiser. All the air conditioning seemed to do was cough lukewarm air at him.

He dozed off and began to dream. In his dream he was running in terror across the orange desert with a giant fly coming after him, its huge throbbing filling the sky.

He could feel the deep vibration even before he heard it, growing as it came towards him. He felt it in his bones as he twitched and mumbled, half-awake, coming closer and closer and getting louder and louder and then right on top of him.

"Wha—?"

The rumble peaked as a slashing red streak seared his raw eyeballs, diminishing with distance. A cloud of pale orange dust enveloped the static police cruiser.

"Sheee-ut!"

Struggling upright in the driver's seat, he fumbled for the pedals and the gear shift.

"Hoo-ray! We got some action!"

Making the siren wail and the lights flash made him feel a lot better. And now he could get some breeze on his face, sucked through the rolled-down window.

He put his foot to the floor and even then all he could do was maintain a steady distance between himself and his target, a red dot far ahead on the grey stripe that split the broiling plain.

Every now and then, the dot would pull away and get smaller. And then it would slow down and get larger again.

"Fuck you!"

Somebody was playing games with him. He slammed his fist on the steering wheel.

Suddenly, the red dot was getting bigger very quickly. It had stopped.

"Okay!"

The Highway Patrolman stepped sideways out of his car and approached his target in textbook fashion, from the back and slightly to the driver's side. As his fingers curled around the worn butt of his holstered .38 Special, he thumbed off the leather safety strap.

"Yew just stay where yew are and keep yer hands on the wheel where I can see 'em!"

Wow! Some car!

It had the power and poise of a big cat, ready to pounce. Bright "rally red" with white go-faster stripes on the hood and along its flanks. Heavyweight chrome and custom wheels, gleaming white upholstery and wood grain trim on the big dash and panelling the doors, more like a luxury yacht inside than a motor car.

It made the Patrolman ache all over. Oldsmobile 442 convertible, with the W-30 badge that said that under that bulging hood lurked the total package.

"Just keep yer hands on that wheel."

He could see long fair hair, flowing down. I might've known, he told himself. One of them fancy rock stars! And California plates. It figgers.

The Patrolman liked to keep his victims waiting, especially the rich ones. He strolled round to the front of the car, all nonchalant.

His jaw dropped.

"Why, howdy, officer…"

She was fantasy made flesh.

"Am I on the right road for Medicine Hat?"

Her long fair hair was like sunshine; her skin was golden like the sand, her voice mellow like the ocean breeze.

"Officer…?"

And she had gorgeous tits. And all she wearing was a skimpy little white bikini bra and tight pale blue running shorts with a white stripe down the sides.

He could see her belly-button peeking at him over the waistband of those sexy shorts. He could see her incredible thighs.

Cat shifted slightly in the driver's seat. The subtle undulation of her spectacular contours made a lump catch in his throat. He was aching so bad he thought he was going to break in half.

"Er…uh…yes, ma'am," he blurted. "Yew jes' keep right on the way yer headin' till yew comes to a fork goin' south. That there'll take yew to Medicine Hat."

Cat looked the Patrolman up and down, long and slow, from the peak of his regulation cap to the toes of his regulation shoes. She saw a stocky young man who filled out his tan uniform nicely, with a ruddy complexion, light blue eyes and a sandy moustache.

The cop made the pages of his notebook rattle nervously.

"Uh…ma'am…d-do yew know what speed yew were doin'!"

Twisting in her seat, she leaned towards him and smiled up at him frankly.

"Yes, officer, it was one hundred and ten miles per hour."

He couldn't believe what he was seeing. Her fingers were actually teasing the knob-end of the gear shift, as she locked eyes with him, smiling.

He thought her tits were going to drop out. Her smile was blinding. Suddenly he was grinning like a high school kid.

"An' I'll betya can cruise at one-ten non-stop from here t'Noo Yawk City in that baby."

Her laugh made her tits quiver. His knees turned to water.

"Oh, I don't even break sweat at that speed…"

She wants me! Jeeee-sus H. Christ! This big city rich bitch wants me!

One hand on his gun butt, he tried to look cool.

"Yep, that there's a mighty big car for a pretty 'lil…"

The car door swung open and she flowed upright out onto the road. The Patrolman's voice trailed away. She was a good two inches taller than he was.

"How fast can *you* go, cowboy?"

The rumble of the massive V-8 made the patrol car tremble. He felt it tingle up through the floor and the soles of his feet.

"Byeee…!"

Cat treated him to a raucous, smoking wheel spin that peppered his dusty windscreen with a spray of small pebbles. She made the tapering tail of the bright red Olds wag at him as the big car flexed its muscles and sprang away, playing a parting fanfare on the twin trumpets of its exhausts.

The Patrolman heard the departing notes of the engine rise into the sky, a faint, mocking *toot-toot-toot* of the horn. Through the veil of pale orange dust that hung over the patrol car, he watched the bright red dot grow smaller and smaller, streaking away down the highway, dissolving in the heat haze.

"Aw…………!"

He was sitting all hunched up in the driver's seat, his right hand handcuffed to his left ankle.

"……………sheeeeeeee-utt!!!"

He was bare-ass naked, except for his boxers, the ones with the hula dancers on them, wedged on top of his head, the elastic waistband pulled down to his ears.

Blushing, he remembered how she'd wriggled and cooed as she talked him into it.

"....oooohh...*I've never done it in a police car...*"
"....*oh, why don't you put those cuffs on, daddy...*"
"...*mmmmmmm...that's right...put them on...like that...oh, it's such a turn-on...!*"
"...*and then, after, if you're very good...you can put them on me...*"

"Awww............Jeeeeeeeeeeeeeeeezzzz!!!"

He glared at the push buttons and tuners for the two-way radio. Sooner or later he was going to have to call in for rescue.

He was never going to live this down.

"...uh, that's right, Sarge...there was five of them...big mothers...coked outta their skulls...two of 'em was carryin' shotguns..."

The Grand Hall had been built in imitation of the great civic structures of classical times, with fluted columns and sculpted friezes that depicted the triumphs of American arms from the Revolution to the Spanish American War. Statues of long gone city worthies looked down sternly from their plinths, draped like Roman senators. Bronze tablets commemorated significant inaugurations and other events of great moment.

"Come to order, please...!"

The lofty marble rang with the excited clamor of two thousand voices.

"Ladies and gentlemen! Order, please!"

The babble diminished to an expectant murmur.

Ladies and gentlemen, it is my privilege to present Mr J. Spencer Warburton!"

There was a rapturous ovation, washing like a giant wave over the speaker's platform. As one, the two thousand crashed to its feet, clapping wildly, their upturned faces shining with hope and expectation.

"Thank you...thank you..."

He was immaculate in a light grey suit and carefully chosen tie. In gilt enamel, the American flag was conspicuous on his lapel.

"...thank you..."

Warburton stretched out his arms, inviting them to sit down. He stood and waited for them to settle and for the cheering to subside.

Placing both hands firmly on the polished lectern, he gazed up at a distant horizon, at some hidden destiny. He held the moment till the hush was absolute.

"My friends...fellow Americans...members of the so-called Silent Majority..."

There was a ripple of recognition in the audience.

"The America that we hold dear...the American values that we cherish...the American flag that we honor...are being contaminated, trampled upon..."

A low rumble of indignation.

"...by dark..."

A snarl of anger.

"... by dark forces of resentment and envy bent on wanton riot and pillage and the destruction of all that we have achieved for ourselves and our children and our children's children...!"

His voice was charged with a messianic fervor. A great noise swelled up from the crowd.

"The silence of the Silent Majority is thunderous..."

People were on their feet, cheering.

"Let it be silent no longer...let the voice of the true America be heard!"

Five miles later, Cat saw a kind of shadow in the shimmering heat haze, by the side of the highway far ahead. As she drew nearer, the shadow took on a shape and solidity and emerged as a modest gas station and diner.

"Just in time..."

Her bladder had been sending her warning signals for the past half hour. And the uppers that she'd popped to keep her wide awake on the road had made her very hungry.

The gas station was a flaking, off-white cabin with a brown shingle roof, in front of a cavernous grey corrugated hanger where the shapes of large machinery glinted dully in the gloom. There were three dark green, out-of-date gas pumps standing in a row in front of the hangar. The nearest had a hand-painted sign hung on it: LAST GAS FOR FIFTY MILES.

"Ooops!"

Cat remembered that she was still wearing the Highway Patrolman's hat. Chuckling, she took it off and sent it sailing out into the desert.

The diner stood a little way off to the right of the gas station, a long faded yellow box with a flat roof and a tin chimney, standing on stubby concrete stilts. Tattered red, white and blue bunting left over from the Fourth of July hung over its plate glass doorway, framing a sign that said "VERNA'S EATS." The heads that could be seen through its long and narrow windows, blurred by a film of grime, all wore broad-brimmed hats or baseball caps. When the doors opened and shut, there was a gust of country fiddle and guitar.

"Yee-hah," Cat muttered wryly.

She let the red Olds roll leisurely onto the large flat area in front of the diner. It looked like something from another planet, next to the row of battered pick-ups and senile Fords.

She saw Confederate flag stickers. Leaning towards the dash, Cat twirled a chrome knob and made her urban funk shout. She saw the cowboy hats in the windows twitch.

Standing aloof from the rank of dusty pick-ups, all lined up like horses at a feeding trough, there was another car that didn't fit, a gleaming black Cadillac with tinted windows. Cat frowned at it as the 442 glided past. It was much too "Establishment" for her.

Cat parked the Olds where she was sure she would be able to see it from the windows. Twisting round, she grabbed a pale yellow shirt tossed down on the back seat. She squirmed into it, leaving the buttons undone.

Switching off the music, she retrieved her shoulder bag from the floor at the foot of the front passenger seat. Reaching into the deep shelf of the glove compartment, her fingers found the smooth pearl grips of the nickel-plated Walther PPK. She checked the magazine, then stowed the pistol in the bag.

She climbed out of the car. Leaning back inside, she flicked a tiny silver switch underneath the column of the steering wheel.

Two fat truckers in red baseball caps and stained blue overalls were thudding down the short flight of steps that led to the dirty glass doors of the diner, scrubbing flecks of cheeseburger from their stubble. They stopped and stared in disbelief at the long-legged vision striding towards them.

"Hey, babeee...!"

They looked up into eyes like chips of green ice.

"Er...'xcuse us...."

The diner was just what she expected.

A long blue plywood counter and blue plywood booths, the table tops and the counter top in matching yellow formica. The floor was speckled blue and white linoleum, the ceiling had been white once but wasn't anymore. Squeaking fans stirred the air tepidly, fanning the aromas of strong coffee and fried onions that wafted from the kitchen, seen through the serving hatch behind the counter. For decoration, there were Wild West scenes, pin-up postcards that went back to the Fifties of strapping girls posing with trucks, advertisements for brands of beer and cigarettes and faded photographs of ball players and B-Western movie stars. Ambiance was provided by the sounds of male conversation, cigarette smoke, cooking smells and seamlessly piped country music.

The baseball caps and cowboy hats all turned in sequence as Cat strolled in through the door, following her progress as she advanced towards the counter. The hum of conversation dipped, and then swelled again, with sharp intakes of breath, inward groans and a wolf whistle or two.

"Jest ignore 'em, sweetheart. They're harmless..."

Verna had been a high school beauty but now she was on the wrong side of forty. A well-built, handsome woman, with a little too much eye shadow and lipstick, her honey-blonde hair was piled high on her head and had pink highlights, under the glaring strips of neon above the counter.

She looked Cat up and down, in detail, smiling wistfully. Cat smiled back.

"What can I get ya, honey?"

"Coffee, black, in a bucket. Ham and eggs."

"How d'ya like yer eggs?"

"Oh, over easy."

"Gotya."

She barked Cat's order at the serving hatch, out of the corner of her mouth. A huge grin set in a shiny brown face appeared and nodded cheerfully.

"Mmm!-mm!-mm! Mah pleasure…!"

The short-order Cook gave Cat a huge wink and she grinned back at him.

"Take a seat, honey," Verna said. "I'll bring it to ya."

Cat glanced hopefully at a door in the corner just beyond the counter.

"I could use the bathroom, if you've got one."

Verna reached under the yellow formica top and came up with a brass key.

"Sure thang. Through thet door, an' it's first on the right. Lock yerself in, though, some o' these boys fergit t'knock sometimes."

The toilet was small and basic but clean. She relieved her nagging bladder and washed her hands, splashing water on her face.

The cubicle exited onto a short dimly-lit corridor. Cat made her way back towards the door that led to the diner.

"Hey there, sweet thang…"

The door opened and a man stood blocking it.

"Now ain't yew somethin'!"

Oh great!

Cat rolled her eyes.

"Excuse me, I'd like to eat my lunch if you don't mind."

The man spread out his arms, placing his palms on the walls of the narrow passageway.

"Aw, be friendly, baby…"

He was tall and lean, with broad shoulders and cords of muscle on his bare forearms, revealed by the rolled-up sleeves of a red-check shirt tucked into tight blue jeans. Lank light brown hair hung down over his ears from under a tattered straw cowboy hat, his upper lip smudged by a wispy moustache. He had the manner of a man who thought he was a lot better looking than he actually was.

I'll just break one leg, before my eggs get cold

The Cowboy leered at her, at all that flesh glistening in the sepia half-light of the corridor, exposed by the open shirt and skimpy shorts.

"I bet yew's one o' them there Playboy centerfolds."

Cat moved towards him.

"Yes, absolutely, now if you'll excuse me…"

The Cowboy was reaching out for her.

"Is there a problem here…?"

The hand that gripped the Cowboy's shoulder was enormous and brown.

The Cowboy gulped.

"Uh…n-n…no, sir, no problem at all!"

The door slammed behind him.

The Cook was a very big man. His dark face shone with sweat from the hot kitchen, a still young but lived-in face, a good face, the kind of face that Cat liked. His chest was massive, straining the olive drab GI T-shirt that he wore under his dirty apron. He had biceps like boulders.

"I saw him watching you," the Cook said. "A lot of men look, but some watch, if you get my drift."

"Thanks," Cat replied. "But I could have handled him."

The Cook laughed, a deep brown bass.

"I know you could. But this way I don't get to strain myself carrying him out of here."

They stood and smiled at each other.

"Your ham and eggs are ready if you are," the Cook said.

"Lead me to it."

"He escorted Cat back into the diner. The Cowboy was nowhere to be seen. The baseball caps and cowboy hats all turned to stare at her again, but looked away sharp when they saw who she was with.

The Cook gazed out of the far window, nodding at the red shape of the Olds 442.

"Nice wheels."

"Thanks. She gets me where I want to go."

"I bet she do. I used to have a Dodge Charger…before…"

"Really? Before…?"

"Uh..well …it was a long time ago…"

The Cook's eyes had a faraway look. Cat waited.

"Good sounds too," the Cook continued. "I heard you all the way back in the kitchen."

"Oh, Miles Davis. 'Bitches Brew'."

"He's the Man. He's evil."

Cat laughed.

"You could say it's my theme tune."

The Cook grinned, touching her arm.

"I'll get Verna to bring you your food."

Cat settled into an empty booth, ignoring all the furtive glances and some openly admiring stares.

"Here ya go, sweetheart!"

Verna came bearing a steaming plate and coffee mug.

"You're a life saver."

Verna laughed.

"We aim to please."

Cat looked towards the busy serving hatch.

"He's an interesting guy, your cook."

Verna chuckled.

"George. He's been quite a learnin' experience for some o' the good ol' boys aroun' here."

"A soldier, if I'm not mistaken."

Verna's eyebrows shot upwards.

"Honey, not jest any soldier. He done three tours in 'Nam. Special Forces I heard. Got medals up to his chin."

She looked mysterious.

"I heard he made it all the way up to Colonel. But then somethin' went wrong. Somethin' he don' like t'talk about."

Cat dug in with her fork and sampled a mouthful.

"Mmmm…well, he makes damn fine ham and eggs."

Cat relished every mouthful, washing it down with good strong coffee. While she chewed, she glanced around the diner. The usual crowd, truckers and farmers and latter-day cowboys.

A few faces stood out from the crowd. Two cute co-eds occupied one of the wooden booths, consuming Pepsi, burgers and French fries. Hippy chicks, a blonde and a brunette, with long straight hair, wearing tie-dyed T-shirts and bell-bottomed jeans. Bulging knapsacks covered in stickers and sewn on patches were stacked on the speckled floor beside them.

Cat smiled, remembering the wide-eyed optimism that she took with her to college. The smile faded, as she recalled her rapid disillusionment. She had found herself stranded between the superficiality of the sororities and their stupid pranks and social rituals, and the earnest muddle-headedness of the so-called "radicals."

Tilting her head slightly, she read some of the badges on the knapsacks: "Keep on truckin'", "Peace"…

"Power to the People…" she muttered into her coffee.

The only people she could get on with at college were the simple-minded, single-minded football jocks. At least they only wanted her for her body and weren't trying to mess with her head. She lasted until mid-way through her sophomore year, before bailing out. Her mother was too busy to notice. Her father blew his top but she just let it all wash over her. Uncle John congratulated her, and promptly took the lock off her substantial trust fund. That was just before he did his own disappearing act, without so much as leaving a farewell note on his desk in Global Tower. Cat, meanwhile, embarked on a journey of twists and turns, of exploration and self-exploration, which at this precise moment found her eating ham and eggs in Verna's diner.

There was another strange face in the diner, another odd-one-out.

Perched on a stool at the far end of the yellow-topped counter, a man was sipping his coffee. Cat looked him over with a trained eye. He was in his mid-forties, of medium height and medium build, with average features, neatly trimmed light blond hair and small ice-blue eyes. His complexion was unusually pale, in this room full of leathery, rugged outdoor tans; and his hands looked soft, amidst all the scars and calluses. In an environment of weather beaten leather and denim, his neatly pressed tan safari suit stood out like a beacon.

Must belong to that Cadillac, Cat said to herself. She noticed that he kept on glancing at the two co-eds and appeared to be favoring the little blonde.

"Refill, honey?"
Verna materialized at her side.
"Yes please."
Verna saw Cat looking at the hippy chicks.
"Ain't they cute? We gets 'em through here all the time, searchin' fer whatever it is they're always searchin' fer."
She laughed.
"I dunno, when I was their age all I was lookin' fer was a boy with a nice car. Now they all wants t'change the world an' I dunno what."
Verna filled Cat's coffee cup to the brim.
"What're yew lookin' fer, sweetheart?"
Cat shrugged.
"Oh, I take it as it comes."
She scooped up another forkful.
"Right now everything I need is right here on this table."
Verna laughed again, squeezing Cat's shoulder.
"Enjoy."
Cat cocked an eyebrow, nodding towards the man in the tan safari suit.
Verna shook her head.
"He ain't from these parts, that's fer sure. I hear there's a lot of new faces aroun' Medicine Hat and Red Springs. Mebbe he's one of 'em."
Verna smiled and went to heed a customer's call. Cat watched Cadillac Man

bring his coffee cup across the room and hover over the two co-eds in their booth. He said a few words to them. They looked at each other. Then they smiled at him and he sat down opposite them.

He was nodding and smiling and when he gestured Cat saw the flash of a gold watch. The girls were smiling back at him and hanging on his every word.

Cat chuckled quietly. She remembered that smile from her teens, the smile that always got her a ride.

She glanced at the black dial of her watch. It was time to hit the road again. Verna was there like magic.
"Check, honey?"

Patting her middle, Cat came skipping down the few steps from the door of the diner and strode out onto the flat dirt of the car park.
The red Olds had company.
"Holy cow! This is some beast!"
She frowned. She was used to her cars drawing a crowd, but she didn't like what she saw.
"A righteous mean machine!"
The "Cowboy" in the dirty straw hat had his hands on her paintwork and was leaning in to peer in at the controls. He had three companions with him. With minor variations, they looked the same as him.
Number One saw Cat coming and nudged the Cowboy in the ribs.
"Well, hey there, sweetcheeks!"
Her brow knitted as she watched his sweaty palm smear the powdering of desert dust on the white upholstery.
"This is some set o' wheels yew got here, baby."

Wait for it...

"This ain't no girly car..." said Number Two.

Here it comes...

"This is a man-sized car," said Number Three.
Cat reached deep into her shoulder bag. Her fingers brushed the butt of the Walther PPK. She was sorely tempted. Just his big toe.

No. They're not worth it

She pulled out the car keys, with the Oldsmobile logo on a little leather tag.
"Well..."

Her mouth was smiling but her eyes were not.

"Why don't you try her for size?"

Startled, Number Three juggled the keys and nearly dropped them. He stood grinning dumbly at his friends.

"Well go on," the Cowboy gestured at the car. "You heard the lady…"

Cat winced slightly as Number Three vaulted the car door and fell into the driver's seat.

"Oooh, mama! Now yew jest watch me make that ol' blacktop burn…!"

Grinning round at Cat, he put the key in the ignition.

"Don't yew worry, baby. I'll bring 'er back in one p—"

His right hand dropped onto the gear shift. He turned the key.

"YOW!"

He snatched his hand away, his face contorted with pain. He stared at his palm with bugging eyes, at a small dot of blood slowly forming there.

"What the heck was thet?" he yelled at Cat. "What in the…?"

His voice trailed away abruptly. His eyes rolled, glazing over. His head lolled forward till his chin was resting on his chest. Sighing, he slumped, sliding down in the driver's seat.

The others stood there gawping. Then the Cowboy came storming around from the other side of the red car.

"Just what kinda game yew playin', sister?"

He stabbed his forefinger at Cat's chest.

"What the hell did yew do t'him? Yew can't—!"

Her face was expressionless. There wasn't a flicker in her eyes, to predict the scarcely visible motion of her left hand, flashing up from her side.

"OW!"

She grasped the offending finger.

"OWOWOWOWOWOWOWOW!"

She hardly seemed to be applying any pressure. Turning beet red, the Cowboy was sinking to his knees.

"OWOWOWO—YEW BITCH—OWOWOWOWOOW!"

Still squirming, he reached round behind him and plucked a slim-bladed knife from his waistband.

"Bad boy."

Cat looked mildly bored. With swift precision, she placed two fingers and a thumb on the Cowboy's neck, just below his ear.

"Uuuuuurrrgghhh….!

The knife slipped from his numb fingers. Everything went black. He fell in a heap at her feet.

Cat kicked the knife far away, making it skitter across the dirt and under a parked pick-up.

"Anyone else?"

She started walking towards the car. Numbers One and Two backed up rapidly.

"Er, no, ma'am."

"It's been nice meetin' yew…"

They hurried away, their boot heels raising dust. She heard car doors slam, an engine ignite and tires squealing.

"Bravo."

The sound of a slow handclap made Cat spin round quickly, her hands coming up reflexively into a defensive posture.

"Neat work."

The Cook was leaning nonchalantly against the high side of a parked truck. Smiling at her, he folded his mighty arms across his broad chest.

Cat appraised him unashamedly, her eyes roving all over him.

"Man," she said. "You're stealthy."

He grinned, strolling towards her.

"You're not so bad yourself."

Cat watched him as he approached, light on his feet for a very big man.

"How much of it did you see?"

"I got here in time to see the whole show. But it looked to me like you were on top of it."

He bent into the car to examine a tiny steel needle that protruded from the black knob of the gear shift. It had a hollow tip, from which a bead of colorless liquid dangled.

He whistled lowly.

"You are one dangerous lady."

Cat laughed.

"That's me."

The Cook lifted Number Three out of the driver's seat, as light as a baby. He laid him out in the shade of the parked truck.

Number Three stirred slightly and mumbled.

"He'll be fine in an hour," said Cat. "He'll just have a bad headache."

The Cook hooked his huge, spade like hands under the Cowboy's armpits and dragged him over to lie next to his friend.

"This one will sleep for quite a while too."

He straightened up and looked at Cat, seeing her in a whole new light.

"Excellent technique."

"Thank you."

"We might have gone to the same school."

Cat laughed.

"Unlikely. I went to an all-girl's school."

The Cook laughed in the deep brown bass that Cat liked very much.
They laughed together.
He glanced towards the red 442.
"Now that isn't standard equipment, not for Oldsmobile anyway."
Cat looked back at him steadily.
"No."
The Cook smiled.
"It's okay. I don't like answering questions either."
He gestured at the prostrate forms laid out next to the truck.
"You'd better hit the road so I can come out and find them."
Cat glanced at her watch again.
"Oh shit. Yes. I'd better."
She looked back at the diner.
"Don't worry," the Cook walked over and nudged the Cowboy with his toe. "These boys won't say anything. They're hardly going to want to have this talked about."

Cat settled into the driving seat. In the rear view mirror, she glimpsed the man in the tan safari suit, ushering the two hippy chicks into his black Cadillac.
"Looks like they got their ride."
"Huh?"
"Oh, nothing."
She reached for the little switch underneath the steering column.
"Aha," the Cook said.
The tiny needle retracted.
"You've seen my secrets," Cat chuckled. "I'll have to kill you now."
The Cook rolled his eyes.
"Verna will kill me if I don't get back to the kitchen soon. My break's almost over."
Cat looked up at him.
"Nice to meet you."
"It's been an experience."
There was a brief pause as they smiled at each other. The Cook took a step towards the car.
"I hope I see you again."
"I hope so too."
She waved as the Olds took off. The sun flashed on her hair.
He watched the car recede until it was just a red dot.
"Mmmm...my oh my...!"
Then he strolled over to the parked truck and stood looking down at the unconscious Cowboy and his pal.
"Dumb rednecks."
Crouching down, he began to shake the Cowboy's shoulder.
"Hey, man! Hey! What's going on? What happened, man?"

CHAPTER 5
Free Love

Dusk settled like a purple cloak and the desert was a vast darkness. The splash of the 442's headlights was a fast-moving firefly. It reflected back in the eyes of a startled jack rabbit, caught the spark of whirring night insects.

Small casualties spotted the windshield. A swish of the wipers cleaned them away.

The mellow drone of the engine underscored the soothing tones of Otis Redding as he sang about tenderness and love.

The reflective surface of the road sign stood out starkly against the surrounding blackness, indicating the fork that led to Medicine Hat. It loomed up and flashed by as she drove past it, straight on down the highway.

Another hour or two and she'd be there.

Fifteen minutes later, some impulse made her slow to a crawl.

Cat pulled the Olds off the road and let it amble a few hundred yards across the hard, stony dirt of the desert, the tires crunching softly. She braked gently and switched off the music, the engine and the lights.

The desert was deep purple. The last trace of the sunset still smoldered on the horizon and the sky was filling with stars.

The temperature had dipped dramatically. Cat buttoned up her shirt.

She took a little plastic bag from the secret place and broke open the seal. Shaking the bag, she made two little white pills roll out onto her palm. She paused, then added a third. Raising her hand to her lips, she tossed the pills into her mouth.

Tilting her face up to the sky, she watched as the stars began to sizzle.

She was walking, walking fast with long determined strides, wading in the deep purple. Suddenly, all she wanted to do was walk away, walk away from everything.

The darkness was humming all around her. The stars above were fizzing and popping, the night air crackling with electricity. Her blood was on fire. She was going to go on walking forever, or until she fell off the edge of the world, fell into the stars.

The ground was rising beneath her feet, leading her towards the uneven crest of a ridge.

A pale, un-natural glow was radiating from the other side of the rise.

Cat heard man-made sounds, a shuffle, and the dull chink of metal on stone. She heard muffled voices.

Instinct took command. Cat crouched down low. Noiselessly, she crawled up the slope to the top of the ridge.

"Come on, hurry up."
"Okay, okay!"

The ridge overlooked a broad and shallow bowl. On the far rim of the bowl, three cars were parked side by side, twin two-tone Police cruisers and the black Cadillac.

The bowl was bathed in a wavering aura, cast by a hand-held lantern. The lantern swung in the grip of an overweight policeman with sergeant's stripes on his sleeves. He was holding the lantern high to light the way for two uniformed subordinates, edging their way gingerly down the slope of the bowl, bowed by the weight of a heavy burden.

At the foot of the bowl, two patrolmen were sweating with shovels, straining to carve a trench in the hard dirt. One winced and stepped back, rubbing his wrist, as the blade clanged on stone.

Standing beside the Cadillac, the man in the safari suit gestured impatiently.

"Will you get on there!"

The patrolmen put their bundle down beside the shallow trench.

Suddenly, Cat's skin was scalding. She ducked back down behind the ridge and rolled onto her back, staring up at the sky. The stars were spinning around.

When her heartbeat had quietened, she inched back up to the top and peered over again.

The bundle was the naked body of the dark-haired hippy chick, lying on her back, arms down straight at her sides. Her face was stark in the lantern light. She wasn't pretty anymore. Her eyes were open wide, standing out in their sockets. The tip of her tongue protruded from between her twisted lips, and there were blue-black blotches on her throat.

"Okay, that's deep enough," the Sergeant said. "Put 'er in."

Cat squeezed her eyes tight shut and then opened them again.

It was real.

She ducked back down. Behind her she heard the sound of the shovels scraping and dirt falling into the hole.

Cat heard the flat of the shovels patting down the disturbed earth. She heard the policemen scuffing over the dirt with the soles of their boots.

She heard car doors, conspiratorial voices, car engines start and rev up and wheels turning, crunching away into the darkness.

Cat sat alone in the deep purple for a long time, until her blood cooled and the stars stopped spinning.

She was suddenly very cold, wrapping her arms around herself.

What to do? No sense in telling the Police. Here the Police buried the bodies instead of finding them.

She burst out laughing, a shrill mechanical reflex.

"Some vacation…!"

She was wading in sand, stark in the hard starlight, under a sky that was full of stars all clashing like cymbals.

The starlight stabbed her eyes. Her brain was frying. Sweat glued the shirt to her skin, turning hot and cold, from acid to ice water.

"OW!"

Cat sat on the sand, rubbing her ankle.

"Damn it!"

She stood up slowly. She wobbled for a moment on one leg, and then put her foot down carefully.

"Shit!"

Cat looked around. The gritty ground was marked by lumps and bumps that didn't fit in somehow with the smoother undulations of the desert.

She scuffed about with her toe. Something took shape and she squatted down to blow the sand away.

"Hm!"

It was a twisted scrap of metal about eight inches long and two inches wide, pierced along its length by oval perforations. When she blew the dust off it and rubbed with her fingertips, Cat was rewarded by a flawless silvery luster, gleaming in the starlight.

She tugged but it was obviously attached to something deeper and heavier. Rising, she moved on to investigate a pronounced scab of earth that had been split by wind and erosion and was crumbling away.

"Ah…!"

The tip of a larger spar protruded from a tussock of dry grass. It was curved and shaped like a T, the color of lead when Cat rubbed the dust away.

Something glinted. She saw scraps of what looked like metallic skin, clinging to the spar.

"Hmmm….."

Cat found a tissue stuffed in a shirt pocket. She smoothed it out and laid it on the ground. Picking delicately with her fingernail, she detached a fragment of the foil, the size of a postage stamp, as fine as silver leaf. Laying it on the tissue, she folded it carefully several times and put it back in her pocket.

The only music was the engine.

Normally, she liked to lose herself in it and savor all the harmonies and counterpoints that were there if you knew what you were listening for. But this night she was oddly distracted.

Her thoughts were all tumbling over each other. Now she wished that she hadn't taken those pills. She was spacey, jangling. She was seeing things.

She kept seeing the dead girl's bloated features, floating like a pale moon in the onrushing darkness ahead of her. She couldn't bear the thought of that lost child lying out there in the desert all alone.

She slammed on the brakes. Taken by surprise, the car squealed in protest, its tail swinging sideways as it slithered to a halt.

"Damn it!"

There was a dull ache pulsing behind her eyes. Her skin was crawling like she was covered with ants. She couldn't stop shivering.

"Fuck!"

Cat scrubbed her face with the palms of her hands. She shook her head from side to side, her long hair floating. She squeezed her eyes tight shut but the contorted death mask was still there, staring at her.

In technicolor, she was back in the diner. The two cute hippy chicks were smiling and laughing, chomping on their burgers, stealing each other's French fries...

...the girls were riding in the big black Cadillac, bouncing on the plush upholstery, grinning at each other. The man in the safari suit was smiling at them in his rear view mirror...

...the Cadillac was bumping over stony ground, driving into the desert. Panicking, the girls were tugging at the locked doors, banging their hands on the sealed, blank tinted glass, clawing at the partition that divided them from the driver...

Stupid! Stupid! Oh you stupid little girls!

...black-and-white patrol cars were waiting in the desert. The Sergeant tossed away a cigarette butt and walked forward as the Cadillac approached. His men were getting out of their cars, sucking on beer bottles...

...red-faced and screaming, the blonde girl ran into the desert...

...they were dragging the brunette from the black car. She shrieked and twisted, her face contorted with terror. They were tearing off her clothes...

...the man in the safari suit watched them for a little while. He told them to hurry up...

...they were putting a leather belt around the brown-haired girl's throat. She screamed at him, begging. He got back into the Cadillac...

...the blonde girl was staggering, gasping, struggling to suck air into her lungs. She stumbled onto her knees. The Cadillac drove up slowly behind her. The man in the safari suit got out and walked over to her. He stood beside her as she sobbed helplessly, her shoulders heaving. He stroked her golden hair...

Cat cried for the dead girl.

"I'm sorry," she told her.

If only. If only she hadn't been flying so high, high on the pills and high on herself. If only she'd been paying attention. If only she'd noticed how wrong they looked together, Cadillac Man and those silly teenagers. If only she'd gone over and offered them a lift instead.

She sat for a long time, in the car skewed across the empty highway, looking back into the huge blackness, into the void.

"I'll be back for you, sweetheart. I promise. I'll take you home."

An insistent beeping pierced the sound of the engine.

Cat plucked the palm-sized handset from its hook under the dash. The curly cord swung, brushing against her knee.

"Hello?"

"Well," said a welcome voice. "You're in range, so you must be getting close."

Cat's face was lit by a huge smile. Suddenly she felt warm all over.

"Hi, Uncle John!"

"Where are you, Princess?"

Cat glanced at her watch.

"Uh…about an hour and a half past the fork to Medicine Hat…"

"Okey-dokey! You'll be there in twenty minutes. I'll send the pick-up to meet you, look out for it."

"Will do."

"See you soon, Princess."

"Love you."

Precisely twenty minutes later, she saw something glint up ahead, caught on the fringe of her headlights.

"Good grief."

It was a genuine relic. A battered 1940 Ford pick-up in various shades of rust and dark brown primer. It had a cracked windshield, spattered with dirt. The radiator grille was missing some of its teeth. Only one headlamp survived, the other was an empty socket with wires dangling from it. The tailgate was long gone and there was just a single red tail-light.

Cat fell in love with it immediately. She wanted it.

"Miss Warburton?"

The Olds rolled towards the ancient pick-up and slowed to a stop.

"That's me."

The driver's door in the tall cab of the Ford creaked open on tired hinges. A pleasant-looking young woman dressed in a simple blue dress climbed down onto the ground. Barely into her twenties, she had a mop of red hair and lots of freckles. Smiling, she walked towards the idling Oldsmobile.

"Papa John said you'd probably be late."

Cat chuckled. Papa John. She loved it.

"He knows me too well."

The girl backed away towards the pick-up.

"Follow me…"

The spaced-out sound of the Grateful Dead wafted on the night air, coming from the cab of the pick-up. It sounded garbled to Cat. She liked a beat that made her hips want to move.

She made the Olds follow the single red tail-light. The path was scarcely defined, the merest smudge in the dirt. Imperceptibly at first, the ground was getting steeper beneath the wheels and the path began to twist and turn in the darkness, meandering between humps and shallow slopes.

The path was lumpy and littered with stones. Not a natural cross-country vehicle, the 442 bounced and wallowed.

"Shit…!"

Cat played on the pedals and experimented with the gears, as the sophisticated engine grated, protesting.

"Sorry…"

Up ahead, the red tail-light was jumping up and down, as the ancient pick-up rattled nimbly up the slanting incline. Cat rarely felt inferior, in the red Olds, but she did now.

At long last, with Cat fearing for her suspension, they reached a kind of summit, a long, low ridge with a gently rounded crest.

Cat brought the Olds alongside the pick-up. The girl stuck her red head out, grinning.

"There it is," she pointed. "Free Town!"

It took Cat by surprise.

She had been half expecting wigwams and campfires, something that looked like Woodstock in the desert.

It was a proper town, a very small town, but a town.

"Far out, huh?"

It had three parallel main avenues, connected by a grid of side streets, all bathed in the soft radiance of old-fashioned gas lamps. Simple houses, like whitewashed wooden cubes, dotted the streets at regular intervals, their small windows lit by the same vintage glow. Old West-style false-fronted stores lined the broader avenues. There were barns and stables and a water tower and a wooden church with a steeple. There was even a town square with a circular bandstand, a Civil War cannon and a flagpole—only the cannon had a bunch of flowers in its muzzle and the flag bore a large peace symbol and a picture of a dove.

"Crazy…" muttered Cat.

Delighted, she burst out laughing. Oh, Dad, if you could only see this!

With a cough and splutter, the venerable Ford banged and clattered away down the slope. The Oldsmobile followed gingerly.

They drove slowly down the gas lit central avenue, side by side. The storefronts were dark, but an old-fashioned saloon was all lit up and alive with the sound of song and laughter. Down every side street, music was floating from open windows.

Young couples were out strolling, their arms around each other: boy and girl, girl and girl, boy and boy.

"You should have called it Free Love," Cat observed, smiling at the young people, who all smiled back at her.

The red-haired girl laughed, leaning out of the cab.

"We almost did. But we thought it might attract too much attention."

They advanced into the town square. On the bandstand, a young man with long hair was plucking the complicated strings of a sitar, before a cross-legged semi-circle of earnest admirers.

Cat could smell the weed from where she was sitting.

"This is where I get off," the red-haired girl said. "You'll find Papa John in the church."

In the church! Cat was incredulous.

"Don't tell me he's got religion!"

The girl just laughed. With a shake, the rusty pick-up accelerated towards the bandstand. It braked and the girl jumped out, joining the semi-circle.

"The church. Okay…"

Cat parked the car in front of the small white wooden church. She didn't flick the little switch beneath the steering column. The Olds was already drawing a flock of admirers, drifting across the town square.

"Crazy wheels…"

"Cool…!"

She trotted up the wooden steps to the tall front doors. There was an antique brass bell pull.

She tugged it. Somewhere inside, the bell tinkled.

"Come in, it's not locked."

Cat pushed the doors wide and stepped through.

She was prepared for pews and a pulpit. What she saw was a luxury apartment that went all the way up to the wooden beams of the pointed roof. The floor was a sumptuously gleaming parquetry of polished woods, the walls lined with stripped pine, hung with iridescent oriental tapestries. At ground level it was one long, enormous space, with richly hued Persian rugs and embroidered cushions tossed around.

Hanging from the beams, brass lamps from Marrakech cast a golden glow. Here and there, incense burners stood on slender tripods, wafting their honeyed musk. At the far end, where the altar would have been, the raised area had been converted into a place for dining, seated on cushions around a long, low table.

"Is that you, Princess?"

Cat craned her head back, looking for the source of that old familiar voice.

"Yes, it is, Uncle John."

"Well, don't just stand there…"

A twisting iron wrought staircase spiralled up to a platform that, supported on flying buttresses, projected almost halfway into the body of the church, creating a huge loft.

"…come on up."

Cat skipped up the twisting stairs so fast it made her dizzy. The loft was split in two. To the right were the sleeping quarters and a great big brass bed.

"We're in here…"

To the left was the bathroom, constructed around a large circular sunken bath, rimmed with marble, fit for a Roman Emperor.

Cat just stood there and laughed.

"Hi there, Uncle John."

Once upon a time, John T. Warburton had been the hub of the Big Wheel, the Puppet Master, surveying his kingdom from the dizzy heights of the Global Tower. With his brother J. Spencer, known collectively as "J.J.," or "The Two J's," he devoted his life to the ruthless expansion of a vast corporate empire.

Then came "the Revelation."

No one ever knew how or why, but one day about eighteen months ago John Warburton disappeared. He simply failed to turn up at the office. For several months, blaring headlines speculated wildly. Theories veered from some kind of accident to kidnapping, from organized crime to alien abduction. The police and the FBI combed the country from coast to coast. Interpol was alerted. There were false alarms and false sightings, suspects were quizzed but all were released.

At the time, Cat, as far as anyone could see, was just a college drop-out, a beach bum, disowned by her illustrious parents.

She was detached from the national debate about the fate of John Warburton. Because two days after he vanished, she had received a brief phone call from him:

"Hello, Princess."

"Hi, Uncle John. How are you?"

"I'm fine, angel."

"What's happening?"

"I've found a better way, Princess. Don't tell anyone. I'm enjoying all the fun."

"Yes, Dad is spitting nails. He had to cancel his golf game with the President."

"I'm sure it's a huge inconvenience for him. Don't worry, I'll put him out of his misery. All will be revealed."

"Sounds mysterious."

"You'll be the first to know. Someone will be coming to see you tomorrow."

"Okay. Look after yourself, Uncle John."

"You too, Princess."

The next morning, Cat saw an anonymous grey Buick turn off the beach road and head towards the house. She slipped on a towel robe.

He was standing on her balcony, peering through the glass doors.

"Miss Warburton?"

"Yes?"

"Your Uncle sent me…"

Hat. Grey suit. Horn-rimmed spectacles. Thin face. Obviously a lawyer.

She slid the doors apart.

"Catherine Warburton?"

He was comparing her to a dog-eared snapshot. Cat plucked it from his fingers.

"Yes, that looks like me alright."

She gave the picture back. Expressionless, he put it in his breast pocket. Cat had the feeling that if she took off the robe and danced naked in front of him, his expression wouldn't change.

"My name is Walter Brownlow, Miss Warburton. I have the privilege of representing your uncle, John Tremaine Warburton."

"Good for you," Cat grinned. "Cup of coffee? How about a spliff?"

His poker face was unflinching.

"No thank you."

The lawyer stepped purposefully into the beach house. He looked around for somewhere to put his briefcase. Cat indicated a small side table. Giving no sign that he had noticed the little packet of silver foil and the cigarette papers, Brownlow snapped open the catches of his case.

He removed a sheaf of documents.

"Boy, those look important."

The lawyer pushed his spectacles up the bridge of his nose.

"Extremely."

He cleared his throat.

Your uncle, John Tremaine Warburton…"

"Just call him John T."

He gave her a frosty look.

"Sorry."

"…John Tremaine Warburton…has relinquished all of his business and commercial interests as well as his various executive positions, including that of Senior Vice-President of the Warburton Corporation…"

Cat clapped her hands.

"Right on! I knew he had it in him. So where is he?"

The lawyer looked dubious.

"Your uncle is currently engaged in the establishment of a new…um… community, in what must remain for the present an undisclosed location. I believe that the term is 'alternative lifestyle'."

"Far out!" Cat laughed.

Brownlow sniffed.

"Yes indeed."

He shuffled some of the papers to the top.

"There is more, Miss Warburton. That pertains to you especially."

Cat was mystified.

"Me? Don't tell me he said I could have his old 'Vette."

Brownlow shook his head gravely.

"It's more than that…"

"And the Cobra?"

"Please! Miss Warburton!"

Cat raised her hands, laughing.

"Okay, okay, I'm sorry. Please continue, Mr Brownlow."

"Thank you."

He rattled the papers, composing himself.

"When you reached the age of fifteen, your uncle set up several trust funds in your name…"

"You're kidding!"

"…which were intended originally to come to you when you attain the age of twenty-five…"

"Wow, well I…"

"…however, in the light of recent events, your uncle has decided to release the funds to you now…"

Brownlow was enjoying himself. That breezy self-assurance had been replaced by stark surprise and she just stood there staring at him with eyes that were getting wider and wider.

"…the sums in question…"

Adjusting his spectacles again, he studied the papers.

"…amount to a grand total of five-and-a-half million dollars…"

Cat blacked out for a moment. She blinked. She shut her eyes tight and then slowly opened them again. The lawyer was still standing there, with the papers in his hands, gazing at her solemnly.

"W-w-what…?"

Her brain was scrambled. She couldn't make her mouth move. All the strength went out of her legs and she sat down with a bump on the floor.

"…your uncle's sole condition was that you, as he put it, 'enjoy every penny'."

"B-b-b-but…"

"…I quote: 'Cat is the only member of this damn family who knows how to have fun'…"

Bending, Brownlow laid the papers on the floor in front of her.

"All the details are here. Once you have read the papers and signed them, if you would kindly return them to my office…"

With that, he tipped his hat and was gone.

"Good day, Miss Warburton."

She sat on the floor for over an hour, staring blankly at the pile of papers. The words all jangled and jumbled and ran together.

"Hi, Princess."

John Warburton sat with the steaming water up to his navel, pearls of moisture glinting in the hair on his broad chest and big belly, his mighty arms spread out along the marble rim of the basin.

"Here at last."

He had the face of a middle-aged cherub, lit by a hearty glow, his blue eyes twinkling behind little round glasses. Long greying hair flowed down to his wide shoulders, complemented by a flourishing walrus moustache.

"It's great to see you again, Uncle John. It looks like you're enjoying yourself."

His impressive biceps were each a pillow for the sleek, blue-black head of a beautiful Chinese girl, the one with a round face like a perfect doll, the other more angular and exotic. Their tawny skin was gleaming, firm breasts bobbing on the water.

The girls looked up at Cat and smiled. She smiled back. The exotic girl twisted sideways to reach a small silver-plated flask. She popped the stopper and poured a golden oil into the water. Instantly, the steam became scented.

"Mmmm..." sighed Cat. "That's nice."

Uncle John stroked the girls' long blue-black hair. Smiling, they squirmed closer to him, resting their heads on his shoulders.

"Why don't you join us?" he suggested.

Cat flashbacked momentarily, to the desert and the secret burial in the night. A sudden chill gripped her spine, cold sweat prickling on her skin.

She felt sticky and stale.

"Why not?"

She tugged off the sneakers and her socks and tossed them aside. The shirt fluttered down beside them. Reaching behind her, she unclipped the bikini top. Thumbs hooked into the elastic waistband, she slid the blue shorts off her hips and stepped out of them. She disposed of the skimpy panties briskly, flicking them aside with her big toe.

Stark naked, Cat stood on the edge of the basin.

"Wonderful...!"

The Chinese girls studied her with admiring eyes. Uncle John was beaming.

"You are very beautiful, Princess."

"Thank you, Uncle John."

She waded thigh deep in the water. The warm scented vapors caressed her.

John Warburton marvelled at the slow roll of her hips as she advanced across the basin, the supple muscle play of her midriff, the surge of her perfect breasts.

"I can't believe that you sprang from the loins of that dull, grey brother of mine."

Cat laughed, a delicious ripple that played little tricks all over her body.

"I don't think he can believe it either."

Letting her legs bend, she dipped her body down into the water, up to her chin, her golden hair spread out on the surface. Then she rose, the water cascading down her spectacular contours. She dipped and rose again, her skin gleaming.

"Mmmmmmmmm....!"

Cat stood with the water lapping at her thighs. She closed her eyes. With a kind of reverence, the doll-faced girl anointed her head with olive-tinted oil. Slowly, luxuriating in the task, she began to wash Cat's long blonde hair.

The exotic girl dipped her hands into a large copper bowl full to the brim with a balm like liquid honey. In a trance, she began to stroke her palms all over Cat's body, smoothing the glistening oil into her skin.

Cat sighed. She smiled, her lips moving, murmuring.

John Warburton watched, enchanted.

Sweet smoke mingled with the perfumed vapors.

"So, how are you, Princess?"

The Chinese girls had donned silken robes and departed to the kitchen. Cat and Uncle John sat smiling at each other across the marble basin.

He leaned over to pass her the joint. Cat took from it deeply. She felt the welcome mellowness creep all the way down to her toes.

"I hope you're enjoying your money."

He wagged his finger at her with mock sternness.

"Now remember, child. I forbid you to spend a single penny of it wisely."

Cat passed the reefer back to him.

"Don't worry, Uncle John. I won't let you down."

His fleshy brow wrinkled.

"God forbid you turn into a dried up stick like your father."

She splashed across to his side and cuddled up to him, laying her blonde head on his shoulder.

"Don't worry, Uncle John. I want you to be proud of me."

He touched the tip of her nose lightly with a fingertip.

"I am proud of you, angel."

He noted the faint lingering trace left by the wire on her breast.

"Selena is too."

Startled, Cat sat bolt upright.

"How—?"

Her Uncle chuckled.

"The Agency isn't a government operation, sweetheart. Where do you think it gets its funds?"

Her mouth popped open like a little girl's.

"Uncle John!"

He put his strong arm around her shoulders.

"I'm sorry to keep secrets from you, Princess, but I didn't want you to feel that I was watching you too."

Cat nodded, smiling.

"Yes, you're right. It's tough enough getting Selena's approval."

"She's something else, Selena."

"How long have you known her?"

There was a slight hesitation.

"Oh, me and Selena go way back."

Cat gave him a saucy look.

"Uncle John! Is there something else you'd like to tell me?"

He laughed, patting her head.

"Never you mind."

They both laughed, making ripples in the steaming water.

"Does Dad know about this? About you and the Agency?"

John Warburton threw his head back and guffawed.

"Hell no! He'd have an apoplectic fit!"

Suddenly, Cat's bright eyes clouded with sadness.

"What's the matter, Princess?"

Surprising him, she shivered abruptly, drawing herself closer to him.

"Something happened, Uncle John. Something I need to talk about."

Hand in hand, they stepped out onto the porch of the old church. In the golden glow of the gas lamps, the night was full of music and laughter.

"You get some sleep, angel," said Uncle John. "And we'll talk in the morning."

The red-haired girl was strolling across the town square towards them.

"Susie here has a room all ready for you in her house."

"Thank you."

She kissed him on the cheek.

"Sleep tight, Princess."

"You too."

The Chinese girls were waiting in the doorway. With a twinkle in his eye, Uncle John turned and flung his arms around them, drawing them back inside.

Laughing, Cat trotted down the steps.

"Can I drive your groovy car?" asked Susie.

"Sure."

Cat stopped in her tracks.

The red Olds was rocking gently from side to side.

"Hey…"

She stifled a laugh, clapping her hand to her mouth.

A young couple was making out on the back seat, oblivious to passers-by and bystanders idling on the boardwalks.

"Hmm," said Cat. "I think we'd better walk."

"…we're right behind you, sir…you speak for the real America!"

Through the plate glass window of his booth, the producer hand-signalled that time was short and calls were waiting.

The show's host waved and nodded.

"Thank you caller, and I think I can say, sir, that you speak for all of us here at Radio Freedom."

Across the table, J. Spencer Warburton cleared his throat, adjusting his headphones.

"Thank you, Mr Culpepper, I have always appreciated your support."

His host, a fat, sweating, red-haired man stuffed into a cream-colored suit, leant over the table towards him.

"If I might take this opportunity to interject," he suggested in an artificially refined Southern drawl. "With a question of my own…"

Warburton was impeccable in a crisp blue blazer and beige slacks with razor-sharp creases.

"Of course."

"A question to which I am sure many of our listeners are eager to know the answer."

"Indeed?"

"When might we expect you to answer your country's call and stand against that… weak man…in the White House?"

Warburton cleared his throat again, as modestly as he could.

"Well, Mr Culpepper, you can be sure that if I was indeed called upon to serve my country, I would be honored to do so."

CHAPTER 6
Strip Search

"This is some place you've got here, Uncle John."

Mornings came bright and early in the desert country, with skies of clear blue crystal.

"We're proud of it, Princess."

He gave her the grand tour of Free Town. He showed her the stores where the currency was barter; the self-sufficient workshops that made anything you needed; the barns and corrals and pens; the cows and ducks and pigs and goats and geese and chickens all laying. He showed her the crops flourishing in the allotments where young men and women bent to their task together, to the accompaniment of guitars.

"It was an old derelict ghost town, they used to make movies here," John Warburton explained. "The Corporation owned it. I bought it."

Cat saw a garage and grabbed her Uncle's hand, hauling him away towards its wide open doors like a little girl wanting to go to the candy store.

"Oh, wow, Uncle John! You've kept them!"

Goggle-eyed, she was admiring a bright red '58 Corvette, the lovechild of a jukebox and a rocket ship.

"Hullo, sweetheart," she cooed, leaning into the glittering cockpit.

"Don't breathe on the chrome," her Uncle joked.

But Cat had lost her heart to another. A beast of prey, stripped down to its bare aluminium, adorned by faded racing numbers.

"Oh God!" she groaned out loud.

An evil gleam picked out the aggressive contours of a low slung Shelby Cobra 427 S/C, fine-tuned for the racetrack.

Oh...it's raw sex...!

Sighing, Cat was all over it, caressing it, pressing her body to its pugnacious curves. John Warburton stood there and shook his head, laughing.

His niece sidled up to him. She stroked his cheek and laid her head on his shoulder, making big goo-goo eyes at him.

"Uncle John..."

He looked at her with mock disapproval.

"After what happened the last time?"

Cat pouted.

"Aw, Uncle John...!"

"It took me six months to rebuild it."

Cat wrapped her arms around him and squeezed him tight.

"I'll be good, Uncle John. I'll be ever so careful…"

"No."

"Please…!"

"No."

"Pleeeeeeze…!"

Cat was ready for the day, in a skimpy cut-off red T-shirt and blue denim shorts trimmed raggedly to the tops of her thighs, her feet sheathed in a pair of fringe-top suede boots.

Squatting down by the border of a cultivated allotment, she threatened the seams of her shorts.

"You have some interesting plants here…"

Her Uncle laughed. He was dressed simply, in a light blue Arab burnoose that hung down to his ankles.

"We grow our own. Top grade."

Cat rose lithely.

"It looks like paradise."

"It's damn hard work. Just about everything you see around you these kids did with their own hands. Everything they know they taught themselves."

"I'm really impressed," Cat said. "I couldn't hack it."

He put his arm around her shoulders.

"You walk a different path. Yours runs closer to the edge. This place is for those who want the simple life."

Cat frowned.

"Sometimes I go right to the edge and look over. Sometimes I almost fall."

She squeezed the big hand that rested lightly on her shoulder.

"Sometimes I almost want to jump."

Scuffling and bumping, goats mobbed a slim, dark-haired girl holding a pail in each hand. Laughing, raising the pails up high, she pushed her way through them, shoving her way towards the trough.

Smiling, Cat watched them jostle and climb over each other.

"They're easy to please."

Her Uncle waved to the girl, who, grinning broadly, was struggling to prise the empty buckets from under the heaving pile of goats.

"The rewards here are uncomplicated, and all the more rewarding for that."

Cat nodded.

"I know what you mean."

Her smile faded. She turned and leant with her back against a rustic fencepost, tilting her face up to the bright blue sky.

John Warburton gazed at her fondly.

"You're flawless, Princess."

She grimaced wryly.

"Looks can be deceptive."

He looked at her again.

"What did you want to talk to me about?"

She told him about the dead girl in the desert. Tears swelled in her eyes.

He stroked her hair gently.

"There was nothing you could do."

"If I hadn't been so high…"

"You couldn't bring her back to life."

She walked away, away from the town, and stood looking out across the rolling desert of sand and scrub, towards the broiling horizon.

Her Uncle waited for a little while before following her.

"If I'd been paying attention…"

"They weren't your responsibility."

The tears welled over, rolling down her cheeks.

"…if I wasn't so busy amusing myself…"

"Princess, there was nothing you could do."

Angry, Cat scrubbed the tears away with the back of her hand.

"Well, I can do something now!"

Medicine Hat was like all the other little towns dotted across this sparse desert state. It offered the bare essentials, a pit stop on the highway from West to East, somewhere to fill up the tank, grab a bite or a night's sleep, stock up on supplies or have a drink. It was the original one-horse town, where you could rub shoulders with the ghosts of the Frontier.

A scabby, three-legged yellow mongrel took it into its head to make a lopsided hop across Main Street. It paused to sniff at something interesting.

"Thank you!"

Cat eased on the brakes.

The dog picked up whatever it was and started to chew. Cat took a look around.

The loafers and passers-by eyeballed the bright red Olds. They looked at her and muttered to each other, grinning.

"Good afternoon," Cat called out cheerfully.

They looked back at her dumbly. It was pretty much what she expected, the usual collection of Stetsons and baseball caps, truckers and twentieth-century cowboys.

The dog finished chewing and stood looking around.

She beeped the horn. The mongrel stared at her balefully and hobbled on.

"Well, excuse me!"

Cat parked the 442. She double-checked that she'd remembered to remove her stash from the secret place. She was clean.

She flicked the little switch under the steering column, climbed out of the car and started across Main Street. She had changed into a blue-check shirt, tied up in a knot, the tails hanging down over her bare midriff, and stonewashed jeans snug on her hips, tucked into the tan suede boots with fringes round the top. Her bag hung from her shoulder, lighter than usual without the gun in it.

Heads on both sides of Main Street turned, following her. The lustful muttering started up again.

Cat pushed through the tall doors of the "General Store."

"Afternoon, Miss…"

The store was trapped in 1917. There was sawdust on its floorboards, a pocked and scarred wooden counter, wooden shelves, drawers and cabinets all the way to the ceiling, brimming over with everything imaginable.

"…I'll be with you in a minute".

A young couple from Free Town were at the counter, bartering jars of homemade honey for a set of hand tools. Two lanky young cowboys were weighing up a selection of rifles and shotguns, racked on the wall. They were eyeing the hippy girl with a mix of desire and contempt. When Cat came in, they did a double-take of disbelief.

Cat turned her back and pretended to be absorbed by a stack of T-shirts on a shelf. To her relief, the hippies, glancing at the cowboys nervously, left without saying anything to her.

The cowboys leered at the hippy girl as she passed by them. They tried the same leer on Cat but it just bounced off her.

The proprietor was a flabby, balding, middle-aged man in a faded blue store coat.

"How can I help you, Miss?"

She laid a handful of assorted T-shirts on the counter. One could never have too many T-shirts.

"I'll take these. Oh, and a carton of Camels, and one of those disposable lighters, mine's out of gas."

"S-s-sure thing."

Spectacular visions like this didn't come into his store very often; in fact, never. He stared at the swell of her breasts, stretching the shirt. He studied the subtle toning of her bare midriff. He admired the span of her hips and the curve of her thighs, sheathed in the tight jeans.

Cat swivelled abruptly and cocked a hip, pointing her rear at him.

"Here, you missed this."

The storekeeper's wife materialized in the doorway behind the counter, a thin, dark woman with a face set in a perpetual frown.

"Henry!"

He turned pink and began counting the T-shirts. The cowboys guffawed.

Cat tossed the T-shirts and the cigarettes into the trunk and locked it. She looked up and down Main Street. It seemed so ordinary. And yet there was a dead girl out there in the desert.

A shiver ran like ice cold water down her spine.

Two men were walking in her direction, on the other side of the street. They could have been twins, with sandy hair and pale eyes, and a muscular build packing their identical, tan safari suits.

"Well," Cat murmured. "How about that…?"

The cowboys had left the store. Side by side, they filled the sidewalk. A colored youth, in his mid teens, was coming towards them, carrying a heavy box in both arms. Red lettering across the back of his white T-shirt proclaimed "A-Z Delivery."

The cowboys saw him coming. The one on the outside clipped him deliberately with his shoulder, and sent the slim boy spinning off the edge of the sidewalk. The box fell in the road, things inside crunching.

"Hey, man…!"

Reeling, the delivery boy struggled to regain his balance.

"Why dontcha watch where yo goin'!"

One of the cowboys stepped towards him, clenching his fists. His companion put a hand on his arm and muttered something.

The cowboys gave the delivery boy a hard look and moved on down the street.

The delivery boy stood in the road looking down at the box.

"Motherfucker."

He looked up and saw Cat strolling towards him, smiling. His face lit up like a beacon.

"Oooo! I feel a lot better now!"

Cat grinned. She nudged the box with her foot. Something rattled inside.

"Shit!" the delivery boy said. "That's gonna come outta my pay."

Cat reached into her bag and came up with her wallet.

"Let me…"

The youth shook his head.

"Appreciate it, but no thanks. I kin take care of my own."

He hesitated.

"I'd like to take a look at your car though."

Cat laughed.

"Sure, go ahead."

He shook his head again.

"Uh-uh! You gotta go wit' me. If the Man see me anywhere near a set 'o wheels like that I'll be busted fo' sure!"

Cat gave him a guided tour. She popped the hood for him and let him goggle at the mighty V-8.

"Ooooo, mama! Yo got the whole W-30 package—and in a drop-top! Man! They only made a few o' these…455 cubic inch…370 horsepower…"

He grinned conspiratorially.

"…'least that's what they tell the insurance companies…I betya got 30-40 more…"

Cat grinned back and winked at him.

"You know your cars."

"I just reads about 'em. I kin only have a ride like this in my dreams."

Flicking the hidden switch to "safe," she invited him to sit behind the wheel. He sat there, stroking it, his eyes lit up with wonder.

Passers-by gave him strange looks. Cat glanced at them sharply and they looked away.

Wistfully, the star struck teenager climbed out of the car.

"Man! She's beautiful!"

Grinning from ear to ear, he stepped back and looked Cat up and down.

"Mama, yo pretty fine yo'self!"

Laughing, Cat feigned blushing modesty.

"Why, thank you kindly, sir."

Scooping up the broken box, the delivery boy set off with a spring in his step. Cat watched him all the way down the street. She suddenly felt very old, at twenty-three.

Cat set the switch again. She noticed a sign that said "Bar." Worth a try, she thought.

She set off briskly, ignoring a chorus of wolf whistles from men sat sucking on beer bottles in the back of a passing pick-up.

A black and white Police cruiser came towards her, patrolling Main Street. The cop in the passenger seat tipped a salute to the good ol' boys in the back of the pick-up as it clattered past.

The cops looked Cat over as they rolled by. She was disappointed. Neither of them registered as one of the faces from the desert, standing over the grave.

"Damn."

Walking in out of the bright sunlight, it took her eyes a moment to adjust to the shadowy interior of the bar. There were puddles of smoky yellow light in a dark brown gloom. In the light were a long bar and bar stools, a few tables and chairs, some booths along the wall. At the far end, there was a squat pool table and the brown monotony was broken by the multi-colored lights of an ancient jukebox, playing seamless country songs.

Hanging from the ceiling, broad-bladed fans turned sluggishly, stirring a tepid soup of stale sweat, tobacco and beer. The bar stools, the tables and the booths were dotted with cowboy hats and baseball caps. Big men in stained overalls were playing pool, feeding coins into the jukebox.

The place went quiet when Cat stepped into the light. Untended, the jukebox finished its song. They all just sat and stared at her, their eyeballs glinting dully.

"Uh...kin I help ya...?"

The bartender was a squat man with a slab-like face and flat nose, making up for thinning hair on top with a bushy black beard. Puzzlement showed in his beady black eyes. It was obvious that the only women who had ever been in the place were the fading pin-ups, cut out of a magazine and tacked up behind the bar.

Cat switched on a big smile.

"Hi! I'll have a beer."

Looking dubious, the bartender flipped the top off a chilled bottle.

"It's okay, I don't need a glass."

He even glanced at her money before taking it, as if he expected something to be wrong with it.

They were all staring at her in stone-faced silence. One of the men at the pool table made a move as if to take his shot, but then straightened up again.

Cat raised the bottle and glugged half of it down.

"Whoo!" she smacked her lips. "That hit the spot!"

Propping her elbows on the bar, Cat leaned towards the bartender.

"Say, I was wondering if you could help me."

"Uh..."

Cat was aware of all the eyes watching her. She swung round and suddenly everyone was looking up, down and sideways.

She noticed that Miss July had been scotch-taped to a worn dartboard hanging by the jukebox. One dart was imbedded in the wall, the others were piercing her obscenely.

"Yes, I'm just passing through, but while I was here I was hoping to look up some people..."

The barman looked increasingly perplexed.

"You can't miss them, they always wear those trendy safari suits..."

Now he was starting to panic.

"Uh...uh........"

Suddenly, he flinched and took a step backwards. Cat turned quickly.

"Yew don't wanta go askin' questions aroun' here, sweets."

It was the pool players, three of them, burly giants in baggy work shirts and overalls, coming towards her.

"I think yew oughta be leavin' now."

Behind her, the bartender had scuttled sideways and was dialling a telephone mounted on the wall. Cat kept the smile nailed firmly to her face.

"No offence, boys…"

The giant frowned.

"Yew gotta leave now."

Cat shrugged.

"Okay. Whatever you say. Just let me finish my beer."

His hand, like an iron clamp, fastened on her wrist. She heard the bones creak. The bottle fell from her fingers.

The giant's buddies stood behind him, grinning.

"Yew go now."

He made to twist her arm behind her back. The bag slipped from her shoulder.

Cat dipped, going with the motion, using his weight and momentum.

"YAAAAHH!"

His imposing bulk suddenly became weightless. She scarcely seemed to touch him, but he was hoisted off his feet in a forward somersault, flipping over and landing on his back with a crash that made everything in the bar-room rattle.

Winded, he groaned, shaking his head, and tried to sit up. Cat's fist only travelled a few inches, from her side to the point of his chin. His teeth clacked together. His eyes rolled like glass balls and he fell back, unconscious.

"Jesus H. Christ!"

The other two rushed her, grabbing and swinging. Dancing on her toes, Cat blocked the clumsy blows on her forearms. Ducking under a roundhouse right, she chopped short and swift, with the edge of her hand.

Eyes bulging, the big man sank to his knees, clutching at his windpipe. He stayed there, kneeling, choking loudly.

Still moving, Cat pirouetted, her leg lashing out in a high kick that smashed into the side of the third man's jaw. The impact hurdled him clean over the bar, crashing down on the terrified bartender.

"B-b-bitch…!"

Wheezing, the second man lurched to his feet and came at her. Twisting her body, Cat let him stumble by. She dropped her fist just behind his ear. He fell flat on his face and lay still.

She wasn't even breathing heavily.

"Anyone else?"

The doors banged open. The two patrol cops burst in, guns in their hands.

Cat leant back against the bar.

Good, right on cue

"That's her!" the bartender yelped. "She's askin' questions and then she starts tearin' up the joint!"

The cops looked at her with their bland faces and blank eyes.

"Yew comin' with us, baby."

Cat bent to retrieve her bag.

"Whatever you say, officer."

The big men were moaning and groaning their way back to consciousness as the cops ushered Cat out of the door and into the waiting patrol car. Everyone watched, crowding in the doorway.

All but one. There was a booth far back where the light barely filtered. Unnoticed, a man sat there, watching everything.

Now he leant forward across the table, thinking. The light glinted on the buttons of his tan safari suit.

The Police Station was a squat red brick blockhouse attached to the end of Main Street, with a concrete yard at the back, girdled by a high wall.

They took her in by the back. At a blast from the horn, the gates swung open and the patrol car rolled into the yard.

"C'mon, out…"

The barred cages of the holding cells were lit by a sickly neon, casting a green tint on the steel walls.

Sleeping it off, the town drunks shifted and mumbled on their cots, and then went back to snoring again. A young black man in a sleeveless vest and baggy pants spotted with dried blood sat hunched over on the edge of his bunk, staring morosely at his bare toes, fingering a large lump under his eye.

"Keep movin'…"

The two cops marched Cat right past the cells. They took her down a flight of concrete steps. There was a heavy wooden door at the foot of the steps.

"Git in there…"

Cat dropped the cigarette butt on the floor and crushed it with the heel of her boot. It joined three others.

She looked at her watch again.

She was sitting on a chair drawn up to a simple wooden table, beneath a naked yellow bulb that lit the cellar garishly. Otherwise, the cellar was bare, a long red brick box with a concrete floor and low ceiling.

There was an old electric fan standing in the corner, but it didn't work. It was hot and stale in the cellar, with the door locked. Perspiration glistened on her forehead.

Keys jangled in the lock. Cat stood up quickly.

The door swung open.

"Well, whadda we got here?"

She recognized him immediately.

"We got trouble, Sarge."

It was him, the Sergeant. Just as she remembered him, out there in the desert, supervising the burial of the hippy girl. The two patrolmen were close behind him.

"She jest walks in and starts askin' questions."

"Does she now?"

He had the face of a sour bulldog, with small eyes like chips of flint and a nose that had been broken more than once. The no-neck, meaty-shouldered bulk that strained his blue uniform told of exploits on the football field, now running to fat that overhung his belt.

He took off his hat and rubbed his close-shaven scalp, glistening with sweat. Dark patches spread from his armpits and where his shirt stuck to his spine.

"Asks questions does she?"

Cat kept her poker face, though her flesh was crawling as the Sergeant looked her over.

"Well now, honey-pie, ain't yew sumthin'…!"

She sat back down in the chair and looked at them coolly.

A tiny muscle twitched at the corner of the Sergeant's mouth.

"Now did I tell ya t'sit?"

Her eyes frosting, Cat stood up slowly. The two patrolmen glanced at each other and grinned.

The Sergeant moved a step closer. His body odor assailed her and he saw the flicker of distaste in her eyes.

His scarred lips twisted in a nasty smile.

"What's the matter, city girl? Yew don't like the way I smell?"

He took another step.

"Yew one o' them California beach bunnies that shits marble and pisses perfoom?"

The patrolmen laughed.

"Yew be careful now, Sarge. That doll knows that there jew-shitsoo and all that stuff."

"That's right, Sarge. Way I heard it she done tossed Big Joe and his boys aroun' like they was rag dolls."

The Sergeant showed his tobacco-stained teeth. He popped the safety strap with his thumb and rested his hand on the butt of a holstered .38.

"Is that right?" his voice was low and laden with menace. "Now yew go an' try any of that gook bullshit on me, sweetcheeks, and I'll blow off yer kneecaps."

He looked at her long and hard.

"Do yew believe me, girlie?"

"Yes, I believe you," she replied evenly.

"That's good. Then we're gonna git along jest fine…"

He saw the shoulder bag, with its beads and fringes, lying on the table.

"Did any one of yew think t'search her?"

The patrolmen looked embarrassed.

"Uh, well no, Sarge, we was kinda waitin' fer yew."

"And, heck, Sarge, she's a white woman…"

The Sergeant muttered a string of obscenities under his breath.

"She's a stranger is what she is. A stranger askin' questions."

He picked up the bag and weighed it, letting it swing by its long strap. He put it down on the table top and peered into it. His broad back hid the bag from view.

He plunged his beefy forearm in up to the elbow, delving around.

"Well, lookee here!"

His hand reappeared, clutching a small plastic bag.

"Now whadda we got here?"

He broke open the seal and white powder spilled onto the scuffed table top.

Cat burst out laughing.

"Oh, that's great! That's just beautiful!"

The Sergeant rounded on her, his heavy features clouding.

"Yew think this is funny, girl?"

Her shoulders were shaking with laughter.

"Sergeant, you should take that magic act on stage!"

He licked his finger, dipped it in the powder and touched it to the tip of his tongue.

"Yew in big trouble now, city girl."

Cat just laughed and shook her head.

He took another step closer, his hand on his gun.

"Strip!"

She stopped laughing.

"Yew heard me. Strip!"

Her face turned to stone.

"I suppose you've heard of the Constitution and the Bill of Rights."

He liked punching women in the belly. He liked the way they bowed to him.

Cat saw the blow coming. He might as well have sent a letter. Tensing her abs, she stood still and let it land.

"UUUUGGH!"

She made it sound worse than it was. It wasn't hard enough to knock her down, but she folded in the middle and let her legs go, sitting down on the concrete floor.

Holding her midriff, Cat sat there with her legs splayed out, letting her body go slack. Her head hung down, long blonde hair tumbling into her lap.

She put on a show, heaving her shoulders and panting loudly.

The patrolmen cackled.

"Aw, she ain't so tough!"

"That were jest a lurve tap, blondie!"

His eyes glittering viciously, the Sergeant stood over her with his hands on his hips.

"Now yew git yer clothes off, slut, or I'll have mah boys put yew across thet table and do it fer ya."

The patrolmen looked eager. Cat's eyes were like chips of ice.

Sitting on the hard floor, she unzipped the suede boots and tugged them off. The Sergeant took them from her, turned them upside down and shook them, stuck his hand in and rooted around.

He tossed the boots down on the table. Her face a stone mask, Cat pulled off her socks and dropped them on the floor.

The Sergeant held out his hand, his lips twisted in a mirthless smile. Expressionless, Cat picked up the socks and gave them to him. He turned them inside out, very slowly, smiling at her all the while. She stared right back at him. He let the socks fall beside the boots.

"And the rest, baby. Yew gotta long way t'go yet."

Cat got to her feet with exaggerated care. She unbuttoned the blue-check shirt and unraveled the knot. She slipped the shirt off.

There was a sharp intake of breath.

She wasn't wearing a bra. She didn't need one. She was perfect.

They gawped at her like they'd never seen a pair of breasts before. And they hadn't. Not like those.

Cat made no attempt to cover herself. She stared back at the patrolmen with lofty contempt.

Remembering to breathe, the Sergeant jerked out his arm and Cat handed the shirt to him. Wrenching his eyeballs from her breasts, he held the shirt up to the light, ran his fingers under the collar, then crushed it between his hands and threw it aside, landing in a crumpled ball on the table.

Cat stood calmly, watching him, hands down by her sides. Her face was a blank but hot wires were twisting in her brain. She was looking straight at them, but all she could see was a grave and the bloated features of the dead girl under the dirt.

The Sergeant rubbed his hand over his face, greasy with sweat, like he was waking from a trance. Swallowing hard, he jabbed with his finger, pointing.

Cat unbuttoned the waistband of the stonewashed jeans. The sound of the zipper was loud in the choked silence.

The men were mesmerized, by the carnal slope of her belly and the swell of her thighs, as she drew the blue denim down from her hips to her knees.

The jeans sank to her calves and piled at her feet. Cat stepped out of them and in one fluid motion stooped to pick them up and hold them out for the Sergeant.

He almost had to grope for them. Suddenly clumsy, he fumbled with the pockets, turning them inside out. Angry with himself, he flung them sideways.

They slid off the end of the table and fell on the floor.

The patrolmen gulped audibly. All she had on now was a pair of simple white panties.

Cat didn't wait to be told. Hooking her thumbs into the elastic waistband, she slid the briefs down her thighs and then let them drop to her feet. Looking straight ahead, she flicked them away with her toe. They slid across the floor, past the Sergeant, to the polished toecaps of the two patrolmen.

"Oh my God…..!"

"Jeeeeeeezzz-us!"

The patrolmen moaned in a perversion of ecstasy.

Cat stood absolutely still, her breathing barely perceptible. In the harsh light of the naked bulb, her skin shone with perspiration and she was glowing, golden.

Suddenly, the cellar was very hot and there was a strong smell of male sweat and lust.

In a dream, one of the patrolmen picked up the white panties.

"Aw, sheee-ut! They're warm!"

Holding them in both hands, he crammed them into his face, inhaling deeply. His colleague let out a shrill giggle, like a child.

Cursing, the Sergeant snatched the briefs from his subordinate and threw them across the room.

"Asshole!"

Pulling himself together, he turned back to Cat.

"Now then, girlie, why don't yew tell us what yew was doin' comin' all the way out here from California jest t'ask questions?"

Her only movement was a shrug of the eyebrows.

"Simple," she said calmly. "I was asking about some people I met out on the Coast…"

"Uh-huh…"

"…they were just passing through."

"Jest passin' through."

"That's right. And they told me that if I wanted, I could find them around here someplace."

The patrolmen were grinning at her, their eyeballs rolling up and down and around her naked body.

The Sergeant sighed the sigh of an old hand.

"Now, baby, I may look like I made too many tackles without my helmet, but I ain't as dumb as I look."

"That would be impossible."

She let him hit her again.

"OOOOOFF!"

But this time he jabbed her with the rounded end of his nightstick, drawn in a flash from a loop on his belt.

It didn't hurt as much as she pretended. But it hurt. Her face contorting, she pressed her hands to her midriff and bent over slowly.

"Uuuuuuuhhh…!"

Clutching herself, Cat sank to her knees.

"Whatsamatter, blondie?" said one of the patrolmen.

"She gotta bellyache," his buddy chortled.

Legs astride, the Sergeant stood over her, rapping the nightstick on his palm.

"Now, yew ain't one o' them long-haired, nigger-lovin' commie hippies out there all smokin' dope an' fornicatin' like rabbits at that…uh…Free Fuck place…"

He went to the table and retrieved the small plastic bag, holding it up between finger and thumb.

"Nope. I thinks that yew is one o' them drug pushers, come out here with yer dirty city ways…"

Lifting her head, Cat glared at him.

"That's ridiculous!"

The Sergeant showed his yellow teeth again.

"Well, who knows what we might find when we takes a good hard look at that pretty car of yours."

Cat made a face.

"I'll bet!"

The Sergeant sheathed the nightstick with a flourish.

"Possession will get yew five to ten in this state, city girl. Now, possession with intent to supply, that's fifteen to twenty. Hard time."

Cat's expression didn't waver.

The Sergeant swept the boots and the shirt and the rest off the table with his arm.

"And if that don't git yer attention, yew gotta couple other places we ain't searched yet…"

The patrolmen sniggered.

"And if yew don't wanna tell me right now who yew are and what yer here fer, I'm gonna ask mah boys here t'bend yew over that there table and take a look."

It had stopped hurting a long time ago. Cat was on her feet quickly.

"I don't think so."

Her fists were clenched at her sides. Her body was balanced and ready.

The patrolmen glanced at each other nervously. The Sergeant looked surprised. He jerked out his gun.

"Now don't yew go gittin'—"

The cellar door flew open.

"Hey, Sarge!"

A patrolman with a thin face pocked with old acne scars came barging in urgently.

"Sarge! You gotta—!"

He was stopped short by the sight of Cat's splendid nakedness. His jaw dropped.

"Uh…uh……."

Cat's eyes narrowed. He was one of the gravediggers from the desert.

Exasperated, the Sergeant grabbed him by the arm and shook him.

"What the hell?"

The new arrival took the Sergeant out of the open door and onto the concrete steps. He was muttering in his ear.

Cat saw the Sergeant's face go dark and contort with anger. He was protesting, but the patrolman, his face creased with anxiety, was insistent.

The Sergeant threw up his hands, defeated.

"Okay, okay!"

Furious, he stomped back into the room.

"Gimme that!"

Mystified, one of the patrolmen bent to pick up Cat's shirt and hand it to him. Scowling, the Sergeant threw it at her.

"Git yer clothes on!"

Ten minutes later, Cat was being marched up the steps and out across the yard.

Without a word, they shoved her out through the back gates and threw her bag after her.

Cat was watched as she stood there bemused, while the gates slammed shut behind her.

She was watched as she walked back along Main Street.

She was watched as she got into her car. And as she drove out of Medicine Hat and turned onto the highway.

Her body ached and her thoughts were all confused. She turned on the music and let sweet Soul soothe her.

CHAPTER 7
A Strange Interview

Cat drove for about an hour, out to where the desert was flat and exposed and where no one was hiding, watching her.

She pulled the car to the side of the road.

It was late afternoon. The blue was thinning and the sky was turning to brass. The air was thick and hot and hard to suck into the lungs. The heat beat off the hard ground in shimmering waves, like melted grease, blurring the horizons.

Cat took a cassette from the glove compartment and pushed it into the slot. The sounds of the surf and seagulls washed over her. Behind the dark lenses of her shades, she let her eyes fall shut and tried to imagine the caress of sea breezes on her face.

"Shit!"

It didn't work. She switched it off.

There was distant movement in her rear view mirror. It filled with the monumental radiator of a huge Mack truck.

It pulled up alongside, big and yellow, towering over the Olds.

"Need any help?"

The driver was leaning out of his cab. He was in his thirties, with regular features and a shock of windblown brown hair.

Cat raised a polite smile.

"Well no, I'm fine. Actually, I was just looking for a place to take a leak."

The truck driver grinned, jerking a thumb towards the large extension at the back of the cab.

I got everything yew need, right here."

Cat hesitated.

"Um..."

"Go right ahead. Be my guest."

"Wow!" Cat jumped down from the cab. "It's like a travelling motel."

The truck driver was down on the ground, admiring the red Olds.

"I got me a beefed up Mustang back home, one of those Shelby jobs, pretty as a picture with them blue racin' stripes. I take 'er to the track whenever I gets the chance..."

They talked cars and engines for a while. The trucker produced a fat joint from the pocket of his denim shirt.

"Do yew partake of the weed…?"

Cat laughed.
"I don't mind if I do."

The sun was lower in the sky and the horizon was starting to glow.
The truck driver glanced at his watch.
"Well, I have a schedule to keep…"
Smiling, he shook her hand.
"It's been a real pleasure meetin' yew."
He climbed nimbly back into the high cab.
"Have a good 'un."
"Safe journey. Take care."
Cat stood by the car, waving as the truck rumbled on its way with a parting blast on its triple horns.
She suddenly felt a lot better.
Leaning into the car, she plucked the two-way radio handset from its hook.

He was there in half an hour. He came bouncing across the desert, out of the setting sun. Trailing a tower of glowing dust, he rode an Army surplus Jeep, its tattered awning swaying from side to side.
"Hello, Princess."
"Hi, Uncle John."
He looked at her intently.
"Did you have any trouble?"
Cat smiled.
"Well, you know how it is, Uncle John, trouble has a way of finding me."
He patted her cheek fondly.
"More likely you go looking for it."
His niece shrugged.
"Well, there's more than one way to go fishing. Sometimes I like to toss a grenade into the pond and see what floats to the surface."
She told him about her trip to Medicine Hat.
"At first I thought it was you who bailed me out. Some of your people were in town getting supplies and I assumed that they must have seen them take me in and called you."
Her Uncle looked puzzled.
"Nope. Not me."
He frowned.
"We have as little as possible to do with the good folks of Medicine Hat. They don't like us very much."
Cat chuckled.
"I gathered that. They think you're all drug-crazed sex fiends and commu-

nists."

Her brow furrowed.

"Somebody was looking after me. And whoever it was has a lot of influence."

They transferred her luggage from the back seats of the Jeep to the trunk of the Olds.

"You sure you don't want to come back to Free Town?"

Cat shook her head.

"I think it's best if I shack up in a motel."

She looked thoughtful. In the mellowing, early evening sun, she seemed to be made out of gold.

"I have a feeling," she said suddenly. "That things are about to happen."

As she opened the car door, Cat saw him rub his chin, struck by a sudden thought.

"Wait a minute."

She hesitated.

"What is it?"

He stroked his long moustaches.

"It may be nothing. Just something that's been nagging at me."

Cat smiled.

"Well, tell me."

He started pacing up and down, like he used to in the office. Cat smiled again, remembering her visits, when she was too small to see over his huge desk, and the treats and surprises that were always waiting for her.

He stopped pacing.

"The girls you saw in that diner. One was blonde and the other was a brunette?"

"That's right."

"And it was the brunette that you saw them burying out here?"

"Yes."

"There was no sign of the blonde?"

"None."

He shook his head, frowning.

"Well, what this amounts to, if anything, I don't know…"

Cat smiled encouragingly.

"Yes?"

"Okay…well, it kind of came to me…"

"Uh-huh…?"

"…that in the past two or three months the only female additions to our community here at Free Town have all been brunettes."

Cat blinked.

"Really? Are you sure?"

"Absolutely. It only dawned on me last night, when I was thinking about what you told me."

Cat took a deep breath.

"Hmmm…"

"Probably just a coincidence."

"Maybe. Maybe not."

"You going to look into it?"

"Yes, I think I will."

"That's my girl."

She remembered something.

"Uncle John, has there ever been a plane crash around here?"

He shook his head.

"Not that I know of. Why?"

"Oh, it's nothing. Not to worry."

Cat gave her Uncle a huge hug. He squeezed her tight.

"You take care," he said. "My golden girl."

"Uncle John…?" she whispered in his ear.

"Yes, Princess?"

"When can I borrow the Cobra?"

"Well," Cat told the girl at Reception. "This is a nice surprise."

The "Starlight Motel" was modern and clean, freshly painted in pastels of pink and blue. Stacked in three storeys, forming a square, its tiled balconies looked inwards over a floodlit courtyard garden and swimming pool. It even boasted a plush restaurant and bar.

The girl smiled.

"We do good business. The middle of nowhere is a place people like to stop and refresh, when they're going from somewhere to somewhere."

To prove her point, a tour bus as long as a city block drew up on the neon-lit forecourt and disgorged a small army of salesmen in tired and rumpled suits. On their way back East from some West Coast convention, most of them were still wearing their name tags.

Shoving in through the tall plate glass doors, they headed straight for the bar. Each and every one looked Cat over from top to toe as they filed past.

"Hey, baby!"

"Guys, we came to the right place!"

Her suite had everything she wanted, and all she wanted right now was a hot bath.

Cat tore the shirt off of her body and threw it on the floor. She kicked off the boots, ripped the socks from her feet and hauled the jeans down her hips and thighs. Screwed into a ball, the stale panties were disposed of, one bounce off the wall and into the waste basket.

She looked at herself in the full-length mirror. In the bland light of the motel room, she had no sheen. She had lost her luster. Shedding those clothes hadn't rid her of the smell of lust and vicious thoughts.

She padded across the carpet and lifted the phone from the bedside table.

"Hello? Room Service."

"Hi. This is…uh…" she glanced at her key tag. "Room 221. Can you bring me up a Screwdriver? A big one. Heavy on the vodka."

"Yes, ma'am."

"Many thanks."

She poured half the flask of scented bath oil into the steaming water, inhaling deeply.

"Mmmmmmmm……………!"

Cat savored the moment. Lowering herself by inches, sliding her body into the perfumed water until the surface was tickling her chin.

Closing her eyes, she made her mind empty. She let herself drift, losing the bad memories along with the bad smell.

There was a knock at the door.

"Hello…..? Room Service…….."

Her eyes opened, the veils parting. She sat up, making water slurp over the rim of the bathtub.

"It's open, come in."

"Ma'am…?"

"Is that my drink?"

"Er…yes, ma'am…."

"Great. Bring it in here."

There was a pause.

"Ma'am…?"

She reclined in the bath like Queen Cleopatra.

"D-d-d-Dios!"

Her gleaming breasts floated on the surface. She extended a bare arm.

"Hand it over."

The Hispanic boy stood open-mouthed.

"Yes…M-ma'am…!

Cat touched her lips to the glass and took a sip. She closed her eyes and sighed.

"Perfect!"

A kind of reverence glowed in the boy's wide eyes.

"Can I…can I get you anything else, Ma'am?"

Cat took another sip and smiled.

"No, this is fine. You'll find a couple of dollars on the top of the dresser."

Suddenly, the boy's face was split by an enormous grin.

"Oh no, Ma'am!" he shook his head vigorously. "That won't be necessary!"

He bolted from the bathroom. Then in an instant he was back, popping his head around the door.

He gazed again in wonder at her breasts.

"God bless you, Ma'am!"

Her sleep was full of dreams.

She was running through the desert at night under a starless pitch-black sky, wallowing in the crunching grey sand. She could hear the Cadillac, coming up behind her, its headlight beams like searchlights in the darkness, veering wildly from side to side.

The sand was transparent and she could see the bloated faces of dead girls. They glared at her with their bulging eyes as she ran by, their swollen purple lips moving, their hands reaching up out of the sand to claw at her ankles.

Cat sat up in bed, wide awake.

She was panting. Cold sweat crawled on her skin. Her nerves were jangling, red raw. She looked at the luminous dial of her watch. It was 1 a.m.

"Shit!"

Stark naked, she crossed the room and peered out through a crack in the curtains. The pool was all lit up and people were swimming, pot-bellied men laughing and splashing with girls in bikinis.

The bar was open, its neon flashing like a giant juke box.

"Hm!"

Cat went to the mirror and ran a quick comb through her hair. She didn't waste time with underwear, slipping on a short pale green silk mini dress that she cinched at the waist with a belt of chain-link silver.

Sliding her feet into a pair of sandals, she grabbed a small black purse and headed for the door.

The bar was full of the noise of salesmen unwinding. Jostling for drinks or linking arms in song; staggering, held up by flashily-dressed girls with knowing eyes.

Cat found a stool to perch on, at the end of the bar. She ordered a cocktail and sat for a while, twiddling the little paper umbrella.

A man in a wrinkled suit took possession of the stool next to her. He looked her over, staring at the unfettered peaks of her breasts, poking though the thin stuff of the green dress.

Cat glanced at him. He was adequate. He was only slightly drunk.

Looking her straight in the eye, the salesman slid a folded bar napkin over to her. Cat looked back at him, and then lifted the corner. A room number was scrawled in pencil. She saw the bills, dealt like a hand of cards.

Cat took a sip of her cocktail. She dabbed the corner of her mouth with the folded napkin, then put it in her purse.

The salesman downed his whiskey, got up and walked out of the bar. Cat finished her drink and left.

He sat on the end of the bed in his boxers and socks.

Businesslike, Cat kicked off the sandals, unclipped the chain belt and lifted the dress up over her head.

The salesman goggled at her, her skin glowing in the soft light of the bedside lamp. She walked over to him. He gazed up at her with glazed eyes. Putting his hands on her buttocks, he pressed his face to her stomach.

He huffed and humped on top of her, grunting. Mechanically, she manipulated and instructed him, until he made her come.

He fell asleep immediately, mumbling. Cat pushed him off. She got up, got dressed and went back to her room.

She took a quick shower and went to bed. As soon as her head hit the pillow, she fell into a perfect, dreamless sleep.

Cat slept through breakfast. She woke up at about eleven, refreshed and very hungry.

She washed her face and brushed her teeth. Tying her hair into a long ponytail, she dug out some clean underwear and pulled on a pair of cream-colored flares and a blue sweatshirt with a big white number 1 on the front and back.

Hunger pangs were hurrying her. Tugging on odd socks, Cat laced up her pink sneakers, slung on the shoulder bag and strode swiftly to the door.

Brunch was uneventful. The restaurant was almost deserted. Through the windows, she could see the salesmen filing back onto their bus, comparing hangovers and telling exaggerated tales of sexual conquest.

"More coffee?"

"Just black, thanks."

Cat sipped her coffee slowly. She lit a cigarette, sat back and watched the smoke drift up towards the ceiling.

Now all she could do was wait. She wasn't good at waiting. She liked to make things happen.

Bored, she hung around in reception, looking at the magazines racked up next to the desk.

"Miss Johnson...?"

The receptionist had to repeat it twice before Cat remembered her alias.

"Oh, yes…sorry…yes?"

The girl was taking something from the pigeon-holes behind the counter.

"There's a package here for you."

It was a thick, rectangular packet in a large brown envelope. All that was written on it, in thick block capitals, was "Catherine Johnson." There was no return address.

"Hm! How interesting…"

She took the package up to her room.

When she ripped the envelope open, three chunky yellow booklets fell out onto the bed.

"What the…?"

The cardboard covers bore lurid illustrations on similar themes: slope-shouldered, knuckle-dragging, ape-like Negroes, with rolling eyes and leering rubber lips, pawed outraged blonde women, ripping the clothes from their bodies.

Cat burst out laughing.

She leafed through the text. It was punctuated by more pictures. Rescue was at hand, in the form of tall, rock-jawed, broad-shouldered white men dressed in a kind of military uniform.

Cat began to read. She stopped laughing.

She put the booklets down and picked up the phone.

"Can I have an outside line, please."

She dialled a long number.

"It's Cat."

"Wait please."

There was a pause.

"The line is secure. Go ahead."

"Hi, Cat."

"Hi, Aiko."

"How's your vacation going?"

"It's been interesting."

"Uh-oh!"

"Listen, I need you to do something for me."

"What've you got yourself into now, Cat?"

"I'll tell you later."

"This was supposed to be a vacation."

"Never mind about that."

"Okay, okay! What can we do for you?"

"Can you tap into the Police missing persons files for, say, the past three or four months…?"

"Okay…anything in particular?"

"For young women, hitch-hiking, on the hippy trail, heading in this direction."

"Looking for...?"
"A common denominator."
"Such as?"
"Well, let's see if anything comes up."
"Very mysterious. Okay. Call back later."
"Will do. Many thanks."
"Take care of yourself, Cat."
"Bye."

Cat settled down to wait. She switched on the television and sprawled out on the bed.

She looked at the booklets again. She read about the threat to the purity of the white race. She was told that the time had come, to reclaim America for the True Aryan American.

She examined the pages; there were no printer's codes that might give a clue. And the title page had no credits for authorship and no publication details.

A succession of re-run sit-coms and quiz shows all blurred into each other. She tried the plastic clock radio perched on the bedside table, but the local stations were all seamless country and western.

The telephone rang.
Jolted out of a doze, Cat grabbed the receiver.
"Hello?"
"Did you get our material?"
A man's voice, flat and expressionless.
"Yes I did."
"Did you read them?"
"Yes. I thought it was very interesting."
"Would you like to know more?"
"Yes I would. Very much."

There was a pause. The man's voice became muffled and distant. He had his hand over the receiver and was speaking to someone.

"Do you know the road to Red Springs?"
"I can find it."

Cat looked at her watch. She had a couple of hours to kill.

She put on her makeup and brushed her hair. Slipping into a chic white bikini, she draped a long pale blue robe over her shoulders, donned her shades and headed for the swimming pool.

Enthroned in a sun lounger, she soaked up some rays, topping up her golden tan. She played the Great White Goddess, making the Hispanic and colored boys jump at her beck and call, fetching her titbits and cocktails.

She put on a show for anyone who might be watching. The mere mortal women, who could never hope to fill a bikini the way she did, gave her sideways, envious looks, and glared at their men when they caught them admiring her from afar.

Back in her room, Cat took a shower. She sat naked in front of the dressing table mirror, wafting with an electric hair dryer.

She chose a crisp white shirt, a short denim jacket and tan slacks, with brown, rubber-soled combat boots. The Walther slipped into a slim shoulder holster.

She went to the phone and dialled the long number.

"Hi, Cat."

"Hi. Do you have anything for me?"

"Well…"

"Yes?"

"Well, this might just be coincidence, but it seems that several young women have gone missing in your neck of the woods."

"Really?"

"Or at least they were heading in your direction. Funny thing though. No comeback at all from the local fuzz."

"Uh-huh. That figures. So what's the coincidence?"

"Well, like I said, this may be nothing, but any bodies found all had brown hair…"

"Uh-huh…?"

"The blondes have just disappeared into thin air."

"Now that's interesting."

"What're you getting into, Cat?"

"Uh, something's going on, and it's more than just coincidence."

"You'll keep us posted, won't you?"

"Sure, Aiko."

She pulled the car over to the side of the highway. The purple dusk was filtering down to the pale glow of the horizon and the first stars were coming out.

Cat walked into the desert. She knew exactly where to go. Every wrinkle and crease in the ground was etched in her memory like lines of fire.

Soon she was standing on the lip of the shallow bowl. She hesitated, then took a deep breath and walked down the concave slope. Abrasive winds had reduced all traces of the grave to a shadow, but she recognized the spot immediately.

She knelt down. Leaning forward, she put her palm down on the earth.

"Sleep tight, sweetheart."

The headlights stabbed into the onrushing darkness. The sign posting "Red Springs" rose up in their glow and flew past behind her.

Making up time, Cat took the turning fast and made the tires squeal, the car leaning sideways on its suspension. Its tail twitched, just a little, but she tamed it and accelerated away, the twin exhausts blaring, red tail-lights diminishing to a pinprick in the gloom.

Cat missed the side-road in the darkness, it was so worn and weathered and overgrown.

"Fuck!"

Angry, she hit the brakes hard and went into a noisy, high-speed reverse, making the car lurch to a stop and then leap forward, swinging into the tight turn.

The Olds bumped and juddered over a long stretch of cracks and potholes, till Cat came off the boil and slowed down.

She stroked the top of the dash.

"Sorry, baby."

The 442 emerged onto a vast expanse of concrete, an ocean of deep blue in the starlight.

"Well, isn't that something."

The concrete was stubbled with tall weeds growing out of jagged cracks. She saw a grid of faded white paint marking out parking bays and rusted steel posts with empty hooks and dangling wires where there used to be headsets.

Above it all, blotting out the stars, loomed the massive curve of the disused screen, now stained and crumbling. Off to one side, a tall signboard still advertised, in those letters that hadn't dropped off years ago, a long forgotten rock 'n roll flick and supporting creature feature.

Cat slid the Olds into one of the parking bays and switched off the engine.

She pulled back the cuff of her jacket and looked at the glowing dial of her watch. She patted the steering wheel.

"Made it with time to spare."

She let her mind wander, imagining all those two-tone, chrome-laden juke boxes on wheels, '57 Chevy, Mercury Cruiser and Plymouth Fury, all rocking from side to side, to the clumsy rhythms of teenage fumbling and groping.

Like pin lights at first, she saw yellow headlamps growing in her mirror, expanding till their reflected glare made her blink.

"Here we go."

The strange car pulled up close behind the red Olds.

"Will you get out please."

A man's voice. Flat, expressionless.

Cat flicked the switch below the steering column and disembarked, climbing out onto the cracked concrete.

"Please turn around."

She heard car doors open and heavy feet crunching on bits of chipped cement.

"Put your hands on your head."

Experienced hands patted her down, her arms, under her short jacket. Nimble fingers plucked the Walther from the hidden holster.

"Well," Cat shrugged. "A girl can't be too careful."

The hands felt around her waist and her hips, brisk and professional, along her thighs and calves, all the way down to her ankles.

"It will be returned to you."

There was a brief, muttered conversation with someone sitting in the car behind her.

"You may put your hands down."

"Thanks."

A silk scarf, folded over into several layers, was wrapped around her eyes. A firm grip clamped on her upper arms.

"Come..."

The hands guided her efficiently into the car.

Cat settled back into the deep upholstery of the back seat, folding her hands calmly in her lap.

"I guess you guys have done this before, huh?"

"Please, no more talking."

They drove in silence. No one spoke.

Disorientated, Cat lost all sense of time. She strained her ears, listening for some distinctive sound that might give her a clue, but all she heard was the monotonous drone of the engine and the sound of the wheels on the highway.

She felt the car turning, a tight turn. Then it was riding on a rougher surface that twisted and turned for a long time.

The car stopped. She heard the doors opening.

"You will get out now."

With the same efficiency, the strong hands extracted her from the car.

"Walk now."

The grip on her arms guided her. Her boot heels were crunching on the gritty surface of the desert. She could feel the cool night air on her face.

"Stop."

Someone was knocking on a door, a signal, one-two-three, one-two. Cat heard the door handle turn.

"In."

She stood quietly, her hands down by her sides.

"Any trouble?"

"None. She was carrying this weapon."

"Leave it here. Wait outside."

"Yes, sir."

Cat waited.

"You may remove the blindfold."

"OUCH!"

Cat raised a hand to shield her eyes. She was looking directly into the searing blast of powerful lamps, beamed straight at her.

She could make out a plain wooden floor and bare walls coated in grey plaster. As her eyes adjusted, she thought she could detect the presence of three figures, behind the yellow glare.

"Your name please?"

The man's voice was even-toned and strangely accent less.

"Catherine Johnson."

He spent the next ten minutes confirming the detailed life history that the Agency had constructed for "Catherine Johnson," available as a matter of public record and easy to look up. There were several Catherines, all false, and each one had an authentic life story.

"That's me."

There was another pause, a brief, whispered conversation behind the lights.

Cat saw a pale hand lift the glittering Walther from a table top, turning it over, examining it. The nickel plate flashed, pearl grips gleaming.

"This is an impressive piece."

Cat smiled.

"German," she said. "The best."

She looked directly into the lights.

"You know how it is. A white woman travelling alone. One needs protection."

The disembodied hand put the gun down.

"Indeed."

Cat had to wait a little while before the voice spoke again.

"We admired the manner in which you conducted yourself in Medicine Hat, Miss Johnson."

"Thank you."

"The way that you dealt with those oafs in the saloon was most impressive."

"Well, I know a trick or two."

"And I feel that we owe you an apology for the behavior of Sergeant Rankin and his men towards you."

"No problem…"

"Although according to our reports, you had the situation well under control."

The floating hand reappeared, sliding one of the lurid pamphlets across the table top.

"What did you think of this, Miss Johnson?"

Cat smiled again.

"Crude. But intriguing."

Fingertips drummed on the cardboard cover.

"Yes, crude. Crude propaganda. Not designed for someone of your sophistication, Miss Johnson. But effective."

Cat made her smile encouraging.

"Well, I found it interesting. I'd like to know more."

Some secret signal was passed. Cat heard the door open behind her.

"Take Miss Johnson back to her vehicle."

The blindfold blotted out the lights.

"If you would be so kind as to remain at the motel, Miss Johnson. We will be in touch again shortly."

She felt the weight of the Walther, slotted back into the shoulder holster.

"I'll look forward to it."

CHAPTER 8
Route 66

"It's Cat."

"Hi, Cat, what's happening?"

"I'm not sure yet."

"How can we help?"

"I'll be sending you a small package. Something I found. I'll need an analysis from the lab."

"No problem. Give us a few days and then call back."

"Will do."

"Take care, Cat."

Cat unwrapped the folded tissue, revealing the scrap of silver foil. She put it carefully into an envelope and sealed it. That envelope went inside a larger one, which in turn went into a third.

In a baggy grey sweatshirt and faded blue jeans, she went down to Reception and mailed the package. The comers and goers and the loafers in the armchairs in the lobby scarcely even glanced at her. She half hoped to see some suspicious figure hiding behind a newspaper, but there was no one.

Cat had an uninterrupted breakfast in the restaurant, lingering over her ham and eggs and having two extra cups of coffee. She sat and smoked a cigarette. She hung around in the lobby for a while, looking at the magazines.

No one approached her. Disappointed, Cat went back up to her room.

The kiddies' cartoons amused her briefly, but the chat shows were irritating.

She was pacing up and down, glaring at the silent phone. She dug the Walther out of a drawer and dismantled it, quickly and efficiently. She examined every part minutely, smoothing over the machined steel with an oily rag. Reassembling the gun in seconds, she tested the action, reloaded the magazine into the butt and put it back in the drawer.

Cat looked at her watch and frowned.

A scratchy old documentary about the Indy 500 saved her from temporary insanity. It accounted for the next hour.

She felt the need for speed. It gnawed in her guts and was a hot fever crawling all over her skin.

Cat glared at the phone again. She snared the receiver.

"Uncle John...?"

At one hundred miles an hour, there was a riot goin' on. The asphalt streaked beneath the wheels, the desert blew by in a blur.

Oooo...baby...!

She drove on a razor's edge. Everything was in tune, her senses in perfect harmony. The wind was in her face, her long hair billowing behind her.

Enthroned in the Cobra's basic black upholstery, Cat was sheathed in a pale blue brushed denim jumpsuit, its voluminous flares hiding pink sneakers decorated with silver stars. Reaching up to her chin, she hooked her finger into the big ring pull and drew the zipper down as far as her navel.

The thrill of the wind on her bare skin made her gasp. Smiling, she tilted her head back and rolled it from side to side, letting the cool breeze wash her face. Her hair was floating like a cloud of gold.

"Hey...?"

There was a blob of white on the blacktop, far ahead.

She put her foot down.

"Woo...! He's shifting."

The needle was nudging past 120 and the white blob wasn't getting any bigger. Cat's eyebrows rose towards her hairline.

"My oh my..."

The other driver had seen the bright spark in his mirror and was slowing dramatically. The Cobra caught up in a rush.

Cat swung the silver car next to the white one. The other driver grinned and tipped her a salute.

"Funky wheels," Cat called out.

A low-slung Dodge Challenger. Lean and clean like the blade of a knife. Its sleek white flanks were spotted and streaked by the dust of a long journey. She saw Colorado plates, OA-5599.

"Not so bad yourself."

The driver of the Challenger was a good-looking man in a white shirt and blue jeans, with dark curly hair and a day's worth of stubble. His eyes had a hard brightness to them. Cat knew that strange light. She'd seen it looking back at her in the rear view mirror often enough. The edge that the pills gave you over long stretches of road.

They were cruising side by side at 70. Cat looked the white Challenger over from stem to stern. She saw the tell-tale "Hemi" badge.

"How fast?"

The other driver just shook his head and flashed his easy grin.

Cat laughed.

"Come on. How fast?"

He laughed back. Beneath their wheels, the asphalt was humming.

His radio was pumping out a smoothly funky instrumental, coming from a local station, with a running commentary by someone calling himself "Super Soul."

"I dig it," Cat shouted above the music and the engines. "Where do you find sounds like that out here?"

The other driver shrugged.

"They found me."

She twisted in the driver's seat, leaning towards him, edging the Cobra so close the cars were almost touching.

"How fast?"

The other driver laughed. His eyes were bright blue.

The Challenger sounded like a beast. They were speeding up, glued together.

"C'mon, man. How fast?"

Laughing, Cat pulled the silver Cobra ahead. She slipped it in front of the Challenger, weaving back and forth across its nose.

When he set up to pull out and pass her, Cat made the Cobra swerve extravagantly, sliding from one lane to the other, keeping her tail in his face. He could see her grinning back at him in her mirror.

"Okay…" he muttered.

He faked to the right, then quickly cut left and the white Challenger slid alongside. They raced side by side, trailing dust. Cat picked up speed, a little at a time. The Dodge stayed with her effortlessly.

Wheel to wheel, they turned their heads to look at each other. The engines raised their voices in a competing chorus.

Cat's eyes flashed.

The Cobra leapt forward and pulled in front again, its twin side exhausts blaring.

The Dodge made to go left. The Cobra slid over to block it.

"Uh-uh!" Cat chuckled.

The Challenger feinted, double-bluffed. It faded to go inside, then swung out.

"Oops!"

Fooled, Cat saw the white car creep up beside her.

"Whoa!"

She saw his shoulder dip as he slammed the gear shift to the top. The Dodge roared as it surged forward explosively, accelerating away from her like a shell from a gun, making distance in the blink of an eye.

Ecstatic, Cat screamed out loud.

"Oh my God!"

She reacted quickly and sent the Cobra streaking in pursuit.

Here the desert was undulating and bumpy and the highway wound its way between scrubby, tufted slopes. They took the first bend hard and fast with the Cobra hanging on tight to the Challenger's tail.

On a short straight, the Dodge held the lead, but Cat reduced the distance as they approached the next curve.

It was a tight one.

The Challenger slowed marginally on the inside, taking the turn with surgical precision. Reckless, Cat came careening round the outside, on the very crest of the bend, in a spray of dirt and pebbles.

Snarling, the cars touched. Just a nudge. Tires shrieking, the Cobra veered off the tarmac and onto the gritty crust of the desert.

The Challenger rocked but held the road and ploughed on, tail swinging, disappearing behind a curtain of dust. Its rival wallowed in a yellow fog, churning sand, the engine grinding, complaining loudly.

"Oh shit!"

Squinting through the yellow haze, Cat juggled the pedals and stick shift and hauled the Cobra back onto the hardtop. Laughing, she accelerated smoothly, everything singing in tune again.

The twists and turns were a leveller. When the desert was flat again and they flew out onto the long straight, they were side by side. The spit and snarl of the engines reverberated off the hard earth and the sky.

Uh-oh!

Up ahead, the highway was halved to a single lane, crossing a sturdy steel girder bridge that spanned a long dead dry riverbed.

Locked together, the silver and white missiles hurtled towards the bridge, each trying to force its way there first.

Above the howl of the Cobra, Cat heard the Challenger surge as it reached for that something extra. By inches, the Dodge began to edge ahead.

The Cobra had a lot more to offer. It had horses to spare.

I can take you, man!

Then she pulled back from the brink.

"Oh well..."

Laughing, she conceded. She blipped the horn and began to brake, coming down through the gears.

As the Cobra rolled to a halt, Cat heard a reply from the Dodge and watched it barrel triumphantly across the narrow bridge, barely wide enough to accommodate it. She shook her head, grinning, as it slammed to a stop on the other side, performing a perfect, squealing 180.

Cat got out of her car. The polished silver was dulled by a film of dust. She walked around and examined the bodywork.

Uh-oh!

She walked around the car a few times, getting down for a closer look.

Oh shit…

She drew a small heart with her finger in the dust on the hood.
"Sorry, sweetheart," she murmured.
The Challenger was rolling back slowly across the bridge. It came and parked alongside the Cobra.
The driver got out and smiled at her.
"Bravo," he said.
"Bravo yourself," Cat laughed. "I was outclassed."
He strolled over and looked into the Cobra's black, functional cockpit.
"You've got the real deal here."
"Yep. How about yours?"
He had a slightly lopsided, easy grin.
"She's hopped up to do over 160."
Cat clapped her hands with glee.
"I knew it! I don't feel so bad now."
He shook his head.
"You could have taken me."
Cat smiled.
"Naw, I funked it."
They walked over to the grimy Challenger. Cat poked her head inside.
"Hmmm…"
He popped the hood for her.
"Oh my…!"
He fished out a pack of cigarettes and gave one to her.
"You know," he said. "You're good. You could do this for a living."
Cat shook her head, her eyes twinkling.
"Been there. I was kicked out. They said I was too dangerous."
He laughed.
"Yeah, I noticed that."
He looked at her appreciatively.
"You're very beautiful," he said.
She smiled, almost shyly.

"Thank you."

They stood close together, next to the white Challenger. Cooling down, its engine was ticking. Time passed.

Cat looked into his eyes.

"Do you want to…?"

His expression sobered. She saw a sadness cloud his eyes, a veil of memories, and loss.

"It's a nice…I appreciate it…but…"

She touched his arm.

"Don't worry. Another time."

He looked down at the ground.

"Yeah. Another time."

He climbed into the Challenger and drove away, back across the bridge. Cat watched the white car get smaller as it sped away down the long highway, towards that distant vanishing point.

She glanced down at her watch.

When she looked up, the highway was empty. The Challenger had disappeared.

The gas station was a crumbling off-white wooden shack with a shingle roof, a porch with a canvas-backed chair on it and two ancient red pumps out front. All around was the baked ochre desert, mottled with green scrub.

A man in faded blue dungarees and a straw hat was sitting in the chair. Like a twist of old leather, he was dried out and berry brown, after a lifetime in the sun.

The old man was roused from a doze by the sound of approaching wheels.

"Hmmgh…hrrmm…phh…!"

His eyes opened wide at the sight of the silver Cobra rolling towards him. He blinked and rubbed them when he saw Cat climbing out, in the pale blue jumpsuit, zipped down to her navel.

"Hi!" she called out cheerfully. "I'd like to wash my car."

The old man came down the porch steps slowly. He took off the straw hat and scratched his head, ruffling a shock of white hair.

"Be my guest," he replied.

He showed her where the stand-pipe was, and handed her a tin bucket and a sponge.

"Many thanks."

"My pleasure."

She saw a small American flag in the filmy yellowed window, and a peeling sticker that said "VETERAN."

Cat filled the bucket and dunked the sponge. The old man sat back down on the porch and watched her, admiring the way her body moved as she went to work, scrubbing away the skin of dust that dulled the aluminium shell.

Smiling wistfully, he enjoyed the swing of her hips, the bobbing and swaying of her cleavage.

Cat paused, standing back to evaluate her handiwork. She saw the old man staring at her.

"I'm sorry," he grinned. "But you're the prettiest sight I've seen in a long time."

Cat laughed, looking down at herself. She was as dusty as her car. She ran her fingers through her long hair, combing out bits of grit.

"Thanks!"

He went inside and came out with some brushes and helped her sweep the dust off the black upholstery and floor mats.

"There!" Cat exclaimed. "As good as new."

He gave her a cold can of soda. She guzzled it greedily.

"Aaaaaahhh…..!"

He stood there openly admiring her. Cat smiled at him. She drained the rest of the can.

"mmm…wow…" she licked her lips. "Perfect!"

She lifted her shoulder bag from the floor of the car.

"How much for the soda?"

He shrugged.

"On the house."

"Thank you."

"No, thank you."

Cat looked puzzled.

"For what?"

"For letting me enjoy looking at you. When I was your age a girl would take pleasure in letting a man admire her. A lot of women nowadays take offence."

Cat laughed.

"I guess I'm just an old-fashioned girl."

Cat pointed at the sticker in the window.

"You're a vet?"

His sloping shoulders squared a little.

"That's right. I fought the fascists from '36 to '45. Enlisted in the Abraham Lincoln Brigade and went to Spain. After Pearl Harbor I joined the 82nd Airborne for the duration."

Cat's eyes widened.

"That's fantastic."

His eyes sparked with sudden bitterness.

"And then Joe McCarthy said that I was a communist because I fought with the Brigade."

He was staring at the little flag.

"I was a teacher, you know, a university professor."

Tears welled in his eyes.

"Now I'm here."

Cat didn't know what to say.

The spark in his eyes flared into flame as he gripped her forearm tightly.

"They're still here," he said, looking at her intently. "The fascists!"

His intense gaze raked the flat horizons of the desert.

"I mean here. Right here amongst us!"

The fire dimmed. Embarrassed, he let go of her arm.

"I-I'm sorry...I didn't..."

Cat smiled, shaking her head. She took his hand.

"No. It's okay."

She hesitated.

"I think you're right."

He gazed at her for a long time in silence, the heat in his eyes mellowing.

"You're so beautiful," he said at last.

"Thank you."

"The girls in Spain were beautiful. It was a special time, of passion and liberty. We believed that anything was possible if you wanted it enough."

An impulse prompted her hands to reach up in a simple, elegant motion, and slip the unzipped jumpsuit off of her shoulders, shrugging out of it so she was bare to the waist.

He stared in wonder at her naked breasts.

"Oh, God...!"

She took him by the hand again and led him onto the porch and inside.

There was a small room at the back, with a narrow, iron-framed bed, bathed in a blue half-light coming from a dirty window.

Cat tugged off her sneakers. She pulled the zipper all the way down and stepped out of the jumpsuit. She wasn't wearing any panties.

Stark naked, she stood in front of him. Her skin was velvet in the soft light, her long hair glowing like pale gold. He stood there staring at her. A sound that was both agony and ecstasy welled up in his chest.

Cat undressed him. He looked down at the floor, ashamed of his dried-out body. Murmuring encouragement, Cat took him to the bed. She caressed and kissed him and gently coaxed him into arousal with her hands and her mouth. He sighed and moaned, groaning when she seized his hands and put them on her body.

She straddled him as he lay on his back, spreading her thighs. As he penetrated her, he cried out in sheer disbelief.

Cat did all the work, smiling down at him, her eyes half-closed. Her hips gyrated with a slow, gentle rhythm. His hands were now roving freely all over her, her skin slick with sweat.

The rhythm of her pelvis became more insistent, as their sighs and groans became entwined, coordinated. Cat threw back her head and laughed as she came, her body leaping. Beneath her, the old man arched his back, shuddering, shouting incoherently.

The bathroom was a wooden cubicle with a washbasin, a chipped enamel tub and barely enough space to turn around in.

Humming to herself softly, Cat washed with cold water and a cloth and towelled herself down. Shaking out her hair, she came back into the bedroom.

The old man was sitting on the edge of the sagging bed, still naked. He looked dazed.

"Boy!" said Cat, clambering back into the jumpsuit. "I needed that!"

He looked up at her. There were tears shining on his leathery cheeks. Cat put her hand on his shoulder.

"What's the matter? You were great."

He put his face in his hands and began to sob, his shoulders heaving. Cat sat down beside him.

"Hey, it's alright…it's alright…"

"Hi, Uncle John!"

Muttering to himself, he went over the Cobra minutely. He found a scratch. And more. Getting down on his hands and knees, he discovered a minor ding or two.

"Uh…gotta split…byeeee…!"

He dashed to the doors of the garage. The red Olds was already halfway down Main Street.

He shook his fist. She tooted the horn and he could see her huge grin in the rear view mirror, even at that distance.

Hands on hips, John Warburton threw back his head and roared with laughter.

"That's my girl!"

Cat let the Olds roll down the ramp to the motel's underground car park. She glided past salesmen's bland saloons and family station wagons, till she found an empty parking space.

She bent down to flick the switch under the steering column, swung the bag across her shoulder and set off towards the dull metal elevator doors, on the far side of the car park.

Fluorescent tubes gave the low concrete ceiling and squat square pillars a green and ghoulish cast. Her footfalls had a thin echo. The cold light seemed to shiver nervously.

Suddenly, Cat reached down and pulled the Walther from its special pocket inside the bag. Aiming from the hip, she directed the muzzle at a nearby pillar.

"Who's there?"

Silence. Then the soft scrape of shoe leather.

"Come out!"

A well-built man with light-colored hair and pale eyes stepped out from behind the concrete column. He was wearing a neatly-pressed tan safari suit.

"And you!"

Cat turned her head slightly, keeping the gun zeroed on the man's chest.

"It's alright," the man said quietly. "Come out."

His twin emerged, close behind her. Cat side-stepped quickly and planted her back against one of the columns, from where she could see both of them, the gun muzzle shifting back and forth from one to the other.

The first man smiled thinly, held his arms out sideways and showed his empty palms.

"You have excellent instincts, Miss Johnson."

Cat frowned at him.

"Obviously I need them. Do you always sneak up on people like that?"

He ignored the question and her frown, the smile unflinching. The other man stood quite still, his hands in plain view, down by his sides.

"You were asked to remain in the motel, Miss Johnson. You were gone for hours. Where did you go?"

Cat shrugged.

"Nowhere. For a burn. Up and down the highway."

She laughed.

"I get my kicks on Route 66."

They stared at her blankly. Then the pale smile was switched on again. Cat noticed that he smiled with his mouth but not with his eyes. His eyes were shards of ice.

"Very well. But we would be grateful if you would restrain these impulses, Miss Johnson…"

"Whatever you say."

"…we would hate to lose you in an accident…"

The second man was lifting his hand towards the hip pocket of his safari jacket.

"Hold it!"

Cat pointed the gun at him, her eyes narrowing, flicking from one to the other.

The first man kept smiling. The second man's hand froze halfway.

"You're very professional, Miss Johnson. I'm impressed."

Cat made a face.

"Like I told your boss," she said. "A woman alone has to know how to take care of herself."

The first man shook his head.

"You haven't met our…boss, Miss Johnson. Not yet. But, if we may…?"

He gestured towards his colleague.

113

"Go ahead," said Cat. "Slowly."

The second man unbuttoned the flap of his pocket and produced a slip of paper. Holding it out between his fingers, he approached her.

Keeping the gun tight to her body, Cat stretched out and took the paper. Both men took dark sunglasses from a breast pocket and put them on. In the strange, subterranean light, the lenses were solid black.

"Be at that place at eleven o'clock tomorrow morning and ring that number and you will be given instructions."

Cat glanced down at the piece of paper.

"Isn't this all just a bit over-elab—?"

The men had gone. A disembodied voice came floating back across the empty car park.

"Don't be late…"

The "PIT STOP" was one of countless diners that made up the dots connecting the miles and miles of desert highway. It was one of the more ambitious efforts, an art deco confection in red brick and cream tiles.

A wide concrete forecourt was sprinkled with parked vehicles, the predictable mix of pick-up trucks, big rigs and company cars with the inevitable suit in a bag hung in the back.

Cat didn't like being without her wheels. It made her nervous. But the written instructions were specific. They said use the motel's taxi service.

She was in for a pleasant surprise. The cab turned out to be a lovingly maintained light blue '60 Impala and, after a while, Cat began to enjoy the ride. It was the driver's pride and joy and he was delighted when she showed an interest. Cat always liked to talk cars.

At a quarter-to-eleven, the taxi deposited her outside the "PIT STOP." There was the phone booth, and she dialled the number on the piece of paper they'd given her.

Cat was dressed for business in the short denim jacket, a plain white shirt tucked into tan trousers, and rugged combat boots. The Walther was snug in its shoulder holster.

She checked her watch again. Five to eleven. The sky above was a singing blue and the desert was starting to cook.

At precisely eleven o'clock, a truck turned off the highway and advanced onto the forecourt.

Cat raised her eyebrows.

It was an ugly US Army surplus two-and-a-half ton six-by-six cargo truck. Olive drab, the big white star on its snout was faded, the stencilled serial numbers wearing away. The buff-colored, high-top canvas awning that shrouded the back was stained and torn in places.

"Miss Johnson?"

The driver was a husky man in brown overalls, wearing a blue baseball cap. The speaker was climbing down from the seat beside him.

"That's right."

Another one! Another one with a strong build, filling out a safari suit, with a blank face and sandy hair, and what would doubtless be pale eyes, behind those black shades.

"Come with me, please."

He ushered her towards the rear of the truck. Stopping, he held out his hand.

"Your pistol, please."

Cat gave him the Walther. She looked up at the high tailgate and the closed curtains of the canvas awning.

"Get in, please."

There was a metal stirrup that made a step up. Cat put her boot in it, reached up with both hands and swung herself effortlessly over the tailgate. She vanished through the seam in the canvas.

The interior of the truck was light by the dim yellow glow of a single electric lantern.

"Hi, guys."

Two burly figures in brown overalls sat opposite each other on fold-down wooden benches, their slab-like features as grey as stone in the feeble light.

"How's it going?"

They said nothing. Their dull eyes looked her up and down once and then they faced front again. Stubby submachine-guns rested on their knees.

Cat sat down on the bench, near to the tailgate and the closed canvas. She heard the slamming of the cab door. The idling engine rumbled into life. The truck lurched and began to roll.

Her watch told her that an hour had gone by.

The hard wood was making her butt ache. It was warm and sticky under the canvas and perspiration prickled on her face.

Her escort sat still and stolid, face to face, the guns glinting on their laps.

"Whoo!" Cat exclaimed, fanning herself with her hand.

They turned their heads slowly to stare at her. She undid a few buttons, exposing a creamy V of skin.

They didn't blink. Just that dull stare. Cat reached out to draw back the canvas flaps.

"We could do with some air in here."

One wrenched back the cocking handle of his gun, the muzzle centered on her chest. The other was beside her in an instant, seizing her wrist in a vice-like grip.

In her mind, Cat twisted him into the path of the bullets, flipped his body out of the truck, then dived and rolled, kicking the submachine-gun out of the other's hands before breaking his neck with a swift karate chop.

"Okay! Okay!" she laughed. "Lighten up, guys!"

He let go, but sat down opposite her, frowning. His partner hesitated, and then pointed his gun down at the floor.

Cat rubbed her wrist.

"Peace, peace…!"

She grinned at them. They stared back sullenly.

They all leaned over as the truck turned suddenly.

It twisted and turned several times in the next half hour, and was going uphill. The turns were tight, the big wheels squealing.

"Whoa!" said Cat, sliding on the bench.

The truck ran on the straight for a while, up a long incline. Then it stopped.

"Here we go again!"

One held his gun ready. The other was brandishing a blindfold.

Holding her by the elbows, they walked her up a long path. Gravel crunched beneath her feet.

"There are some steps now."

She heard the faint creak of an old-fashioned bell pull and the bell sounding far away. After a short pause, a heavy door clanked open.

"The Colonel is expecting us."

"Yes sir. Come in."

Cat's feet slipped and slid on a smooth and polished surface. It was a long walk. The hallway must be huge.

"Now we go up the stairs."

The stairs went up and up, in a long, sweeping curve. It seemed to take forever. She almost stumbled once, but the grip on her arms supported her.

When she reached out for the next step and it wasn't there, she knew they'd arrived at the landing. There was another long walk, now she waded in lush carpeting.

Boot heels crashed to attention, making her jump.

"We have an appointment with the Colonel."

"Sir!"

There was a knock on a door. A voice inside responded—"Enter!"

She heard the door open.

"Go on…"

Cat was walked forward, stopped, turned, walked forward a few paces and stopped again.

"Leave us."

"Yes, sir!"

She heard the door close behind her.

Cat stood absolutely still, her hands hanging down by her sides. In the darkness behind the blindfold, she willed her heart to beat evenly, and prepared her mind for everything and anything.

"You may remove the blindfold."

She reached up promptly and unwrapped the scarf.

"Take your time."

Blinking, she got used to the light. The room swam into focus. It was enormous, with curving walls that formed an oval. There was floral wallpaper bordering panels with classical motifs. The furniture was heavy and ornate, with elaborately carved and gilded frames and red velvet upholstery that matched the curtains with their gold fringes and tassels. Up above, a gilt and crystal chandelier hung from the center of a flamboyant rosette.

"Alright now?"

The whole room focused on a vast, marble-topped Louis XV desk, smothered in gilt carvings. The desk lamp was gold and crystal, the inkwells were solid gold.

Please be seated, Miss Johnson."

Cat barely smothered the laugh that jumped into her throat.

The man rose, extending an arm towards a mighty red and gold armchair.

"Please."

He was too small for his desk. His shoulders were too narrow for the massive gold epaulettes that jutted from them, matching the gleaming buttons and the heavily braided cuffs that went almost to the elbows of his Confederate grey tunic. His torso was disproportionately longer than his legs, which were too thin for the tight-fitting pale blue trousers with their yellow stripe, tucked into knee-length boots that gleamed like black glass.

"Thank you."

I should have come dressed like Scarlett O'Hara

"This is a wonderful room," she said, smiling like she thought a Southern belle would smile, descending gracefully into the plush red velvet depths of the armchair.

"I'm glad you like it."

Gazing all around to admire the period furnishings helped her keep a straight face. She found it hard to look at him.

"May I offer you some refreshment?"

He indicated a tall crystal decanter and long-stemmed glasses.

"That's very kind, but I'm fine, thank you."

Cat forced herself to look at him, smiling directly into his eyes.

"If you're certain...?"

His eyes were small and dark and blinked irregularly, behind the thick lenses of spectacles with small oval rims, perched on the thin bridge of his nose. He could have been in his mid-forties, but the skin of his face was as smooth as a child's, its startling paleness emphasized by the jet blackness of his receding hair, slicked back from his high white forehead. A small black moustache and pointed goatee beard further highlighted the peculiar porcelain quality of his skin.

"No, I'm okay, thank you," Cat was very thirsty, after the long hot, jolting trip in the truck, but safety came first.

He sat down again and gazed at her for a little while, stroking his beard. Cat noticed that his hands were very small and white.

"I apologize for all that cloak and dagger business and the discomfort of your journey."

Cat stifled a grin. His accent was that of a Southern Gentleman and was as phoney as the rest of him.

"But security is of the essence."

Cat leaned towards him in the chair, smiling.

"I quite understand."

His thin lips curved slightly.

"I knew you would."

He dispensed an amber liquid from the decanter into one of the crystal goblets. Holding the moment, he took a slow sip, reflected, then another.

"Are you sure you won't...?"

Cat's mouth was parched.

"Well, perhaps..."

His lips curved again in that bleak parody of a smile.

"I admire your caution, Miss Johnson."

He filled another glass and rose from the desk, bringing it to her.

"Thank you."

The sherry was crisp and refreshing.

"This is excellent."

He bowed slightly.

"I thought you would appreciate it."

He crossed the room and stood beside a marble bust of Robert E. Lee, his elbow resting on the base.

"You must forgive my manners, Miss Johnson. I haven't introduced myself."

He bowed again, deeper this time.

"I am Johnston Harwood Beauregard the Third."

He was the most ridiculous thing she had ever seen.

"Colonel, now retired."

Colonel my ass. County dog catcher most likely
She gave him another smile.
"I knew that you were military man."
His backbone stiffened. He puffed out his puny chest.
"I am descended from a long line of military men. My ancestors were among the flower of Virginia aristocracy and fought and died with pride under the Stars and Bars!"
There were two hot pink spots on his pale cheeks. His eyes were blinking rapidly.

Yeah, sure. And I'm the Queen of Sheba

"Really? That's fascinating."
He drained the sherry, then stood for a moment gazing at some distant horizon, as if he could see the battle flags and hear the bugle call.
Cat had to look down at the carpet quickly to mask the grin that was threatening to crease her face.
He heaved a dramatic sigh.
"But those were different times. When everything was in its proper place. Before the world turned upside down."
Cat looked sympathetic.
"I know what you mean."
He fixed her with a penetrating stare.
"Do you?"
He strode briskly back to his desk and sat down. He looked smaller than ever.
"I wonder if you do, Miss Johnson."
He pulled open a heavy, ornate drawer and took out a blue cardboard folder. His small hands spread its contents out on the gleaming marble desktop.
He looked up at her. Cat gazed back at him expectantly.
"You made a considerable first impression on my people in Medicine Hat, Miss Johnson."
"I did?"
"You conducted yourself with considerable aplomb in dealing with those clods in the bar…"
"Oh, well…"
"And you endured the…unfortunate…indignities inflicted upon you by our local constabulary with admirable sang-froid."
"Thank you."
Behind the thick lenses, his small black eyes were flicking all over her. Cat sat quietly, smiling at him. Her flesh was creeping.
"You displayed true breeding, Miss Johnson. The very essence of superiority. In the finest traditions of your race."

Cat looked puzzled.

"My race?"

"Indeed." His thin fingers shuffled the papers in the file. "Johnson...might I inquire...?"

Cat smiled.

"Oh yes, I see. The name used to be Johansson, but it was Americanized when my great-grandfather came to this country. My family comes from Sweden."

The wintry smile flickered again.

"Of course. I knew it."

Cat's blood went cold. But she kept smiling.

"One of the Aryan tribes."

His busy eyes were examining her in detail.

"And if I may say so, Miss Johnson, you are a true credit to your race."

She felt nauseous. She looked flattered.

"You are a perfect specimen. You represent a physical ideal."

I'm going to puke!

"Why, thank you...I don't...I don't know what to say..."

He leant forward across the desk, transfixing her with a piercing stare. The thick lenses enlarged his eyes abnormally. Cat resisted the impulse to recoil in her chair.

"Colonel Beauregard" stared at her for a long time. Cat maintained her air of calm expectancy.

Whenever he was about to speak, his eyelids would blink rapidly.

"I wonder, Miss Johnson..."

"Yes?"

The Colonel lifted the lid on a tortoiseshell box embossed with an ornate regimental crest. Extracting a cigarette, he screwed it deftly into the socket of a long gold and amber holder. The match-head rasped on the side of an antique silver matchbox. He sat back, swivelled slightly in the red leather desk chair and gazed up contemplatively, watching the curling tendrils of smoke rise towards the carved ceiling.

The muscles around Cat's mouth were straining to smile. But she sat soberly, her hands folded in her lap.

"Your breeding is impeccable. That is obvious, one only has to look at you. You are physically perfect..."

"Well, I..."

With a grandiloquent sweep of his arm, he indicated an oil painting on the wall above and to the right of him.

"As you can see..."

The hairs on the back of her neck prickled. It was a prime example of Nazi art, a quartet of naked Rhine maidens, disporting on the river bank. Flaxen-haired all, they were strapping and sculptural, with vacant, flawless features.

Cat made herself look suitably modest and flattered.

"I...I never quite saw myself as a work of art..."

He swivelled back to look directly at her.

"A work of nature! And the very pinnacle of nature, the Aryan race! Not an aberration, a freak of nature, like the Jew or the Black!"

I'm definitely going to puke!

The Colonel's eyelids were a blur. He sucked hard on the gold mouthpiece of the cigarette holder and exhaled the smoke with a hiss.

"But I do wonder, Miss Johnson..."

"Yes...?"

"Whether your thoughts are true to your blood."

Cat put on her puzzled face.

"I don't understand."

"You exhibit all the traits of the superior race, in the way that you conduct yourself, in the way that you dismiss the insults of your inferiors."

"Um..."

He was leaning across the marble desktop again, looking deep into her eyes.

"And yet your behavior is sometimes...contradictory."

"Oh. I'm disappointed. How?"

Sucking on the cigarette holder, he leant back in the chair.

"That should be obvious to you."

Cat adopted her blank face. It worked, he was plainly pleased with himself.

"I am told that you listen continually to those pagan jungle noises that pass for 'music' amongst the Blacks..."

"Ah."

"...and you have been observed on many occasions conversing on what appears to be an almost sociable level with colored menials..."

Cat smiled reassuringly.

"Oh, yes, of course, I see what you mean."

She leaned forward in the armchair. She was persuasive, eager to please.

"Now, Colonel, I'm not one who believes that all the Blacks should be expelled from the US of A."

She even managed to raise a chuckle.

"I don't think that we have to ship them all back to Africa."

He looked interested.

"Indeed...?"

Cat laughed.

"No. My belief is that the Black should know his place, and then everything will be fine."

"I see..."

She was on a roll now.

"I can dig Jazz and be polite to delivery boys and still believe in white supremacy. The Blacks are fine by me as long as they're playing my music, batting for my ball team or washing my car..."

"Quite..."

"And even if we were inclined to give them what they want—and I say they want too much—heck, they're not ready for it."

"Absolutely."

"We can't all of a sudden get down on our knees and turn everything over to the leadership of the Blacks. At least not until we've been able to educate them to a point of responsibility. And I don't believe that would be possible."

The Colonel was impressed.

"You are plainly a sophisticated thinker, Miss Johnson."

Cat very nearly burst out laughing.

He rose from behind the desk and began to pace the plush carpet, every inch the man of destiny.

Cat sat still, trying to look humble.

"The next question, Miss Johnson..."

"Yes, Colonel?"

"...is whether you are prepared to transform your beliefs into action."

CHAPTER 9
Secret Army

"I see you are impressed, Miss Johnson."

Cat was speechless.

The Colonel ushered her out into the sunlight, onto the broad sweep of a glistening white marble terrace.

"What do you think?"

The sky was a singing blue, the hot sun directly above them, at high noon. The sizzling glare of the marble made Cat fumble for her sunglasses, in the breast pocket of her jacket.

"I'm amazed Colonel."

They were leaning on the balustrade that fenced the edge of the terrace. Below them, stretching as far as the eye could see, blurring into the heat haze, were lush green gardens, the geometric order and elegance that belonged to an eighteenth century chateau.

Glowing with pride, the Colonel led Cat down a long curling flight of marble steps. The grass was plush beneath her feet and then their boot heels were crunching as he took her down manicured gravel paths, flanked by great flowerbeds, bursting with color. Through ornate, iron wrought gateways in tall, dark hedges she glimpsed secret gardens adorned by classical statuary. Fountains tossed up their tinkling, glittering cascades.

She was genuinely impressed. The Colonel puffed out his narrow chest.

"I had everything transported from Europe and reconstructed here in the desert. A complex feat of irrigation, I can tell you."

Cat shook her head in wonderment.

"It's...it's...impossible..."

The Colonel paused by the statue of an ancient warrior, standing over the body of a slain enemy. He struck one of his Napoleonic poses.

"Anything is possible, my dear Miss Johnson, if one has the vision and the will!"

Cat smiled at him ingratiatingly.

"Yes indeed, Colonel. The triumph of the will."

She made her eyes shine with admiration. Nausea nagging in her guts, she forced her eyes to lock on his and hold the moment.

Okay, mein Fuhrer. I'll play your Eva Braun

The little Colonel obviously got the message she was pretending to send. He was positively glowing.

Stepping closer, he took her gently by the elbow. She turned cold when he touched her, and overpowered the urge to snap him in half.

"Come, Miss Johnson. I have much to show you…"

She saw stark arenas, with bare sandy floors, ringed by high walls of dark red brick. Beyond them, stood row upon row of long prefabricated huts with sloping corrugated roofs.

"Move it!"

"On the double!"

Raw recruits with pale, sweating faces and crew cuts, the back of their necks red from the sun. In olive drab T-shirts and gym shorts, they were being worked hard by bellowing muscle-bound drill instructors. Grunting and groaning, sweat dripped from their faces, spotting the sand—running on the spot, jumping astride, push-ups and squat thrusts.

Elsewhere, the pale recruits were being familiarized with a variety of small arms: automatic pistols, carbines and submachine-guns, learning to strip and reassemble them blindfold, timed with a stopwatch.

Ragged volleys rose up from the shooting ranges, peppering targets in the form of human silhouettes. Some standing, some prone, men who had been there long enough to get an even tan were lined up shoulder to shoulder, blazing away, while their instructors paced up and down behind them, pausing to admonish or encourage.

It all looked familiar to Cat. Reminiscent of the gruelling training regime that had followed her recruitment by Selena's secret "Agency."

"This is quite an operation you have here, Colonel."

His eyes burned with a deep, dark fever.

"When the time comes, Miss Johnson, we will be ready."

Watching all the activity closely from behind the black lenses of their sunglasses were pale-faced men with sandy hair, wearing tan safari suits.

The Colonel indicated another gateway, in yet another bland brick wall.

"This, I believe, will be of special interest to you, Miss Johnson…"

They entered the bricked-off arena, with the sun beating off the yellow sand.

"I like to think of these gentlemen as our Special Forces."

There were five of them. They were different. Their hair was shaven to a stubble cropped close to their glistening scalps. Their faces were blank, slab-like, their thick necks sunk into shoulders packed with muscle. They had bulging biceps as hard as rock and huge forearms like corded steel. They were carved out of granite and steel, all in black, black T-shirts and track suit trousers.

They seemed unusually pale, un-tanned. There was even a tint of greyness in their strange pallor.

"Perfect physical specimens, aren't they, Miss Johnson?"

A cold finger ran down Cat's spine. Their eyes were all the same color, very dark, almost black, impenetrable, and unblinking. They looked at Cat without a flicker of expression, checked her over from top to toe, mechanically, making a mental note of her. They had shark's eyes. Their eyes fixed on her the way a shark identified its prey.

Then their eyes all switched to the Colonel, as they stood in a line, shoulder to shoulder.

The spell was broken. Cat swallowed hard.

"Y-yes, very impressive…"

The Colonel was as pleased as a boy showing off a favorite toy.

"We're still training them. They're not the finished article."

He was looking at her, appraising her. Cat steeled herself for what she knew was coming next.

"Perhaps you would care to assist us with our training program?"

The blank black shark's eyes all rotated to stare at her. Cold went hot and Cat felt a sudden sweat prickle all over her body.

"Would you care to give us a demonstration of your skills?"

Suddenly it was very hot and the sandy yard was a brick-lined oven.

"Sure."

She shrugged off the short denim jacket.

"Colonel…?"

He stepped forward and took it from her, admiring the thrust of her breasts beneath her shirt. Then he took a few quick paces backwards, his eyes gleaming with anticipation.

Cat took a long deep breath and let it out slowly, calming herself, emptying her mind. She let her hands hang down loosely by her sides. The men in black were all watching the Colonel.

The Colonel looked from Cat to the five men in black and back again. He savored the moment. Then he lifted his small hands and clapped them together once.

"YAAAAAAHHH!!!"

The first man exploded off the blocks. From a standing start, he was hurtling across the sand, a missile of muscle and bone.

"UGH!"

And then he was lying flat on his face. A twitch, a shudder. Motionless.

Cat stood over him, her feet slightly apart, thumbs hooked into her belt, gazing calmly at the other men. The rise and fall of her breasts beneath her shirt was barely perceptible. There was just a hint of perspiration on her forehead.

The Colonel's mouth dropped open. He snapped it shut and swallowed hard.

He raised his hands again and clapped twice.

"Two and three!"

The next two stepped forward together. They advanced on Cat, shoulder to shoulder. She stood her ground, hands down, feet apart, perfectly balanced.

The men separated. They moved sideways, on the balls of their feet, circling to the left and right, flanking her. Cat's eyes flicked from one to the other, but she remained motionless, inscrutable.

"YAAHH!!!"

With a shout, the men sprang into a martial pose, coiled springs. They held the pose, ratcheting up the tension, every muscle quivering.

Cat didn't move. She was serene.

"AAAAAAIIIEEEE!!!!!!"

They attacked, with scything arms and kicking feet.

"AAYAAAHHHH!!!!"

Cat advanced to meet Number Two. With concise, economical gestures, she blocked his chopping blows on her forearms. Feinting right, and then leaning left, she flicked out her right leg in a short backwards hook-kick as her opponent surged past her.

Her heel impacted on the back of his knee. The man yelled as his brawny limb seemed to crumple like paper. He lurched and fell awkwardly, off balance, arms flailing.

"HAH!"

It was a short punch delivered with a twist of the wrist. Cat's fist only travelled about eight inches before arriving at the base of his skull, but the man was propelled forward as if he had been struck by a battering ram. He rolled over twice before coming to rest in a tangle, unconscious.

"YAAAAAA!!!"

Instinct made her sway sideways.

The edge of a big hand, like an axe blade, fanned her face and flicked her swirling hair.

Number Three lunged past, braked, pivoted on his heel and came at her again, his arms wind-milling. Cat kept moving sideways, bobbing and weaving, blocking the hail of blows.

For an instant, his sheer momentum and physical weight pierced her defences. She only just deflected a blow intended to crush her throat, downwards onto her chest, and was rocked back a few paces. He clutched at her as she retreated and Cat felt the shirt being ripped from her shoulder.

Now she was balanced again and was using her backwards motion to bring him on to her. Encouraged by her retreat, the man in black came forward quickly, reaching for a stranglehold.

Suddenly, Cat planted her feet and, twisting her body, used his onrushing energy to throw him, flipping him up and over in an extravagant somersault.

As he flew, he took the shreds of her shirt with him, leaving a few tatters dangling from her waistband.

The Colonel gasped.

The brassiere that Cat was wearing was built more for action than for fashion, but was all the more erotic for it. She was breathing heavily now and her skin was glowing with sweat.

Number Three was struggling to his knees. Cat strolled towards him across the churned sand. He saw her blurred form advancing and tried to hurl a handful of sand into her face as he lurched up at her. She let the coarse spray go by with a disdainful shrug of her bare shoulders. Grains of sand glittered on her gleaming torso.

Without breaking stride, Cat snaked out a leg. The high kick took her boot heel to the point of his chin. The crunch of his teeth coming together rang off the brick walls.

Cat was starting to enjoy herself. Blowing strands of long golden hair out of her face, she smiled at the two remaining men in black.

"Next?"

The men in black stood stolidly, shoulder to shoulder. They were looking at the Colonel, and seemed utterly unmoved by Cat's performance or her state of undress.

The Colonel's face was beet red and sweaty. He was staring at Cat in a kind of daze.

Furious, he jerked himself together, clearing his throat loudly. He clapped his hands.

"Four!"

His thin lips twisted into an unpleasant smile.

"Knife!"

Number Four walked towards Cat. Reaching behind his back, he produced a heavy combat knife, its six-inch blade stained black to eliminate reflection.

Cat waited for him. She was smiling.

She let him come close. Then, on bent legs, in a crouch, she began to circle sideways. The man in black circled with her, making slow passes and little feints in the air with the blade.

He made to cut at her belly but slashed at her face. She wasn't fooled, swaying safely out of harm's way.

They circled. There was blood on the sand, vomited by the man with the broken teeth. Cat's foot slithered.

Her opponent lunged. Cat felt the needle point of the dagger trace a fine red-hot line of fire on her bare skin, just below her ribs. The sweat made it sting.

"Ah!"

Sensing an advantage, Number Four was all over her. Cat parried his knife hand with her forearm. Abandoning finesse, she brought her knee up into his groin with all the force of her powerful thigh.

"Four down...and one...to go..."

Brushing back her hair with both hands, Cat got her breath back. The sweat was now trickling freely on her skin.

Her pose, with her hands behind her head, was magnificent. The Colonel was enraptured.

Cat looked across at the last remaining man in black.

"Well, we wouldn't want to leave anyone out, would we, Colonel?"

The Colonel smiled his thin smile. The handclap echoed off the bricks.

"Five!"

Cat stood waiting with her hands held loosely by her sides. She was puzzled when Number Five, instead of coming to do battle, simply stayed where he was, about fifty feet away.

They stayed like that for some time.

"Uh, Colonel, I don't think he heard—"

Suddenly, there was a gun in his hand. Cat recognized it with a flash of alarm, a stubby little machine-pistol, favored by tank crews for close quarter combat.

"Uh-oh!"

He opened fire, the little gun rattling in his hand. Some instinct made Cat twist and jump sideways just as his finger tightened on the trigger. She heard the crack of the bullets close by her head.

With a yell, she was flying towards him across the sand, closing the distance rapidly in a series of spectacular cartwheels.

As Cat bore down on him, the man in black kept firing, the bullets kicking up spurts of sand behind her.

The machine-pistol had a small magazine and by the time Cat was upon him, Number Five had drained it. She was a whirling blur of arms and legs and golden hair and gleaming flesh and then all of a sudden she was standing in front of him and a big grin was the last thing he saw before oblivion came crashing down on him.

She towelled herself down with the tattered remains of her shirt.

"Colonel, your boys have a lot to learn."

He strode swiftly to her, offering her jacket.

"You are magnificent, Miss Johnson! A true Valkyrie!"

Men in white overalls came running. They lifted the sprawling forms of the men in black onto stretchers and carried them away quickly. The stretcher bearers looked more like lab technicians than medical staff.

She was given a black T-shirt, to replace her ruined shirt.

"Shall we retire to more pleasant surroundings, Miss Johnson?"

Delighted with himself, the little Colonel escorted her back into the manicured gardens. He suggested an ornate iron wrought bench set before a melodious marble fountain.

"Thank you, Colonel, this is much nicer."

He waited for her to sit, and then settled down beside her, smiling.

"Indeed. But I suspect, Miss Johnson, that you find yourself equally at home in more...rugged...surroundings?"

Cat looked cool.

"I can take care of myself."

The Colonel laughed, an unpleasant bark.

"You gave a very efficient demonstration of that, Miss Johnson."

Brisk footsteps crunched on the shining gravel path. An oriental manservant in eighteenth century livery came bearing a crystal jug and two glasses.

"May I offer you some lemonade?"

Cat drank the chilled drink gratefully. The Colonel stared, admiring her.

"Thank you, Colonel."

He was stroking his moustaches.

"I would say, Miss Johnson, that you get...how can I put it...a distinct gratification from physical competition...from conquering an opponent...?"

She grasped the jug and refilled her glass.

"You could say that."

He looked at her keenly, his sharp eyes boring into her.

"And I'll wager that you don't shy away from the notion of receiving—or giving—pain."

Cat looked straight back at him.

"I'm not squeamish, Colonel."

They were back in his office. The Colonel was enthroned behind his desk. Cat was occupying one of the gilded armchairs.

Suddenly, he leant across the desk towards her, gazing at her intensely.

"Do you believe in white supremacy, Miss Johnson?"

"Yes I do."

"And do you believe that the supremacy of the white race is under threat as never before?"

"Yes."

He sucked on the gold stem of the cigarette holder, exhaling abruptly.

"I asked you before, Miss Johnson, whether you are prepared to translate your beliefs into action."

"Yes..."

"And you didn't give me an answer."

She looked him full in the face, her eyes unblinking.

"The answer is yes, Colonel."

She leant forward in the armchair, her whole body persuasive. His eyes dropped to the swell of her breasts beneath the T-shirt.

His thin hand twitched, jabbing a button hidden by the carved gilt rim of his desk. Cat heard the doors behind her open.

Her blood ran cold.

In his crisp safari suit, it was the man from the diner, Cadillac Man, the smiling man who had driven away with two giggling teenagers, who had supervised the digging of a grave in the desert.

"Colonel?"

He barely glanced at her, as he walked forward towards the huge desk. There was no salute; it appeared that they regarded each other as equals.

"I believe," the Colonel said. "That Miss Johnson is both willing and able to do the job for us."

He sat back in his chair. He looked at her and she looked straight back.

"You saw everything," the Colonel continued. "What do you think?"

Cadillac Man turned slowly to look at Cat but she remained attentive to the Colonel. She smiled back when he smiled at her.

"I think you are correct, Colonel."

Delighted, the Colonel clapped his hands together, barking his nasty laugh. "Excellent!"

Tugging open a desk drawer, he scooped out a fat cardboard file.

"If you please, Miss Johnson…"

He passed the folder to the man in the safari suit, who leant over Cat, holding it out to her. His bloodless lips flickered briefly in a cold smile as she took it, his ice blue eyes gleaming.

"Now, Miss Johnson," said the Colonel. "I will explain your mission to you."

In the late afternoon the desert was like molten honey, as the blue of the sky began to thin at the edges and blend into pale gold.

The baking waves of heat that rose from the long grey ribbon of the highway muffled the sound of the V-8 to a sonorous drone.

Cat looked relaxed, with one hand on the wheel, with her shades on and her long blonde hair floating in the breeze, letting the red Olds cruise at 90 while mellow grooves washed over her.

Inside, she was turning over. Her thoughts were scrambling, re-winding then fast-forwarding, falling over each other.

She wrenched the radio handset from its hook under the dash.

"Uncle John? Do you copy?"

Static.

"Uncle John? Do you read me?"

The static was interrupted.

"I'm here, Princess."

Cat smiled. She felt a lot better.

"Where are you, Uncle John?"

"It's cool, sweetheart, I'm here waiting for you."

He was as good as his word. Right where he said he'd be, standing by his Jeep.

Cat rolled the Olds up alongside him.

She flung open the door and jumped out. He gave her a big hug. She clung on to him.

With his strong hands on her shoulders, he stood back and looked at her.

"Are you in some kind of trouble, Princess?"

Cat shook her head gravely.

"I'm onto something, Uncle John. It's big. But I don't know what it is yet."

John Warburton nodded.

"Well, what can I do to help?"

Bending into her car, Cat opened the glove compartment and retrieved a cassette tape with a funky track listing scrawled on the label.

"If you put this in a machine," she explained. "It'll just play music. But if you transmit it to Selena and—"

Her Uncle chuckled, taking the cassette from her.

"Yes, I know, angel. It'll wipe the music so she can hear your message."

Cat rolled her eyes, laughing.

"Sorry, Uncle John. I forgot that you and Selena are…"

He laughed with her.

"Are just good friends, missy."

"Sure, Uncle John, whatever you say."

She sobered suddenly.

"It has my report…as far as it goes…"

He looked down at the cassette, turning it over in his hands.

"Don't worry, Princess. I'll radio the Agency as soon as I get back."

She stepped forward and wrapped her arms around him.

"I'm so glad you're here, Uncle John!"

Tears were brimming in her eyes. He squeezed her tight.

"I'll always be there for you, angel."

He ruffled her golden hair gently.

"Now get going."

She reached the outskirts of the city as dusk fell and all the lights around the Bay began to twinkle. It was a good feeling.

The posters gave some life and color to the drab, functional offices, tucked away in a modest side street. A bright tribal print of yellow and green, emblazoned with a black clenched fist, and a single word in bold red: "ADVANCE!"

Although it was well past midnight, the lights still burned and bleary-eyed campaign workers with rolled up shirtsleeves toiled at desks piled high with paper, sustained by overflowing ashtrays and coffee cups. Typewriters clattered, tired voices intoned into telephone receivers.

"Yes, Reverend Jones will be at the march on Sunday…"

Framed like an icon, the focal point of the office was a huge photograph of a gravely determined man in vigorous early middle age, with iron grey hair and a square goatee beard, his intense eyes framed by heavy horn-rimmed glasses. Dark preacher's robes draped his broad shoulders and his large hand grasped an ancient leather bound Bible.

"…that's right, the Reverend has been told that he will be arrested if the march goes ahead…"

Footsteps pounded on the stairs. At the desks, heads jerked up in alarm.

The double doors crashed open. Three huge men heaved their bulk through, surging into the office. They could have been triplets, with shaven skulls gleaming like polished ebony, eyes masked by impenetrable shades, shoulders straining the seams of their black suits.

They came to a halt in the middle of the office, looking urgently in all directions. The campaign workers were all standing bolt upright at their desks.

"Is he here?"

"What…?"

"The Reverend, man! Is he here?"

"No, he's supposed to be at the hotel with you."

"Well, he ain't."

"Whaddaya mean he ain't!"

"I mean we put him to bed like always and then when we went to check on him later he was gone."

"Aw, shit, man! Not again!"

The taxi rolled to a stop.

"Keep the change."

The man that climbed out onto the motel forecourt had a battered trilby pulled down to his ears, the collar of his overcoat turned up to the tip of his nose and was wearing dark glasses.

Grinning, the taxi driver tipped him a knowing wink.

"Have a good time, man."

The man in disguise flinched and turned his back quickly. Tugging a scrap of paper from his coat pocket, he double-checked the address scrawled on it.

"Okay…" he muttered.

The "Ace Motel" was a shabby, unmemorable grey concrete block, its neon askew and missing a few letters.

"Jesus…!"

There was a brass key scotch-taped to the piece of paper. He ripped it free and traced the number stamped on it with his fingertip.

Looking anxiously left and right, the long coat flapping around his ankles, the disguised man jogged across the cracked asphalt forecourt, his arms wrapped around himself as if he thought that would make him invisible.

He trotted up some iron steps to the second storey balcony that ran all along the front of the motel.

"Twenty-seven…"

Haste made him clumsy and he fumbled with the key and the lock. With a last worried glance over his shoulder, he opened the door a crack and slid inside.

The room was what he expected, lit by a dull yellow bulb. A bed with a single grey blanket. A battered armchair, a small table and a lamp. Through an open door he could see a cracked toilet bowl and a small towel hanging on a rail.

The disguised man pulled back his cuff. There was the flash of a jewelled watch on a heavy gold bracelet, starkly out of place in these drab surroundings.

"Shit! You'se late, bitch."

He yanked a half bottle of whiskey from his coat pocket and unscrewed the cap. He took a swig, and then another, smacking his lips. Some of it spilled on his lapel.

"Fuck!"

He screwed the cap back on and stowed the bottle away. He looked at his watch again.

"C'mon, whore!"

He sat in the chair. He got up again.

He took the hat off. And the glasses. And the coat.

Underneath the coat was a blue suit. It had a button pinned on it, a yellow and green button with a black fist and the word in red: "ADVANCE!"

In the suit was the Reverend Jones. He looked just like his picture.

There was a knock at the door.

The Reverend jumped. He froze, staring at the door. The knock was repeated.

He went to the door and put his face close to it. Suddenly his face was shiny with sweat, in the pale yellow light.

"W-who is it…?"

He heard a feminine chuckle.

"Your dreams come true, honey."

He pulled the door open a short way and peered out.

"Well, hi, daddy…"

Cat's golden hair was piled high on her head. Her long false eyelashes fanned up a breeze as she batted them at him. The alluring mask was made complete by deep blue eye shadow and glistening red lipstick.

"Ain't ya gonna let me in?"

Her hardboiled twang went with the face. She was wearing a shiny leopard skin print mini dress and knee-high boots that looked like white plastic.

The Reverend gaped, his jaw dropping. The dress had a neckline that plunged in a V to her diaphragm and below that there was a diamond cut-out that exposed her navel.

"G-G-God Almighty!"

Grabbing her wrist, he pulled her in and slammed the door shut behind her.

Cat giggled shrilly.

"Hey! What's yer hurry, lover? We got all the time ya want."

And then she was all business, standing there with one hand on a cocked hip.

"An' time costs money, man…"

Staring at the pale mounds of her half-exposed breasts, the Reverend rooted in an inside pocket. He unfolded a fat crocodile wallet and dealt out notes onto her outstretched palm.

"Oooh, daddy! We're gonna have us a party!"

Smiling at him, Cat slipped off his jacket and let it fall on the worn carpet. Taking him by the arm, she steered him into the sagging armchair. With nimble fingers, she un-knotted his tie and disposed of it, her fingers fluttering down the buttons of his shirt.

She stepped backwards, still smiling at him.

"Now yew just relax, honey…"

She reached up briefly and her long hair came tumbling down over her shoulders.

"Ah….." the Reverend sighed.

Cat reached down and pulled the skimpy dress up and off and over her head.

"AAAAHHHH…..!"

She wasn't wearing any underwear.

He was hypnotized. Her hips swaying extravagantly, Cat undulated towards him, sinking slowly to her knees.

There was a dark car parked in the shadow of some trees, in the far corner of the forecourt.

The red tip of a cigarette glowed for an instant within the car, before being cupped by a hand.

"Watch it…!" a man whispered.

"Sorry."

A rustle and shuffling. The seat creaked.

"Let's get ready."

"Okay."

Indeterminate sounds, metal sounds.

"Okay?"

"Okay."

"Let's go."

The Reverend sprawled in the armchair, his shirt unbuttoned to the waist, his legs splayed wide apart. His wide eyes stared at her over the dome of his belly.

Stark naked and smiling, Cat was crawling slowly towards him on her hands and knees, making her hips swing from side to side.

When she reached him, she reared up lithely, smoothing her hands along his thighs.

Her fingers grazed his crotch. The Reverend groaned and closed his eyes.

She reached his belt buckle. Slowly, she began to unzip his flies. His eyes popped open. She looked up at him from between his knees. The tip of her tongue passed slowly across her moist, red smile.

"Oh you dirty bitch!" he moaned. "You filthy—!"

The door was kicked open.

"Smile…!"

With a yell, Reverend Jones struggled to sit up straight, his arms flailing.

Squealing, Cat hung on to his belt, forcing him back down. Pointing her bare backside in the air, she hid her face in his groin.

"You're on Candid Camera!"

In the confined space, the blast of the flashbulbs blanked out the whole room.

The pictures splashed the front pages of the gleeful tabloids.

"LEADING RADICAL CAUGHT WITH PANTS DOWN WITH MYSTERY BLONDE IN MOTEL ROOM!"

All that could be seen of Cat was a mass of swirling blonde hair. Her naked backside was discreetly censored. The startled features of the Reverend Jones were, however, unmistakable, glaring with horror straight into the lens.

The phone rang in the beach house later that morning.

"Miss Johnson?"

"Colonel. How are you?"

"I have just seen the morning news broadcast and I am delighted, Miss Johnson."

"Yes, it went very well, Colonel."

"You were superb, my dear."

"Thank you."

"You may rest assured that we will have other assignments for you in the very near future".

"Thank you, Colonel, I'll look forward to it."

J. Spencer Warburton's army of pin-striped assistants had to cross an acre of ankle-deep carpet before reaching his modern steel and ebony desk.

His office, at the top of the Global Tower, occupied an entire floor. It embraced a "hospitality zone," with plush black leather furniture and a gleaming glass and chrome bar, and a long oval conference table overlooked by a wall of TV monitors that could be tuned in to interested parties worldwide.

Panoramic windows, from floor to ceiling, gave J. Spencer Warburton a 360-

degree view of the city. His city. He was the Puppet Master, pulling the strings.

There was a battery of color coded telephones on his desk. A green one rang.

"Warburton."

"Have you seen your morning paper?"

"Yes, I have."

The voice on the line was one of wealth and influence, cut from the same cloth.

"I think we may safely assume that the Reverend Jones will no longer be an obstacle to our interests."

"So I believe."

"In fact, I understand that the Reverend will be announcing his resignation later this morning."

"I saw the pictures."

He hung up the phone and leaned back in his hi-tech swivel chair. He sat for a long time, gazing out of his high window, at a point far beyond the distant horizon.

Cat paced the floor. She made coffee but was too distracted to drink it. She put some music on but hardly heard it.

She snatched up the phone and dialled the secret number.

"Hi Cat."

"Hi Selena."

"You did a nice job."

"Yes, it all went like clockwork."

At the other end of the line, Selena could sense Cat's misgivings.

"What's the matter?"

"Well, you know…does the end justify the means…in the long run will it be worth discrediting a man like that?"

"Yes, but…"

"Okay, so he gets his kicks with hookers in cheap motels, but he does stand for something."

Cat couldn't understand why Selena was laughing.

"Oh, sweetheart…"

"What? What is it?"

Her laughter was making Cat's ears ring.

"Honey, you know who's going to be pissed the most about the fall of that so-called champion of civil rights?"

"What? No. Who?"

"Why, J. Edgar Hoover. That's who."

"What!"

"That's right, Cat. The Reverend was an FBI informer!"

CHAPTER 10
The Raid

"Touche!"

Cat's broad grin glimmered behind the mesh of the fencing mask.

"You got me that time. Let's go again."

The clash of steel rebounded off the glaring white walls of the gymnasium, merging with the sounds of quick feet and the squeak of rubber soles on the glossy wooden floor.

"Hah!"

Cat reached up and lifted off the mask. Her eyes were bright and excited. Beads of perspiration sparkled on her face.

"Now we're even," she chuckled.

Breathing heavily, she rolled her head from side to side, shaking out her long golden tresses.

"Three-three. Want to go for the decider?"

A sword's length away, Cat's opponent unmasked.

"Enough," panted Selena. "Let's settle for the tie."

Adjourning to the changing rooms, they showered in adjoining cubicles and then stepped out gleaming and naked, to towel down.

"You've been keeping fit," Cat observed.

As they dried themselves, Cat admired Selena frankly. Her superb body was ageless, her suppleness and strength evident in the slightest, most casual movement.

"I try and go a few fast falls with Aiko whenever I can."

She leant towards Cat and patted her toned midriff.

"You're not so bad yourself, golden girl."

Cat laughed.

"Oh, I get a lot of exercise."

Smiling, Selena shook her head.

"Yes, I read your report. I almost felt sorry for that poor dumb cop."

Selena sheathed her body in a bronze silk mini dress with a subtle paisley pattern, cinched in by a gold chain at her waist. Cat pulled on a white track-suit with red go-faster stripes down the arms and legs.

"Well, you're full of surprises too, Selena."

"Oh yes?"

"Yes. What's all this about you and Uncle John?"
Laughing, Selena reached out and ruffled Cat's hair.
"When you're older, dear...."

In Selena's office, amidst the tribal hangings and carvings, the mood was businesslike.
"Your report made interesting reading, Cat."
Cat settled into the jungle upholstery.
"Well, your guess is as good as mine, but something's going on down there. That toy soldier isn't putting together his own private army for nothing."
Selena's long golden fingernails rapped on the desktop as she pondered for a moment. Cat sat watching her.
"And those characters he's got with him, the ones that all look the same...?"
"And dress the same, in those square safari suits."
"That just sounds plain freaky to me."
"Really weird."
"And evil too. Dead chicks buried in the desert."
Cat's eyes clouded.
"Yes. It was awful."
Selena looked at her sympathetically.
"We'll get to the truth. The truth is out there."
"Yes it is."

There was a knock on the door.
"Come in."
The door swung open and Aiko strode in briskly, in a short green jacket and billowing black trousers. She had a fat cardboard file tucked under her arm.
"Hi Cat!"
She stooped to kiss her on the cheek.
"Hi, Aiko, it's great to see you."
Aiko plopped herself into a vacant zebra-striped armchair. They all smiled at each other.
"So," said Selena. "Have they finished the tests?"
The file was resting on Aiko's lap. She flipped it open and withdrew a sealed transparent envelope. The strange silver foil glittered through the plastic.
Cat shivered suddenly, remembering the desert.
"Are you okay?" Selena asked.
"Yes, yes...I'm fine..."
She swivelled towards Aiko.
"What did you find out?"
The Japanese girl frowned.
"Absolutely nothing."

Cat's brow furrowed.

"Nothing?"

"Nothing. We did every test in the book, and then we made up some new ones. Whatever this stuff is, there's no name for it."

Cat shook her head slowly, lips pursed.

"Crazy…"

Selena slapped her palm on the desktop.

"Well, keep trying."

She reached out for the file and Aiko leant forward from her chair to hand it to her. Selena began shuffling through the contents.

"I'm beginning to wonder…" she mused.

Cat waited but Selena fell silent, turning over the papers.

"Wonder what?"

"…it's all happening at once…"

"Yes, isn't it," said Aiko.

"What is?" demanded Cat impatiently.

Selena smiled at her.

"We have what looks like Black Militants killing cops here in the city, and bombing city politicians…"

"While a black civil rights leader is caught in a honey trap and a White Nazi army is drilling in the desert," Aiko continued.

Cat nodded.

"Yeah, it's like total war's about to break out."

Selena looked doubtful.

"It doesn't feel right."

"No it doesn't," Cat agreed.

"There's a pattern to it," Aiko added. "But it's not the pattern you see on the surface."

"A hidden agenda."

"Correct."

Cat uncoiled from the depths of the armchair and sat up straight.

"We need to look into these so-called Black Militant killings."

Selena laid her hand down flat on the file.

"We are. We have an agent on the case."

Cat looked slightly disappointed. Selena smiled again.

"You're already doing enough, Cat. You keep in contact with the Colonel and see where that takes you."

Cat grinned.

"Oh, I'm very popular with the Little Colonel. I'm sure it won't be long before I hear from him again."

The young watchman was a pale and scrawny kid whose baggy grey uniform was a size too big for him. Mousy brown hair straggled from beneath his cap as he blinked at the world through coke-bottle lenses.

"Somethin's comin'."

The old watchman was a retired Irish cop, a waddling, wheezing fat man with thinning grey hair and the florid, blotchy features of a long-term serious drinker.

"C'mon, wake up and get out here!"

He banged his fist on the door of the small wooden gatehouse. The younger man was jolted out of a doze.

"Okay, okay!"

The wooden shack guarded high gates of heavy mesh, hung with signs that said "DANGER! KEEP OUT!" The gates merged into a tall perimeter topped with curling strands of razor wire. Within this secure enclosure was a complex array of huge generators and pylons, all humming softly.

Security cameras were mounted on the gates, and on lofty pylons inside the fence. Floodlights on stalks made the power generating station an oasis of light, in the middle of the night, in the vast, dark and deserted industrial outskirts of the city.

The cameras noted the splash of approaching headlamps, on the asphalt drive running up a shallow slope to the gates. Shielding their eyes from the glare, the watchmen peered through the mesh.

"Great!" the old man grunted. "Now what?"

A pale blue truck slowed to a stop in front of the gates, a familiar City Power and Light truck. The driver's door slid open and a man in pale blue overalls stepped out.

"Hey, man..."

He was a bland, inoffensive-looking young man, sporting a jaunty baseball cap. His dark face creased into a grin as he strolled casually towards the gates.

"How ya doin'?"

The old watchman frowned at him.

"What is it this time?"

The grin didn't waver.

"Oh, probably nothin'. The boys at Central say they gotta red light on their board so they sent me to take a look."

The old man hawked and spat a gob of saliva on the ground.

"They oughta check their damn board sometime!"

The man in the overalls laughed.

"Yeah, right."

Shrugging, the old man nodded at his young colleague. The young watchman blinked back at him.

"Well, go on!" the old man barked.

The young man retreated to the door of the hut. Reaching inside, he depressed a lever. The gates quivered and then began to slide apart, creaking.

"Thanks, man."

The man in overalls jumped back into the cab of his truck and drove on through. He parked his vehicle a little way past the guardhouse and then dismounted again.

He grinned at the younger watchman.

"Say, ain't ya supposed to look it over?"

The older watchman looked bored and impatient. The young man blushed.

"Oh, yeah. Sure!"

He walked quickly around to the rear of the truck, twisted the handles and pulled open the double doors.

"Hey—?"

He stepped back suddenly, his eyes blinking rapidly, enlarged by the thick lenses.

Thwack!

The young watchman flung out his arms and lurched backwards. His glasses flew off and shattered on the tarmac.

Thwack! Thwack!

He sprawled on his back, a dumb look on his face. A dark stain was spreading slowly on his chest.

"What the fu—!"

The old man took a step forward, groping for the pistol at his hip. The man in overalls was close behind him. A steel sliver flashed. The old man's face contorted in agony.

"Aaaagghhh…!"

His legs crumbled. The man in overalls stepped back to let him sag downwards, groaning, crumpling shapelessly to the ground.

The man in overalls slapped his hand on the side of the truck.

"Let's go!"

Four men sprang nimbly out of the truck, landing lightly on silent, rubber-soled shoes. Dark men, dressed darkly, wearing shades in the middle of the night, in black leather jackets buttoned down over black turtlenecks, black pants, black shoes.

Two of the dark men were wielding ugly submachine-guns. One took his station at the gates, the other went into the guardhouse. The other two were hefting a weighty canvas holdall between them. Lead by the man in overalls, they jogged deep into the humming, floodlit enclosure and were soon busy amongst the generators and pylons.

At the same time, throughout empty industrial districts that were scattered around the city, watchmen were dying. Knives flashed and silenced automatics coughed bullets. Dark men dressed in black were working quickly, attaching devices and setting timers.

And at one a.m. precisely, there were dull reverberations that rattled windows miles away and balls of orange flame blossomed in a ring around the city. The vast glowing grid of streetlights flickered and went out. In the clubs and discos the glitter balls ceased their effervescent revolutions, the flashing strobes went black and the pulse of the music that was the city's heartbeat stopped instantly.

The warehouse doors opened and then shut behind the pale blue City Power and Light truck.

The driver left his cab. He opened the back and let the dark men out. The air in the huge space of the empty warehouse had a chilly metal tang, lit by hanging strip lights.

"Over here!"

At the far end of the warehouse, a pale man in a tan safari suit was standing beside a long metal table. In the bleary light his fair hair and blue eyes were almost colorless.

"On the double!"

The driver and the dark men ran all the way. There was a grey box on the table, with luminous dials and switches and wires coming from it. The wires were connected to a silver, bell-shaped lantern, which the pale man held in his hand.

"Quickly!"

Without hesitation, the men stripped naked. They formed a line, face front, standing shoulder to shoulder, a wall of solid muscle.

The man in the safari suit bent over the grey box and touched something. There was a faint drone, a subtle vibration. In his hand, the strange, multi-faceted crystal of the lantern was glowing, purple.

A web of grey steel girders supported the great span of the warehouse roof. Someone was up there, watching.

"One!"

The driver took a pace forward. Starting at his bare feet, the fair-haired man washed his skin with the violet light. As he did so, the darkness thinned, the pigmentation fading away, a paleness emerging.

"Two!"

While the city groped about blindly, small bands of dark men were being transformed into pale men by the eerie purple light. The Black Power regalia were exchanged for anonymous casuals, the blue trucks for inconspicuous cars.

The watcher in the roof waited, suspended high above the gleaming concrete of the floor. He was a big man, but quick and nimble as a spider, as he swung down onto a narrow metal gantry. A short dash took him to a heavy skylight, which he hoisted effortlessly, with arms that swelled with muscle. Up and out lightly, he negotiated a sloping boardwalk that led to a long iron ladder, running down the corrugated cliff face of the warehouse.

His car was submerged in the shadows. The sound of the engine igniting proclaimed considerable power.

The city was on a short fuse, just waiting for an excuse. Looters went shopping in teams, forming chains that stretched out into the streets from the smashed store windows, handing out TVs and hi-fi's and designer clothes on racks, passing them from hand to hand, on down the line.

The ghetto boiled over and flooded uptown, invading the fashionable malls and arcades. The have-nots seized their chance to have some just for once. Police helicopters circled nervously high overhead, sweeping the mob with searchlights.

In their secret places, the Black Militants seethed with frustration. This wasn't the way, this only played into the Power's hands. Ministers on the steps of their churches and other community leaders standing in the middle of the street tried to stem the tide but the dam had broken and it rolled right on by. The helicopters counted hundreds, then thousands.

The white radicals, the sincere kids from "good" homes, they couldn't believe their luck. But they didn't want do any shopping. They came out to destroy, bearing Molotov cocktails and incendiary devices in shoeboxes and shoulder bags, concocted by long-haired, intense young science graduates. They staged an assault on capitalism and its infrastructure. Banks and post offices were burning.

It took the cops a while to gather their strength. Sirens wailing, they came in fast-moving convoys, their headlights making wild shadows leap down the blacked-out avenues and concrete canyons. Armored in riot gear, they sprang from their trucks, but they were heavily outnumbered. The mob just sucked them in and spat them out, helmets rolling on the sidewalk.

Martial law was declared. The National Guard came rushing from its barracks. They came in full combat gear, in flak jackets and carrying M-16's. They even came with tanks. The shooting started.

The *crump!* of the gas grenades and the occasional rattle of gunfire carried thinly to the dizzy heights of the Global Tower, lit by its own generators. A faint tang of tear gas could be tasted all the way up there.

"Jeez! What a mess!"

"Those jigs are havin' a street party alright."

In the eerie colorless half-light of the emergency lighting, the expanses of the Tower lobby were chill and echoing. Their faces bathed in the flickering blue glow of the screen, two uniformed guards were watching the news flashes on a small, portable TV.

"Oooh! That's gotta hurt!"

"Yep, that's an old trick I learned on the Force. Dumb jig thinks ya gonna club down on top of his head, but ya fakes it and jab him in the balls instead."

"Jeez! Ow!...Ooooh!"

They were distracted by movement on the forecourt beyond the giant plate glass revolving doors.

"Hey, what's that?"

An anonymous grey truck opened at the back and disgorged four burly men in overalls. They began unloading heavy equipment.

"Beats me."

The driver's door slid back and a tall man in a black suit got out. He had fair hair and was wearing dark shades in the middle of the night. His passenger came walking round from the other side. They could have been twins.

While their assistants carried on unloading, the men in suits strode up to the glass doors. The driver pressed the intercom.

The security guards frowned.

"Yeah?"

"Special Security Service. We have to sweep the building."

The guards looked doubtful. The men in suits held glittering gold badges up to the glass.

The buzzer rasped loudly in the great empty spaces. The men in suits came quickly through the revolving doors and advanced towards the desk. Outside, on the dark and empty forecourt, the men in overalls stood waiting, holding heavy objects between them.

"So, what's the problem?"

The dark shades were impenetrable.

"We had a bomb warning. We have to go up top and check it out."

The guards were dubious. They glanced at each other nervously.

"Well, we ain't heard nothin'…"

One of them reached for a red telephone.

"We gotta get clearance before we can—"

The men in suits reached into their hip pockets. Something silver glittered in their hands.

"Hey—!"

The guards jumped out of their chairs, grabbing for their guns. Their faces blank, the men in suits held out their hands. They showed the guards small silver discs with odd symbols etched on them.

"What the hell is…?"

The silver discs were glowing, a translucent purple. A deep note throbbed throughout the deserted hallways.

"Uuuuuhh......"

The guards seemed to deflate. They sagged back into their seats. Their eyelids drooped, chins dropping onto their chests. They began snoring.

The men in suits signalled to the others waiting on the far side of the glass doors.

The Global Tower's emergency generators kept the maintenance elevator running. The invaders rode it all the way to the top.

"Hurry!"

The roof bristled with spires and tall pylons and elaborate antennae, with satellite dishes of various shapes and sizes, some fixed and some revolving. There was a constant humming that swelled and diminished with the ebb and flow of the whistling wind.

Far below, the blacked-out city was a shadowy mass, with only the occasional pinprick of light. Blotches of red fire were glowing where the forces of law and order battled the mob, jabbed by the circling searchlights of Police helicopters.

"Over there!"

Moving swiftly despite their bulky load, the men in overalls jogged in and out of the maze of towers and aerials. They stopped at a singularly impressive dish, rotating slowly on its complicated stalk.

Quickly, expertly, the four men constructed a small tower of their own, of a strange grey metal that gleamed dully. With cables that were made of a clear, flexible material, they connected it to the base of the rotating dish.

They mounted a control box on their tower. Then they stepped back to make way for the men in suits. Their pale fingers flickered and dials marked with jagged hieroglyphics began to glow purple. The purple fizzed along the hollow cables.

The spectral luminosity infused the turning dish, which slowly became transparent, like glass. The eerie transmission lasted for several minutes before the purple glow faded and disappeared.

"Go!"

The men in overalls sprang into action. The cables were disconnected and coiled, the tower vanished in seconds.

They took the service elevator back down to the lobby, marched out past the sleeping guards and climbed into the truck. The men in suits paused at the desk to replace the tape from the security cameras with one that would depict an uneventful night in an empty lobby.

The doors slid shut and the truck drove away slowly.

Half an hour later, the guards snapped wide awake, their memories wiped clean.

"Jeez! What a mess!"

"Those jigs are havin' a street party alright."

Selena frowned.

"What's wrong with this picture?"

Aiko thought for a while.

"I don't know. What?"

They were gazing up at the bank of TV monitors behind Selena's desk.

"Number one. There is a picture."

"Meaning...?" asked Cat.

"Meaning they didn't knock out the security cameras..."

"...and their faces are uncovered."

"Exactly. They even parked their truck right under the cameras. It's like they were putting on a show."

"Quite a show," Aiko commented. "Like a full-scale military operation. I didn't think the Militants could stage anything like that."

Selena nodded.

"That's number two."

She played with some buttons in a console on her desk, making the flickering images fast forward and rewind.

She made the picture freeze; the dark men, cutting down the hapless watchmen, laying their charges.

"Number three..."

"There's more?"

"Take a look."

Aiko looked. She turned to Cat. They both shook their heads.

"I don't get it."

Selena smiled.

"Well, I know we're all supposed to look alike but—"

Cat burst out laughing.

"But these guys really do."

Selena's sweeping gesture embraced all the screens.

"They all do. Every last one of them. We seem to be dealing with gangs of black quintuplets."

Selena picked up the phone.

"Give me a secure line."

She waited for a few seconds and then dialled a number.

"I've seen the tapes. There's something very strange going on here. It's not what it seems. What have you seen?"

Selena listened. Suddenly, she sat up straight, astonished.

"What!...no way!.......you're kidding!............uh-huh........uh-huh..........."

Frowning, she replaced the receiver slowly. Cat glanced at Aiko, who shrugged and raised her eyebrows in puzzlement.

"Well, now," Selena murmured. "Ain't that something..."

Cat was almost falling out of her chair.

"What? What's going on?"
Selena swivelled to look up at the flickering screens.
"The world turned upside down," she replied.
"Huh?"
Selena smiled.
"Black is white," she said. "And white is black."

CHAPTER 11
Double Agent

Cat was dreaming.

In her dream she was walking in the desert. A brassy sky was boiling and the sand was like smooth glass beneath her, scalding the soles of her bare feet. She could see through the transparent sand. The watery, wavering forms of the dead girls were reaching up to her with their white hands, their dark staring eyes huge in their pale faces.

And then she was walking on hot asphalt, down the middle of Main Street. She was stark naked and the sun was baking her skin. There were faces at the windows and people lining the sidewalks were staring at her. Her father, immaculate in blue blazer and grey flannels, walked right past her, brushing her shoulder, looking through her, without a word. She caught a glimpse of Selena, arm in arm with Uncle John, turning into a shop doorway and she tried to call out their names but though her lips were moving no sound came out, the words withered in her throat.

Suddenly, the ground was shaking and she was stumbling, arms flailing, the faces and the windows blurring, whirling around her. The sun in the bright blue sky was spinning, flashing, dazzling her. With a crack, a great ragged gash opened up in the road and she lost her balance, falling forward into blackness.

Cat sat bolt upright. The bed was vibrating beneath her. She was naked and her skin was slick with sweat. The single silk sheet clung to her thighs. She wrenched it away and stood quickly, the snub-nose .38 that she kept under the pillow cocked and ready in her hand.

She could feel the powerful vibrations through the floorboards of the beach house, through the soles of her bare feet. Flashing lights illuminated the shadowy interior, alternating red and green. Her ears were battered by a raw, mechanical droning, an unmistakable whirring clatter.

Ducking low, Cat padded swiftly across the bedroom, over to the window looking out over the beach. The sand was like silver in the moonlight, edged by the sparkling froth of the surf.

"Huh?"

She was right. It was a helicopter, parked on the sand, its rotors blurring. Red and green navigation lights twinkled on its nose and tail, a sleek, streamlined machine that gleamed like black glass, an executive toy.

The shape of the pilot was indistinct, but Cat could see the two passengers quite clearly in the moonlight, as they marched across the silver sand towards the wooden steps that led up to her balcony.

"Well, I'll be....!"

This was hardly a stealthy ambush, so Cat let down the hammer of the Smith & Wesson. Her towel bathrobe lay crumpled by the bed. Stooping, she seized it and slipped it on. Just in case, she put the small gun in her pocket.

They were knocking on the door.

"Good evening, gentlemen. To what do I owe the pleasure...?"

The burly blond twins in their tan safari suits stared back at her, unsmiling. The sight of Cat so obviously naked beneath the robe appeared to make no impression on them.

The one in front took off his black shades and looked at her with his unblinking, almost colorless eyes.

"Please get dressed, Miss Johnson. We have an important assignment for you."

Every wrinkle and fold stood out starkly in the moonlight, flowing by below, as the lean black helicopter flew low across the desert, every blister of stone, every dot and cluster of scrub.

Cat looked at her watch again, the luminous markers glowing in the dimness of the padded passenger cabin. Peering out through the thick lens of the porthole, she saw some lights twinkling in the distance, but nothing she could identify.

The men in the safari suits sat opposite her on upholstered benches, their pale faces like wax in the half-light.

"We'll be there soon."

"The Colonel is waiting for you."

For the first time Cat noticed that they not only all looked alike, they also sounded alike. They had the same voice, flat, dry and accent less.

The police were baffled.

Here and there, on disused, derelict industrial sites, on rubble-strewn waste ground reclaimed by weeds and brambles, missing City Power and Light trucks were turning up, burnt out, black and gutted. Reduced to charred skeletons, they were barren, offering nothing to the experts from forensics.

The big man parked his powerful car discreetly. Masked by the smoked glass of his raked-back windscreen, he watched the experts in their gloves and boiler suits shake their heads and shrug wearily. He didn't bother to get out of his car, after the police had packed up and gone.

Sheathed in perforated black leather driving gloves, his strong fingers drummed on the wooden rim of the custom steering wheel. He reached for the radio handset, hung on a hook under the dash.

"Like I thought," he said in a deep brown voice. "They didn't leave a trace.

I'll hang around a day or two to see if I can pick up any whispers."

Cat felt it in the pit of her stomach as the helicopter dipped suddenly.
"Oops!"
She looked out of the cabin window, but all she saw was the stark desert sand, like frozen waves, mottled with brush and scraps of tufted grass.

There was a jolt as the helicopter touched down. The desert was blotted out by a cloud of dust which thinned as the grinding rotors slowed and with a low whining sound became still.

One of the blond twins stood up quickly and heaved open the sliding cabin door. He jumped out onto the sand. His companion nodded at Cat and she followed. The desert night was cool and clean.

"This way…"

They were stepping out ahead of her, leaving a trail of footprints in the sand. Cat jogged after them. Behind her, the helicopter coughed and spat into life, the whirring rotors lifting it into the star-spangled sky.

They walked for a while in silence, save for the sound of the gritty sand crunching beneath their feet. It was cold in the desert at night and Cat was glad to have her Lee "Storm Rider" jacket, turning up the corduroy trimmed collar. All she had on under the blue denim was a tie-dyed T-shirt, tucked into maroon crushed velvet flares that flapped around the toecaps of her shiny banana yellow and caramel boots.

The exaggerated bell-bottoms snagged the heels of her boots and made her stumble.

"Hey, slow down, guys. You didn't tell me we were going hiking."

The men in the safari suits turned and looked at her with blank faces.

"We are here now."

Cat looked all around, puzzled. All she saw was sand and scrub.

"Here? Where?"

The men pointed. Halfway up the rising slope ahead there was an imposing outcrop of sand-colored rock, like a giant scab on the skin of the desert.

"There."

One of the men took a small metal cube from his pocket. His thumb depressed a button. Muffled gears meshed down below. Amazed, Cat saw a huge boulder move aside slowly and smoothly, as a slit of pale yellow light expanded into an ample doorway in the stone.

"Miss Johnson…?"

Stepping forward, Cat peered into the light. She saw a polished metal staircase, spiralling downwards.

The man in the safari suit stepped through the luminous portal.

"Follow me, if you please…"

She didn't hesitate, striding forward into the light.

Lingering behind, the second man produced what looked like a small, silver flashlight. But the light it gave was a pale violet. He trained the beam along the sand, back the way they had come. The sand seemed to quiver, the grains jostling, shifting, until the trail of footprints had disappeared completely.

Satisfied, the man switched off the purple beam and vanished through the glowing entrance. The rock slid shut behind him and the desert was dark and empty again.

The big man was at home in the 'hood.
"Respec', mah bruther..."
It was his turf.
"Hey, gimme some skin, mah man!"
He could always park his car safely. No one was going to scratch it or spray paint it or drive it away. No one was going to touch the equipment.
"It's me. No, nothing. The jungle drums didn't have anything to say...uh-huh...yeah.....uh-huh...I'm gonna give it another day or two and then hit the road..."

The shimmering spiral staircase wound down and down within a shaft of polished stone. Its tight curl was starting to make Cat dizzy. Her voluminous velvet flares kept catching on her boot heels, making her lurch and grab for the shining steel rail.
"Hey!" she gulped. "Can't we slow down?"
The man in front was descending at a trot. The man behind was catching up fast. Cat wasn't used to feeling clumsy, and it was starting to annoy her.
Suddenly, the man below her veered sideways and disappeared.
"This way..."
Cat emerged onto a narrow steel gantry with a pierced latticework floor and a safety rail constructed from twisted steel cables. It hung high on the rim of a massive stone bowl, part machined out of the rock, part natural underground cave formation.
"Wow!" she exclaimed.
Thick veins of quartz glistened on the curved walls of the bowl, in the bright light cast by powerful hanging lamps. Far below, the floor was polished grey granite, occupied by ranks of busy computers housed in tall steel cabinets, attended to by serious-looking men in long white lab coats, brows furrowed as they annotated their clipboards.
Men in tan overalls sat side by side in a long row of metal cubicles, operating high-powered radio equipment. Bulky headphones clamped on their heads, they spoke into microphones, their voices providing a constant background murmur that merged with the hum and chiming of the mighty computers in a symphony of technology.
"Welcome, Miss Johnson!"
The centerpiece of this high-tech assembly was an enormous table. Its illu-

minated rectangular top was composed of a huge and highly detailed map of the United States. It made for a dazzling display, with various regions color coded in every shade of the rainbow.

"Please come down and join me."

A flight of metal steps zig-zagged down from the gantry to the stone floor of the great bowl. Cat descended carefully, wary of tripping over her flares.

"It's a pleasure to see you, Colonel."

"The pleasure is all mine, Miss Johnson."

He stepped forward and saluted her. Clicking his heels, he stooped to kiss her hand. She felt his hot breath on her skin and her flesh crawled.

"Welcome to my Command Center!"

The Colonel had exchanged his Civil War dress uniform for modern combat fatigues. Clad in crisp and spotless jungle tiger-stripes tucked into mirror-polished paratrooper's boots, he was crowned by a green beret adorned with brass insignia. There was a Colt .45 automatic holstered on his hip, enhanced by pearl grips.

Now he thinks he's General Patton!

His small black eyes were roving all over her. He was disappointed by her ensemble.

"You dress like one of those damn pinko hippies, Miss Johnson."

Cat looked apologetic.

"I'm sorry, Sir. Your boys were in such a hurry. Had I known I was coming to see you…"

She had pleased him. The Colonel shrugged, emitting the nasty bark that was his laugh.

"No matter, my dear. After all, you are working undercover…"

He laughed again.

You don't know how right you are—shithead!

The Colonel took her by the elbow and steered her towards the illuminated map table.

Cat put on her impressed face.

"This is really quite something, Colonel."

He beamed at her, his thin face contorted in the warped semblance of a smile.

Glancing up, Cat saw a long steel terrace running along the curved wall of the bowl high above them. Set into the stone were cabinets made of an odd, dull metal, with dials in a jumble of geometric shapes, all glowing in varying intensities of purple.

"What's that for, Colonel?"

His smile wavered. His grip tightened for an instant on her elbow. The technicians on the balcony were all wearing tan safari suits.

"Nothing that need concern you, my dear Miss Johnson..."

They reached the map table. The Colonel spread out his arms to embrace it.

"This, however, might interest you."

Up close, Cat saw that all the major cities were marked by a small electric bulb. Some of these little lights were lit, bright red—cities like Detroit, Chicago, and her own city by the Bay.

"What do they mean, Colonel?"

He was smiling again.

"Every one of these lights indicates a city in flames, Miss Johnson. A city in turmoil, torn by riots and looting. A city out of control, a city crying out for a strong hand to take charge and bring order!"

It can't be. You're the puppet master? But how? How are you doing it? You? You pathetic little man!

She looked suitably impressed.

"That's amazing, Colonel."

He puffed out his narrow chest.

"Yes, everything is going according to plan."

Then he frowned and bent over the table, leaning on it with his palms on the glowing map.

Consumed by revulsion, Cat willed herself to move close to his side, almost touching him.

"Is there a problem, Sir?"

He didn't reply, gazing down at the map, every inch the Great Leader, weighed down by his awesome responsibilities.

Creep!

Cat didn't know whether to laugh or throw up.

The Colonel straightened slowly, still looking at the map. Cat saw that he was fixed upon the tiny lamp that marked her city, and its beach, her home.

"Yes," he said slowly, carefully, as if he was building up to something. "You might say that we have a fly in the ointment..."

Cat's stomach turned to ice.

Then he barked his laugh again, sneering.

"Or a nigger in the woodpile, one might say. That would be a better way of putting it, if you get my drift, Miss Johnson?"

Cat relaxed, the cold fist in her guts unclenching.

"Yes, I believe I do, Colonel."

Suddenly, he was looking straight into her eyes. They were very close. She was taller than he was and he had to look up. He didn't like that and took a step backwards. Cat managed not to smile.

"Have you ever killed a man, Miss Johnson?"

Cat's cool expression didn't waver. She looked straight back at him.

"Oh, I've left a few for dead, Colonel."

He twitched his twisted smile.

"Excellent!"

There was a very slim file perched on the corner of the map table, a skimpy cardboard folder with only a few sheets of paper in it. The Colonel opened it, frowning.

"Someone has been asking questions, Miss Johnson. Too many questions."

"I see."

"An investigator, working undercover. We believe that he is acting on behalf of that so-called Black Militant scum, who will obviously be anxious to disassociate themselves from some of the more extreme actions carried out by our agents recently."

Cat made her eyes go wide with dawning revelation.

"So…so it was your men…and not…who…who…?"

The Colonel basked in the warmth of her admiration.

"You catch on quickly, Miss Johnson."

Cat was positively gushing.

"Yes! I mean…I understand…I see…I…you amaze me, Colonel…"

He accepted her tribute with a gracious waft of the hand. Then he was back to business, the Great Commander.

"This man is becoming a threat. He has excellent instincts and has been trying to make connections, moving back and forth between the city and the desert."

Cut furrowed her brow.

"He sounds dangerous."

"Indeed he is. He is very skilful."

From the slim file, the Colonel extracted a grainy, indistinct black and white print. All that Cat could make out was a husky, dark and definitely male figure, seen from the back, half in shadow.

"This is the only photograph that we have been able to obtain."

Cat picked the picture up and studied it.

Phew! Well, whoever it is, it's not me, that's for sure!

"Not much to go on…"

The Colonel's smile was a bleak grimace.

"What we do have on reasonably good authority is that he drives one of those customized street racing machines…"

Oh yes?

The Colonel took one of the papers from the file.
"Yes...here it is...possibly a...Plymouth Barracuda..."

Oooh, baby!

The Colonel sniffed disdainfully.
"...with special tinted glass, apparently..."

Mmmm, cool!

"And it is rumored that he frequents the kind of...establishment...popular with the gaudier elements amongst the young urban blacks. That should give someone with your intuition something to go on, Miss Johnson."

He sounds like fun

The fires died down although the city nights still smoldered uneasily. Police patrols roamed the streets in armored cars, snuffing out any remaining embers of resentment with ruthless overkill before they could be fanned into flame.

Doors were unchained and boards came off the windows. The tang of burning was carried off on the breeze. Warily at first, the pleasure-seekers reclaimed the night, re-emerging in their feathers and furs, like exotic animals freed from captivity and released back into the wild. Soon, as bold and brash as ever, the night-time economy was booming again.

The Scene was happenin' again, one big bright whirling glitter ball. It was time to get back into the Groove. The "Par-tay!" just picked up where it left off.

In the Golden Age, it had been the local movie house, a cream-colored Art Deco wedding cake with geometric trimmings of green tiles. In the daylight, you could still just about trace where it had once said "THEATRE ROYALE" but by night its neon hailed "**THE JOOK JOINT**." Once, the posters flanking the gleaming glass and chrome doors had proclaimed the new Cagney, Gable, Harlow or Garbo picture, now they offered an "all-nite" carnival and superstardom for everyone on the dance floor.

The old neighborhood that had once served the "ROYALE" was long gone and gutted. The houses surrounding it were abandoned, burned out and demolished. After the derelict picture house had been acquired and restored by sharp-eyed entrepreneurs the mounds of rubble were smoothed away to create ample parking space for the hedonistic herd.

Under the hard floodlighting of the car park the sleek Corvette gleamed like a sword blade.

"Mmmm...sweetheart..." Cat murmured. "You're in good company tonight."

Tires swishing smoothly on the tarmac, she let the Stingray glide down the lanes between the parking bays. She saw exotic badges—Porsche, Ferrari…

"Out you go."

Cat retracted the pop-up headlamps, restoring the clean edge of the Stingray's snout. The yellow 'Vette was purring, a deep rumble that made her tingle.

"That's right, darling. There are lots of pretty faces here tonight, but you're the Prom Queen."

With pinpoint precision she slipped the low-slung sports car in between two hulking, gaudy pimpmobiles. Shaking her head, she smiled, amused by shocking pink and purple paintwork, the sheer tonnage of glittering, superfluous chrome, radiator grilles like castle gates, a vinyl roof in psychedelic paisley, a steering wheel studded with rhinestones, white fur and leopard skin upholstery.

"Dee-lite-ful…!"

Cat laughed out loud. She switched off the engine and climbed out of the open T-topped black leather cockpit.

She looked at her watch. It was two a.m. and this was the third place she had visited that night. But the pills were kicking in and she was buzzing. The bright floodlights were ringing like bells and the air was crisp and cool and she was sharp and ready for anything.

Cat toured the car park, making a show of admiring the exclusive metal on display. Suddenly she stopped and laughed again.

"Well, how about that! Third time lucky?"

It was a lean mean machine, re-painted matt black with just a ghost of the go-faster "hockey-stick" stripes along its flanks. It had tinted glass like dark brown smoke. The big black air cleaner sticking out through the hole in the "shaker hood" was pure evil.

She read it out loud: "Hemicuda…"

Cat felt it in her loins. She wanted to moan in ecstasy. Instead, she exhaled a low whistle.

"Oooooo…! Looks like I've come to the right place."

Feet scuffed on the tarmac behind her. There was laughter.

"Yo sure have, mama! This is the place alright!"

Cat turned quickly. Her hand slipped into the embroidered shoulder bag, finding the gun in its special pocket. Then she relaxed.

"This is where it's happenin', baby…"

He was stepping out of a snow white stretch limo. Under the floodlights his narrow face was very dark. Tall and slim, he sported a broad-brimmed black hat with a snakeskin band around the crown. A long coat hung down to his ankles, made of shiny caramel leather with enormous dark brown lapels. His suit was claret colored velvet, with a flourishing yellow silk cravat, voluminous flares brushing the pointed toecaps of his stack-heeled snakeskin boots. Dark shades masked his eyes, with lenses shaped like stars, the frames picked out with real diamonds.

His giggling chorus was provided by a quartet of pretty girls, two black, one oriental and the fourth a pale red-head. Bedecked in skimpy feathers and spangles, their ample charms were on display.

"Oooh, mama!"

Sliding his shades down the bridge of his nose, the pimp took a good look. "Now ain't yo sumthin'!"

Flowing down to the small of her back, her hair shone like pale gold. She had put on the war paint, accentuating her exotic eyes, her lips glistening, hot pink.

"Ow! Baby!"

Her breasts were thinly veiled by a halter top that was a mere scrap of ice blue silk, somehow supported invisibly. Barely clinging to her hips, secured by a twist of golden cord, were billowing harem pants, iridescent like mother of pearl, her feet shod in dainty golden sandals. A green emerald that matched her cat's eyes was twinkling in her navel. Her face and the bare flesh of her midriff and flaring hips were lightly powdered with a silvery glister.

She was luminous, like a moonbeam. The four hookers stared at her with shameless envy.

Grinning broadly, the pimp strode towards her. His teeth were impeccable and very white in his dark face. A diamond sparked in one of them.

"Yo is fine, mama! An yo' is jes' what I bin lookin' fo!"

He jerked a thumb back at the four girls standing behind him. A battery of gold rings flashed on his fingers, making Cat blink.

"As yo kin see, I'se color-blind, baby, an' I needs a long cool blonde like yo' fine self to complete mah excloooo-sive stable…!"

He was handing her a business card. There was a phone number on it and in flowery print it announced: "Birds of Paradise—whatever you desire."

Cat was smiling as she read the card. She was flattered.

"Mmmm…why, thank you…I'll think about it…"

The "**JOOK JOINT**" was a wonderland of sound and light. A boogie wonderland where you brought your reinvented self, where you left reality at the door and became a superstar for the night.

It was a riot of light, whirling spotlights and strobes and colored gels and glitter balls. Sparks and lightning bolts and showers of stars, effervescent rainbows that washed over the heaving mass on the dance floor.

And the Beat. Always the Beat. Seamless, relentless, intoxicating, the best drug of all. One great almighty high.

Smiling, Cat inhaled deeply. It gave her a rush, the heady cocktail of thick sweet marijuana, hot sweat and sex, sex, sex.

She looked like she was made out of starlight, her bare skin glistening, the pearly silk gleaming. She had an aura, she was supernatural.

Already men were staring at her, men prowling the fringes of the crowded dance floor, like a giant chessboard of luminous, multi-colored squares, lit from below. Men with silk shirts unbuttoned to the waist, with heavy gold medallions clanging on their hairy chests.

Cat looked without appearing to look and one by one the predators tried to look cool, and not disappointed, when she passed right by them. She stalked along the edge of the dance floor with her long slinky strut. The men watched her, hungrily.

Cat wandered onto the dance floor. It was irresistible. Her dance was subtle at first, her feet hardly moving, hips twitching to the beat. Slowly, she became more expansive, until her whole body was working in lavish, voluptuous undulations and gyrations.

The predatory males were sizing up this new beast in the jungle. She made them nervous. There was something primitive and strong, something elemental, a force of nature that was made all the more intimidating, packaged in a "long cool blonde."

A few took up the challenge and tried to dance with her. They gave up quickly. Cat didn't seem to notice them. Soon she created a space around her, filled by her aura. Men dancing with their women couldn't tear their eyes away and the women were stabbing angry looks at her.

Though she seemed to be lost in a world of her own, Cat saw everything. She was picking out faces, hoping that something in one of them would trigger her instincts.

She could be seen all the way from the long chromium bar way at the back, its display lit up like a Christmas tree. The bartender was a slim young man barely out of his teens, with a spectacular afro that was as wide as his narrow shoulders.

"Man!" he said grudgingly. "Bitch got some funky moves, fo' a white chick."

Opposite him, across the polished counter, a big dark man was adding an extra squirt of soda to his whiskey. He swivelled on his stool to look. His broad shoulders tensed.

"Goddamn!"

He slid off the stool quickly and stepped out of the pool of light that bathed the busy bar, vanishing into the crowd. Shrugging, the bartender finished the whiskey for him.

When he lowered the glass, Cat was standing in front of him.

He blinked. He'd never seen a real woman with a body like that, not in the flesh, not living and breathing instead of on a billboard or the front cover of a magazine that was all about a world that he didn't belong to.

And she was looking at him.

"I'll have a bourbon. On the rocks."

And so much flesh. Bitch was hardly wearin' nuthin'. So much tanned and toned flesh that glistened as she breathed. He could feel her heat, fresh from the dance floor, warm waves of expensive perfume, wafting over him.

"Uh...comin' right up..."

He could smell her flesh.

The ice cubes tinkled. Cat took a sip, savoring the slow burn of the bourbon. Dipping two fingers into the glass she hooked out an ice cube. She smoothed the ice across her forehead, glinting with perspiration. She anointed her cleavage.

"Mmmmm…!"

Pretending to polish a beer glass, the young barman was looking at her sideways. Suddenly he wanted to hurt her badly.

Cat could feel the hate radiating from him. It disturbed her, but she stayed in character. She popped the ice cube into her mouth, rolling it on her tongue from cheek to cheek. She sucked on it slowly until it had melted entirely.

She tapped the empty glass on the polished surface of the bar top.

"I'll have another."

When the young bartender hesitated, an older colleague stepped up beside him.

"Yes, miss?"

He poured her a refill. Cat rapped the glass on the chrome top again as the older barman made to move away, to see to other customers.

"Hey."

"Yes, miss?"

"I'm looking for the man who drives the evil black Barracuda that I saw parked out in the lot…"

The senior bartender kept his poker face, but Cat saw a flicker of recognition in the younger man's eyes.

She turned to look at him with a slow undulation of her body. The older man swallowed audibly. The young man looked angry.

"Do you know him?" she asked in a way that said that she knew that he did.

The young man frowned.

"What business d'yo have wi' him?"

Cat showed her teeth. Her body language was eloquent.

"Oh, I'd just like to meet the man who can ride an animal like that."

The older man gave his colleague a quick sideways glance. The young barman glowered.

"I don' know the man."

Cat downed the bourbon in a gulp. She shrugged.

"Okay…"

She slipped off the barstool and was strolling away, hips swinging.

"It's his loss…"

The barmen stood shoulder to shoulder, watching her as she weaved her way back to merge into the crowd, mesmerized by the extravagant rotations of her backside.

"Aw shit!"

"What?"

"The ho' ain't paid fer her booze!"

Hidden in the crowd, the big dark man was watching too. He watched Cat retrieve her shoulder bag from the check-in and leave through the side doors that led to the car park.

He went back to the bar. The two barmen were waiting for him.

"That one's trouble," the older man said.

"Naw," his junior replied. "She jes' one o' them rich honkey bitches that likes the taste o' dark meat."

The big man looked thoughtful, studying the empty glass with a smudge of hot pink lipstick on the rim.

Cat strode swiftly across the floodlit car park.

I know you're here, man

She made a beeline for the matt black Barracuda.

Oomph! You are a beast!

She settled down to wait, leaning decoratively on the flank of the car parked opposite. She looked at her watch. Five minutes later she looked at it again.

Come on man. They must have told you. I put on enough of a show

She glared at her watch again. She delved into her shoulder bag and lit a cigarette.

So come on!

Cat heard the sound of footsteps, heading towards her. She looked up expectantly.

Shit!

Three ragged men, pale unshaven scarecrows with dirty hair straggling down from under tattered baseball caps, in a motley patchwork of denim and army surplus.

"Hey sweet thang…!"

Marvellous!

They lined up in front of her, looking her up and down, goggle-eyed, their bodies galvanized by a nervous eagerness.

"Hey, baby…!"

Their leader was taller and broader than the others. He stumbled forward and his body odor made Cat wince.

"Whaddaya got in the b-bag s-s-sweetcheeks...?"

I really don't need this right now!

He was clearly strung out, his eyes very bright and getting crazy.

"G-g-got any b-b-bread...b-baby...?"

Close behind him, his two companions were leaning towards her greedily, their eyeballs rolling around. Cat's first impulse was to kick the crap out of them. But she had more pressing business.

She reached into the deep bag and came up with a fistful of crackling greenbacks.

"Here, man, get yourself a fix."

The scarecrow stepped back, surprised. Behind him, his accomplices looked at each other. This was too easy.

"Uh...wha...?"

Cat stamped her foot impatiently.

"Go on, take it and get out of here!"

Confused, the hophead hesitated. Then he grunted and grabbed the money.

"Well?"

He was still standing there. He was staring at her, licking his lips.

Oh great!

He was actually drooling.

"Uh...m-mebbe ya g-g-g-got sumthin' else I wan'...b-b-b-b-bitch...!"

He pulled a knife from his pocket. The blade gleamed like the crazed lust in his eyes. The others were shuffling forward, emitting a kind of cracked and nasty cackle.

Fuck this!

Cat stubbed out the cigarette in his left eye. It stuck there, sizzling. The knife clattered on the tarmac. With a piercing shriek, the scarecrow stumbled backwards, clutching his face.

He staggered into his pals and sent them reeling. One collapsed on his hands and knees. Cat kicked him deftly on the side of the head, a quick flick of her foot that laid him down splat, spread eagled on his face.

His twin tugged a long rusty butcher's cleaver from under his threadbare coat. He lurched towards Cat, mumbling curses and swinging.

Cat stood her ground until he was almost on top of her. Then she stepped sideways, blocking his downswing with her forearm. The cleaver fell from his numbed fingers. Planting her feet to take her strength from the earth, Cat put the whole of her body into a short, crisp left hook that whipped his head round sideways in a spray of spittle. His eyes staring blankly, the junkie fell back against the door of a parked limo and slid down limply, sitting in a crumpled heap, dribbling blood.

One hand clapped to his eye socket, the leader ran away wailing into the night. Frowning, Cat blew on her knuckles.

That's just wonderful!

There were spots of blood and spit on her bare shoulder. She reached into the bag, searching for a tissue.

"You're impressive, alright."

The nickel-plated Walther appeared like magic in her hand.

"I said to myself when I first met you..."

The deep brown voice was very familiar. Suddenly Cat was confused, her thoughts tumbling over each other.

"...That is one very special lady..."

The familiar voice was coming from behind an outrageous pink and yellow, chrome-smothered pimpmobile. Cat aimed the PPK at it.

"Step out so I can see you!"

His bass laughter made a very pleasant sound. Something was starting to register.

"Don't shoot, I'm on your side..."

Her eyes went very wide. Her hand with the gun in it dropped down by her side.

"What...? You!"

He was grinning at her.

"Me."

It was George, the short-order cook from "VERNA'S EATS." Only he wasn't wearing his apron. He was looking sharp in a black three-quarter length coat made of exclusive leather, hanging open over a dark grey cashmere turtleneck tucked into the tightest black leather pants, with a fancy belt and a gold and enamel buckle that matched the buckles on his shiny Italian shoes.

Cat stood there gaping.

"You...you look...fantastic...!" she managed.

Smiling, the big man nodded at the black Barracuda, as Cat took a step back and bumped up against it.

"You go together well."

Then it hit her like a brick.

Oh Jesus! It's him! He's the one!

CHAPTER 12
Hit Squad

Cat led him all the way back to the lonely beach house. The bright moon raced them, hanging high above the horizon. In the early hours the coast road was deserted and she drove very fast, the yellow Corvette like a streak of light. Hard on its tail, the matt black Barracuda seemed to soak up the moonlight, a shadow.

Long tubes of neon lit up the cavern of her garage, cut deep into the cliff face, between the tall stilts that supported the house.

George parked the 'Cuda alongside the Stingray. Smiling, he admired the suppleness of Cat's curves, as she vaulted lightly out of the open cockpit. She smiled back at him as he opened the driver's door and stepped out.

He saw the red Olds 4-4-2. And the blue Chevelle. And an orange Dodge Charger 500 up on blocks with its wheels off, its body shell a patchwork of grey primer.

"That's quite a collection you got there."

Cat grinned.

"My family," she nodded at the black Barracuda. "Your baby will have someone to talk to."

Chuckling, George patted the roof of his car.

"Yeah, she's my baby…"

The steel shutters of the garage slid shut behind them. She took him out onto the sand, shining like silver in the moonlight, into the fresh sea breezes and the distant murmur of the glittering surf.

They stood for a while, side by side, looking out to sea.

"Nice spot you have here," he observed.

Cat inhaled deeply.

"It's where I come to find peace."

All the while, her thoughts were racing.

Oh Christ! It's him! He's the one! What am I going to do?

And hidden eyes were watching, from the cliff tops, looming black and scraggy against a sky full of stars.

He followed her up the wooden stairs that ran up from the sand to her balcony.

"Be it ever so humble…"

Cat unlocked a metal screen that barred the doors. Sliding the tall glass panels apart, they advanced into the lounge with its throw-down rugs on a bare wooden floor and cushions heaped about. She moved around, switching on standing lamps with bell-like shades, filling the room with a glow like smoked amber.

Hands on hips, George was looking at one of the jazz festival posters.

"I was there."

Cat was crouching over the stereo. She looked up, wide-eyed, flicking back her hair.

"Yeah? It was a real blast wasn't it?"

"Righteous."

His eyes were devouring her. He was looking deep into her.

Cat chuckled.

"And some of the finest grass I ever had. Man, I was high!"

He laughed. His deep brown bass made her spine tingle. She looked at him.

What am I going to do?

She made her selection, sliding the black disc out of its cardboard sleeve, vintage Otis Redding, at his most mellow.

"Ah," said George. "The Man."

"Oooh yeah…" Cat murmured, moving her hips.

George was watching her hips move. His eyes clouded.

Cat hip swayed elegantly through the swinging bead curtain and into the small galley. He heard a cupboard open and close, the scrape of a drawer and a chink of glasses.

She was back quickly, bearing a wooden tray, a dark bottle, two wine glasses and a large corkscrew.

"If you'd do the honors," she said cheerfully. "I want to freshen up."

She set the tray down on a small side table. Then she was heading for the bedroom and the bathroom beyond it.

"I won't be long. Make yourself at home."

George watched her walk away. The slow swinging span of her hips was hypnotic.

The door closed behind her. He could hear her moving about, humming a tune, harmonizing with Otis. She had a nice voice.

Slowly, George picked up the corkscrew and went to work on the cork. It gave in easily. Glowing ruby red, the wine slurped into the glasses. He raised a glass and sniffed delicately. He took a sip.

"Mmm….!"

He read the label. His eyebrows lifted. He was impressed.

George put the glass down on the little table and took off his leather coat, laying it down beside a heap of floor cushions. He was wearing a compact blue-black automatic in a shoulder holster. He slipped off the clever straps and slings and hid the gun and holster under his coat.

He settled into the cushions, took another sip of wine and let the honeyed voice of the late great Otis Redding wash over him. He could hear the muffled sound of water running beyond the closed door of the bedroom and Cat's pleasant voice raised in song.

George was frowning. Sliding the gun out from under his jacket, he flicked off the safety. He weighed the gun on his palm, looking at the bedroom door. He took a deep breath, tensing as if about to rise. Then he let the air out slowly and relaxed back into the deep cushions, stowing the gun away.

His brow creased in thought, the big man sat staring at the floor. Then he grunted softly, making a decision. Rooting in his jacket pockets, he found a little tin box. He prised the lid open with his thumbnail.

A tiny yellow pill plopped into Cat's wine glass. George lifted the glass, stirring carefully. A few bubbles trailed up to the top, in seconds the pill had vanished.

He studied the contents of the wine glass, holding it up to the light. Satisfied, he replaced it on the table beside him.

Cat sank back into the cloud of fragrant stream, letting herself submerge until the bathwater was tickling her chin.

"Mmmmmm………….!"

The scented oils did their work, anointing and soothing her, soaking away the musk of the disco, the sweat and stale perfume.

She lost all track of time. She could hear the muted mellow music creeping under the door. She slipped into a doze.

"You okay in there?"

There was a soft rapping on the door. Water splashed over the rim of the tub as Cat sat up, startled.

"Yes…fine…sorry…"

She pulled the plug and stood up in the bathtub. The water, suffused with iridescent oils, cascaded over her lithe contours, making her skin sleek and glossy.

Why him?

The water gurgled in the plughole, descending to her calves and then her ankles. Cat reached out for the showerhead, lifting it from its mount on the tiled wall.

Come on! Think!

On the other side of the door, the big man was listening, his brow creased, frowning. Behind him, Otis finished his song.

"...I'll be out in a second. Put another record on..."

He heard her moving about inside, and the whine of a hair dryer. Light on his feet, he retraced his steps, crossing the room to the stereo deck.

Cat's sounds were stacked on the floor in three big piles next to the deck. George was crouched down beside them as she emerged from the bathroom.

"See anything you like?"

He looked up. A kind of wonder lit up his eyes. Cat was wrapped in a short pale peach silk dressing gown that came down to her thighs, cinched in tight at the waist by a rope with long tassels. In the amber glow of the lamplight, she was lustrous, golden.

George swallowed hard.

"I see everything I like."

Strolling towards him, Cat laughed deliciously.

"I meant the music."

Otis Redding gave way to Lester Young and his airy, ethereal sax, adding deft highlights to the matchless beauty of Lady Day.

"Gorgeous," Cat sighed, subsiding elegantly into the cushions.

"Yes," said George, looking down at her.

Cat smiled up at him. He had a good, strong face. Under the soft second skin of the dark turtleneck his torso was stacked with muscle.

You're pretty damn gorgeous yourself, man. Oh, this isn't fair!

"Come down and join me," she said softly.

She pushed some cushions together and he sat down beside her. He picked up his wine glass and handed her the other.

"Here."

"Thank you."

Their eyes locked.

"Cheers."

"Good health."

They raised their glasses and drank.

Cat listened to the music for a little while. She took another sip, her head tilted back, eyes half closed. George watched her. His mask slipped momentarily, a spasm of regret.

She shook herself awake, gazing at him intently.

"You're not really a cook are you?"

He had a very handsome smile. He made her ache in all the good places.

Ohhhhh...!

"Why, didn't you like your eggs and bacon?"

Cat shook her head, grinning. She took a gulp of her wine.

"The food was great. But being a short-order cook isn't your main occupation, is it?"

She looked straight at him. He looked straight back.

"And you, lady, ain't one of the plastic people like you pretend to be."

Suddenly, she was serious.

"Who are you?" she asked.

"You first," he replied.

Cat opened her mouth. Her lips moved but nothing came out. Her tongue was numb.

She looked puzzled. Her eyelids fluttered, the green orbs rolling up till only the whites showed. A thin string of saliva dangled from her lower lip.

The wine glass slipped from her limp fingers and rolled across the floorboards. Her eyes closed.

George stood up quickly and looked down for a long time at Cat sleeping her drugged sleep, deep in the cushions.

His troubled features were a map of the debate raging within. He had the gun in his hand. It was pointed at her heart, where her breasts were rising and falling under the thin silk.

Outside, the sand shone like silver in the moonlight and the murmuring surf was a long line of glittering froth marking the edge of the beach. The cliffs looming behind the beach house were huge and black against a wash of twinkling stars.

And keen eyes were watching from the grassy cliff tops, fixed upon the amber glow of the windows.

And someone was watching the watchers.

"Mmmmm....mgh...hh......."

Cat was thrashing in deep dark waters, rising rapidly towards the light.

"Ah!...ahh..hh...uuuuhh-h-h-h.......!"

Gasping, she broke through the glassy, shimmering surface.

"Oooohhhh........"

The light seared her eyeballs which grated like there was sand in the sockets. She squeezed her eyes tight shut then opened them cautiously, blinking.

A dull ache throbbed in her temples. She had a sour taste in her mouth. Nausea was a fist clenching in the pit of her stomach.

Icy chills washed over her, cold sweat crawling on her skin.

You fool!

She was sitting on the floor, propped against the wall, her legs stretched out in front of her. Her hands were behind her back, manacled in heavy duty police handcuffs. The short peach-colored silk dressing gown was still wrapped snugly around her, the silken tassels on her bare thighs.

"Here..."

The big man was walking across the room towards her. He had a tall glass in his hand, half filled with a milky fizzing liquid.

Cat made a face. Her head was aching and she felt dizzy. Her stomach churned violently, making her gulp.

"Uh! What the hell did you give me? I'm going to throw up!"

George sidestepped so as to stay out of range of her long legs. Offering the glass, he hunkered down beside her.

"Drink this. It'll make you feel better."

She glared at him.

"Well uncuff me then."

He shook his head, smiling.

"I don't think so, sister. I've seen what you can do."

He raised the fizzing glass to her lips. She pouted, then tilted her head forward and took a sip.

"Ugh! Terrible!"

"Drink it all now..."

Cat frowned but did as she was told. The effect was electric. She felt better at once. The pounding ceased. Her head was clear and the nausea evaporated.

"Ah...uh...wow!"

George rose and walked away. He put the empty glass down on the small side table. He laid his gun beside it and sat cross-legged on the cushions.

He gazed at Cat, looking her over from top to toe.

You damn fool! He took you like a baby!

She gave him a big smile.

"Aren't you going to search me for concealed weapons? They all do."

The big man was serious.

"Who are you working for?"

Her smile didn't waver. She shook her head.

"I don't know what you mean."

He got to his feet quickly, very quick for such a big man.

"You found me, you drew me out and you brought me here. What for? Who are you working for?"

You let me find you. You're one jump ahead of me, man...

"I'm sorry...?"

He took a step towards her, his massive fists like rocks clenching by his sides.

Her smile vanished. She looked up into his eyes.

"Are you going to hurt me now?" she said quietly.

He stopped.

"You know I won't tell you anything."

His eyes clouded, looking at her. His fists uncoiled slowly. He turned his back on her abruptly and marched across to the corner where the telephone sat on the floorboards.

Cat watched him dial a long number. She heard him speak softly into the receiver. She heard him say something very familiar.

"…give me a secure line…"

She sat up straight, the handcuffs rattling.

"Hey—!"

George was speaking again. He was giving a full and detailed report of his encounter with Cat at "**THE JOOK JOINT.**"

Cat was trying to stand up. Her bare feet slipped on the polished boards and she slid down with a thump.

"Ow! Hey! Wait a—!"

She saw the big man go rigid, his mouth open. He shot her a startled glance.

"You're shittin' me!…stop laughing…what?…Selena!"

He was staring at her, astonished, as he listened to the voice at the other end of the line. Cursing, Cat heaved herself upright, her hair falling across her face.

"Selena?" she gasped. "Hey, what the—!"

George was holding the receiver out towards her. She recognized the faint and tinny laughter.

"Selena!" Cat yelled. "This isn't funny! I—!"

He spoke briefly, then put the phone down. He was walking towards her again, but this time he was relaxed and grinning broadly.

"It looks like we're on the same side, Miss Catherine Warburton."

Cat was hopping mad. She glared at him through a veil of hair. In her struggles to stand the dressing gown had come loose and a bare breast was showing, pale gold and coral-tipped.

Shaking his head, George gently tucked the two halves of the silk together, restoring her modesty. Cat tried to stay mad, but burst out laughing instead. Puffing, she blew hair out of her eyes.

"Well, big guy, you'd better get these damn cuffs off me, because we're in deep shit here."

Long ropes uncoiled, snaking down from the scraggy cliff top to the sloping roof of the beach house.

Silhouetted against the stars, bulky figures with guns slung across their shoulders stepped off the edge and came corkscrewing swiftly down the ropes in quick succession.

Their rubber-soled combat boots scuffed softly as they dashed along the broad slanting roof, crouching low. They hardly made a sound as they swung down lightly onto the wooden balcony.

Cat slipped the palm-sized transmitter back into the pocket of her dressing gown.

"Relax, guys…"

There were five of them. Burly, indistinguishable figures dressed for combat in a mottled olive drab, their pale faces daubed by dark grease. They sported plain black berets, commando-style, hefting submachine-guns with folding skeleton stocks.

"The job's done."

Cat stepped aside to let them see past her. She picked up the wine bottle.

"See?"

An exotic rug was rumpled up under the heavy shape that sprawled across it. The big man was lying on his chest, his face turned away, legs all crooked, his right arm trapped underneath him. His left arm was stretched out on the bare floorboards, an empty wine glass rolling from his limp fingers.

Cat laughed.

"No trouble at all."

She cupped her breasts in her hands, making the silk whisper.

"Not with these weapons."

She jabbed the prostrate figure with her toe.

"He was too busy thinking about these. He didn't see me coming."

Smiling smugly, she brandished the wine bottle.

"He'll have a big headache when he wakes up."

They had left a sentry on the cliff top. The submachine-gun balanced in his arms, he stood looking down at the roof of the beach house, gleaming dully like pewter in the moonlight.

A slim shadow flitted in the corner of his vision. He half turned, lifting the gun, opening his mouth to shout an alarm.

Thin wire glinted, looping around his throat. The shout was strangled.

A gurgle. Boots scrabbling in the long grass. The sling slipped off his shoulder and the gun vanished over the edge.

"Oh shit…!" someone whispered.

Cat stepped back. She took a swig from the bottle, smacking her lips.

"He didn't have much to say, but I'm sure the Colonel will want to question him."

Three commandoes hung back, standing in a line. Slinging their guns on their shoulders, the other two stepped forward and stood over the body.

With a crash, the sentry's gun landed on the roof.

Instinctively, everyone looked up. The muzzles of the submachine-guns were jerked towards the ceiling.

George rolled over. The hand underneath his body was holding his compact automatic.

Cat's yell distracted the men standing over him. Confused, they turned towards her, fumbling to un-sling their weapons. Swinging her arm upwards, Cat smashed the wine bottle on the edge of the small table. She lunged forward and thrust with the jagged edges. The commando staggered backwards, clutching at his throat. Blood spurted through his fingers.

He collapsed, dying, his throat a ragged ruin. His face was expressionless.

Propped up on his elbow, George fired twice. One-two, neat black holes appeared between their eyes, as the submachine-guns clattered on the floor. They went down, one falling across the other.

The slim shadow was coming down the rope. Alighting on the roof, it paused to scoop up the submachine-gun.

It dashed on and swung down nimbly onto the balcony.

As he untangled the sling and raised the muzzle towards her, Cat kicked the gun out of the commando's hands. Instantly, he drew a long-bladed fighting knife and came at her, cutting and slashing.

Cat tossed the broken bottle aside. Bobbing and weaving, she kept moving in a circle, evading his energetic attacks. Suddenly, she feinted to go one way, then the other, then jumped in close, took him by the wrist and dipped her shoulder under his arm.

"YAAAHH...!"

He went up and over and came crashing down on his face. His legs kicked once, twice and then he didn't move. Cat could see the point of the knife protruding from his back.

George was rolling fast across the floorboards, firing the pistol as he rolled.

"SHIT!"

Hit in the ribs, the last commando staggered but kept firing his gun, spraying the room with bullets.

"Whoa!"

Cat flung herself down flat as hot lead sizzled past her, a slug flicking her hair.

Cursing, George was tangled in a heap of cushions. The slide stayed open, the magazine empty.

"Fuck!"

His face oddly blank, the wounded commando was tugging another magazine from his belt, slapping it into the breach of the submachine-gun.

"Oh fuck!"

Sliding across the floor, Cat grabbed the broken bottle and threw it at him. It hit the commando on the side of the head, slashing his cheek open in a rush of blood.

He didn't seem to notice. Wrenching back the cocking bolt, he came walking forward.

George was fumbling in his jacket pocket, searching desperately for a spare clip. Cat was scrambling on her hands and knees, reaching out, groping for one of the fallen weapons.

Blood dripping from his face, the commando was taking aim. They were going to be too late.

The commando's chest opened up like raw meat as bullets entered his back and ripped right through him. A long burst held him upright, his body juddering.

The firing stopped. Expressionless, the commando crumpled and dropped heavily to the floor.

"Hey wha—?"

George struggled to sit upright, wallowing waist deep in cushions.

"Jeez!"

Cat was on her hands and knees. Panting, she scraped the tangle of hair away from her face.

"And who the hell are you?"

A slim figure leant nonchalantly in the doorway to the balcony, cradling a submachine-gun. It was obviously feminine, with supple contours in a sleek black cat suit, its features concealed by a matching ski mask.

It looked at them and laughed.

"Hi guys. Having some trouble?"

She knew that laugh. Cat rolled her eyes and groaned.

"Oh, I don't believe it!"

Aiko removed the ski mask, swinging her head from side to side to shake out her shining blue-black hair.

"Pull yourself together, Cat."

Cat's breasts were escaping the front of her dressing gown. Muttering, she tugged at the silk, covering herself.

"I might have known," she said, getting gingerly to her feet.

She stomped towards Aiko, who was grinning at her like a wicked kitten.

"Selena said I could come out to play."

Cat glared at her, spitting a stray strand of hair from the corner of her mouth. Then she burst out laughing and flung her arms around the Japanese girl in a crushing embrace.

"Oh baby! And am I glad you did!"

Letting the gun slip down to the floor, Aiko returned Cat's embrace. Laughing, they squeezed each other tight.

Stepping out of the heap of cushions, George cleared his throat.

Breathless, the girls parted. Cat gave the big man a knowing look.

"I take it that you two have met?"

Smiling, George winked at Aiko.

"Uh, yeah, we've met…"

Aiko ate him up with her eyes. Twinkling saucily, she nudged Cat in the ribs.

"Isn't he a hunk? Isn't he gorgeous? He's just your type, Cat."

George looked positively bashful. Cat gave Aiko a shove.

"Why, Cat, you're blushing!"

Cat could feel the heat on her cheeks. It was ridiculous. She had never blushed in her life!

She shot a glance at George. He looked straight into her eyes and swallowed hard. Aiko giggled. Cat glared at her.

She stepped back and nearly fell over one of the dead men. Cold reality came back hard.

"Shit!"

Aiko's grin vanished.

"What is it?"

Grabbing Aiko's forearm, Cat turned her wrist over so she could read the Japanese girl's watch. She frowned.

"It's not over yet."

She touched Aiko lightly on the shoulder.

"You'd better make yourself scarce."

Aiko nodded. Quickly, she reached down to retrieve the submachine-gun.

"I'll go back the way I came."

This time a swift embrace, and Aiko was gone. Cat stood looking out onto the empty balcony.

When Cat turned back into the room, George was down on his haunches, taking a close look at one of the dead commandoes.

"Notice anything funny about these guys?"

Cat seemed slightly distracted.

"Uh…no…what…?"

George tweaked the camouflaged tunic, soaked in blood that swelled from the jagged rent in the dead man's throat.

"They could be killed alright. But they didn't feel any pain."

Cat shrugged.

"Maybe they were all on something. It's been done before."

George touched the cold face with a fingertip. The dead eyes stared back at him sightlessly. The skin had an odd, wax like texture, and even for a corpse the grey tint to its paleness was strange.

The big man rose to his feet. He was frowning.

"Yeah, maybe…maybe…"

Cat was looking at him.

"We don't have much time," she said flatly.

George nodded. He looked unhappy. Cat smiled at him.

173

"Come on. You know what to do."
His smile was bleak. He nodded.
"Yeah. I just don't want to do it."
Cat shrugged again. She was still smiling.
"It has to be done."
She laughed suddenly.
"And I have complete faith in your technical expertise."
George's gaze dropped to the floor.
"Yeah I'm an expert alright. I learned all my skills in 'Nam…"
Cat was surprised to see his eyes welling up.
"…till they asked me to use them on a…"
And brimming over, a single tear trickling down his cheek, glinting on his dark skin.
"…he was just a kid…he couldn't take it…"
Cat was standing close to him. She leant forward and kissed the tear away. He stared at her, confused.
Smiling, Cat pointed to her side.
"Here."
He was rocking back and forth on his heels. Cat pointed again.
"Come on. Here."
His fists were clenching and unclenching. The sleeves of the grey turtleneck were rolled up to the elbow and the muscles of his forearms rippled like cords of steel.
Cat's smile evaporated.
"Do it!"
His face turned to stone. His right fist rose in a short arc and impacted on her ribcage.
"UHH!"
Cat's face contorted. Puffing out her cheeks, she bent over.
George stepped back as she stumbled towards him, his features etched with regret.
"Oooooo….!"
Cat straightened slowly, beads of sweat glistening on her face. She grimaced, shaking her head.
"Harder…" she gasped. "It's got to be real…"
A veil came over his eyes. He stepped in close and hit her again.
"UUUGGHH…NNNNGG…GGG…!"
Her face went beet red, shiny with sweat. Then she turned white and sank slowly to her knees, clutching herself with both hands.
"Aaaaaahh-h-hh-hh-hhh…that's b-better," Cat groaned. "I…I think you've c-cracked a rib…!"
George turned away from her, rubbing his hand over his face.
"Aw, Jesus!"

Grunting with pain, Cat lurched to her feet and stood swaying, her hands pressed to her side.

"C-come on...you just got s-started...make it look g-g-good..."

His powerful shoulders were rising and falling as he took great gulps of air, cranking himself up. He swung back suddenly and grabbed a fistful of the silk nightgown.

"UH!"

"AHH!"

"UGH!"

"AH!"

"AGHH!"

He slapped her back and forth, rocking her head from side to side, her long hair flailing, holding her upright with one hand when her legs gave way.

"URGH!"

"AH!"

"UH!"

He lowered her tenderly to the floor. She was glassy-eyed, her face mottled with lurid yellow and purple bruises.

"Oooowww...www...ww...www...!"

She sat in a rumpled heap. Blood was dripping from her nostrils and oozing over her swollen lips. A long string of blood and saliva dangled from her chin.

Cat made to wipe her battered mouth with the back of her hand, then winced, clutching her ribs.

"AAAAAA...HH!"

The dressing gown had fallen open and spots of blood were dotting the heaving mounds of her breasts, gleaming with sweat.

"I...I'm sorry..."

Gently, George covered her up.

Cat smiled weakly through the blood.

"D-d-don't b-be...," she mumbled. "You're d-d-doing a...fine...job..."

Her face contorted with pain.

"N-now finish it..." she panted. "You know wha...what I m-mean..."

He hung his head again. Cat raised a shaky hand and let it fall on his shoulder.

"It has to b-b-be...extreme...s-s-so they...believe...it..."

George couldn't look at her. He shook his head.

"I can't!"

Her hand slid down his arm, over the bulging muscle as hard as rock.

"You...have t-t-to..."

She laughed suddenly, pink bubbles on her lips, making a face and grabbing her side.

"Only I...I'd rather n-not...be awake...when...you do it..."

He lifted his eyes to look at her. His hands were very soft as he cupped her battered face between them.

"You're special," he murmured in his deep brown voice. "A very special lady."

Cat looked back at him warmly.

"I'll let…you…remind m-me of that…later…" she whispered. "I'll let you…make m-me…feel…special…"

George smiled, looking into her eyes. His hand slipped down, stroking her hair, down to where her neck melted into her shoulder in a lovely curve.

He pressed slightly.

"Uuuuuuuhhh…"

Her eyes closed as her head lolled forward slowly. She went limp in his arms.

He lost all track of time, standing over her. It was only seconds, but it seemed to go on forever, an eternity, an agony of indecision.

"Fuck!"

The big man squatted down next to Cat, stretched out unconscious on the floorboards. He took the little finger of her left hand and broke it quickly with a dull snap.

"Nnnnnnn…."

She stirred slightly.

He broke her index finger.

"Mmmnnmmm…"

He lit a cigarette. He took a deep drag, then another.

He applied the glowing tip of the cigarette to the sole of her bare foot.

"NNnnghh..hhh…!"

To the curve of her naked thigh.

"MMMmmnn…nnghh..!"

He pulled apart the folds of the silk.

"NNNNnnn…ggg..ghhhh!"

He lurched to his feet and staggered into the small bathroom, where he vomited violently into the basin. He rinsed away the mess and stood staring at himself in the mirror until his face was absolutely calm.

He picked up the phone, dialled the long number and asked for a secure line. His report was brief and to the point.

"Yeah, that's right…send a team to plant the seventh body…Yeah, seven…Yeah, there's one on the cliff, bring it into the house…There have to be seven bodies in the house, six of them and one for me."

The big man bore her unconscious weight effortlessly, out onto the balcony, down the wooden stairs and onto the starlit beach. He scuffed up the silvery sand to simulate a trail made by someone crawling and laid her down carefully about two hundred yards from the house.

"Mmmm…nnn…nn…?"

Drifting in and out, consumed by pain, Cat was dimly aware of hasty activity within the beach house. Then everything was quiet.

"Nnnn...nnn...nn..."

The room full of dead men was engulfed instantly by a conflagration that burst the confines of the wooden house, billowing out of the shattered windows.

"UH?"

On the sand, the detonation jolted Cat back into consciousness.

"AAAAAHHH!"

As the huge fireball bubbled outwards, orange and black, she felt the searing heat and began to crawl away from it, towards the glittering surf. Her body was one great mass of pain and every movement wrenched a groan from her lips, crusted with blood.

She stopped crawling when she felt the water tickle her groping fingertips. Grunting with pain, she rolled onto her side and looked back at the beach house.

"Oh...C-C-Christ...!"

Already it was a blackened shell, devoured by raging flames that lit up the sand and made dancing reflections on the waves. Through a blur of pain, she mourned it, and grieved for her record collection.

Gasping, she fell back and lay looking up at the stars. At least her babies would be safe, secure in the fireproof garage. Likewise her other toys, sealed in the vault of her arsenal.

"Oooooooo....!"

The stars went fuzzy and began to dim as she lapsed back into unconsciousness.

She woke to a clatter of whirring metal wings. The sand billowed like silver sparkles in the night sky as the sleek black helicopter descended.

"Miss Johnson...?"

The men in safari suits were looking down at her, their pale faces glowing pinkly in the leaping firelight.

They turned abruptly as the wreckage of the beach house tottered and came crashing down in a towering cloud of red sparks. The shockwaves fanned the lashing flames, making them take a step back.

"He's d-dead..." Cat muttered feebly. "They're...all...dead...he took them all with him..."

The blond men looked at the black ruin and the daunting flames. They began to walk towards it, but then came back, obviously frustrated.

"All d-d-dead..."

They bent down and picked her up and lifted her onto the floor of the helicopter. They weren't gentle and Cat screamed and lost consciousness again.

CHAPTER 13
Not of This World

"Uuuuunnn…nnn…nnn…"

Cat was floating in a bubble of bright light. Her body was supported on a cushion of air, her long hair floating in a radiant halo.

She felt warm all over. There was no pain.

This must be what it's like to die

She was stretched out on her back, her arms by her sides. When she lifted her head to look down the long shining column of her body she saw that she was stark naked.

"NNNnnn…nnn…!"

Cat tried to move, straining every muscle. She could barely make a finger quiver.

"AHH!"

When she tried to move, the pain came back abruptly, severely, an admonishment. She relaxed, gasping.

"Please keep still, Miss Johnson."

Figures took shape, emerging from the bright white light, shimmering and ghostly. They became more substantial as they approached, two blond men in tan safari suits.

"You must keep still for the procedure to work."

They drew close and stood over her, gazing down at her blandly with their pale eyes. They seemed unmoved by her nakedness, displaying a mere, mild technical interest as they walked slowly around her, surveying her injuries.

Her face was raw and discolored, lips swollen and crusted with dried blood. Lurid yellow and purple bruises mottled her ribcage. Two of the fingers on her left hand stuck out at crooked angles. Her skin was dotted by angry red burns.

"NNghh!"

Cat's body went rigid, arching slightly, as one of the men touched her side. Suddenly she was covered in sweat, her naked form shining under the light like alabaster.

The two men withdrew into the light, their shapes melting, transparent.

"AAAAAAAHHHHH……!"

The light was suffused by pale lavender, bathing her in its eerie glow. Cat screamed as the sweat on her skin turned cold, as if she had been plunged abruptly into a bath of ice water.

"OOOOOOOOHHH-HHH-HH!"

She moaned, shivering. The purple light was pulsating, darker and lighter.

"OOOOOAAAA-AAAHH-HHH-HHH!"

Her body, galvanized by a kind of icy electricity, was juddering and jerking. Her muscles flexed, gripped by uncontrollable spasms.

"UH-AH-AH-AGH-AH-AH!"

The crust of blood on Cat's mouth began to crack and flake and fall away. Her swollen lips were restored slowly to their former beauty.

The raw redness and discoloration faded from her face. The bruises on her ribs were shrinking until they were gone altogether.

"MMmmmmm....!"

The purple thinned to pale lavender and was pure bright white again. Cat moaned, her head rolling from side to side, eyes half closed, her long eyelashes fluttering.

The pale men re-emerged from the light. They were wearing gauntlets fashioned from a gleaming silver mesh. They moved around her floating body, touching her. They stroked her burnt flesh and massaged her crooked, broken hand.

"AAAAAGGHH-GHH-HHH!"

They laid hands on her side. Cat's body convulsed, her eyes open wide. She screamed until her voice cracked hoarsely.

The bright light imploded in upon her, onrushing blackness crushing it to a searing pinpoint in her skull.

Then nothing.

Cat awoke to the smell of perfume and the sound of elegant chamber music. Her blurred vision focused slowly. She saw brass lamps, floral wallpaper and baroque oils depicting nymphs and shepherds.

"Uhh...."

She was in an antique four-poster bed, lying on silk sheets. Above her was suspended a royal purple awning fringed with gold. A plump quilt embroidered with golden fleurs-de-lys was tucked up to her chin.

"Mmph!"

Cat sat up abruptly. Her hair was silken soft, washed and combed and scented. Someone had dressed her in a billowing Regency nightdress with intricate lace collar and cuffs.

She realized suddenly that there was no pain. There was a gilt hand mirror on the ornate bedside table. Hesitantly, she looked at her reflection.

"Wha—?"

Her flawless, gorgeous self was looking back at her. Not a mark. Cat pressed a hand tentatively to her side. Nothing, not a twinge.

She and her reflection raised their eyebrows at each other, mystified.

There was a knock at the door.

"Miss Johnson...?"

Cat laid the mirror down.

"Come in."

The Colonel strode swiftly into the bedroom, the toy soldier in one of his ridiculous dress uniforms.

Now he's given up on Patton and is back to being General Lee

She gave him a welcoming smile.

"Colonel, I'm so glad to see you again."

He clicked his heels and bowed.

"The pleasure is all mine, Miss Johnson. How are you feeling?"

Cat touched her ribs.

"A bit weak, Sir, but fully mended."

She gazed at him quizzically.

"Your people can work miracles, Colonel."

The Colonel merely looked mysterious. He pulled up a gilded armchair and sat, suddenly brisk and businesslike.

"You did well, Miss Johnson."

"Thank you, Sir."

"Although it was disappointing that he could not be taken alive for interrogation. It appears that he perished in the flames, along with six of my best men."

Cat was contrite.

"I'm sorry, Sir."

He favored her with his thin smile.

"Not at all, my dear. You lured him most adeptly. You were exceptional."

Cat looked suitably grateful. The Colonel rose and began pacing the plush carpet. Suddenly he stopped and leant towards her eagerly.

"The black swine tortured you?"

Cat lowered her eyes.

"Yes."

"He beat you and burned you with a cigarette?"

Jeez! Stop drooling!

"Yes, he did."

He took a step towards her. There was a strange, eager light in his eyes.

"And did he abuse you in any way?"
"No, he didn't."

Sorry to disappoint you

He did look disappointed. Then he pulled himself together, retreating towards the bedroom door.
"You look tired. Rest a while."
He turned back to beam his bleak smile at her.
"I say it again, Miss Johnson, you are a credit to your race. I have great plans for you!"

Wisps of grey smoke were still seeping from charred heaps of wreckage piled high on the fashionable Boulevard. The ruins of exclusive interiors, raked out of gutted establishments that served the very best to the very best people.
The Boulevard was a hive of activity. Workmen in hard hats and overalls were clambering in and out of the gaping, ransacked store fronts. Showers of sparks fizzed from rasping blowtorches. Drills were grinding and hammers pounding. A fine mist of concrete dust filtered the pale morning light.
Teams of insurance representatives in grey suits were filing in and out, carrying clipboards and doing a lot of pointing. All along the Boulevard, knots of radio and TV reporters brandished microphones and cameras in the over painted faces of fashion gurus and their celebrity clientele, who were putting on a show of flowery bravado. Amidst laughter and applause, the venerated head of one of the mighty Houses sold a diamond bracelet to a fur-caped movie star, from a small trestle table set up on the sidewalk.
In front of each scorched shop front, a National Guardsman had been posted, looking tough in full combat gear and flak jacket, wielding his carbine.
"Atten-hut!"
J. Spencer Warburton cut quite a dash in his National Guard uniform. Lean and fit, with his hawkish, patrician features, he looked good in olive drab, a single star on his shoulders, a Colt .45 automatic holstered on his hip.
He advanced with long, swift strides, a flock of subordinates trailing in his wake.
"My God, Sir!" blurted a young lieutenant with a bland pink face. "It's like Rome after the barbarians got through with it!"
Much to their annoyance, the celebrities found themselves abandoned abruptly by the reporters, who swarmed around the commanding figure of Warburton, clamoring and thrusting their lenses and microphones at him.
There were trees and ornate benches, along the Boulevard. Warburton climbed nimbly onto a bench and stood looking down with barely disguised contempt on the media pack in its feeding frenzy.

A curt gesture prompted instant silence.

"What you see here before you, and in other parts of our city," he told them. "Is an attack on the very fabric of our society, an assault incited by spite and envy, an attack by the basest elements—who aspire to nothing but destruction and anarchy—upon the very best of our values and accomplishments."

He held a dramatic pause. One reporter was brave enough to step into it.

"Mr...er, General...Warburton...every time there are riots and disturbances like these the call gets louder for you to declare your candidacy for the White House..."

Cat's dreams were disconnected, fragments of her life all jumbled and jangling. Familiar faces came and went, all muddled together.

Her father, in his club blazer and flannels, was getting on down on the dance floor, disco-dancing with a glorious, gleaming half-naked Selena.

George the Cook, in his green beret and tiger-stripe jungle fatigues, was stumbling towards her, crashing through thick undergrowth, through dripping fan-like fronds and stalks of bamboo, an M-16 slung across his broad shoulders. He was carrying the broken, bloody body of a child, a tiny little girl with shining black hair, an oriental doll. Tears were shining on his dark face.

Cat was running. She was naked. The sweat on her skin was like acid and then like ice. She looked down and her bare feet were treading on dead faces, bloated and grey, with bulging eyes. The rotting flesh was pulpy and oozing. It squished between her toes and she gagged on the stench.

She was running down a dark alley with high walls pressing in on either side of her. Darkness was above, behind and in front of her. Something in the darkness was chasing her.

"UH!"

Cat woke with a jolt. She was sitting upright in bed. Sweat glued the thin stuff of the nightdress to her skin.

"Oh...hh...h...."

Through chinks in the heavy curtains, slivers of moonlight picked out the highlights of gilding on the furniture, a curve, a curl, a corner. The faces of martial portraits on the walls were a pale glimmer in the deep blue gloom, their epaulettes glinting dully.

"Mmph!"

Cat threw back the covers. She swung her long legs off of the bed, sinking her bare feet into the deep carpet and standing in a single, fluid motion. With the embroidered hem of the antique nightdress billowing around her ankles, she strode quickly to the tall window.

She drew the heavy velvet folds aside slightly and poked her nose through the gap.

"Hm!"

She was on the second floor. Below lay the broad sweep of the marble patio with its ornate balustrade, and beyond the complex geometry of the vast gardens were the barrack roofs and brick walls of the exercise courts. All was bathed in a wash of silver by the bright moonlight, dappled with deep blue pools of shadow. High above, the desert sky was full of stars.

Turning back into the bedroom, Cat caught sight of her ghostly reflection in a full-length standing mirror. She thought she looked ridiculous, in the diaphanous nightdress with its floral lace collar.

Can't say I'm exactly dressed for the occasion

Moving swiftly around the room, a pale ghost in the semi-darkness, she tugged at ornamental gilt handles, opening inlaid drawers and doors. She found nothing. It was all empty, just there for show.

"Marvellous!"

Cat studied herself in the long mirror. With a sharp intake of breath, she reached up with both hands and tore the frothy lace to bits, wrenching downwards with a ripping sound to create a ragged V neckline.

"Ha!"

Bending, she grabbed the generous hemline and reduced the long nightgown to a mini dress, ending two inches above the knee.

Now that's more like it!

Reaching through the slit in the curtains, she pushed open the tall windows, slowly, in case they creaked. The long panes opened out onto a small marble balcony, like a box, its rail of fluted columns coming up to her waist.

Cat peeked out. She could see nothing moving. The gardens were absolutely silent. The night air was cool on her face.

She stepped out onto the balcony. The white marble chilled the soles of her bare feet.

"Ssss...!"

She hunkered down and peered out between the columns of the railing. Twisting her body, she looked left and right. In line with the floor of the balcony, a narrow ledge ran along the face of the mansion, linking other small balconies that projected from tall windows. Two windows along to her left, thick dark vines clung to a web of trelliswork, from the roof above with its fancy gables and chimneys to the glistening marble patio below.

Instinctively, Cat was up and over the railing and was inching her way along towards the vine. Her bare toes curled around the lip of the ledge, her back pressed to the wall. The bricks were cold through the thin remains of the nightdress.

Halfway to the next window and its boxlike balcony, she froze. A sentry, a rifle slung on his shoulder, had rounded the distant corner of the chateau and was advancing along the broad patio, a small black shape on the expanse of stark marble.

Scarcely breathing, Cat remained motionless, her feet apart, arms held out wide from her sides, her back glued to the wall.

The sentry was directly below her. The merest tickle of a breeze made the shreds of the nightdress flutter about her naked thighs.

If you look up now, man, you'll get a view you didn't expect

The guard carried on. Cat watched him walk slowly away from her until he vanished around the far corner.

Breathing normally again, she resumed her careful progress, inching gingerly along the ledge. When she reached the next balcony, she saw that the curtains behind the window were closed and all was dark.

Cat vaulted lightly onto the balcony and ducked down to check out the elaborate expanses of the gardens, spread out below. Satisfied, she stepped out onto the ledge again. She was halfway to the next balcony when another sentry appeared and came down towards her along the wide patio.

This time, as luck would have it, he stopped to light a cigarette, directly below her. He stood for a while, smoking.

Don't look up! Don't look up!

The cold brick was making her back ache. She curled her toes tighter around the lip of the ledge. Perspiration chilled on her forehead.

Come on, motherfucker! Move! How long does it take to smoke a goddamn cigarette?

A momentary cramp stabbed into her calf. Cat grimaced with pain. It spasmed again, more violently this time, like a red hot dagger point jabbing into her flesh. She ground her teeth, biting back the yelp that leapt into her throat. Lifting her foot slightly, she flexed it upwards to stretch her nagging calf. For a moment, standing on the ledge on one leg, she almost lost her balance and alarm was a fist of ice twisting her guts.

Jeeeeezus!

The sentry took a last drag, tossed down the butt and ground it out with his boot heel. Adjusting the rifle sling on his shoulder, he moved on.

Cat released her trapped breath in a long sigh and then sucked in the cool night air gratefully. She flexed her foot a few more times, very carefully. The cramp had gone.

She took another long, slow deep breath and then resumed her journey along the precarious ledge. When she reached the next balcony, bordered by the convenient vine, she saw that it was longer and fancier than the others. And there was lamplight behind the heavy curtains, which were glowing royal purple.

"Uh-oh…"

Her bare feet were silent as she vaulted feather light onto the balcony. There was a crack low down in the purple drapes through which the brassy light was shining. She couldn't resist it.

She was looking into the Colonel's bedchamber. His bed was fit for a king, a monumental four-poster hung with cloth of gold. The slender form of a naked girl was spread eagled upright at the foot of the bed, her arms out flung and wrists lashed to the carved posts up above her head, her legs forced wide so her ankles could be secured by short lengths of rope to the feet shaped like carved eagle's claws.

The girl's head was lolling from side to side, her face in shadow, her hair a halo rimmed by the glowing lamplight. Her lithe coppery body was drenched with sweat and twitched and jerked spasmodically. From her shoulders down to the backs of her thighs there was a criss-cross, random pattern of vivid welts, oozing blood.

Oh, you son-of-a—!

Cat moved slightly so she could see more. Her eyebrows shot up towards her hairline.

The Colonel was standing in the middle of the room. He was wearing a Roman centurion's helmet with its towering horsehair crest and a breastplate embossed with antique designs and battle scenes, gleaming like brass in the lamplight.

He was naked below the waist and his thin legs looked like pipe cleaners, dangling down below the barrel-chested breastplate.

In his right hand, the Colonel was holding a vicious buggy whip. The fingers of his left hand were hooked into the tight curls topping the head of a second girl, who knelt stark naked at his feet with her hands tied behind her back, her head bobbing as she pleasured him with her mouth.

Cat caught partial glimpses of the kneeling girl's face and saw that her eyes were screwed tight shut, her cheeks wet with tears.

A cold fury consumed her.

You evil piece of shit…! You're going to get yours! I promise!

But not now. Now she had other business to attend to.

Cat watched for a few harrowing moments more, to ensure that the Colonel was fully occupied. Then she crept along the balcony to the far end where the clinging vines ran down.

There was a sentry passing by below. Cat waited. From inside, she heard the muffled whistle and slash of the whip, and a piercing soprano shriek rise up and then descend into contralto groans. Her blood boiled, but she smothered the urge to go crashing headlong through those tall windows and rip his throat out with her bare hands.

When all was clear below, Cat rose cautiously and stepped up onto the marble rail of the balcony. Reaching out, she tugged at the dark mat of foliage that clung to the wall. Its grip seemed firm enough.

Satisfied, she swung out off the balcony and began to climb down.

The sleeping gardens were dappled with silver and blue. Cat waded deep in the pools of shadow cast by the manicured hedges and sculpted bushes. Submerged, she was invisible.

She heard boot heels crunching and crouched, motionless, holding her breath. A lone sentinel trudged along the glistening ribbon of a gravel path, stark silver in the moonlight. He passed within yards of her, oblivious to her presence.

The clipped grass was smooth and cool beneath her bare feet as Cat sprinted noiselessly across a narrow patch of moonlight that divided great lakes of shadow. Swallowed safely by the darkness, she slowed to a walk, treading lightly on the balls of her feet, listening intently. It was cold in the desert at night and beneath the skimpy fabric of the remodeled, tattered nightdress the chill tingled on her skin, an electric charge that invigorated her.

Reaching the far side of the gardens, Cat skirted the dark and empty exercise courts, with their high brick walls. She was aiming for the long, low sloping corrugated roofs of the barracks, grey prefabricated huts laid out in rows.

Ah-hah!

There was one structure that was larger and set off a little way from the rest. And there was light glowing in its small square windows, while elsewhere all was dark and slumbering.

The hut was set in a sea of gravel. As Cat crept towards it she put her feet down carefully. She took a zig-zag path, keeping to the mottled patterns of shadow.

Shit!

There were screens inside the windows, made of a fine wire mesh. They turned everything inside to a fuzzy blur.

Cat moved along the grey flank of the hut. She tried the next window and then the next. She got lucky. The mesh had parted from its frame, curling back slightly.

She peered through the gap.

She saw a face. The face of a pretty girl in her late teens, framed by blonde hair spread across a pillow. The eyes in the face were empty and staring, though the bare breasts with their virginal pink nipples were rising and falling slightly.

Cat moved to the next window. She found that if she tried hard she could see through the mesh. In soft focus she saw another blonde head staring straight up at the ceiling with blank eyes. The girl was completely naked, held down on a bunk bed with straps on her wrists and ankles. There were tubes coming from her arms.

If Cat twisted to peer through the mesh at an angle she could see a file of bunks take shape. Each was occupied by the pale naked form of a girl with fair hair, lying still and staring vacantly.

What the...?

There was movement beyond the mesh in the next window.

Cat saw a strange chair, a throne of grey metal, with something like a cone-shaped bell hanging above it. Transparent cables snaked from the tip of the cone, down behind the back of the chair. Other cables ran from the base of the chair, to a fat crystal bulb perched on a grey cabinet, the height of a tall man.

There was a naked girl sitting in the chair. Metal cuffs clamped her forearms and ankles. Eyes wide and glaring with terror, her mouth was screaming although her screams were stifled by a brutal ball gag. She was sweating, struggling madly, her flesh bulging against straps that secured her body. Drops of sweat flew from her flailing blonde hair as her head thrashed wildly from side to side.

Two men flanked the metal throne, pale men in tan safari suits. One stood observing the struggling girl, his face composed blandly. The other hovered over a panel cluttered with dials and odd hieroglyphs that glowed an eerie purple.

A hand made motions over the control panel. The cone began to descend slowly and then stopped, inches above the frantic girl's head. Beads of purple light coursed through the transparent, hollow cables, from down behind the chair and up to the hovering cone.

A purple beam fanned out from the bell of the cone, bathing the girl's squirming body. Instantly, she stopped struggling and went rigid, every muscle in her body clenched. Her eyes became fixed and staring.

The beads of purple light began to flow along the cables that extended from the base of the chair. Slowly, the strange bulb on the grey cabinet began to fill with a glowing lavender mist. When it was full, the hand moved over the control panel again. The light retreated along the cables, which became empty and transparent. The curtain of purple rose from the girl's body and was sucked back into the cone.

The girl went limp, her body suddenly slack and flabby, sagging in her bonds. Her head lolled forward slowly, eyes wide open. Her bare breasts were moving slightly.

What kind of a madhouse is this?

Cat watched the men unclamp the girl and carry her to a vacant bunk. She saw them lay her out flat on her back and attach the tubes to her arms.

The lights dimmed inside the hut. The men were heading for the door.

Her head in a spin, Cat retreated to the shadows.

She lay awake for a long time, staring into the darkness above her bed. Eventually, she sank into a troubled, disjointed sleep.

When she awoke, shafts of searing sunlight were slicing through the gaps in the heavy drapes.

"Ow-w-w...!"

The light hurt her eyes, making her blink. She was fuzzy-headed and her tongue was sticking to the roof of her mouth. She sat up in bed, yawning. Images from the night before flashed by like a rapid-fire slideshow. At first she thought it was just another dream. Then, coldly, she remembered that it wasn't.

Cat swung her long legs out of the bed and stood up quickly. She stripped off the ragged tatters of the nightdress.

The bathroom was palatial, in panels of gleaming marble and a blaze of mirrors, lit by polished brass lamps with shades like frosted glass flowers. An old-fashioned tub had faucets that were miniature dolphins made of gilt bronze.

"Just what the doctor ordered..."

Cat poured a cocktail of scented bath oils into the steaming water. She wallowed in the fragrant steam for a long time, the water tickling her chin, lapping at the lip of the tub.

"Aaaahhh...!"

There was a knock on the door.

"Ma'am...?"

Cat sat up in the bathtub and water splashed on the marble floor.

"Uh, I'm in the bath!"

Through the half-open door of the bathroom, she could make out the petite form of the Hispanic maid in her stiff black-and-white uniform. She was holding something.

"Your clothes, Ma'am. The clothes that the Master would like you to wear."

Cat's mind boggled.

What now? Scarlett O'Hara? Eva Braun?

"I'll leave them on the bed, Ma'am."

The maid bent to pick up the shredded remains of the nightdress and was standing there, her brow furrowed, looking at them.

Cat laughed, making the water slosh onto the floor again.

"Oh, sorry about that. I was just trying to make myself comfortable."

The maid frowned.

"Yes, Ma'am."

Cat heard the door close. She luxuriated a while longer, till the water became lukewarm. Then she stood up and washed her hair, with the hand-shower fashioned like a gilded conch shell.

When she was all done, Cat strolled back naked into the bedroom. She stepped into a shaft of bright sunlight and stood looking at herself in a long mirror. With her fair hair and tawny skin she was a glorious sculpture fashioned from precious gold.

Stark snapshots from the night before were still flashing behind her eyes, images of frantic, terrified girls being transformed into staring zombies. The velvety warmth all over her pampered body suddenly vanished and was replaced by ice.

With a shiver, Cat turned away from her eyes in the mirror. She walked across to the bed.

"Hm!"

She was mildly disappointed. Crisp and freshly laundered, an unpretentious pale blue bra and matching panties, grey socks and a pair of rugged desert boots with thick rubber soles. Spread out flat across the rumpled sheets there was a one-piece heavy duty jumpsuit that zipped up the front, in plain olive drab. It had baggy pockets on the chest and thighs and across the left breast pocket a tag with yellow lettering that said: "C. JOHNSON."

Cat picked up the basic garment and returned to the mirror. She held the jumpsuit up in front of her.

"Well," she chuckled. "It looks like I've enlisted."

Muffled by the window panes, Cat heard tires crunching on gravel. She crossed over and looked out through the crack in the curtains.

A convoy of three cars was pulling up on the forecourt below the marble patio. Plain grey cars dulled by desert dust, with dark windows and licence plates deliberately obscured by streaks of dirt.

"Hello…?"

As each car stopped rolling, tall, fit young men in windbreakers and slacks, sporting crew cuts and sunglasses, jumped out from the front passenger seat and opened the rear door. The men who got out were older, with iron in their cropped hair, their burly frames not quite right in their civilian suits because they strode with a brisk and martial gait up the marble steps.

"Uh-huh…"

At the top of the steps, the Colonel was waiting, in his crisp jungle fatigues and green beret. He saluted each arrival in turn and shook his hand before ushering the entire party into the chateau, below and out of Cat's field of vision.

It was then that Cat noticed the two fair-haired men in their tan safari suits, standing a little way off down the marble terrace, pale figures in the morning sun. Shoulder to shoulder, the men held back for a moment, before following the party into the building.

Cat got dressed. She slid the panties up her long, smooth thighs and made them snug on her hips. She slipped on the bra with a shimmy of her shoulders. Climbing into the GI jumpsuit and zipping it up, she sat on the edge of the bed to tug on the socks and lace up the boots.

She inspected herself in the mirror.

"Well, baby," she told herself. "It's goin' down."

Cat glanced out of the window again. The tall young men were standing guard by the dusty cars.

"Hmmm…"

Smiling, Cat slowly lowered the brass zipper of the jumpsuit.

The War Room was a stark iron box with cold steel walls and a low ceiling hung with strips of neon that gave everything an eerie greenish cast. A long metal table shaped like a stretched oval filled the room, ringed by chairs fashioned from steel tubing and padded black leather.

All along the wall, running the full length of the table, there was a map of the United States. It hung in semi-darkness, indistinct.

There was no chair at the head of the table. Instead there was a large screen of thick, opaque glass, set into the wall.

"Gentlemen. If I may call this meeting to order…"

A low masculine murmur faded. In his crisp combat fatigues, the Colonel occupied the seat to the right of the head of the table. The two pale blond men sat opposite him. They had removed their impenetrable sunglasses to reveal their almost colorless eyes.

"Thank you."

At intervals around the table, nine chairs were occupied. By men who sat up straight, the way they'd learned at West Point and Annapolis. Middle-aged men who looked fit, with hard faces and keen eyes.

The Colonel swivelled in his chair to look up at the screen at the head of the long table.

"We're ready for you, Sir."

Instantly, the dull grey glass came to life, with a pale yellow glow that shimmered on the polished table top and made bright pinpoints in the men's eager eyes.

"Good morning, gentlemen…"

The voice was very deep and disguised by some electronic filter. It sounded like it was issuing from the bowels of a crypt.

"I assume that all the proper security measures have been taken with regard to your attendance here today?"

Around the table all the men were nodding. Behind the glowing screen there was a silhouette, a blank, black anonymous cut-out of a man.

"Excellent. Now if you will turn your attention to the map..."

Suddenly, the huge map of the United States leapt out of the shadows, as light bloomed all over it. It was a military map, with codes and symbols denoting military entities and objectives, a jagged, jangling slash and thrust of arrows and numbers and icons that could be decoded only by a mind steeped in khaki.

The major cities, and the civil ports and airports were highlighted by tiny bulbs. The main roads and highways and railway lines were different colored arteries and tributary veins of light. Important bridges over any river broad enough to represent an obstacle were circled. Regimental and Divisional Codes denoted the military bases and airfields.

"The plan, gentlemen, remains essentially the same. There are a few modifications which you will find in the supplementary files provided for you. Please take a few minutes to acquaint yourself with them..."

On the gleaming table top, each man had a pale blue cardboard folder with his name on it. Quickly, they flicked back the covers and began to read.

The Colonel was quivering with excitement. His eyes were glinting in the cold light as he looked around the table, darting a quick glance at the silhouette behind the glowing screen.

The two pale men in their safari suits sat impassively, staring straight ahead.

Morning, boys..."

Cat came strolling down the sweep of marble steps that led down from the patio. The white marble glistened in the morning sun, which was climbing high into a singing blue sky.

"Beautiful morning, isn't it?"

As she advanced, she tweaked the zipper of the GI jumpsuit to just below her navel. She came down the steps slowly, seductively, walking like a model, hips swaying.

Her boots crunched in the gravel as she sauntered towards the tall young men grouped around the dusty grey cars. Raising her hands, she fluffed out her long golden hair, letting it flow down over her shoulders. The motion made her creamy cleavage swell in the cups that strained to confine it.

The men were all staring at her, from behind their dark glasses. Cat stopped, put her hands on her hips and grinned at them.

"My oh my, ain't this my lucky day," she drawled. "It looks like the Army is in town."

She saw their faces tighten. Thin-lipped, they exchanged quick glances and then stared back at her blankly.

Cat laughed deep in her throat, doing "that thing" with her long hair. She made her eyes flash like green fire.

"Aw, c'mon, guys! Someone tell me what's going on."

A slightly older man, with the burly authority of a non-com about him, turned his back on her and muttered something indistinct but insistent to the group. As one, they turned on their heels and walked away, going to the rear of the line of parked cars.

Scratching her head, Cat shrugged, grinning wryly.

"Oh well. I guess my mojo ain't workin' today."

"Thank you, gentlemen..."

All around the table, the men closed the blue folders. They sat up straight and looked at the map again.

"We will proceed as per the plan. The country will be placed under martial law, divided into the following districts and administered as follows..."

On the map, the entire West Coast was shaded deep blue.

"Admiral Stockbridge..."

The Mid-West became orange.

"General Cooley..."

Piece by piece, from coast to coast, from the Gulf of Mexico to the Canadian border, the map was transformed into a patchwork quilt of many colors.

"General Martin..."

"General Fuller..."

"Admiral Brewster..."

And one by one, each in turn, the men sat up a little straighter, the fire in their eyes igniting. Now they were all looking at the black silhouette in the radiant screen.

"Remember, my friends. The fate of our nation is in your hands!"

CHAPTER 14
Coup d'Etat

"How was your meal, my dear?"

The dining table was long enough to land a jet plane on. Its polished surface gleamed like dark glass.

"Just perfect, Colonel..."

Oak panelled walls were hung with panoramic tapestries illustrating ancient victories, punctuated by stag's heads, heraldic shields and crossed pikes and broadswords. Tattered, fading battle flags adorned the wooden beams and buttresses up above.

"...It's all quite perfect."

They were dining alone, in the glow of many candles. The elaborate dinner service was blue and gold and bore the Napoleonic cipher. There was exquisitely cut crystal for the wine and the cutlery was solid gold.

"Some more wine, perhaps?"

"Mmm, please, yes."

The decanter was mounted on a little gold wagon. With a flick of his hand, the Colonel sent it rolling down the length of the table, from one end to the other. Cat's touch brought it gently to rest.

"Thank you."

She topped up her glass, then raised it to her mouth and sipped. The Colonel watched, his eyes fixed upon her lips as they caressed the rim of the glass.

"You look magnificent, Miss Johnson."

Setting down the wine glass, Cat dipped her head modestly in acknowledgment of the compliment.

"Thank you, Sir."

I look ridiculous!

Her costume was pure "Gone With The Wind." Green satin trimmed by frothy white lace, with billowing sleeves and layer upon layer of flaring skirts, the bodice cut to bare her shoulders and offer a generous display of cleavage.

The dainty dress shoes were killing her feet.

Owww...!

"A worthy consort..."

Cat looked up sharply. Tonight, the Colonel was dressed for the regimental mess, in a white dinner jacket trimmed with gold braid and epaulettes and dark blue trousers with a broad red stripe.

"I...I'm sorry...?"

Enjoying the moment, the Colonel took a long, slow sip of his wine, and then sat back in the tall chair, stroking his small pointed beard.

"You have all the necessary qualifications, Miss Johnson."

Cat raised her eyebrows.

"I do? I mean, I'm very flattered, Colonel, but—"

He dismissed her doubts with a waft of his hand. Slipping a gold cigarette case from an inside pocket, he lit up and watched the smoke curl upwards to the roof beams. Cat sat and waited, gazing at him with what she hoped was the proper anticipation.

The Colonel took another drag and exhaled. He shifted in his chair and looked about to speak and Cat responded by leaning towards him eagerly. His eyes locked on her swelling cleavage and there was a repeated twitching at the corner of his mouth.

He sucked on the cigarette again and blew out smoke. His eyeballs weighed a ton as he struggled to lift them from the pale gold slopes of Cat's breasts.

His Adam's apple bobbed nervously. He cleared his throat.

"You are a perfect physical specimen, Miss Johnson. Quite flawless. The very embodiment of the purity of your race."

Cat made her eyes go wide with wonder.

Aw, shit! These fucking shoes are murder!

"And your philosophy concerning the supremacy of the white race and the proper subservience of the Negro, is similar to mine."

Asshole!

Rapt, Cat gazed into his small black eyes. She let him rant on for a while, expounding upon his bizarre world vision. Nodding, her eyes shining with enthusiasm, she made urgent, affirmative sounds designed to stimulate him.

It was working. He was becoming shrill. Perspiration glinted on his forehead. Cat let the tip of her tongue tease her ripe ruby lips. She made her bosom palpitate. Her green eyes gleamed behind long lashes lowered to half mast.

Flecks of spittle flew from his thin lips.

"I am offering you an empire, Miss Johnson! I want you to rule beside me!"

Cat bent forward towards him till her straining breasts were almost resting on the table top. Her voice was husky and breathless.

"And I want to serve you, Sir...in any—in every way—that I can..."

The salesman rubbed a peephole in the fog on the car window and peered out into the night. He saw nothing but the looming grey ghosts of concrete columns that supported the curve of the deserted flyover high above. Receding into the surrounding gloom, he glimpsed the scrubby, rubble-strewn wasteland that girdled the industrial outskirts of the city.

"MMmmph-h…!"

As his body shifted on the slippery upholstery there was a muffled complaint from down below.

Sprawled awkwardly across the back seat with his pants snagged down around his ankles, the salesman looked down at the tousled mane bobbing between his legs. He frowned at his watch.

"C'mon, babe…" he muttered. "Nothing's happening…!"

The hooker glared up at him through a tangle of hair, with eyes that had thick rims of mascara. Her bright red lips grimaced as she squirmed and re-adjusted. Her pendulous, pale breasts were flopping out of a leopard-print halter top.

"Jeez!" she grunted. "Hold still then, why don't ya? How can I—?"

A quiver. A distant vibration. Swelling and coming closer.

"Wha—?"

A mighty rumble. The ground beneath the parked car was shaking.

"Jeez! It's a fuckin' earthquake!"

The car was rocked and juddered, battered by a great roaring and clanking that came crashing down out of the blackness.

"OH, MY GOD…!"

The hooker tried to get up. The salesman tried to get down. They were wedged together, screaming.

Their screams were drowned by a cacophony of grinding and crunching.

The tank crushed the car like a tin toy and rolled on. Behind it came another, and another, and more, and behind the tanks there were half-tracks and trucks full of men, moving into the city.

"This way, my dear…"

The imposing, carpeted staircase coiled upwards from a floor of black and white marble. Its baroque railing was carved and heavily laden with gilding; its stately curving progress observed all the way up by stern Civil War generals and Marshals of France.

"Yes…Sir…"

Cat stumbled, reaching out to grab the ornate rail. The wine glass slopped, spilling on the stair carpet.

"…coming…Sir…"

She was pretending to be drunk, just drunk enough to encourage him. Clutching her wine glass, skirts flouncing, she hurried in his wake. The Colonel led her briskly along the landing and down a long corridor lit by brassy lamps, past tall doors and marble busts of ancient Romans.

"After you, Miss Johnson…"

Cat half expected to be confronted by a naked girl strung up for whipping, but the master bedroom was empty.

Other than that, it was exactly what she expected. Epic proportions, suffused by the ruddy glow of a massive white marble fireplace that was a riot of carved garlands and heraldry. The walls were covered with richly inlaid panelling and Renaissance tapestries. Persian rugs and an impressive assortment of English Regency, Louis XV and exotic oriental furniture were scattered about the room. From intricately fashioned rosettes on the ceiling, hung spectacular chandeliers, their crystal strands and droplets catching the firelight in ten thousand sizzling, scintillating sparks.

"Oh my, Colonel, isn't this just…?"

Dominating the room, was the towering four-poster, draped in gleaming cloth-of-gold. Cat stopped and stared at it. In her mind's eye, she saw the spread eagled girl, writhing under the whip.

Beads of cold sweat pricked her spine. She barely suppressed a shudder when the Colonel stepped up to her side.

"I have it on unimpeachable authority, Miss Johnson, that the Emperor Napoleon himself slept in that bed."

His eyes were exploring her cleavage. Cat wanted to hurl the contents of her wine glass into his nasty, leering face. In her mind's eye the whipped girl screamed and twisted.

Instead, she took a gulp of wine and swayed slightly, smiling sloppily.

"I hope," she chuckled. "That they've changed the sheets since then."

The Colonel twitched one of his brief, bleak smiles. His narrow eyes were glinting. They were saying *she's mine tonight!*

He took her by the elbow and was leading her sideways, at an angle away from the bed.

"Come, my dear, there's something I would like you to do for me…"

His touch made her flesh creep.

"Why surely, Colonel, whatever you—oh!"

Out of place in these period surroundings, she saw a brace of studio lights on chromed stands, framed by their silvered umbrellas, thick cables snaking across the extravagant rugs to a small, squat black transformer.

An eager light in his eyes, the Colonel took his station beside a tall telescopic tripod, supporting a silver and black Hasselblad.

"A hobby of mine…"

Cat switched on her modest face.

"Oh, well…I…I never saw myself as a model, Sir…"

His thin smile flicked on and off.

"Nonsense, my dear. You have all the qualifications."

He indicated a small side door on the far side of the room.

"You will find a selection of costumes in there. The choice is yours…"

Oh this is just marvellous!

Cat smiled at him and set her wine glass down on an ornamental side-table. She pivoted and headed for the narrow door.
"I am most intrigued as to which it will be."

Jesus!

The costume cupboard simulated a theater dressing room, with a wide mirror framed by light bulbs. An assortment of outfits and accessories hung from hooks mounted on the walls.

Jeee-zus!

There were bullwhips and cat-'o-nine-tails. Black leather hoods and ball gags and harnesses and cuffs studded with steel spikes. Coils of rope, shiny handcuffs, chains and spiked collars and heavy manacles that clanked as Cat brushed past them.

You have got to be joking, man!

Stacked on narrow shelves were devices that she could identify as metal clips and clamps of various shapes and sizes. And some that she could not even guess at.

Cat studied a small black box, about the size of a shoebox. It had dials and a crank handle on the side. Thin wires ran from the back of it, tipped with little crocodile teeth.

She picked up what appeared to be some kind of brass pump, with a long plastic nozzle at the end of a rubber tube. Grimacing, she put it down quickly.
"Ugh!"
Cat stopped short, her jaw dropping.
Standing in a row like trophies on display, she saw a file of plugs and phalluses. They started short and fat. Then they were very long and slim and some were curved.

Others were perfect replicas of the male organ. They started big and grew to the impossible. It made Cat groan, just to look at them.
Some were obviously electric. Some had large bulbs at the tip, or ribs or rubber studs.
One was covered in tiny steel needles.

No way!

Her stomach churned. She turned away quickly and found herself facing the costume rack.

It was all quite predictable; and strangely comic, after the violence and perversity on the opposite wall. There was a mail-order harem outfit, with transparent Turkish trousers and a cheesy bra with spangles and fringes. Or a riding costume: tight breeches, boots and blazer. And a tea chest stuffed full of frilly Victorian undergarments.

Smiling, she held up a pair of lacy bloomers. The smile vanished. There was blood on them.

She moved on…a schoolgirl uniform…a set of contrived dungeon rags…

"Aha!"

Cat burst out laughing.

"This will do nicely!"

When she came back into the bedroom, the Colonel was loading spare magazines for the Hasselblad.

"Ah, welcome back, my dear. Did you—?"

His voice trailed away. Cat smiled at him.

"You have an interesting mind, Colonel…"

Cat was dressed in black, from head to toe. She was in uniform. An S.S. uniform. The silver skull and crossbones glinted above the shiny peak of her cap. The jagged runes adorned her collar. A swastika armband made a splash of crimson on her sleeve. Her belt and boots gleamed like black glass. In her right hand she carried a slender silver-handled riding crop.

The Colonel gaped at her. He muttered something under his breath, it sounded like an incantation.

"…very interesting."

He swallowed hard. Sweat shone on his forehead.

"Wha-what…t-took you so long…?" he gulped.

Cat tapped the side of her boot with the tip of the riding crop.

"Your toys, Colonel. I was admiring your collection."

A kind of thrill went through him. It was visible.

"Ah! Yes…"

Suddenly his collar was very tight. Cat was smiling at him. The wicked leather switch was stroking her strong thigh, sheathed in the tight black breaches.

"Perhaps one day we might both play with your toys, Colonel…?"

Joy and disbelief flared like a fever in his eyes. Wild visions of Cat in all her blonde majesty, flaying slim brown backs and devising ever more inventive cruelties, tumbled over in his brain. In his excitement he almost knocked the tripod over.

"Yes!" he gasped. "Absolutely! Yes! You'll be an inspiration I'm certain!"

Cat looked pleased. Making little passes in the air with the crop, she strolled over to the camera. She stooped to peer into the viewfinder, glancing up at the lights.

"So, how would you like me, Colonel?"

He put on some music.

I might have known!

"Mood music, Miss Johnson. Marches of the Third Reich."

Yow…! Fun-kay…!

He positioned her by the enormous marble fireplace.

"Just one moment, my dear…"

There was a large painting above the fireplace, protected by purple velvet curtains. Reaching up on tiptoe, the Colonel tugged a tasselled cord.

"There!"

The curtains parted.

"Oh…!" Cat exclaimed.

In his customary brown tunic with its iron cross and Party badge, the Fuhrer stood on the terrace at Berchtesgaden, a man of destiny, gazing out upon an idealized alpine landscape bathed in a golden sunrise.

The Colonel looked at Cat in her black uniform, standing below the painting.

"Perfect!"

Cat leant elegantly on the marble mantelpiece, looking up at the Fuhrer. The shutter clicked.

"Excellent!"

She advanced a few paces and stood hands on hips, legs astride, the riding crop dangling by a thong from her wrist.

"Superb!"

Dealing with the silver buttons swiftly, Cat took off the tunic. She was naked underneath. She was naked to the waist, in the S.S. cap, the tight black breeches and boots.

"Aaaah-h…!" the Colonel exhaled.

Cat turned a chair round and straddled it. She stared straight into the lens. The riding crop caressed her cheek.

"Wonderful…!"

By day, the manicured lawns and groves and ornamental ponds across the river from the State Capitol were a haven for the lunchtime crowd, the young professionals in their suits and crisp skirts. Toddlers ran about on the grass and mothers chatted as they wheeled their baby buggies along the paths.

By night, the park had a change of personality. A very different society was formed, in the darkness beyond the lamp lit pathways and under the arches of the stone footbridges.

Needle park. Where deals were done for dreams.

"Hmgh…mmmm…mm…!"

Mumbling, the junkie rolled over on his back. The syringe slipped from his fingers and was snagged on the short grass.

A slight, shaggy figure in a faded plaid shirt and ragged blue jeans, he lay looking up at the night sky with half-closed eyes that glinted dully, his thin face pale in the moonlight. He felt good. He felt like he was wrapped in cotton wool, a deep warmth expanding slowly from the middle of his chest, down his arms and legs to his fingers and toes.

"Hmm…uuhh…?"

His eyes opened wide.

"Uhh…?"

There were flowers blooming in the sky. White flowers in the black sky. Spreading their petals. Strings of white flowers way up high. Floating. Drifting. More and more of them.

"Mmmmmm….."

The flowers were beautiful. So bright and white in the black sky. They were coming down. Getting bigger.

The flowers were enormous. They were filling the sky. There were hundreds of them. They were so pretty. And there were people in the flowers. People in the flying flowers.

"F-f-far…out……!"

He hardly felt the knife that cut his throat.

"Go! Go! Go!"

Commands were given in urgent whispers. Cocking their carbines, the paratroopers dashed across the bridges that led to the Capitol.

The Colonel's hot breath raked Cat's face. His hands were all over her naked body. Revulsion made her bowels churn, her skin crawling.

"Colonel…!"

His hands were clumsy and incompetent. He sprawled across her as she lay on the bed, losing his balance and falling on her. He was panting, his eyes feverish.

Flexing her strong body, Cat squirmed out from under him and sat up. She put a hand on his narrow chest to restrain him.

"Slow down, Colonel," she said breathily. "We have all night."

Arching her body towards him, Cat looked deep into his eyes, her moist lips parting slightly. She raised her hand from his chest and touched his hot cheek.

"All night…"

Her hand slid downwards, stroking his neck. The Colonel's body quivered. He groaned behind clenched teeth.

Her fingers delved beneath the high collar of his mess jacket. They found the point where his neck merged into his shoulder. She began to squeeze, increasing the pressure slowly, slowly…

"Uuuuhh-hh…"

The Colonel closed his eyes. His head fell forward. His body seemed to deflate. He sagged, sliding off the edge of the bed and crumpling to the carpet.

Cat strode quickly over to the discarded S.S. tunic, her bare feet sinking deep into the luxuriant carpet. Digging into a breast pocket, she produced a slim syringe filled with a colorless liquid.

She squatted down beside the Colonel's limp body and removed the tiny plastic cap from the tip of the needle. Holding the syringe up to the light, she made a squirt of liquid jet from its tip.

"Never leave home without it…"

Rolling up his sleeve, Cat injected the contents of the syringe into the Colonel's puny bicep.

"Sleep tight."

There was an ancient musket mounted on the wall. Cat popped the empty syringe into the muzzle and heard it rattle all the way down. She stepped over to the huge Imperial four-poster bed and rumpled up the sheets until they looked convincing. Then she hunkered down again and hooked her arms under the Colonel's body. With a grunt, she straightened her long legs, lifting him.

She dropped him onto the bed. Quickly, she stripped him. Her face was a mask of cold contempt, at the sight of his scrawny physique and meagre endowment.

"Go to red!"

"Red on!"

At the heart of command and control, men and machinery were saturated by a deep crimson glow, the false night that tuned their eyes to the darkness in the real world above the surface.

"Up periscope!"

The river was like black glass, wrinkled by its sluggish whorls and eddies. The periscope made a slit that left a faint white streak behind.

"Up periscope, aye aye, Sir!"

Reversing his cap so the brim faced backwards, the Captain leant forward to peer through the eyepiece. A blurring film of water cleared in an instant and snared in the cross-hairs he could see the familiar dome of the State Capitol, stark in the moonlight.

With a grunt of satisfaction, the Captain stood back.

"Down periscope!"

"Down periscope, aye aye, Sir!"

The Captain turned to a burly figure, standing beside him, in the helmet and mottled battledress of the U.S. Marines.

"We're there, Major. From here on in, the rest is up to you and your men."

The Colonel was jerked into consciousness.

"Uh! Wha—?"

Blinking, he sat up in bed, raising a hand to shield his eyes.

"Good morning, Colonel…"

The bright morning flooded the bedroom as Cat drew back the heavy curtains. With the light behind her, her pale dressing gown was transparent and he could see the silhouette of her long legs as she advanced upon him.

"Time to get up."

She was bending over the bed, offering him a dainty blue and gold cup embossed with the heraldic Napoleonic "N." The front of the dressing gown parted as she leant towards him and he glimpsed a bare breast.

"Uhhh…ah…what…?"

The inside of the Colonel's mouth was like blotting paper, sucking up the thick sweet coffee. His tongue was numb and felt twice its normal size. There was a dull ache behind his eyes and a nagging throb in his temples.

He gulped the coffee while Cat hovered over him attentively. He tried to remember and drew a blank.

"Wha…what happened? D-did we…?"

Cat leant forward and gave him another fleeting glimpse of her breast. She smiled, her eyes glowing.

"You were glorious, Sir!"

Dickhead!

The Colonel drained the cup and handed it back to her. Squinting, he looked around the bedroom, at the trail of discarded garments that led to the rumpled bed.

"You were magnificent!" Cat declared, as she took the empty cup away and returned immediately, bearing a billowing robe of royal blue silk, spangled with gold fleur-de-lys.

"Er…yes…Yes…!"

Heaving himself out of bed, the Colonel strained to hide his confusion. Beaming, Cat helped him into the sumptuous robe, which billowed copiously, too big for his thin body.

"…ah…er…you are an inspiration, my d-dear Miss Johnson…!"

His brain was scrambled with fractured images, of golden hair and green eyes and tawny flesh.

Cat brought him a pair of velvet slippers and knelt down so he could slip his small feet into them. Knotting the golden cord of his robe, the Colonel studied his Imperial reflection in the large mirror on his antique dressing table. The sight of him as he liked to see himself made him feel a lot better.

He looked down at Cat who still knelt at his feet, gazing up at him.

You disgusting little shit!

He liked to see her kneeling before him. With what he fancied to be a gesture both imperious and gracious, the Colonel extended a hand and raised her to her feet.

You make me want to puke!

He sneaked another peek at himself in the mirror and then bestowed his thin smile upon her.

"There are great deeds afoot, my dear Miss Johnson. And I want you by my side to share the glory with me!"

The President liked flying in Air Force One. It made him feel Presidential. He got to wear a jacket with the Presidential seal on the breast. The headrests on all the seats had the Presidential seal on them. The cups and saucers had the Presidential seal on them.

"Your papers, Mr President…"

And there were his official box files and briefcases, with the Presidential seal on them.

"Thank you, Sam."

Sam was a well-scrubbed and fit young man with a blonde crew cut who packed his neat blue suit well.

"More coffee, Sir?"

The President was a square-jawed, stocky individual in his early fifties with thinning reddish hair and bright blue eyes set close together in a square head set on a short, thick neck. He had the look of an old College football player, the kind of guy who, in the privacy of his study, would still wear his sweatshirt with the faded letters across the chest.

"No thank you, Sam. I'm fine."

The President spread the documents out on the small formica-topped table that extended across his lap. The papers had the Presidential seal on them.

Opening a slim crocodile skin case, he extracted his gold-rimmed reading glasses. He adjusted them on the bridge of his battered nose and reached out for the gold fountain pen, unscrewing the cap. The pen had a tiny Presidential seal on it.

He began to read, scribbling notes in the margins.

"Sir...!"

He hated being interrupted. Frowning, the President pushed the spectacles downwards and peered up over the top of them.

"Yes? What is it, Sam?"

His aide was stooping to see out of the small TV-shaped cabin window.

"We have company, Sir."

"What?"

His frown growing darker, the President extricated himself from behind the table and crossed the carpeted aisle to look out of the window.

"Good God!"

In the singing blue sky, high above a mantle of white cloud that hid the earth below, like a sleek pale grey dart, an Air Force jet fighter was hanging parallel to the wingtip of the Presidential Boeing 707.

The aide went from port to starboard.

"And there's another one over here, Sir."

Two men entered the President's cabin. One burly, the other tall and lean, in dark blue Air Force uniforms adorned with silver braid.

The President glared at the burly man.

"Major, would you mind telling me just what the hell is going on?"

The Air Force Major lifted his hand. There was a big black .45 in it.

"Please sit down, Mr President."

The President went bright red in the face.

"What!" he spluttered. "What the—?"

His aide took a step forward, his right hand slipping quickly under his jacket.

The .45 boomed. In the confines of the cabin the detonation was louder than sound. It was a physical sensation like a buzz saw ripping across the skull.

Sam jacknifed in the middle. Lifted clean off his feet, he was hurled backwards and hit the bulkhead housing the cabin door. With a look of wide-eyed surprise frozen on his face, he sat down hard then slid sideways, a big red stain spreading on his white shirtfront.

"My God! Major! Wha—?"

The huge bore of the .45 zeroed in on the President's heart.

"Please sit down, Mr President."

"Please sit down, Mr President."

In the cold iron box of the War Room the Colonel's voice had a thin and frosty echo. He was wearing his neatly pressed jungle fatigues.

"Mr President..."

The strips of neon gave the President's face a waxy, corpselike pallor. He was standing at the head of the long metal oval table, between two of the fair-haired pale-eyed men in their crisp safari suits.

He took a deep breath, squaring his shoulders. The chair at the head of the long table was a recent addition, a throne of padded black leather and chromium tubing, with a high adjustable headrest. Straps and buckles dangled from the back of the headrest and from the arms of the chair.

The President glanced at the chair nervously.

"I prefer to stand."

His thin lips compressed, the Colonel made a quick impatient gesture with a hand holding a gold-tipped swagger stick.

"Gentlemen…"

The blond twins stepped in close and took the President by the elbows. He was still a strong fit man but their strength was supernatural. They handled him like a small child. Pulling him down onto the black throne, a single hand spread on his chest was enough to hold him there while the straps and buckles were secured tightly around his forehead and his wrists.

Sweat shone on the President's face, a face turning red with anger and indignation. Tiny veins pulsed in his temples.

"What is the meaning of this? Who are—?"

For the first time, he noticed the large opaque glass screen, high on the wall at the far end of the table, as it became suffused by a pale glow that shimmered on the steel walls and polished table top.

"Good afternoon, Mr President…"

The anonymous silhouette spoke in its deep disguised voice.

"As I am sure you will appreciate, I will come straight to the point"

Beads of sweat dropped from the President's forehead. His face contorted and the sinews corded in his thick neck as he clenched his fists and heaved against the straps with all his might.

"Resistance is futile…"

Panting, he gave up the struggle.

The Colonel sneered, tapping his thigh with the tip of the swagger stick. The pale blond men stood impassively, flanking the chair, staring straight ahead at the glowing screen.

"This nation, so woefully handled by you and your pitifully weak and liberal administration, is now in the safe hands of forces dedicated to the restoration of order and strong government"

The President's face was a frozen mask of horror and amazement. He was breathing heavily.

"What! W-who are you? You're insane!"

There was a slight stiffening of the shoulders, barely detectable, in the silhouette framed in the luminous glass. The distorted voice droned on relentlessly.

"You will now do your country a service by broadcasting to the American people a short speech that we have prepared for you"

One of the blond twins leant across and placed a blue cardboard folder on the steel table top in front of the President's chair. He flipped the folder open to reveal a solitary neatly typed sheet of paper.

The President glared up at the screen, straining against the straps again.
"Go to hell!"
"I am afraid you have no choice, Mr President..."
One of the pale men took something from the deep hip pocket of his safari suit. Two small cubes made of a colorless crystal. His face expressionless, he turned towards the figure trapped in the black chair.

The President was sweating again, breathing quickly. Wide-eyed, he looked across the table at the Colonel.
"What are you doing? Who are these people?"
The Colonel's thin smile flickered coldly.
Bronze bolts projected from the strap that secured the President to the high headrest, in line with his temples. The crystal cubes clipped onto them neatly.
"What is this? You can't do this to me...!"
The blond man stepped back from the throne. His twin placed a small grey metal box on the table. It had winking purple pin lights and asymmetrical projections etched with jagged symbols.
"This is your last chance, Mr President..."
"Go fuck your—!"
The blond man touched the box with a fingertip. Instantly, the crystal cubes glowed a pale purple.
"Aaaah-hh-h!"
The President's face turned chalk white. His eyeballs bugged out in their sockets.
"AAAAA-AA-GG-HHHH...!"
"UUUUU-UUGG-GHH-HHH!"
"G-GG-GHAA-AAAGH-H-HH-HHH!"

CHAPTER 15
State of Emergency

"My fellow Americans..."

The networks asked their viewers to tune in for a special broadcast from their President at precisely 7 p.m. Disturbed by the unaccustomed sight of tank columns on their highways and guard posts on their street corners, the citizens gathered anxiously in front of their TV screens.

"I am speaking to you at a grave and significant moment in our history..."

Wearing a sober suit suitable for the occasion, the President was seated at a large desk set against a backdrop of heavy blue drapes. The desk had the Presidential seal on it and behind it, over the President's shoulder, was the American flag.

"For too long now, our great nation has been under attack from within by the cancer of reckless radicalism and disorder..."

If his voice seemed a little flat and colorless, no one really noticed. A steady monotone was pretty much this President's normal style.

"Our college campuses have become a hotbed of revolution and our inner cities a breeding ground for crime, wanton destruction and violence. Decent law-abiding Americans no longer feel safe on their own streets..."

The President's face looked a little pale and waxy, but that was probably the unflattering studio lights. And with those battered football player's features, he was never going to win any beauty contests anyway.

"But now the time has come to take action against the dark forces that are polluting the sanctity of our ideals and the purity of our noble race..."

A few eyebrows were raised here and there. That wasn't his normal prose style.

"These criminals and so-called revolutionaries will be dealt with ruthlessly. This cancer will be excised from the body of our nation...!"

What no one noticed was that the President's eyes never blinked, not once during the course of his entire broadcast.

In the smoldering heartland of the ghetto, the Black Militants tried to defend their headquarters, firing from the windows and the rooftop, the dark mass speckled with winking muzzle flashes.

Their bullets pinged uselessly off the steel flanks of the armored troop carriers that bulldozed through the barricades made of rubble and burnt-out cars. They could only watch in frozen horror as a tank turret rotated slowly, angling its long cannon towards them.

A tremendous flash. A roar. The earth shook. Dust billowed and the sidewalk quivered like a drum skin. The building imploded and crumpled in on itself, folding slowly, floor by floor, down to the ground. Where it once stood was a vast column of dust and smoke, glowing red in the night sky.

In the desert the sky was full of silver stars.

Like the silver stars on the shoulders of the men being chauffeured in a camouflaged collection of jeeps and brawny all-terrain vehicles, men with keen hawkish features and long hunting rifles.

The vehicles were drawn up in a shallow crescent on the crest of a low ridge. Slab-faced drivers in olive drab kept the motors running, a steady drone that rose up above the boundless, rugged plain, stark and silvery in the moonlight.

The Colonel looked up at the Moon.

"A perfect night for a hunt, my dear."

They were standing in the wide open back of a heavily adapted pick-up, with buffers and rails fitted with mounts for heavy-caliber machine-guns. The Colonel had dressed himself for the occasion as the Great White Hunter, complete with broad-brimmed bush hat.

"Yes. Yes it is, Sir."

Cat had been provided with a basic one-piece jumpsuit mottled in shades of sand and earth. A short M-1 carbine was slung over her shoulder.

His face suffused with excitement, the Colonel gazed out left and right along the line of vehicles poised on the crest of the long low ridge.

"An excellent idea, I think, to celebrate this great moment in history in this way. A traditional recreation and festivity for the rulers of men, from ancient times!"

In the crisp clear moonlight the keen anticipation on the faces of the other members of the party was plain to see.

"Yes, Colonel," Cat produced a convincing smile. "I'm certainly looking forward to it."

He turned to admire her. She stood tall, with an athletic poise. Her body was magnificent, her long hair shone like white gold in the moonlight.

The Colonel beamed.

"You grace us with your presence, my dear Miss Johnson. You are a true Amazon!"

Cat opened her mouth but couldn't think of anything to say. So she just smiled again.

The Colonel glanced at his watch. In the other vehicles, the men with stars on their shoulders were becoming impatient.

"Well, Colonel...?"

"Come on! Let's go!"

The Colonel showed his teeth in a thin smile. He lifted his arm and pointed.

"Don't worry, General. Here they come."

Down below the ridge, in the distance, a plume of dust was a pale glow advancing towards them. Within minutes, the dark blob at its heart took shape and revealed itself to be a drab Army truck, its canvas sides swaying from side to side as it crunched and rattled across the broken ground.

"Aha! At last!"

"That's right, Admiral. Not long now."

The truck crunched to a halt at the foot of the slope. There were rough, urgent voices from inside its covered back, and lighter, frightened ones.

Burly figures in khaki jumped down onto the ground. Two stood back, their M-16s at the ready. Others made chains and bolts clatter as they lowered the heavy tailgate.

"Come on! Out! Out!"

Two slender forms half jumped, half fell out of the back of the truck, stumbling to their knees as they landed on the stony sand.

"Stay there!"

Caught in the glare of the headlamps were two girls with frightened faces, a pale brunette captured on the road and a colored go-go dancer. Their hair was in disarray. They had been stripped to their skimpy bras and panties and their skin gleamed with terror sweat.

"Well, Colonel, you sure do things in style!"

"I thought you might like it, General."

Kneeling on the sand, the girls stared up at the semi-circle of vehicles with eyes that were wide and full of fear.

Oh surely not...!

Cat's blood turned into ice water. The Colonel turned to rake her with a smile that cut her like the edge of a razor. Her flesh crawled.

"What do you think, my dear? Inventive, yes?"

She was paralyzed. It took all of her strength to make her head nod.

"Yes indeed, Colonel. Quite a novelty."

He was very happy. There were excited voices coming from the vehicles all around.

"I thought our guests might appreciate it. The military man is a hunter by nature, and his prey is human."

He gestured at the soldiers standing by the truck down below. Reaching down, they seized the girls by the hair and hauled them to their feet. The girls screamed. They stood there with their bare feet on the jagged ground, swaying, holding their arms across their near naked bodies.

The Colonel produced a hand-held megaphone and aimed it at the frightened girls.

"*YOU WILL HAVE ONE HOUR'S HEAD START...*"

The girls glanced at each other, confused.

"*...AND THEN WE WILL COME LOOKING FOR YOU. IF YOU CAN ELUDE CAPTURE UNTIL DAWN YOU WILL BE ALLOWED TO LIVE...*"

The girls were trembling visibly. Their eyes were huge.

"*...BUT IF YOU ARE CAUGHT BEFORE DAWN COMES THEN YOU WILL BE KILLED...*"

The girls were moaning with terror, their bodies shaking.

Cat almost turned away, her gorge rising. But she summoned up every ounce of her will and remained rigid, staring straight ahead. There was only a flash of light in her eyes, which the Colonel interpreted as excitement.

The Colonel gestured again and the soldiers seized the girls by the scruff of the neck. Screaming and protesting shrilly, the captives were sent stumbling out into the forbidding vastness of the desert.

"*RUN! RUN AS FAST AS YOU CAN...!*"

The thin bark of his laughter chased them into the darkness as the girls staggered into a clumsy jog and were swallowed up by a great pool of shadow.

Under the cover of darkness, the round-ups continued.

Army trucks rolled onto the college campuses and disgorged squads of heavily armed troops that kicked down the doors and stormed up and down the stairways in the dormitories.

Screaming and protesting, young men and women in jeans and T-shirts, some in their underwear, some stark naked, were dragged out by the hair and hurled into the trucks. If they resisted they were kicked into submission by the soldiers' heavy boots or smashed in the face with rifle butts.

"*IT'S TIME!*"

Engines revved in a concerted roar. With the coordination of a chorus line, the camouflaged vehicles dipped from the ragged crest of the ridge and rolled down the shallow slope.

"*GO! GO! GO!*"

When they hit the floor of the desert, the jeeps and reinforced pick-ups accelerated, stirring up a luminous tower of dust. Searchlights blazed into life, as their searing beams lanced deep into the darkness that retreated before them.

Panting, the girls ran for their lives.

The chill night air rasped raw in their throats. Their legs ached and their hearts pounded until they thought their ribs would crack. The rough, brittle surface of the desert made their bare feet bleed.

They ran and ran till they could run no more. On the down slope of a wrinkled dune they staggered to a shambling halt.

"Ooo-hh-h-h...!"

The hippy chick sagged until she was sitting slumped on the sand. Her companion stood bent over, head hanging down, her hands on her knees. They were gasping, breasts heaving as they strained to suck in air. Their bare skin was glistening all over and the sweat was streaming down them. Chilled by the night air it was almost scalding.

Dancing lights glowed on the jagged black horizon, erasing the stars. There was a distant mechanical drone.

"Oh...G-G-God...!"

Moaning with terror, the girls struggled upright and stumbled into a run again.

"Driver! Stop!"

In response to Cat's hand signals, the Colonel called a halt.

"What is it, Miss Johnson? Have you seen something?"

He gripped his elegant hunting rifle tightly. Cat tried to look keen and cunning.

"No, Colonel, just a feeling."

She put on her predatory face. The Colonel was interested.

"Indeed?"

Cat surveyed the moonlit silver sands and crumbling outcrops, the dark dots and smudges of scrub. She weighed the M-1 carbine in her hands, every inch the huntress.

"You may be right, Sir," she mused. "They may just run and run until they drop..."

"But?"

"But my instincts tell me that they may go to ground and simply try to hide and wait it out till daybreak."

The Colonel was very pleased with her. She had obviously entered fully into the spirit of the thing.

"Yes...perhaps...but I..."

Before he had time to think, Cat had vaulted out of the back of the pick-up and was standing on the sand.

"There's a lot of cover around here, Colonel. With your permission I'd like to stay for a while and try my luck. You can come back for me later."

The Colonel looked doubtful for a moment. But he was a man of decision. He nodded.

"Very well, my dear. It would be a shame were you to miss out on the kill, but so be it."

Cat smiled up at him. He liked looking down at her while she smiled up at him.

"Ah yes, Colonel," she said. "But it's the thrill of the hunt. The hunt is the thing!"

The Colonel barked his nasty laugh.

"Yes indeed, my dear Miss Johnson! Good hunting!"

Cat waited until the Colonel's tail-lights had diminished to pinpricks, until they were gone altogether.

Okay...

Slinging the carbine, she reached deep into a side pocket and tugged out a small grey metal box that fit snugly in her palm. She pulled out a stubby chrome antenna.

I hope this works...

There was a tiny button set into the side of the little box. Cat pressed it. Then she sat down cross-legged on the sand and waited.

There was always another dune to climb, on bloody feet and aching legs that were turning to water.

"Uuuuuhh-hh-hhh-hh...!"

The crusty lip at the summit crumbled and the colored girl lost her balance.

"AH!"

Instinctively, the two girls grabbed for each other but only succeeded in bringing them both down.

"AAAAA-AA-HHHGH-HH!"

Limbs flailing, they rolled and tumbled heavily, all the way to the bottom of a long, steep slope, rubbed raw on a carpet of rubble and small stones. There they sprawled, one on top of the other, the sweat making the scrapes and bloody scratches sting horribly, sand and grit stuck to their bare skin.

They heard that distant drone again, only now it seemed a little louder. The moving glow on the skyline looked brighter.

"Ooohh-hh nn-n-noo-o-o...!"

"Hullo, Uncle John!"

As he heaved his billowing, kaftan-clad bulk out of the jeep his niece ran across the sand, threw her arms around him and hugged him hard and for a long time.

"Hey! Hey! Hey!" he chuckled, a deep resonance that tingled and warmed her. "I'm glad to see you too, Princess."

He was surprised to see tears brimming in her eyes.

"Oh, Uncle John, these people are pure evil...!"

In a rush, her eyes bright with a kind of fever, she told him about the hunt.

"We have to stop it! We have to save them!"

John Warburton shook his head sadly.

"We can't, angel."

Cat took a step back. Her eyes were huge.

"But—!"

Her Uncle laid his big hands gently on her trembling shoulders.

"We can't interfere," he said softly. "It would ruin everything."

Cat shook her head fiercely, her golden hair swirling. Stepping close, her Uncle cupped her face in his hands. Her hot tears trickled through his fingers.

"We'll stop them, my darling, don't you worry," he said soothingly. "Now tell me everything."

In a subdued murmur, pausing every now and then to collect herself, Cat gave her Uncle a detailed report. And when she had finished, her Uncle put his arms around her until she recovered.

The girls were screaming.

Cables were looped around their ankles. The trucks drove round and round in a great circle, beneath a pall of silver dust, dragging the girls across the jagged ground.

Clustered in the back of the trucks, the hunters swigged from beer cans and champagne bottles and watched the shrieking girls with glaring eyes and open mouths.

Alone again, Cat could hear it all. The cacophony of the engines and the coarse shouts and laughter, pierced through by the terrible screams.

I'm going to kill you, Colonel. And I'm going to enjoy it

By dawn the football stadium was full to the brim of its towering terraces.

Many were bloody and bruised, some with bayonet, bullet and shrapnel wounds. Some lay packed close together on the grass of the field, unconscious or groaning, their blood soaking into the ground. The rest were ordered to sit or kneel with their hands on their heads, watched over by young soldiers with blunt hard faces, carrying black M-16s and ready to use them.

Officers were going through the crowd, snapping out orders. Occasionally, a group or an individual would be commanded to stand up and would be taken away into the bowels of the stadium. There the facilities had been transformed into interrogation centers and the corridors way down below echoed with angry shouts and screaming.

There was sullenness and defiance on some faces, mostly male, black faces. Even a look of defiance could be rewarded with a blow from a rifle butt, but the black faces wore their bruises as a badge of pride.

There were middle-aged white professors and a few writers and artists who tried to reason and debate with their captors. An officer simply lifted his .45 and dropped one of them with a single bullet through the head and that was the end of the debate.

Most of the white faces were very young and very frightened. The boys who tried to give the near naked and naked girls their sweatshirts or T-shirts were clubbed senseless and the naked girls were forced to kneel with their hands behind their heads while the young soldiers stared at them.

A sleek private helicopter came and hovered for a while over the seething anthill that was the football stadium seen from that height.

It gave the man in the passenger's seat enormous satisfaction, to look down upon it all. This was his natural position in life. It was his destiny!

Another night. Another hunt. And two more girls died screaming in the desert.

The geometric gardens of the Colonel's chateau slumbered beneath the stars, dappled with stark silver and deep blue shadow. The only movement was the regular passing of a sentry.

A fleeting flicker, the merest sliver of a shadow that flitted unseen, was tacking quickly between the great lakes of darkness that dappled the swathes of silver.

The figure was lithe and slim and all in black. It moved with swift suppleness, now crouching low, now springing lightly over some obstacle, a clipped hedge or marble parapet. The bulging pack slung on its back seemed weightless.

Every now and then, submerged in a pool of shadow, the figure would pause. It would pluck from the backpack something small and metallic. These cryptic objects it planted in the shrubbery, completely hidden, or concealed in the nooks and crannies of the ornate statuary.

In the Command Center, a pale blond man stiffened suddenly and hunched a little closer over a glowing screen.

His twin was instantly at his side.

There was an electronic grid on the screen, marked out in intersecting squares and triangles. A line of tiny hieroglyphics had flashed up on the screen, below a single red dot that was winking urgently. The dot was moving, crossing the border of one square and entering its neighbor.

The blond men glanced at each other. One of them nodded.

Some instinct made the slim figure in black twist and turn quickly.
"HUH!"
The sentry's rifle butt swished by harmlessly.
"UH!"

The lithe shadow struck like a snake with the hard edge of its hand. The sentry crumpled to the ground.

Heavy boots crunched on the gravel. A squad of slab-faced men in khaki overalls came running down the long path that led from the barracks. They were brandishing short clubs.

With eyes glinting dully and expressionless faces, the squad formed a circle around the slim figure in black. There was a pause. Then, as one, swinging their clubs, they moved in to attack.

"HAAA-YEEEE-AHH!"

Dancing on its toes, the intruder bobbed and weaved, dodging the clubs.

"YAH!"

A leaping, spinning kick jerked one man's head back and felled him, unconscious.

"YAH!"

The spin flowed into a feint, a quick sidestep and a short punch to the next man's chest. The force of it paralyzed him. Now the edge of the hand slashed across his adam's apple and he crumpled, vomiting blood.

"HUH!"

A third man, his onrushing bulk exploited in a smooth hip throw, flew in a yelling backwards somersault and bowled over two of his companions.

Four and Five coordinated their attack, coming in from front and back, swinging their clubs. At the very last split-second, their black-clad quarry, with a supple twist, appeared to simply dematerialize. Unable to stop himself, Number Four laid Number Five out cold with a crushing blow to the side of the head.

"Uh...?"

Number Four stood dumbfounded, looking down at his prostrate colleague in confusion. His adversary stepped up behind him without making a sound on the gravel. Slender black-gloved fingers were placed deftly on the spot where his bull neck merged into his shoulder.

"Uuuuuhhh...hh...hhh...."

His eyes rolled up until only the whites showed. His jaw dropped. He drooled. His legs buckled and he sat down on the path and then rolled over, fast asleep.

Numbers Six to Ten were forming a rank on the grass a little way back from the path.

"HAH!"

The intruder made a move towards them, a bluff that worked, making them take a nervous step backwards.

Then the figure in black turned and ran and was poised to leap and disappear into a great lake of shadow.

Like a statue carved out of silver, a man stepped out into the moonlight, directly in the intruder's path, a pale blond man in a safari suit, with unblinking colorless eyes.

"AH-YA!"

Halting, the intruder struck a defensive pose. The pale man stood there impassively. He raised his hand. It was holding a stubby metal baton.

The baton had a crystal tip and seemed to be vibrating slightly.

"Aaaa-aa-a-hhh-gghh-hh…!"

The figure in black lost its poise. It swayed. Clapping its hands to its hooded head, it staggered and fell on the silver-washed grass.

"Uuuuu-aaa-a-a-hhh-ggghh-hhh…!"

The pale man walked forward slowly, his arm extended, aiming the baton. Groaning, the intruder clutched its head, writhing in agony.

A rhythmic feminine grunting rebounded off the polished wooden walls.

"Ugh…ninety-five…!"

"Unnghh..hh…ninety-six…!"

As she heaved the twin black barbells up in a smooth bicep curl, Cat admired her form in the full-length mirror in front of her. She was wearing a sleeveless white singlet made of a thin synthetic stuff, pale blue running shorts and scuffed yellow sneakers over fuzzy grey gym socks.

"Uhh..ghh…ninety-seven!"

A healthy glow of perspiration shone on her face, on her strong sculpted shoulders, her bare arms and thighs.

"Nnn..nn..gghh…ninety-eight!"

The gym was a huge barn set way at the back of the great gardens, behind the low slung barrack huts. Its great curved ceiling was supported by a web of steel beams. The high walls, hung with climbing bars and ropes, had a skin of highly polished pine. The gleaming parquet of the floor was stacked on several levels linked by short ramps, and cluttered by the very latest in fitness technology.

"Uunn..nn..gh…ninety-nine!"

There were tall green doors at the far end of the gym. They opened quietly. The light of a bright morning blurred the edges of the figure that stepped inside.

"Mmm..mmff…one hundred!"

Cat swung round fluidly to set the barbells down in their place on a tall rack of varied weights. Hands on hips and feet astride, she surveyed herself in the tall mirror, her shoulders rising and falling quickly.

She took a long, deep breath, inflating her chest slowly. The hard points of her breasts pricked the thin stuff of the vest.

There was a sharp intake of breath from behind her. Cat turned swiftly.

"Bravo, Miss Johnson! Your conditioning is excellent!"

The Colonel applauded her, the handclaps echoing sharply off the gleaming walls.

Shit! Now what?

"Good morning, Sir."

For today, he had chosen to adorn himself in an officer's cap with gold braid and a patent leather peak, a neat khaki battledress jacket and tan chino's tucked into mirror polished riding boots.

Cat stood to attention. The Colonel's eyes gleamed, locked on the thrust of her superb breasts.

Staring, he swallowed hard.

Creep!

Then he gestured magnanimously with a gloved hand.
"Please, stand easy, my dear."
Cat relaxed and he was able to wrench his gaze away from her chest.
"If you are done, Miss Johnson, I would like you to accompany me…"
He was indicating the doors. Nodding, Cat plucked down a large towel that was draped on the wall bars. She dabbed her face, then began to mop the sheen of sweat from her arms and her thighs.

The Colonel watched, his thin lips parting slightly to show his teeth and the nervous tip of his tongue. Cat took her time, enjoying his barely concealed agitation.

Finally, she flung the towel down on a long wooden bench. From the depths of a blue sports bag, she pulled a pair of baggy sweatpants and tugged them on, cinching the drawstring waistband securely. Then came a matching red track suit top with white stripes along the shoulders and the arms. She shrugged into it and zipped it up from her waist, up and over her breasts to her chin. The Colonel looked disappointed.

She gazed at him expectantly. Clearing his throat, the Colonel smiled abruptly.
"Ah! Right. Yes…"
He jerked an arm towards the doors.
"Please come with me, my dear. I have an amusing diversion for you…"

The stadium was full of screams.

Pale men in identical safari suits, with fair hair and colorless eyes masked by impenetrable shades, were walking amongst the knots and rows of kneeling prisoners.

Supervised by the pale men, squads of stone-faced young soldiers stopped and started, turned this way, then that, wending their way through the throng, wading through the tightly packed bodies and the moans.

Suddenly, a pale man would stop, look and then point. The soldiers would spring forward. Twisting and screaming, a young woman would be seized by the arms and hauled to her feet. Any protest or attempt at intervention was crushed instantly by a blow from a rifle butt or the thrust of a bayonet.

Sobbing, the selected girls were dragged and half-carried to a line of empty Army trucks parked in the long tunnel that led out of the vast humming bowl of the stadium. Crying out in fear and pain, they were lifted up by the arms and the legs and the hair and tossed roughly into the semi-darkness inside the olive drab canopies. The metal tailgates crashed shut behind them, chains and bolts clattering.

The convoy drove out of the stadium and out of the city. It took the seemingly endless highway into the baking desert.

In the stifling darkness, the girls huddled together, their bruised bodies aching, their throats raw with thirst. If any of them had been capable of noticing anything, through a fog of terror and exhaustion, she would have noticed that she and all of her companions were blonde.

The cellar door was a grim ironbound slab of dark wood.

"After you, my dear..."

The Colonel gripped the heavy, corroded ringbolt and twisted it, an effort for his thin wrist. He heaved and the mighty door swung open slowly, its ancient hinges grinding.

"Thank you, Colonel, I—"

As she stepped in through the doorway, the groans were like a gust of wind in her face.

"I...I......"

Cat stopped in her tracks. She stood and stared.

"Oh!"

She had passed through a gateway in time.

"What do you think, Miss Johnson?" The Colonel was smiling. "Do you like my little playroom?"

The floor was constructed of glistening stone slabs. Walls of crude brick and stone masonry were spanned by rough-hewn heavy beams and buttresses high above. Torches set in rusting iron brackets on the walls cast a musty glow. Oily tendrils of smoke snaked up and twisted around the dark beams.

An assembly of ropes and pulleys dangled from the beams up above. The walls were garlanded with strands of heavy iron chains and manacles. Long metal tongs, pincers and claws hung on hooks, like a grotesque bouquet, between the garlands of chains. There was a table, its scarred top mottled with old stains, heaped with coils of rope, tossed down beside dull black clamps and screws and more mysterious devices. In the corner, a brazier squatted on tripod legs, the wooden handles of the irons thrusting from coals that glowed deep red.

"Every detail is authentic. Many of the pieces you see here are genuine."

There were indeterminate, mechanical sounds and then the loud groans gusted in Cat's face again.

"UUU-AAAA-AA-RRRRGG-GGG-GG-GHHH...HHH...HH...!"

The centerpiece of the torture chamber was a heavy wooden structure, like the hollow frame of an enormous bed, raised about waist height from the floor on stout legs. At the foot of this frame was a thick crossbeam with two iron hoops hammered into it, set wide apart at the corners. The head of the "bed" was occupied by the drum of a heavy roller, a thick log, with a windlass at each end, fitted to a construction of iron gears and ratchets.

"UUU...uuuu...hhhhh..hhh....gghh..."

A spread eagled figure sagged limply inside the giant frame, its bare buttocks brushing the stone floor. Ropes secured to its ankles extended to the iron hoops at the foot of the bed and from its wrists ran up and around the wooden roller.

"Uuuu...uuu...nnn....hhh..hh...."

Cat went very cold. It was Aiko.

"uuuu..hhh...hhh...hh..."

Displayed within the frame, her sagging body was stark naked. Her head fell back, long blue-black hair hanging down lank and sweaty. Her pale lithe body, dripping with sweat, gleamed in the torchlight.

Smiling, the Colonel strolled across to stand by the rack. The room was full of the sounds of Aiko's labored breathing. The Colonel twisted his body to smile at Cat, who stood frozen, just inside the doorway.

"As you can see, my dear, I am something of a traditionalist."

Cat was consumed by horror and dismay. Her grimace just about convinced as a smile. It took every ounce of her physical strength to manage a curt nod of her head.

He even had his minions in costume. Two of them, manning the windlasses at either end of the wooden roller, their muscular frames encased in studded leather jerkins. They waited patiently, their dull eyes in their slab faces fixed upon their master.

For the first time, Cat noticed that one of the pale safari-suited men was standing in the half-light off to one side. He was frowning.

His voice was flat and accent less.

"This is an unnecessary waste of time," he stated. "We have the facility to simply probe her mind."

The Colonel barked.

"Ha! Yes, I'm sure you do, my friend. But this is so much more...creative...and more enjoyable, don't you think?"

The blond man looked at him blankly, and then walked out of the cellar. The door crashed shut behind him.

"Ha!"

The Colonel seized a fistful of Aiko's damp hair, pulling her head up. Her eyes had a feverish glare in them and narrowed, sparking, as they met Cat's frozen stare.

The Colonel didn't see Cat's face cloud with regret and then go hard with anger. He was twisting Aiko's hair in his fist to force her to look at him, her face contorting with pain.

"Now, my little yellow slut, are you going to tell me what I want to know?"

Aiko was panting. Sweat shone on her face and was trickling on her skin.

"G…g…g-go….t-t-t…t-to……he..ll..lll…!" she gasped hoarsely.

The Colonel released her hair and let her head loll down.

"Again!" he snapped at his assistants. "Stretch her again!"

Cat's eyes squeezed shut. She forced them open.

The torturers bent to the long spokes of the windlass. The stone chamber echoed with the winding drum's dull creak and clatter. Aiko's limp body rose from the floor and was spread out taut within the frame.

"Begin!"

She felt the ropes grip wrists and ankles. A sharp creak. The ropes tightened and squeaked. A sudden tearing pain wrenched her limbs and body.

"UUUAAA…GGGHH…HHH…!"

The inexorable click and clack of the ratchet. The creaking of the strained ropes. Pain scorched her sinews. She was screaming with her eyes. The sounds that burst from her gaping mouth were more animal than human.

"GG-HAAAGGGHH-GGHUUAAA-AA-AAAGGG-GGHHH-HH!"

"Well!" the Colonel demanded. "Are you going to speak?"

Gasping, Aiko lifted her head and glared at him.

"N-never…!"

Cat watched. Her heart was bursting.

Oh, Aiko, I'm so proud of you!

The Colonel sneered. He nodded to his henchmen. The drum swung back a half-turn and tightened with a jerk.

"HH-HHAAA-IIIEEE…AAAA-AAGGHH-GGUUGHHH…!"

Agonized sweat rolled over Aiko's distended and quivering body, dripping down onto the flagstones.

The Colonel lifted his hand. The torturers paused. Aiko's outcries subsided into low moans and panting.

Slowly, his hand descended upon her taut, sweating flesh. It wandered over her heaving chest, pinched the two nipples lightly, stroked her concave, strained stomach, the silky patch of dark hair at her groin.

Through a fog, Cat became aware that the Colonel was smiling at her. Extending his bony arm, he indicated the roller and the windlass.

"Perhaps, you would care to participate, Miss Johnson?"

Bile that scalded like acid rose into Cat's throat. Her smile came up twisted and ugly but she straightened it quickly. She could look away from Aiko's abused body but could not escape the sounds of her tortured breathing.

"Uh…no thank you, Sir. I prefer to leave these things to the professionals."

The Colonel shrugged.

"Continue!"

The creak, a groan, a stifled shriek. A wait. Another squeak…

"AAAAGG-GH…AAAAA…aahhhh…uuuuuu…hhh…hhhh…."

Aiko's scream faded to a moan and then silence as she lapsed into unconsciousness. Utterly drained, Cat was weak with relief.

The Colonel lifted Aiko's head again and then let it fall back. He frowned.

"Hmph! How disappointing."

He glanced at his watch.

"Never mind. I have business to attend to. We can begin again later."

He strolled over to stand beside the glowing brazier, toying with the handles of the irons. "Perhaps the little slant will feel more inclined to talk when she can smell her own flesh burning."

Cat was breathing slow and deep, restoring her strength. She almost flinched as the Colonel materialized at her side, taking her by the elbow.

"Come, my dear, I have more to show you…"

They rode in the steel cage of an elevator. Cat felt that sudden rising sensation in the pit of her stomach as the cage descended sharply. It was all the more acute, in the grip of a dull nausea deep inside.

The elevator went down and down and down. Cat was glad that she was encased in her track suit because underneath she soaked in cold sweat. When the Colonel wasn't looking she mopped her glistening forehead with her sleeve.

The Colonel twitched his lightless smile at her.

"Almost there…"

The cage jolted to a sudden halt. Cat gulped as a fist grabbed her guts and twisted. The barred gates rattled open and the Colonel stepped out briskly.

"Here we are!"

The cold steel of the War Room sheened dully in a murky half-light, its source a single lamp mounted at the head of the metal conference table. The Colonel indicated the chair furthest from the large screen on the wall. Cat took her seat, hidden in a splash of shadow.

The Colonel advanced to the head of the table where the light was brighter. The light had a sinister cast, and his sharp features with the small pointed beard looked positively Satanic.

He glanced back over his shoulder to ensure that Cat was totally invisible.

"Please keep perfectly still and quiet, Miss Johnson."

There was a small panel of switches and knobs set into the polished steel table top. His bony finger flicked a switch and the screen in front of him began to glow softly. He glanced back again but the light only advanced about halfway down the table. Cat remained in total darkness.

The Colonel stood to attention.

"I'm here, Sir."

In the darkness, Cat raised an eyebrow.

Aha! I knew it. I knew you weren't the Main Man!

She raised both eyebrows when the blank black silhouette took shape within the frame of the glowing screen.

The deep, distorted tone of the disguised voice startled her. Her chair shifted slightly but the small sound didn't carry.

"My compliments, Colonel. I have seen for myself and it would appear that everything has gone according to plan"

The Colonel was quivering with pride.

"Yes, Sir! Like clockwork. Just as you anticipated. Your strategy was impeccable. In fact, if I may say so, Sir, it has exceeded our expectations. I—!"

"And our friends? Are their needs being catered to as I instructed?"

The Colonel snapped back to attention.

"Yes, Sir! Even as we speak. The women have been selected and are being transported here. Everything will be in place, for our friends' arrival."

"Excellent, Colonel. I shall look forward to your next report"

The Colonel saluted as the silhouette vanished and the glow faded from the screen. He turned to smile into the gloom behind him.

"We are making history here today, my dear! And you are part of it!"

There was a pause before Cat's voice came out of the darkness.

"I'm honored, Colonel…"

She rose and stepped into the weak light.

"I suppose I'd be wasting my time, asking who that was?"

The Colonel had the look of a man inspired.

"A man of destiny! When the time comes he will reveal himself and lead us to greatness!"

Cat stared into the mocking blankness of the screen. In the pale light her eyes were like pieces of ice.

CHAPTER 16
The Master Race

"I'm afraid that I shall have to leave you to your own devices tonight," the Colonel said. "I have a great deal to attend to."

Cat looked suitably disappointed.

Perfect!

She smiled at him.

"Don't worry, Sir. I'm sure I can find something to do."

Her clenched fist hammered dully on the dark wood. A square metal shutter squeaked open and a sullen face peered at her through a pitted and rusty grille.

"Uh?" the face said.

Cat frowned at it.

"I'm here to question the prisoner."

She waited while heavy bolts grated loudly. Ancient hinges groaned as the great ironbound slab of the door was heaved open slowly.

"Uh....?"

Cat strode in quickly, brushing past him. There were two guards, stone-faced and dull-eyed, their sturdy frames packing drab khaki overalls. They both opened their mouths but couldn't think of anything to say.

Cat glared at them imperiously.

"The Colonel knows I'm here. I have his full authority!"

The guards stepped back and stood shoulder to shoulder, against the rough masonry hung with manacles and diabolical instruments.

In the torchlight, Cat seemed to be made out of gold. The guards stared at her, a slight sheen tinting the dull bulbs of their eyes. She was wearing a flawless white safari shirt and tan riding breeches tucked into high-topped brown boots.

"UU-uuu-uu...hhh...hh...."

Her body sagging within the frame of the rack, Aiko stirred, returning to semi-consciousness. Stale sweat glistened on her naked flesh.

A terrible weight descended on Cat. Her throat was very tight and tears of rage pricked her eyes. But she conjured up a mask of cruel contempt and strolled coolly across the stone floor to stand over the rack.

"Ah, sleeping are we...?"

With a flick of the wrist, she slapped Aiko back and forth across the face.

"Come on," she cooed viciously. "Wake up ...!"

"Mmm…mmgh….mmph!"

Aiko opened her eyes. Cat's face swam into focus.

"H-h-huu…hhh….uhhh….?"

Cat saw confusion in her friend's eyes. She put a hand over Aiko's mouth and bent very close, till their faces were almost touching. Cat's eyes were full of pain, burning with a fierce fire.

I'm going to get you out of here!

"So….."

Cat stood up straight and took a step back. She smiled down at the spread eagled figure on the rack.

"We're going to have a nice little talk, you and me. I'm sure that you have lots you want to tell me."

She saw the light dawn in Aiko's eyes.

That's it, baby. We're going to play a game…

Slowly, Cat unbuttoned her crisp white shirt. She shrugged out of it and held it out behind her by her fingertips.

"Hang that up will you."

The guards gulped. Jaws dropping, they stared, mesmerized by the revelation of her superb torso, the pale gold mounds of her firm breasts scarcely contained by black satin cups with a subtle trim of lace.

"Well!"

They stepped forward together and collided. Cat curled her lip. The shirt was plucked from her fingers and hung with great care on an unoccupied steel hook projecting from the wall.

Cat stood gazing down at Aiko. She looked thoughtful. The Japanese girl lay still, gazing stoically up at the vaulted stone ceiling.

"Hmmm…."

Cat sauntered round to the head of the rack. She placed her hands on the spokes of the geared windlass. A kind of dumb eagerness lighting their eyes, the guards stepped forward quickly. Cat glared at them and they jumped backwards.

"I can manage, thank you!"

She looked deep into Aiko's eyes.

Ready…?

She turned the spokes and the great wooden drum rotated. The pawl dropped into the ratchet with a loud clack. Just one notch.

Aiko gasped. Cat's mouth contorted into a sneer. Her eyes were gloating.

Clack! Another notch.

Careful...careful...

Aiko ground her teeth, stifling a groan.
"B-B-bitch...!"
Cat laughed and turned the windlass again, another notch. Aiko moaned. One of the guards was chuckling, a guttural, brutish sound.

...they're buying it...

Cat ruffled Aiko's sweat-soaked hair with her fingers. She stroked her slippery belly with her palm.
"That's it. Nice and tight."

...but not too tight...

She swivelled away from the rack, hands on hips, surveying the scene. The guards were staring her with crude adoration.
"Mmmm... What lovely toys..."
The coals were glowing dimly in the squat brazier. Cat seized the wooden handle and drew an iron out. Its tip was a blunt spear point. Wisps of smoke curled from a crust of ash.
"Bah! Barely lukewarm!"
She rammed the iron back into the coals and scowled at the guards, who squirmed like naughty children.
When she snapped her fingers, one of the guards wrenched a small wood and leather bellows from its hook on the wall and almost ran over to the brazier. He began pumping energetically.
"Much better!"
The tip of the iron was glowing cherry red, its reflection making sparks of fire in Cat's eyes.
"Stand there!" she took the iron and ordered the guard to wait at the head of the rack. Then she walked around the rack slowly, making slow passes over Aiko's naked body with the searing brand.
"Now...where to begin...?"
In the humidity of the chamber, Cat's near naked torso was glistening with perspiration. Fresh trickles of sweat laced Aiko's skin, her taut body quivering, wide eyes fixed on the ceiling. The faces of the guards were greasy, beads of sweat spiked on their stubble.

There was a hiss, a sizzle, as hot metal came into contact with sweating flesh.
"AAAAA-AA-GG-GGGHHH!!!!"

Light on her feet, Cat whipped round and lunged with the iron, thrusting like a fencer. The glowing point pierced the guard in the throat, emerging at the base of his skull.

"GGGGHH-GGHH-HH…!"

Eyes bulging, a bloody foam spilling from his twisted lips, the guard collapsed. As he fell his clawing fingers hooked the spokes of the windlass and the drum turned another notch.

"AAAII-IIEEE!"

Aiko screamed. The second guard looked at her. He looked at Cat. He looked at his colleague, who lay twitching in a lake of blood. He looked at Cat again. He completely forgot that he had a holster on his belt with a gun in it.

Cat was vaulting over Aiko and the rack. Impeccably balanced, her landing flowed into a high hooking turn-kick that caught the second guard on the side of the jaw, whipping his head round in a spray of sweat and snapping his neck with a loud crack.

"Hah!"

Aiko exhaled a long sigh of release as Cat un-cocked the ratchets and slackened off the drum, lowering her gently to the floor.

"How do you feel?"

Tenderly, she loosened the loops of rope that bound Aiko's bruised wrists and ankles. With an arm around her waist, Cat helped her sit up. Aiko grimaced.

"Taller."

Laughing softly, Cat stroked the Japanese girl's damp, dark hair.

"You were marvellous."

Flexing her arms gingerly, Aiko managed a brief smile.

"You're not so bad yourself," she replied, in a voice hoarse from screaming.

Frowning, Cat looked at the corpses sprawled on the stone floor.

"Bastards!"

Her body seized by sudden cramps, Aiko's features spasmed with pain. Concerned, Cat cupped her face between her hands.

"Do you think you can walk?"

Wincing, Aiko put an arm around Cat's strong shoulders.

"Just watch me!"

They both laughed this time.

"Then let's get out of here!"

The sloping skylight stood on a section of flat roof, in the shadow of a tall chimney.

"Careful…"

Cat opened it, just a sliver and peered out. Nothing. No patrols. The roof was empty.

"Okay, come on…"

She emerged into the moonlight, which bathed her in silver. She had flung her shirt back on and tied it up at the front in a knot with long tails, baring her midriff.

"Uuggh-hh…"

Aiko's strained features rose into view as she strove to heave herself up and out onto the rooftop. Cat crouched down to help her and Aiko rolled out and lay on her back, panting.

"Thanks!"

Aiko was wearing the dead guard's khaki overalls. They were very baggy on her. Cat grinned.

"You look cute in those."

Aiko wrinkled her nose.

"The son of a bitch didn't believe in taking a bath!"

They crawled on their bellies to the edge of the flat roof and peered through the short fat columns that fenced it. They looked at each other, wide eyes shining in the moonlight.

"Jeez!" said Aiko. "What's going on?"

Cat shook her head.

"Beats me."

Down below, the gardens were a blaze of light. Beneath searing floodlights a bustling construction site was expanding rapidly, while an army of workers in drab overalls crawled all over it like ants. Jets of orange sparks fizzed from welding torches; there were loud volleys from rivet guns. In sections lowered by mighty cranes, a vast, polished steel platform rose on stilts above the lawns and hedges and flowerbeds.

Cat was mystified.

"Any ideas?"

Aiko shrugged.

"Nope. But it's a lucky break. It's keeping everybody occupied."

Cat went rigid as her keen eyes picked out the unmistakable figure of the Colonel, in his neatly pressed battledress. He was striding about, pointing and barking out orders. But it was plain to see that the pale men in safari suits were in charge.

Cat glanced at the luminous dial of her watch.

"Well, there's no time to figure it out now."

Rolling onto her side, she looked back across the flat roof, dull grey in the moonlight.

"If I'm right, there's a ladder down at the side there."

She reached out to take Aiko's hand.

"I can sneak you out to the perimeter," she whispered. "After that you're on your own."

Aiko ducked her head close. Their lips brushed lightly.

"Don't worry, I'll be fine. I know what to do."

Cat's laugh was a soft sound deep in her throat.

"I'll give you an hour's start, before I discover your escape."

The first hint of dawn was a fine pale pink line along the rugged horizon of the desert. But the windows of Free Town were already glowing with lamplight and busy with figures moving behind them as the inhabitants woke and readied themselves for another day's chores. People were on the streets, heading out to the fields.

"Thank you, sweetheart."

Wrapped in an embroidered robe, the doll-faced Chinese girl was pouring scented oils into John Warburton's steaming bathwater.

Identically garbed, her more exotic companion approached the enormous brass-framed bed, bearing a silver tray etched with intricate Arabian artistry. There was an immaculately rolled joint on the tray.

Stark naked, John threw back the black silk sheets and sat up in bed. He beamed at the Chinese girl, his merry blue eyes twinkling.

"Go to work on a spliff," he chortled. "That's what I say!"

Taking a deep drag, he heaved his bulk upright and padded on bare feet across the polished wooden floor. The sight of his great big pink and hairy nakedness, with his mighty, matted chest, long silvery hair and spectacular moustaches, made the Chinese girls smile at each other and giggle "Daddy Bear."

"Now then, now then," John Warburton chuckled. "Don't you go making fun of your Papa."

Playfully, he patted the behind of the doll-faced Chinese girl as she bent over the bath. Still giggling, the exotic girl took him by the hand and led him to a small side table with another tray on it, this one piled high with ham and eggs.

John Warburton grinned broadly, stroking his big belly with relish. The doll-faced girl pouted.

"No! Bath first! Not eat. Eat first bath get cold!"

The exotic girl frowned, stamping a delicate foot.

"No! No! Bath first food get cold!"

The two girls began arguing.

Laughing, John Warburton rolled his eyes, waving his hands to placate them.

"Peace! Peace!" he said, in their language. "Do we have to go through this every morning?"

Picking up the plate of ham and eggs, he strode towards the sunken bath.

"I have the perfect compromise," his Mandarin was flawless. "I'll do both at once. Now you two just..."

There was a muffled commotion in the street outside, agitated voices.

"Papa John! Papa John!" a young voice was shouting.

Instantly, their faces were serious. The doll-faced girl took the tray from John's hand. The exotic girl was at his side, helping him into a tent-like blue silk robe.

His door was always open. A group of his young people came spilling in, boys and girls, very excited. They had someone with them.

"We were halfway to Red Rock, Papa John…!"

"She just came out of nowhere…!"

John's bushy eyebrows shot skywards.

"Aiko…?"

She could hardly stand. Her matted hair was clogged with sand and bits of grit. There was sand in the creases of the baggy overalls and glued to the crust of stale sweat on her face.

When she saw John Warburton Aiko shook herself from the supporting grip of the young people and staggered towards him. After a few faltering steps she swayed and began to fall. John lifted her in his strong arms, as light as a feather.

"Re…p-p-port…" Aiko mumbled. "M-Must m-m-make…a…re…port….!"

Thanking them, John Warburton ushered the kids out.

He looked tenderly into Aiko's glazed eyes.

"Don't worry, darling. We'll take care of it."

The Chinese girls undressed Aiko and washed her hair and bathed her. They massaged her with soothing oils and ointments for her bruises and abrasions and tormented sinews. Then they put her to bed and watched over her as she slept.

There was a small room behind the bedchamber, stacked to the ceiling with a tower of radio equipment.

"TZ-243 calling AO…TZ-243 calling AO…come in please…"

John Warburton twiddled and fine-tuned until the buzz of static in his headphones evaporated.

"…AO calling TZ-243…read you loud and clear…"

John Warburton grinned.

"Hey, mama, is that you?"

He could hear the smile in Selena's voice.

"It's me, big man. What's happenin'?"

He was deadly serious.

"It's all happening, mama. It's going down. Any time now."

There was a slight pause at the other end. He heard Selena take a deep breath.

"Well, we're ready. How about you?"

John's massive fist thumped a metal ledge, making the microphone jump.

"Let's rock 'n roll!"

The Colonel looked like he was going to burst with sheer excitement.

"It has come! The great day has come!"

He was hopping from one foot to the other, like a little boy. Lined up along the high marble terrace that overlooked the gardens, the generals and admirals were looking at him sideways.

"*They* are coming!"

He was dressed like a Napoleonic field marshal, in a blue coat with long tails, bejewelled with gold buttons and epaulettes, tight cream-colored trousers tucked into glossy black boots. A curved cavalry saber hung at his hip, supported by a red silk sash.

"Er…who's coming, Colonel?"

Cat was encased in the olive drab GI jumpsuit, zipped up to her chin.

"Wait and see, my dear Miss Johnson. Wait and see!"

She was nervous. Very nervous, as she saw a stocky figure in khaki approach and heard him mutter in the Colonel's ear.

"…search parties…still looking…haven't found her…"

The Colonel was frowning.

"That yellow slut is proving to be very resourceful."

Cat looked suitably concerned but the Colonel was far too excited to care. He waved his subordinate away.

"No matter! Whoever she is, she cannot turn back the tide of history!"

Feigning keen anticipation, Cat placed both hands on the marble rail and leant out, looking down into the gardens below.

The great platform was complete. The size of a football field, its surface appeared to be a skin of white ceramic tiles, reflecting the glare of the mid-morning sun in subtle shimmering ripples.

Three ranks deep, men in uniform surrounded the platform, in parade drill, at attention, but ready for action with helmets and rifles. There were the Colonel's stone-faced commandoes, in black and tan; and representing the rebel junta of generals and admirals, marines in their mottled camouflage, paratroopers and plain GI's. The dull glint of their helmets formed a metal frame around the gleaming platform.

Cat turned to look at the Colonel.

"This is very impressive, Sir. But what's it all about?"

Along the marble rail beyond him, she saw the jaws of the admirals and generals drop.

The Colonel almost jumped off the ground, as though he had been jolted by an electric shock.

"That!"

He was pointing up at the sky.

"That's what it's all about!"

Startled, Cat craned her head back. With one hand raised as a visor, she strained to penetrate the daunting brightness of a flawless blue sky.

The glare made her blink. She strained but couldn't see anything. But she felt something, a slight, then slowly intensifying pressure in her ears.

"There!" the Colonel exclaimed, his voice shrill. "Don't you see it?"

The pressure was a sound now, a distant humming that swelled and became a steady pulse.

Cat's heart seemed to jump into her throat.

"Oh…m-my…"

Now she could see it. A bright spark high in the sky.

"…G-G-God…!"

The silver shape was descending, growing, a gleaming cylinder. The sky was throbbing. The dull metal frame around the platform was now a pale rim of upturned faces, pocked with gaping mouths and wide eyes.

The ground was trembling. She could feel the vibrations through the soles of her combat boots. The noise was an almighty droning that was squeezing her skull. All around the platform, the soldiers were reeling, dropping their rifles and clapping their hands to their ears.

"Jesus Christ!" Cat yelled but the sound sucked her voice away. "It's huge!"

The tiled surface of the platform was shivering, the ripples of light racing along its length. Its expansive proportions had a purpose. The silver craft fitted it exactly.

Suddenly, the crushing drone began to diminish, shrinking to a soft and bearable humming. The great cylinder came to a complete stop, hovering about fifty feet above the surface of the platform.

Harried by their barking non-coms, the soldiers picked up their guns and pulled themselves together, perfecting their ranks again. For the first time, Cat was able to take a good look at the strange craft. She was met by a complete blank. It was huge and silver and cigar-shaped, and that was about it. It was smooth and featureless and seamless. It gave nothing away.

Seconds ticked into minutes, minutes stretched into an eternity. No movement. Not a sound, save for that faint humming.

Oddly, Cat wasn't as surprised as she thought she ought to be.

"Aha!" said the Colonel.

She saw three pale men in safari suits, walking out from the shadows below the terrace. They strode swiftly towards the platform and up a flight of metal steps, to stand beneath the blunt tip of the silver cylinder.

Then it came to her.

Well, now I know what that weird wreck in the desert was

"Aha!" the Colonel said again.

A dark, vertical aperture was materializing on the under slope of the nose of the gleaming cylinder. It extended slowly into a blank, black oblong.

The Colonel was rubbing his hands together, his body rocking from side to side. Cat had reached a stage where nothing was going to surprise her anymore. She was totally calm.

Like a long silver tongue, a ramp was descending towards the platform, floating on air. As it finished uncoiling, there was movement in the dark opening. Two figures emerged, pale men with fair hair and colorless eyes. Except that they weren't wearing safari suits. They were clad in a glistening skin of pearly mesh, which sparked with every color of the rainbow.

The Colonel gripped Cat's arm, making her wince.

"They're magnificent! This is the true Master Race!"

That's just great. Nazis from outer space!

The shining beings stood on the platform, flanking the silver ramp. The three men in safari suits stood shoulder to shoulder, gazing up at the dark portal.

And here comes the Boss

He was much taller, and sparse, with long, lean pale features and golden eyes. His hair was snow white and flowed down to his shoulders. He was swathed in a billowing cape that was woven from light and made him appear to be floating, as he came down the ramp.

As the Leader reached the platform, the men in safari suits were bowing deeply to him. Advancing, he acknowledged them with the wave of a hand with fantastically long and slender fingers.

Suddenly, there were doorways appearing and ramps uncurling all along the shining flanks of the great silver cylinder. A huge noise went up from the assembly as the alien craft disgorged an army of pale figures in their pearly mail, wielding odd stubby carbines that appeared to be made out of glass. It took many minutes for the steady stream of them to cease and there were enough to make three ranks, forming a wall all around the edge of the mighty platform.

"By God!" one of the generals exclaimed. "Nothing can stop us now!"

From loudspeakers spiked on high posts, a brassy fanfare brayed.

With a synchronized crash of boot heels, the troops presented arms. The admirals and generals were standing to attention. The Colonel saluted.

The men in safari suits were preceding their Leader, coming down the steel steps from the platform and across the grass and immaculately raked gravel.

Suddenly, the Leader stopped, his cloak of light shimmering as he seemed to hover on the spot.

Oh!

He was looking up. He was looking at Cat. He was looking deep into her eyes.

Aaaa…aaa…hhhh…!

Her heart was racing. She was light-headed, giddy. She was afraid, exhilarated. Those golden eyes were enormous and she felt like she was about to lose her balance and fall and be drowned in them.

In ten thousand sparks and darts, candlelight scintillated in every strand and pendant of the crystal chandeliers.
"My friends, a toast!"
It flashed like red rubies in the Colonel's raised wine glass.
"To our allies. And the world at our feet!"
At the head of the dining table, the Leader responded with a slight incline of his head. In the candlelight he was lustrous, his eyes glowing and golden.
Flanking him, the men in safari suits sat with sober faces, looking straight ahead. In their dress uniforms, the generals and admirals all swivelled like a chorus line, joining in the toast, their eyes bright with an eagerness verging on lust.
"OUR ALLIES! AND THE WORLD AT OUR FEET!"
From the oak panelled walls, the stuffed stag's heads looked down dumbly with their glass eyes. With an equal blandness on their slab faces, attendants stood around the table, half in shadow, their muscular frames crammed into white mess jackets with gold buttons and braid.
The Colonel drained his glass. Smacking his thin lips, he sat down, glowing with satisfaction.
"You didn't join in our toast, my dear."
Cat occupied the Colonel's right. Her long golden hair was coiled on top of her head, emphasizing the sensuous grace of her neck, and her bare shoulders, elegant as she was in a strapless black satin evening gown.
She smiled at him.
"Oh, I'm sorry, Sir. I was transported. It's all…like a dream…"
She paused to sip her wine. The Colonel watched as her lips touched the rim of the glass.

At the head of the table, the Leader was staring at her intensely. The gold of his eyes was swirling, molten.

Her mouth was very dry. She took another sip.

"I didn't realize that your plans extended to the whole world, Colonel."

The Colonel's mouth was smiling but not his eyes. His eyes were black and hard, like pieces of flint.

"Oh, indeed they do, my dear. And it is such a shame that those plans won't include you."

What?

Her vision blurred momentarily, and then cleared. An odd warmth crept along her limbs.

"Wha…? What do…do you….?"

Her tongue was twice its size and seemed to have become disconnected somehow.

"…m-m-mean…?"

The edge of her sight was watery and shimmering. The shapes of the white-suited waiters that materialized on either side of her were wavering, insubstantial.

The wine!

The guns in their hands were very real. They were pointed at her head.

She wanted to stand up but her feet didn't belong to her. She was looking at her feet through the wrong end of a telescope and they were miles away from her brain.

The Colonel's laugh was a tinny rattle.

"You did very well, I must confess, my dear. You had us all fooled, for a while."

Suddenly, he backhanded her hard across the face. The pain was distant and dull. There was a warm wetness on her lips.

"But you underestimated us."

One of the pale blond men was standing behind her. Leaning over her sagging shoulder, he placed a small grey box on the table in front of her. It had a glowing green screen, about five inches across. The screen was filled with tiny moving figures. Blinking the mist from her eyes, Cat saw herself in miniature, rescuing Aiko from the torture chamber.

Oh you…damn…fool…!

Cat's hands and feet were hot and tingling. Her stomach was churning and she was dizzy. The Leader's glowing eyes were gigantic. She was falling into them.

Her head had become a block of concrete that weighed a ton. It lolled forward until her chin was nudging her chest.

"Oh no, my dear Miss Warburton. Stay with us. There is someone I want you to meet."

The Colonel seized a fistful of Cat's hair and pulled her head back sharply. The pain cut through the fog and she cried out.

"I want you to meet the man whose genius and resources, whose divine inspiration, have made all of this possible!"

Cat cried out again. A shriek wrenched out of her by pure shock and horror.

"Hello, Catherine."

Her father was standing before her.

"D-d-dad...?"

No! No! I'm dreaming!

He was very real. He looked immaculate, in a razor-sharp tuxedo. The admirals and generals gaped at him, their faces lit by a dawning revelation.

"Yes, Catherine. I am the one."

Suddenly, she was very weak, slumping in her chair. He was looking down at her gravely, his arms folded across his chest.

His daughter shook her head in disbelief, her mouth opening and closing, emitting tiny incoherent sounds. The Colonel snapped his fingers and the burly attendants seized her and dragged her to her feet, twisting her arms up viciously behind her back.

The pain ripped through the stupefying veils and was a white hot knife slashing at her. She tried to scream but could only gag and choke, going red in the face, as her churning bowels rose into her throat.

Her legs crumpled and she sagged in the cruel grip of her captors. With an effort that made beads of sweat stand out on her brow, she lifted her head and looked at her father, through eyes blurred with tears.

"D-D...D-Daddy...!"

The only discernable expression on his face was one of cold disappointment. Her father turned his back on her.

The darkness rushed in upon her from all four corners of the room. With a low moan, Cat collapsed limply, her long hair unravelling and falling across her tear-stained face.

The Colonel was hurrying to catch up with J. Spencer Warburton, who was making a grand exit with generals and admirals trailing in his wake.

"Take her away! We will deal with her later!"

Beneath the battering sun of high noon, the smooth silver skin of the vast cylinder seared the eyeballs of the soldiers if they tried to look at it.

They didn't have time to stand and stare, harried by their red-faced non-coms, chivvied in their turn by over-eager lieutenants.

"C'mon! C'mon! Show some hustle! Get a move on!"

In the shadow of the great craft, an alien army was establishing itself. Broad ramps had been lowered and the pale human-like beings were ushering huge dull grey crates etched with multi-colored hieroglyphics down onto the tiled platform. Some were the size of freight wagons, but they were weightless, sliding downwards on a cushion of air.

"This is merely the vanguard!" the Colonel exulted. "This is only the beginning!"

Her hands cuffed behind her back, Cat was marched through the bustling gardens. Blinking in the harsh sunlight, she shook her head, trying to clear the fog in her brain. Her tongue felt like sandpaper and bitter bile rose and scalded her throat.

"You're...insane...!" she croaked. "You c-can't let them...d-destroy the world...!"

His mouth contorted into a vicious leer, the Colonel seized a fistful of Cat's long blonde hair and twisted. She grimaced, tears of pain welling in her eyes.

The Colonel's face was very close, his hot breath raking her face.

"I wouldn't concern yourself with the fate of humanity, my dear Miss Warburton," he hissed. "I would worry about what lies in store for you!"

He twisted her hair again, harder. Cat gritted her teeth, glaring at him, refusing to give him the satisfaction of a scream.

"UGH!"

His fist ripped into her solar plexus. Her legs gave and she sagged, her hair falling forward, masking her face.

"I assure you that it will be most unpleasant."

Cat's feet scuffed the gravel as she was dragged away.

On the high platform, the rampart of grey boxes was growing.

"C'mon! On the double!"

At the furthest reaches of the gardens, the exercise courts were silent. The barracks were empty. Their occupants, the Colonel's stocky, stone-faced commandoes, had merged into the hullabaloo engulfing the landing platform and the alien craft.

The secluded laboratory, housed within its pre-fabricated walls, was full of sound and activity.

Oh Christ!

A dismal chorus was like a sudden gale stopping Cat in her tracks, as the guards shoved her in through the doorway.

"Fascinating, is it not, my dear?"

A chorus of shrieks and moans.

"A science far beyond our understanding."

Narrow grey metal tables were ranged down the entire length of the laboratory. At the head of each table was a tall grey cabinet lit up with geometric dials and shifting grids of winking lights. Each cabinet was crowned by a squat, semi-transparent drum of hollow crystal, pale purple and glowing.

At the foot of each table stood one of pale beings with its colorless hair and eyes, clad in a clinging skin of pearly mail.

Jeee-zus...!

The fearful wailing was coming from the tables, from blonde girls, stripped naked and strapped down by their wrists and ankles. Thin wires snaked from electrodes attached all over their bodies, dangling down to the floor and plugged into the grey cabinets. Each girl wore a kind of shiny metal skullcap from which an opaque and flexible tube looped all the way to an elaborate socket on the crystal drum atop its cabinet.

Pulses of purple light, like luminous beads, were coursing along the transparent tubes, flowing from the metal skullcaps to the crystal drums. The pale lavender glow within the drums was intensifying slowly, becoming deeper and brighter.

The guards pushed Cat a few steps closer. She was still wearing the strapless black evening dress. Sweat glued its thin material to her body and in the hard light of the laboratory was glinting like beads of glass on her face. The piled coils of her hair had come undone, hanging down loosely.

The pale man-like creatures stood and observed the tables impassively. Occasionally, one would move round to the tall console, to make a minute adjustment that would prompt an upsurge of screaming from the girl on the table.

"Fascinating..." the Colonel breathed in Cat's ear. "You see, this is indeed the true Master Race..."

He was gazing at the pale aliens with a kind of rapture.

"These are the true Aryans. And that which flows in their veins is the very essence of racial purity..."

Cat opened her mouth but nothing came out. Behind her eyes, she could see the blonde hippy chick, laughing and gobbling her burger and French fries in "VERNA'S EATS."

"It is an essence which must be harvested throughout the Galaxy. And here on our unworthy planet they have found that essence to be at its purest in the bodies—no, the very souls—of our fair-haired females!"

Shrill ululations spilled from the girls' gaping mouths, their eyes bulging with terror. Drenched in sweat, they writhed insanely, their bodies arching and straining.

Cat squeezed her eyes tight shut, but she couldn't wipe out the sound. She couldn't cover her ears, with her hands cuffed behind her back.

She couldn't blot out the Colonel's voice, like a white hot needle piercing her brain.

"And I intend to provide our new allies with a limitless and convenient supply of that essence, so they need wander the Galaxy no more. I will establish a system of…of…yes, of breeding farms…producing a crop of flaxen-haired females to meet our friends' needs…"

The screams were one great concerted howl that was crushing Cat's skull. Everything was spinning round.

"…and in return…well, put simply, my dear Miss Warburton…your father…and I…we will rule the world!"

The guards were ripping the fragile evening dress from Cat's body, down from her shoulders to her ankles. Shredded like tissue paper, it lay crumpled at her feet, leaving her with only a tiny black G-string. She staggered and they seized her arms with fingers like steel clamps, gripping down to the bone. Cat shouted something obscene, lost in the screaming.

The Colonel's gloating sneer roved over her sweating body.

"If it was left up to me, my dear, I would punish your betrayal with a lingering and painful death. But the Leader has selected you personally. You belong to him now!"

The guards twisted her arms till the bones creaked.

Everything went black. She was falling into a deep, deep darkness.

CHAPTER 17
A Reckoning

"LET'S ROLL!"

Uncle John's voice boomed from the bullhorn clasped in his big fist.

"YEEEEEEEEEE...

A great concerted bellow and grinding of motors, in a haze of blue-grey vapors.

"...EEEEEEEE-HAH!"

A cheer went up as the convoy lurched into motion. It picked up speed, making a trail of desert dust that glowed in the bright sunlight, like the long tail of a comet.

It was a rag-tag caravan, over one hundred strong, of assorted pick-ups that went back to the 40's, and surplus jeeps and Army trucks. There were even bright yellow dune buggies, hopping and skipping over the broken terrain.

The motley vehicles were crammed with determined young faces, young men and women in combat fatigues, brandishing semi-automatic rifles.

John Warburton's jeep was weaving in and out of the convoy, as he kept a keen eye on the young faces. He was dressed for the occasion in faded jungle stripes, like those he had worn as one of the first "special advisors" sent by JFK to South Viet Nam.

Suddenly, the years rolled away and he saw again those fresh young Marine Corps faces, as they came ashore, showboating for the cameras, before the terror and disillusionment crushed the gung-ho out of them.

He looked up from his jeep into the trucks and the grins and thumbs-up and V-for-Victory signs that greeted him. A great sadness weighed in his chest. Some of those young faces would not be getting any older.

Then everyone was tilting their heads back and looking up, shielding their eyes, up into the bright blue sky. Suddenly the weight lifted from Uncle John's heart.

"YEEEEEEEE-HAH!"

The young people were pressing their hands to their ears, their eyes wide as saucers, grinning at each other, as a rolling thunder passed overhead.

Cat was floating.

"Uuuu-uu-uuu-hhh-hh..."

She was rising up out of deep dark waters. The water turned from black into blue and the blue became paler and faded altogether as she rose towards the light.

"UH!"

Someone was slapping her face, short sharp stinging blows. The pain was distant at first and then immediate, jolting her back to consciousness.

"Ah, so you are back with us."

Her eyes fluttered open. The Colonel's face swam into focus. He was leaning over her, his black eyes glittering, his mouth warped in that familiar thin smile.

"Nnn...ghh...hhh!"

Instinctively, Cat tried to stand up. She couldn't. Gritting her teeth, she strained with her entire body but couldn't budge.

The Colonel was laughing.

"I'm afraid you are quite helpless, my dear..."

Reality came crashing down on her.

"...there is no hope for you now."

She was seated on a high-backed grey alloy chair, secured by tight straps. All she wore was the tiny black G-string, and the electrodes with their trailing wires, fixed to her body.

She felt the presence of the strange metal cone, suspended like a crown. Glancing sideways, she glimpsed the transparent cable attached to the crystal drum on top of its tall cabinet.

Cold sweat broke out on her creeping flesh.

The Leader was watching her, with his golden eyes set in his long pale face. Her father was standing next to him.

"D-Daddy...!"

She was consumed by a sensation she had never felt before, a kind of chill paralysis that gripped her limbs, scrambling her brain. It was fear. Fear was new to her and it was horrible.

"D-Daddy...you c-can't let them d-do this...!"

In his razor-sharp blue blazer and cream flannels, J. Spencer Warburton stared at his daughter with a face of stone. Then he turned his back and walked away. The Colonel jumped to follow him, trotting at his heels.

"D-DADDY!"

The doors of the laboratory slammed shut behind them. Cat slumped in the chair, all the strength drained from her body. A tear trickled down her cheek.

The Leader signalled with a flutter of his long fingers, his lustrous cloak shimmering. One of the pale men in safari suits was standing by the tall grey metal cabinet. His hand hovered over the glowing dials.

Instantly, Cat was galvanized.

"AAAAAHH...HHH...GGHH...!"

It wasn't pain. A hideous ice cold terror engulfed her like an onrushing darkness. Her face contorted. Her body was seized by violent convulsions. Above her, the crystal drum began to glow faintly.

BOOM...!

BOOM...!
The earth shook.
BOOM...!
BOOM...!
BOOM...!
The splendid gardens were reverberated by a chain of dull explosions.
BOOM...!
BOOM...!
In rapid succession, the devices that Aiko had secreted in the shrubbery and in the nooks and crannies of the ornate statuary detonated with a flash of white heat and a jolting concussion. Anyone within twenty feet was rendered unconscious. Up to fifty feet they were bowled over, dazed and confused, the soldiers in khaki and aliens in their silver glister sprawling on the gravel paths and in the flowerbeds.
BOOM...!
BOOM...!
Fountains of orange sparks fizzed from some of the devices, spaced amongst the stun grenades. They spewed a thick and oily grey smoke that spread out rapidly, hugging the ground to a height of about fifteen feet, clogging the gardens with a dense fog.

"GO! GO! GO!"
High above in the singing sky, a fleet of silver-skinned DC-3's was disgorging its cargo.
"GERONIMO!"
In long strands, tiny figures fell out, jumping into the void. One by one their parachutes opened, like a string of pearls.
Blundering about in the grey fog, those on the ground didn't see the parachutes coming down upon them, carpeting the gardens. Suddenly, nimble figures in hooded black cat suits were all around and in amongst them, with submachine-guns blazing from the hip.

"AAA-A-aaa-rrrg-ghhh-hhh...!"
Resistance meant pain.
"NN-NNNGGHH-HH...!"
Pain was something that Cat could handle. Pain was familiar. Pain was a challenge.
"UUNNN-nnngg-gghh...hhh...hhh...!"
She ground her teeth, her features contorting. Every muscle in her body strained against the straps that secured her to the grey metal throne. Her flexing body gleamed. Sweat was dripping from her face; drops of sweat flew from her flailing hair, as she shook her head from side to side.

On top of the metal cabinet, the squat crystal drum was suffused by a throbbing purple glow. The beads of light were coursing through the transparent cables. But their progress was hesitant, erratic.

The Leader's long features were warped into a frown. His golden eyes were dark and smoldering.

"NNNN-NNGG-GGHH-HH!"

Cat was glaring back at him, her lips drawn back in a snarl from her clenched teeth. The beads of purple light were faltering.

The fog was pierced by darts of light that spat from odd-looking carbines that seemed to be made out of glass. Impaled by a shard of light, a slim cat-suited figure threw up its arms and screamed in agony, then crumbled, a husk of charred flesh and bone.

The riposte was a rattle of submachine-gun fire. Struck by a short, scything burst, the silvery alien was blown backwards off its feet, its punctured chest oozing a thick colorless slime.

"YAAAH!"

John Warburton moved fast across the marble terrace. His mighty boot reduced the towering French windows to matchwood and glass splinters, as they shattered inwards with a rending crash.

"Holy fuck!"

The splendor of a Louis XV drawing room came as a shock after the heat and dust of the battle raging outside. Uncle John stopped short in his tracks, his mouth open, scrubbing the sweat out of his eyes.

"Well, brother..." said a familiar voice.

John Warburton turned quickly, the muzzle of his .45 automatic zeroing in on the source of the voice.

"...I might have known."

Impeccable in his blue blazer and crisp flannels, J. Spencer Warburton stood within the gilded frame of the doorway, at the far end of the long room. There was a stainless steel revolver in his hand.

The brothers walked towards each other until the muzzles of their guns were almost touching. J. Spencer was sneering. Uncle John looked sad.

"I might have known that you would oppose me," said J. Spencer Warburton. "You're pathetic! We might have shared the world between us, but you had to throw it all away!"

John Warburton sighed heavily.

"I feel sorry for you, J."

Anger sparked in his brother's steely grey eyes.

"Feel sorry for yourself, John! You let yourself and your class down."

Remembering, Uncle John frowned, angry with himself.

"What have you done with Cat? What have you done with your daughter?"

J. Spencer curled his lip.

"I have no daughter. You saw to that. You turned her against me."

"Where is she, J?"

"Where she belongs. She is getting what she deserves."

John's knuckles were white, his fingers clenched around the butt of the .45.

"Not if I can help it!"

J. Spencer tilted the barrel of his gun so it angled towards his brother's face.

"I don't think so, John."

John Warburton took a quick step back. His shoulders seemed to sag.

"So," he said softly. "We've come to this."

Tears welled in his eyes.

"This is terrible, J."

J. Spencer Warburton shrugged.

"You brought it to this, John. It was you who deserted me."

Uncle John looked at him sadly, shaking his head. J. Spencer lifted the muzzle of his pistol till it pointed up at the ceiling decorated with cupids and voluptuous maidens cavorting in the clouds.

"Shall we do this like gentlemen?"

John Warburton heaved another enormous sigh.

"Whatever you say."

J. Spencer gave a curt nod.

On the count of ten then," he snapped. "Like gentlemen. Agreed?"

John nodded wearily.

"Yes, yes...ten..."

They turned and stood back-to-back. Then they began to walk away from each other.

J. Spencer did the counting.

"One!...Two!...Three!..."

The tears were brimming over and trickling down Uncle John's cheeks.

"...Four!...Five!...Six!..."

J. Spencer's eyes were slits of fire, his lips drawn back to show his teeth.

"...Seven!...Eight!...

John Warburton turned on eight. In the long drawing room, the sound of the .45 was like a thunderclap.

There was a *whack!* and bits of fluff and stuff thrown up by the impact between J. Spencer's shoulder blades.

"UH!"

His immaculate shirtfront became a ragged, bloody mess where the bullet exited. Eyes wide open and surprised, he was hurled forward and fell, lying face down, his arms out at his sides, the pistol slipping from his lifeless fingers.

John Warburton stood over his brother's corpse, a pool of blood lapping at the toecaps of his army boots.

"I'm sorry, J. But I'm no gentleman."

The beads of purple light were in motion again.
"UUUNN-NN-NNNN…!"

Cat was starting to weaken. Droplets of sweat were pattering down on the concrete floor. Her entire body was one great awful draining pain, the resolve in her mind and her muscles seeping out of her.

Focus…focus…!

She tried to concentrate on the face of the dead girl in the desert, anger giving her a surge of new strength.

"UUUUuuu…uuuhh….hhhh…!"

But the girl's face melted and merged and became the long silver features of the Leader, his golden eyes enormous, swallowing everything.

Her taut and straining body was beginning to slacken, her head hanging down.

"uuuhh…hhh…hh…"

Somewhere, in the distance, through the blur of agony, Cat thought she heard a sound, a familiar *pop-pop-pop*. Then she heard muffled shouts. And that *pop-pop-pop* again.

"huuhh…?"

The Leader's long face, floating like a demonic mask in a red haze of pain, appeared to fracture and spew out pieces and pulp. Gobs of something sticky splattered her bare flesh.

"Switch that motherfucker off!" she heard someone say.

The red mists were fading. The crescendo of pain ebbed away and left her with a dull throbbing in her temples and aching limbs. She felt the weight of the metal cone being lifted from her head. Nimble fingers were plucking the electrodes from her skin. Strong hands wrenched the straps apart.

I must be dreaming!

Blinking to clear her watery vision, Cat saw three faces smiling down at her as she sat slumped in the metal chair.

"Wha…?"

"Hey, mama."

It was George the Cook, that brown-eyed handsome man. Transformed, in his old green beret and tiger-striped jungle fatigues, the M-16 like a toy in his massive fist.

"My turn, Cat."

Aiko. Refreshed, restored, in a black silk blouse tied up at the middle, and billowing black slacks snug on her hips. She had an old M-1 carbine cradled in her arms.

"Wha…?"

"I thought I'd join the party, baby."

Selena. The Goddess of War. Dressed to kill in a sleeveless olive drab T-shirt cut off to bare her hard midriff and baggy Army pants tucked into paratrooper boots. She was adorned by a criss-cross of webbing hung with pineapple grenades, hefting a .30-cal MG as light as a feather, the long belt of brass cartridges slung over her shoulder.

Cat stared in amazement, her mouth opening and closing. Selena smiled at her.

"The gang's all here, honey."

Slowly, everything swam into focus. Three pale men in safari suits were sprawled in a heap in the aisle between the metal tables. The purple lights were extinguished and the shrieking girls had subsided into moans and welcome unconsciousness.

"Ugh!" said Cat.

The Leader was now a shapeless thing, crumpled up at her feet. Her bare toes were dabbling in the pulpy mess that used to be his head.

She winced as Aiko, with an arm around her shoulders, helped her carefully to her feet.

"Oww...!"

"How do you feel?"

"Like I've been through a meat grinder."

Suddenly, the stale sweat was ice cold on her bare body. She shivered. George found a blanket and came forward to drape it around her. Cat shook her head.

"No, I'm okay. I want to fight."

Selena grinned.

"That's my girl. But you ain't gonna go out there half naked like that. You'll put George off his aim."

George, who was gazing at Cat with frank admiration, gulped and looked away.

"Aw, now, big guy," Selena chuckled. "Are you blushing?"

Aiko was laughing.

"They're both blushing! Again!"

There were shouts, the sound of running feet and gunfire, coming from outside. They sobered instantly.

"C'mon," said Selena. "We got business."

The blonde girls' clothing was scattered around. Cat grabbed a pale blue denim shirt and put it on. It had flowers embroidered on it and seemed hugely inappropriate.

"Here."

George plucked a .45 automatic from a holster on his belt and gave it to her.

"And some spares."

She stuffed the clips into the breast pockets of the shirt.

"Thanks."

She touched his hand. They smiled at each other.

Selena cleared her throat.

"Are we ready?"

Cat took a deep breath and worked the slide of the auto. The sound made her feel good.

"Ready!"

Keeping tight, they raced through the smoke-filled gardens. The strange shapes of the manicured bushes and fancy statues loomed up out of the grey fog as they dashed by.

"On the left!"

George shouted and Aiko whirled catlike and fired twice, knocking down the figures in khaki that were stumbling towards them, lifting their rifles.

Gravel crunched beneath their feet. Ahead of them the path blended into the fog. Suddenly, two men in safari suits were blocking the way, shoulder to shoulder, the strange glass weapons in their hands.

The others jumped sideways to seek invisibility in the mist. Glaring, Cat stood her ground.

"Fuck you!"

The big .45 bucked in her hand. One of the pale men staggered and toppled across the path. With a yell of alarm, Cat fell flat on her face, pressing her nose into the gravel, as his companion sent bright bolts spitting from his glass carbine, sizzling by above her.

"Jesus!"

There were muted muzzle flashes in the mist. The pale man spun sideways and fell.

George emerged onto the path. A wisp of smoke curled from the muzzle of his M-16. He was laughing in his deep brown voice.

"You can get up now, sweet thang."

Rolling over and grinning up at him, Cat held out her hand so he could pull her to her feet. Behind him, Selena and Aiko were shaking their heads reproachfully. Looking sheepish, Cat brushed gravel off the front of her shirt.

They paused over the bodies. Aiko nudged one of the glass carbines with her toe.

"What the hell are these things?"

"Dunno," Cat grinned. "But I want one for my collection."

She reached down to pick it up. Clucking her tongue, Selena tapped her on the wrist.

"Work now. Play later."

They moved on quickly. All around them, in the fog, the sounds of battle were becoming more sporadic. They glimpsed shadowy figures standing with their hands up.

"It looks like our people are mopping up the Colonel's goons," Aiko observed.

Lithe, cat-suited shapes darted across their path. Recognizing Selena, they stopped and saluted.

"We've got them on the run, Ma'am."

Cat was surprised. The voice coming from the hooded figure was distinctly female. And the shape was most definitely feminine. The matter was settled when the hood was tugged off and shoulder length light brown hair came tumbling down, framing a pretty and determined face.

"Well done, Wanda."

The cat-suited girl-squad moved on, vanishing into the artificial mist. Cat looked quizzically at Selena.

"That's right," Selena smiled. "I thought it would do the girls good to get out of the office for a change."

They jogged on, keeping to the path as some source of orientation in the fog. The grey smoke had an acrid tang. Cat wrinkled her nose and coughed.

"I think you might have overdone it, Aiko."

The Japanese girl snorted.

"Rubbish. It's perfect."

"And I don't like the color."

"Oh well, I'm so sorry. Next time, I'll—"

"LOOK OUT!" shouted George.

The marble steps leading up to the terrace had materialized in front of them, thrusting out of the mist. There were figures coming down towards them, oddly translucent in the smoke, aliens garbed in their silvery glister, the crystal carbines glittering.

This time, Cat flung herself sideways off the path, as the searing bolts zipped by. One flicked her long hair and singed it.

Cat went left. George and Aiko were diving right. Selena stayed where she was. Legs astride, she cut loose with the big .30-cal, firing from the hip, her whole body steeled against the juddering recoil, heedless of the bright bolts flashing past her. Spent cartridges rained down, tinkling on the gravel around her feet.

"Fuck!"

Cat put down the .45 and stuck her fingers in her ears.

When the noise stopped, she crawled to the fringe of the path and peered out through the mist. The marble steps were clogged with corpses, ripped ragged by a hail of lead.

"You may be superior beings, but you ain't bulletproof, motherfuckers," Selena muttered.

Cat was approaching her with eyebrows raised. Rising up from behind a convenient hedge, Aiko and George were wide-eyed with amazement.

"Okay, okay!" Selena said. "We all get carried away sometimes!"

Then they burst out laughing, the kind of laughter that has an edge to it.

George stopped laughing.

"Hey, look there!"

Behind them, the massive bulk of the alien craft was looming up above the mist, vast against the pale wash of the sky. The ramps were busy with figures and equipment, all going upwards and inwards.

"It looks like they're getting ready to leave," said Aiko.

"They must know that their leader is dead," added Cat.

Some of the ramps were already retracting into the hull.

"And they won't be coming back in a hurry," George concluded.

The sounds of battle were now reduced to the odd rifle shot or spurt of machine-gun fire. Stepping over the pile of alien corpses, they climbed the marble staircase and strode onto the terrace in front of the chateau.

Then they all flinched and ducked down, clapping their hands to their ears. With a crushing drone that threatened to crack their skulls, the alien craft detached itself from the great platform and rose into the sky.

"Hey," said Cat, looking at the demolished French windows. "It looks like Uncle John's been here."

Picking her way through the wreckage, she led them into the elegant drawing room.

"Princess!" his face lit by joy and relief, John Warburton was striding swiftly towards her.

Like a little girl, she flung out her arms and ran all the way down the long room to meet him. Her Uncle wrapped her up in a great big bear hug, lifting her off the floor.

"Oh, Uncle John! We won! We—!"

Over his shoulder, she saw her father's body.

"Oh…"

John Warburton released her. Glancing at each other, her companions hung back, their smiles fading.

Cat stared down at her father.

"It never occurred to me…" she whispered.

The seconds ticked by, as she stood looking down. Then she raised her eyes suddenly.

"Did you know?"

Her Uncle's eyes were full of grief. He couldn't meet her steady gaze.

"We…" mumbled Aiko.

"We suspected," said Selena. "But we had no proof."

Cat nodded, not looking at any of them.

"I'm sorry, Princess…" said John Warburton in a voice that ached with regret.

Smiling, Cat reached out and took his hand, squeezing it tight.

"Don't worry, Uncle John. It's alright."

She didn't look at her father again. Keeping hold of his hand, Cat led John Warburton across the room, to join the others by the broken windows. As she approached, they regarded her somberly, searching her face.

"Hey, I said don't worry," she was smiling again. "I'm okay, honest…"

The smile didn't reach her eyes.

"…I don't feel anything."

Cat let go of her Uncle's hand and stepped back out onto the sweeping terrace. The others hesitated for a moment, and then followed her.

The terrace was above the smoke, which dissipated slowly towards the far reaches of the vast gardens. The afternoon sun was beating down fiercely. Down below, through the thinning veils, they could see long lines of prisoners being marched away towards the barracks.

Cat stood with her palms resting on the carved marble rail that fenced the terrace, her head down, thinking. The others stood patiently, watching her.

Yes, of course. That's how it'll be…

She nodded, standing up straight. Turning to them, she embraced each in turn solemnly. She removed the teardrops from her Uncle's cheeks with the tip of her finger. She smiled when George doffed his green beret and pressed it to his heart. And when Aiko kissed her. And when Selena framed her face between strong hands and looked deep into her eyes.

Cat turned back towards the house.

"I'll see you all later. I have a score to settle."

The sun banged like a gong, reflected off the polished tiles and burnished copper that adorned the domes and towers and turrets worn like a crown by the chateau.

"I thought I'd find you here, Colonel."

A glass hatchway opened and Cat stepped out onto a section of flat roof large enough to accommodate a tennis court.

"I've been waiting for you, Miss Warburton."

He was decked out once more in the blue and gold of a Napoleonic Marshal, traversed by a red silk sash, with tight white breeches tucked into gleaming black boots.

Yes, up here above it all, letting others do your fighting for you

He was seated in a small wood and canvas chair. His tall hat, with its red, white and blue cockade and white ostrich plumes, was set down beside him on a folding campaign table. A curved saber lay across the table in its decorated sheath hung with red tassels. There were maps, a brass telescope, and a crystal decanter whose contents glowed like a dark ruby.

Appraising her coolly, the Colonel took a sip from a wine glass with an intricately twisted stem.

"I see that, as usual, you are undressed for the occasion."

The pale blue denim shirt was stained and torn in several places, unbuttoned down to her breastbone. Her bare knees were smudged with dirt and there were livid red scratches on her calves and thighs. Her face was dirty, her long blonde hair tangled and a shade darker, matted by dust and sweat.

"And in the thick of it as always. Although you betrayed me, I do still admire you, my dear."

Cat's face was a blank, staring back at him. The Colonel set down his glass. He lifted the corner of one of the maps and withdrew a nickel-plated Colt Frontier with gleaming ivory butt plates.

The rooftop was suspended in an immense bubble of silence. The click of the hammer being cocked was very loud.

Cat merely raised an eyebrow.

"Aren't you getting your periods a little mixed up, Colonel? Trying to be both Marshal Ney and General Patton?"

The Colonel stood up quickly, holding the gun at his hip. Black sparks glittered in his narrow eyes.

"I'm going to enjoy this. I'm going to shoot you in both knees. And then in the belly!"

Cat lifted her hand. The sun flashed on the blade of a heavy cavalry saber.

"I thought you believed in tradition, Colonel."

The black light flared in his eyes. His lips drew back, baring his teeth. Releasing the hammer, he slapped the pistol down on the table top. Smiling at her, he slipped off the sash and removed his blue coat. Underneath, he was wearing a white shirt with a high collar and frothy cravat.

"Yes," he hissed viciously. "This will be much more satisfying…"

He tugged the cravat loose and tossed it aside. His saber rasped from its sheath.

"…I feel bound to warn you, my dear, that I have been schooled by the finest fencing masters in Europe!"

Cat stood quite casually, with the blade of her weapon resting lightly on her shoulder.

"And I, Colonel, was once selected for the Olympic team."

Only I got sent home because of that…business…with that Cuban boxer…

His smile twitched for an instant.

"Really? Then it will make a pleasant change to have some genuine competition. I grow weary of decapitating the clods I have to practice on."

He stepped away from the table, moving sideways, into the open spaces. Cat moved with him. When they stopped they were facing each other, about ten feet apart.

The Colonel indulged in a few deep knee bends. He performed a series of flourishing passes with the saber, the flashing blade painting broad brushstrokes of light.

Cat just stood and watched him. She took long slow deep breaths. She was as cold as ice.

"Ready?"

"Ready."

"EN GARDE!"

First, there was the sparring. Probing, testing each other's blades and instincts.

"Hah!"

The Colonel experimented with a feint, shaping to cut at Cat's head but slashing at her flank. Cat parried deftly.

"Uh!"

She stayed well within herself, leading him on, wanting to see what he was made of. The Colonel attacked in flurries, like combination punches. She blocked them all.

"Uh!"

"Hah!"

"Ah!"

Their blades rang like clanging bells.

Cat was patient, waiting—then, drawing the Colonel in close, she turned a measured retreat into a dummy and a quick sidestep, and counterpunched: a parry, a lunge, a swift cut.

"AH!"

There was a slit in the thin white stuff of his shirt, a patch of crimson on his upper arm.

Frowning, his brow furrowed in concentration, the Colonel was more cautious now. And when he was thoughtful he was very good. Cat tried all of her tricks but his defences were impenetrable.

And suddenly she was very tired. It was all beginning to catch up with her, the torture, and the battle.

Her concentration slipped for an instant.

"AAH!"

And in that split second, she felt pain like a red hot poker drawn across her thigh and a warm wetness seeping. Her vision blurred. She heard the vicious bark of the Colonel's laughter.

He was indulging himself, playing to an imaginary gallery. Strolling over to the table, he took a sip of wine.

"I think you're getting tired, my dear. But then we have been keeping you busy."

A flood of sweat had glued the denim shirt to Cat's body. It was cramping her movements.

Damn it!

Angry with herself, she ripped the shirt off and threw it away. She was naked, except for the tiny black G-string.

The wine glass slipped from the Colonel's fingers and shattered on the grey surface of the flat roof. His eyes were blazing.

"Oh, this will be exceptional!" he exulted.

He advanced towards her, brandishing the saber.

"I will relish carving that magnificent body of yours!"

Sensing her tiredness, he mounted a sustained attack. His blade was a whirlwind. Cat tried to stand her ground but was slowly forced back.

"AAAHH!"

A white hot streak across her midriff. She felt the blood trickling down.

"AAAGH!"

Her hip.

"UUUAAGH!"

Her thigh again. Sweat made the cuts sting. He was toying with her, pulling his punches, cutting her, but not too deep.

He was laughing at her.

"I'm going to slice you up in little pieces…"

"AAAAUUUGGHH!"

Her breast. Just a nick. The pain was nauseating. She swayed, the blood and sweat dripping from her body and making dark spots on the rooftop. She was panting, her chest heaving.

"Now, where next…?"

"YAAAAAHH!"

There was a red roaring behind her eyes, a scarlet mist that blinded her. She felt a tremendous jolt that jarred her shoulder.

The mist thinned. The Colonel had disappeared. She looked down.

"Uuuuuuhh…hhh…"

He sprawled at her feet, clutching his face. His saber was skidding away across the roof.

Blinking, Cat shook her head to try and clear it.

"B…b…b-bitch…!"

She had lashed out with blind instinct and smashed him in the face with the heavy brass hand guard of her saber, the one move that his sophisticated fencing brain hadn't counted on.

"The noble art of street fighting, Colonel," she panted.

She stood over him, raising her saber.

Time to die, fucker!

Something cold and hard was pressed to the back of her neck. She heard a familiar double-click.

"Drop the weapon," said a bland, accent less voice.

She let the sword fall from her hand. She knew what to expect before she turned round. A pale blond man in a safari suit, with a cocked revolver pointed at her face.

Cat stared into the colorless unblinking eyes. It was him. Cadillac Man, the man from Verna's diner.

"So, there's still one of you bastards left."

The Colonel was scrambling to his feet. He had a lurid black eye, all puffy and yellow and purple. He was spitting with fury. The man in the safari suit stood impassively, the pistol unwavering.

The Colonel calmed himself. His thin lips curved in a pale imitation of a smile.

"My first instinct is to disembowel you here and now, Miss Warburton…"

He turned away from her, walking quickly towards the table.

"…but first…"

There was an enormous campaign chest on the far side of the table, an iron-bound crate of dark wood.

"…I want you to suffer the indignity of witnessing my escape…"

He lifted the lid and removed something big and heavy. A contraption of tubes and nozzles and straps, centered on twin tanks similar to a diver's oxygen cylinders, and a control handle with what appeared to be a lever and a throttle with a twist grip.

"Yes indeed. I intend to live to fight another day. Which is more than I can say for you, my dear."

The Colonel shrugged his shoulders into the harness that secured the tanks on his back. His eyes rolled all over Cat's near naked body.

"Such a waste…"

Then he turned to the pale man standing behind her.

"When I am gone, kill her!"

His thumb depressed a red button on the tip of the handle. There was a muffled detonation and a burst of blue-grey vapors from the nozzles that angled down and rearwards.

"But be sure and give her ample time to savor her defeat!"

His fist released the lever and rotated the throttle. With a loud cough, the nozzles ignited, twin hissing lances of an opaque blue flame. The soles of the Colonel's boots detached from the rooftop. He rose almost imperceptibly at first, inches, then a foot, then ten feet, then upwards maybe thirty feet where he hovered for a second or two before he moved off sideways out over the gardens.

"AYAAH!"

Cat whirled in a raking pirouette, her right leg coming up and around to knock the gun from Cadillac Man's hand.

"HAH!"

She made that movement flow into another, a wind milling assault with both hands that drove the pale man backwards to the edge of the roof. She felt the blows, but she didn't see him. She saw the hippy girls in the diner, smiling up innocently at him. She saw them laughing as they got into his car and drove away with him.

"HA-YAH!"

Without a sound, his face expressionless, he went over. Cat heard him hit the marble slabs of the terrace far below. She looked over and saw him lying motionless with his arms and legs at crooked angles, his head resting in a spreading stain of colorless slime.

She saw her friends, jumping back, startled. She saw them look up. Uncle John and Selena were pointing. George shouted something, tugging back the bolt of his M-16. Aiko was lifting her carbine.

The Colonel had increased height to about a hundred and fifty feet and was making his way steadily towards the far end of the gardens, still blurred by the thinning veils of grey fog. From the ground, he was invisible, and with all the activity below, the hiss of the nozzles was just another anonymous sound mixed in with all the rest.

George was taking aim.

"NO!" Cat screamed. "HE'S MINE!"

She sprinted to the table and grabbed the Colonel's fancy .44. Dashing to the edge of the roof she knelt down, resting her forearms on the low wall that fenced it.

She took a slow steady breath and held it, gripping the revolver in both hands.

You're mine, you murdering bastard!

She fired.

The Colonel was laughing at all the little ignorant ants, scurrying about below, glimpsed through clear patches in the smoke.

Fuck!

She fired again.

The Colonel stopped laughing when he felt the jolt and heard the *dong!* of the slug puncturing his left tank.

He heard liquid slopping out and sizzling on the hot pipes.

"OH MY GOD...!"

WHOOOSH!

He was engulfed in a bubbling fireball. The jetpack went spiralling out of control, making a corkscrewing smoke trail up and up and up, high into the bright blue sky.

The fireball hung motionless for an instant, at the peak of its crazy arc. Then, rolling over and over, it came down like a meteor, out past the gardens and into the desert.

The Colonel screamed all the way down. The screaming ended in a dull *whomp!* and a pillar of fire that became a black mushroom cloud, rising above the far distant wall of the gardens.

"Nice shooting," said George.

"All-State pistol shooting champion at sixteen," said Uncle John proudly.

Cat emerged onto the terrace. She was wearing the Colonel's blue coat, with its shiny gold buttons and epaulettes.

"It suits you," Aiko reached out to free the long blonde tresses where they had snagged on the high collar.

Cat offered the nickel-plated .44 to Selena.

"Here, a souvenir."

"You keep it."

"I don't want it."

Cat stood looking down at her feet. Selena stroked her hair and Cat raised her head and looked at her with eyes that were overflowing with pain and confusion.

"It didn't make you feel any better, did it?" asked Selena gently.

Cat shook her head.

"No, it didn't."

Selena took Cat's hand.

"I'm sorry about your father."

Cat's brow furrowed.

"I had no father."

A great shiver convulsed her.

"No. There's one more thing I have to do. Then everything will be alright."

The desert was cold at night. The stars were like flecks of ice.

Cat was cold. She had the snow white soft-top of the red Olds buttoned down and the onboard heater was blowing warm air at her. But she was still cold, even when she tugged the ring pull on the zipper of her yellow jumpsuit all the way up to her chin.

The desert had a thin crust that crunched beneath the wheels. She had left the highway nearly an hour ago. All around her was a fathomless darkness, her world confined to the yellow pool of light cast by the headlights, going before her.

Marvin's soothing tones were oozing from the speakers. But even he couldn't heal her. Not this time. She switched him off.

"Sorry, man…"

It seemed like years since she had been here last but she knew exactly where to go.

She stopped the car. When she got out she left the motor idling so it stayed warm.

She was cold, and very tired. She yanked on the zipper but it wouldn't go any higher.

"Hullo, sweetheart…"

In the splash of light from the headlamps, Cat could make out the slight mound that marked the grave.

"I've come back. I said I would…"

There was a small bunch of blue wildflowers in her hand. Cat stooped to lay them on the ground.

"I'll tell them where to find you, darling. And then you can go home to your Mama and Papa and you won't be lonely any more."

Suddenly, she wrapped her arms around herself and sank to her knees beside the grave. Her body was racked by great convulsive sobs, and scalding tears were flowing on her face.

Poor baby…! Poor baby…!

The Persian lamps bathed the elevated bedchamber in their honey glow. Fragrant incense tinted the air.

Pampered, oiled and perfumed, Cat's nakedness was lustrous in the golden lamplight, as she came fresh from the sunken bath and into the bedroom.

"Feeling better now?" asked Uncle John.

Smiling, Cat yawned and stretched and ran her fingers through her long silken hair.
"Yes, much."
"Then come to bed," said Uncle John.
"Right on!" said George.
"Please come to bed," said Aiko.
"Right now!" said Selena.
"Okay, okay!" Cat laughed. "I'm coming!"

If you enjoyed this book, call or write for a free catalog

**Midnight Marquee Press
9721 Britinay Lane
Baltimore, MD 21234**

**410-665-1198
www.midmar.com**

www.ingramcontent.com/pod-product-compliance
Lightning Source LLC
LaVergne TN
LVHW021657060526
838200LV00050B/2389